PRAISE FOR *Year of the Griffin*

"This boisterous spoof of the campus novel reads like a cross between David Lodge and a particularly buoyant incarnation of J.R.R. Tolkien. One exuberantly inventive adventure follows the next all the way to the pleasing conclusion. Great fun."

—*Publishers Weekly* (starred review)

"The sequel to *Dark Lord of Derkholm* retains the goofiness of its predecessor, continuing Jones' spoof of traditional fantasy conventions. This book may help impatient Potter fans cope with the wait for Harry's next adventure." —ALA *Booklist* (starred review)

"I found *Year of the Griffin* filled with splendors and delights, sparkling plays of wit, and high flights of fancy—in short, Diana Wynne Jones at her finest."

—Lloyd Alexander

"Diana Wynne Jones chooses the most outlandish subjects and treats them with such aplomb that the reader never blinks. Her humor is deft. All the worlds that Jones creates have her trademark integrity."

—Megan Whalen Turner, author of *The Thief*

"*Year of the Griffin* was a pleasure to read, and not only do I look forward to reading it again somewhere along the line, but I am already looking forward to her next book. It can't be too soon." —Margaret Mahy

ALSO BY DIANA WYNNE JONES

Archer's Goon
Aunt Maria
Believing Is Seeing: Seven Stories
Castle in the Air
Dark Lord of Derkholm
Dogsbody
Eight Days of Luke
Fire and Hemlock
Hexwood
Hidden Turnings:
A Collection of Stories Through Time and Space
The Homeward Bounders
Howl's Moving Castle
The Ogre Downstairs
Power of Three
Stopping for a Spell
A Tale of Time City
The Time of the Ghost
Warlock at the Wheel and Other Stories

The Worlds of Chrestomanci
Book 1: Charmed Life
Book 2: The Lives of Christopher Chant
Book 3: The Magicians of Caprona
Book 4: Witch Week
Mixed Magics (Stories)
The Chronicles of Chrestomanci, Volume I
(Contains books 1 and 2)
The Chronicles of Chrestomanci, Volume II
(Contains books 3 and 4)

The Dalemark Quartet
Book 1: Cart and Cwidder
Book 2: Drowned Ammet
Book 3: The Spellcoats
Book 4: The Crown of Dalemark

DIANA WYNNE JONES

Year of the Griffin

❦

A GREENWILLOW BOOK

HarperTrophy®
An Imprint of HarperCollins*Publishers*

Year of the Griffin
Copyright © 2000 by Diana Wynne Jones
All rights reserved. No part of this book may be used or reproduced in any
manner whatsoever without written permission except in the case of brief
quotations embodied in critical articles and reviews. Printed in the United
States of America. For information address HarperCollins Children's Books,
a division of HarperCollins Publishers, 10 East 53rd Street, New York,
NY 10022.

Library of Congress Cataloging-in-Publication Data
Jones, Diana Wynne.
Year of the griffin / by Diana Wynne Jones.
p. cm.
"Greenwillow Books."
Sequel to: Dark Lord of Derkholm.
Summary: When Elda, the griffin daughter of the great Wizard Derk,
arrives for schooling at the Wizards' University, she encounters new friends,
pirates, assassins, worry, sabotage, bloodshed, and magic misused.
ISBN 0-688-17898-7 — ISBN 0-06-029158-3 (lib. bdg.)
ISBN 0-06-447335-X (pbk.)
[1. Griffins—Fiction. 2. Magic—Fiction. 3. Schools—Fiction. 4. Fantasy.]
I. Title.
PZ7.J684 Yc 2000   99-048522
[Fic]—dc21   CIP
                                                                           AC

Typography by Hilary Zarycky
❖
First Harper Trophy edition, 2001
Visit us on the World Wide Web!
www.harperchildrens.com
12 13 14 15 OPM 15 14 13 12 11 10

FOR SUSAN HIRSCHMAN

ONE

NOTHING WAS GOING right with the Wizards' University. When High Chancellor Querida decided that she could not change the world and run the University as well, she took herself and her three cats off to a cottage beside the Waste, leaving the older wizards in charge. The older wizards seized the opportunity to retire. Now, eight years after the tours ended, the University was run by a committee of rather younger wizards, and it was steadily losing money.

For forty years before that, the University had been forced to provide for Mr. Chesney's off-world Pilgrim Parties. Wizards had also been made to provide magical events for the tours. Tourists from the next universe had come in droves every year, expecting to have adventures with elves, dwarfs, dragons, and the powers of darkness, and most years this left the world laid waste. The wizards then had to put it straight for the next year. Mr. Chesney, whose orders were backed by a powerful demon, had been very strict in his requirements, and he had paid for this service in gold. When almost everyone in the world united to put a stop to the Pilgrim Parties, the payments naturally stopped, so it was small wonder that the University was short of funds.

"We need to make the place *pay* somehow," the Chairman, Wizard Corkoran, said anxiously at the beginning-of-term meeting. "We've raised the student fees again—"

"And got fewer students than ever," Wizard Finn pointed out, although to hear the shouts and the bang and scrape of luggage from the courtyard outside, you would have thought most of the world was currently arriving there.

"Fewer, yes," Corkoran said, looking at the list by his elbow, "but the ones we *have* got must all come from very rich families, or they couldn't afford the fees. It stands to reason. I propose we ask these families for money; we could put up a plaque with their names on. People like that."

Wizard Finn shot a look at the lovely Wizard Myrna, who turned down the corners of her shapely mouth. The rest of the committee simply stared at Corkoran with different sorts of blankness. Corkoran was always having ideas, and none of them worked. The students thought

Corkoran was wonderful. Many of them imitated his style of wearing an offworld necktie over an offworld T-shirt—both with pictures on—and did their hair like Corkoran in a wavy blond puff brushed back from the forehead. Quite a few of the girl students were in love with him. But then they were only *taught* by him, Finn thought gloomily. They didn't have to wrestle with his ideas of how to run a university.

"We can't afford a plaque," said Wizard Dench, the Bursar. "Even with all the fees paid, we can only just afford to pay the staff and buy food. We can't afford to mend the roofs."

Wizard Corkoran was used to Dench saying they couldn't afford things. He waved this away. "Then I'll float a commemorating spell," he said. "We can have it circling the Spellman Building or the Observatory tower—transparently, of course, so it won't get in the way." When nobody said anything to this, he added, "I can maintain it in my spare time."

Nobody said anything to this either. They all knew Corkoran never had any spare time. All the time he could spare from teaching—and much that he couldn't spare, too—went to his research on how to get to the moon. The moon was his passion. He wanted to be the first man to walk on it.

"That's settled then," said Corkoran. "Money's bound to pour in. If you just take my first-year tutorial group, you can see the possibilities.

Look." He ran a finger down the list beside him. "There's King Luther's eldest son—he's Crown Prince of Luteria, and he'll own all sorts of land—Prince Lukin. And the next one's the sister of Emperor Titus. At least I believe she's his half sister, but I'm sure we can prevail on the Empire to make a large donation. Then there's a dwarf. We've never had a dwarf before, but they all come from fastnesses stuffed with treasure. And there's this girl Elda. She's the daughter of Wizard Derk, who—"

"Er—" began Finn, who knew Elda quite well.

"Wizard Derk is a wealthy and important man," Corkoran continued. "Did you say something, Finn?"

"Only that Derk doesn't approve of the University," Finn said. It was not what he had been going to say.

"Obviously he changed his mind when he found his daughter had talent," Corkoran said, "or he wouldn't be paying for her to come here. All right. That's agreed then. Myrna, you're married to a bard. You know how to use Powers of Persuasion. You're in charge of sending a letter to the parents of all students who—"

"I, er, have another idea," Wizard Umberto put in from the end of the conference table. Everyone turned to him hopefully. Umberto was quite young, rather fat, and almost never said anything. The general belief was that Umberto was a brilliant astrologer, except that he never said anything about his work. He went pink, seeing them all looking at him, and stammered, "Oh. Er. I think we should, well, you know, be able to set up a scheme to let people pay for magical information. You know, come from miles away to be told secrets."

"Oh, don't be silly, Umberto," said Wizard Wermacht. Wermacht was the youngest wizard there, and very proud of the fact. "You're describing just what we do, anyway."

"But only for students, Wermacht," Umberto stammered shyly. "I thought we could, er, sell everyone horoscopes and so forth."

"But then they wouldn't be secrets!" Wermacht said scornfully. "Your usual muddled thinking. I suggest—"

"Umberto and Wermacht," Corkoran said, "you are interrupting the Chair."

At this Umberto went pinker still, and Wermacht said, "I'm *so* sorry, Corkoran. Please do go on."

"I'd nearly finished," Corkoran said. "Myrna is going to send out a letter to the parents of all students, asking for the largest possible donation and telling them their names will go up in a spell with the ones who give most in big letters at the top. We're bound to get a good response. That's it. Now forgive me if I rush away. My latest moon studies are very delicate and need watching all the time." He gathered up his lists and stormed out of the Council Hall, with his tie flapping over his shoulder.

"I hate these meetings," Finn said to Myrna as they walked out into the stone foyer together, where the shouts and rumbles from the arriving students echoed louder than ever.

"So do I," Myrna said dourly. "Why do I always end up doing the work for Corkoran?"

Finn found Myrna the most ravishing woman he knew. She had brains and beauty. He was always hoping she might be persuaded to give up her bardic husband and turn to him instead. "It's too bad," he said. "Umberto just sits there like Humpty-Dumpty, and Wermacht throws his weight about and then crawls to Corkoran. Dench is useless. It's no wonder Corkoran's relying on you."

"Of course he does," said Myrna. "His head's in the moon. And I didn't notice *you* offering to do anything."

"Well," said Finn. "My schedule—"

"As if I hadn't enough to do!" Myrna went on. "I've seen to all the students' rooms, and the college staff, and the kitchens, and the bedding, and there's probably going to be an outcry when someone realizes that I had to give Derk's daughter the concert hall to sleep in. She's too big for anywhere else. How is it, anyway, that Corkoran's teaching her? Why does he always grab the most interesting students?"

"That's just what I was going to say!" Finn

cried out, seeing his chance to be truly sympathetic to Myrna. "I've met most of those students. I knew them as kids when I was Wizard Guide on the tours, and I tell you it's going to serve Corkoran right for hogging the ones he thinks are best, or richest, or whatever he thinks they are."

"They probably *are* best," Myrna said, barely listening. "I did the admissions, too. The University secretaries nearly went mad over that, and they'll go mad again now they have to get this letter out. And on top of it all, I've just discovered I'm pregnant!"

"Oh," said Finn. There, he thought, went his hopes of Myrna's leaving her bard. All he could think of was to say lamely, "Well, anyway, Corkoran's in for a shock when he sees one of his new students."

Finn was right. Next morning Corkoran hurried into the tall stone tutorial chamber and only just managed not to stand stock-still, gaping. He bit his teeth together. He knew better than anyone that his fine, fair good looks caused most students to hang adoringly on his words. He thought of his face as his best teaching aid and was well aware that letting his jaw hang spoiled the effect. So he plastered a smile across it. But he still stood rooted to the spot.

Blazing out of the decidedly motley set of young people in the room—like a sunburst, Corkoran thought dazedly—was a huge golden griffin. He was not sure he was safe. Not exactly a *huge* griffin, he told himself hastily. He had heard that some griffins were about twice the size of an elephant. This one was only as large as an extra-big plow horse. But she—he could somehow tell it was a *she*; there was an enormous, emphatic *she*ness to this griffin—she was so brightly golden in fur and crest and feathers, so sharply curved of beak, and so fiercely alert in her round orange eyes that at first sight she seemed to fill the room. He noticed a dwarf somewhere down by her great front talons—and noticed with irritation that the fellow was in full war gear—but that was all. He very nearly turned and ran away.

Still, he had come to teach these students and also to find out, if possible, how wealthy their parents were, so he pasted the smile wider on his face and began his usual speech of welcome to the University.

The students gazed at him with interest, particularly at his tie, which this morning had two intertwined pink and yellow dragons on it, and at the words on his T-shirt under the tie.

"What's *MOON SOON* mean?" rumbled the dwarf. Probably he thought he was whispering. It gave a peculiarly grating, surly boom to his voice.

"Hush!" said the griffin, probably whispering, too. It sounded like a very small scream. "It may mean something magical."

The dwarf leaned forward with a rattle of mail and peered. "There's another word under his tie," he grated. "*SHOT*. It's *SHOT*. Why should anyone shoot the moon?"

"It must be a spell," small-screamed the griffin.

Corkoran realized that between the two of them he was being drowned out. "Well, that's enough about the University," he said. "Now I want to know about *you*. I suggest each of you speaks in turn. Tell the rest of us your name, who your parents are, and what made you want to come and study here, while the rest of you *listen quietly*. Why don't you start?" he said, pointing at the large, shabby young man on the other side of the griffin. "No, no, you don't have to stand up!" Corkoran added hastily as the young man's morose-looking face reddened and the young man tried to scramble to his feet. "Just sit comfortably and tell us about yourself. Everyone can be quite relaxed about this."

The young man sank back, looking far from relaxed. He seemed worried. He pulled nervously at the frayed edges of his thick woolen jacket and then planted a large hand on each knee so that they covered the patches there. "My name is Lukin," he said. "My father is King of Luteria—in the north, you know—and I'm, er, his eldest son. My father, well, how do I put this? My father isn't paying my fees. I don't think he could afford to, anyway. He doesn't approve of

9

my doing magic, and he, er, doesn't want me here. He likes his family at home with him."

Corkoran's heart sank at this, and sank further as Lukin went on, "Our kingdom's very poor, you know, because it was always being devastated by Mr. Chesney's tours. But my grandmother— my mother's mother, that is—was a wizard— Melusine, you may have heard of her—and I've inherited her talent. Sort of. From the time I was ten I was always having magical accidents, and my grandmother said the only way to stop having them was to train properly as a wizard. So she left me her money for the fees when she died, but of course the fees have gone up since her day and I've had to save and economize in order to be here. But I do intend to learn, and I *will* stop having accidents. A king shouldn't spend his time making holes in things." He was almost crying with earnestness as he finished.

Corkoran could have cried, too. He made a secret mark on his list to tell Myrna not to waste time asking King Luther for money and asked, "What kinds of accidents do you have?"

Lukin sighed. "Most kinds. But I'm worst when there's anything to do with pits and holes."

Corkoran had no notion how you put a stop to that kind of trouble. Perhaps Myrna did. He added another scribble to remind himself to ask Myrna. He said encouragingly, "Well, you've come to the right place, Lukin. Thank you. Now you." He pointed to the large young woman sitting behind the dwarf. She was very elegantly dressed in dark suede, and the elegance extended to her long, fine, fair hair, which was drawn stylishly back inside an expensive-looking scarf to set off her decidedly beautiful hawklike face. From the look of command on that face and the hugely expensive fur cloak thrown casually over the chair behind her, Corkoran had no doubt that she was the Emperor's sister.

She gave him a piercing blue-eyed look. "I am Olga," she said.

"And?" invited Corkoran.

"I do not wish to say," she replied. "Here I wish to be accepted as I am, purely for magical ability. I have been raising winds and monsters since I was quite a small child." She sat back, clearly intending to say no more.

So the Emperor's sister wishes to remain incognita, Corkoran thought. Fair enough. It could be awkward with the other students. He nodded knowingly and pointed to the tall, narrow, brown-faced fellow half hidden behind Olga and the griffin's left wing. "And you?"

"Felim ben Felim," the young man replied, bowing in the manner of the eastern countries. "I, too, wish to say little about myself. If the Emir were to discover I am here studying, he would very likely dispatch assassins to terminate me. He has promised that he would, at least."

"Oh," said Corkoran. "Er, *is* the Emir likely to discover you?"

"I trust not," Felim replied calmly. "My tutor, the wizard Fatima, has cast many spells to prevent the Emir from noticing my absence, and she furthermore assures me that the wards of the University will be considerable protection to me also. But our lives are in the laps of the gods."

"True," Corkoran said, making a particularly black and emphatic scribble beside Felim's name. He did not know Wizard Fatima and certainly did not share the woman's faith that the University could protect anyone from assassins. Myrna must definitely not send a letter to Felim's parents. If the answer came in assassins, they could all be in trouble. A pity. People were rich in the Emirates. He sighed and pointed with his pen at the other young woman in the group, sitting quietly behind Lukin. Corkoran had her placed in his mind, almost from the start, as the daughter of Wizard Derk. He had met Derk more than once and had been struck by his unassuming look. Quite extraordinary, Corkoran always thought, for the man whom the gods had trusted with the job of setting the world to rights after what Mr. Chesney had done to it to look so modest. The young woman had a similar humble, almost harassed look. She was rather brown and very skinny and sat huddled in a shawl of some kind, over which her hair fell in dark, wet-looking coils on her shoulders. She twisted her long fingers in the shawl as she spoke. Corkoran could have sworn her dark ringlets of hair twisted about, too. She gave him a worried stare from huge greenish eyes.

"I'm Claudia," she said huskily, "and the Emperor of the South is my half brother. Titus is in a very difficult position over me, because my mother is a Marshwoman, and the Senate doesn't want to acknowledge me as a citizen of the Empire. My mother was so unhappy there in the Empire, you see, that she went back to the Marshes. The Senate thinks I should renounce my citizenship as Mother did, but Titus doesn't want me to do that at all. And the trouble over me got worse when it turned out that the gift for magic that all Marshpeople have didn't mix at all with Empire magic. I'm afraid I have a jinx. In the end Titus sent me here secretly, for safety, hoping I could learn enough to cure the jinx."

Corkoran tried not to look as amazed as he felt. His eyes shot to Olga. Was *she* Derk's daughter then? He switched his eyes back to Claudia with an effort. He could see she had Marsh blood now. That olive skin and the thinness, which always made him think of frogs. His sympathy was with the Senate there. Perhaps they would pay the University to keep the girl. "What kind of jinx?" he said.

A slightly greenish blush swept over Claudia's thin face. "It goes through everything." She sighed. "It made it rather difficult to get here."

This was exasperating, Corkoran thought. Something that serious was almost certainly incurable. It was frustrating. So far he had a king's son with no money, an obviously wealthy girl who would not say who she was, a young man threatened with assassins if the University admitted he was here, and now the Emperor's jinxed sister, whom the Empire didn't want. He turned with some relief to the dwarf. Dwarfs always had treasure—and tribes, too, who were prepared to back them up. "You now," he said.

The dwarf stared at him. Or rather, he stared at Corkoran's tie, frowning a little. Corkoran never minded this. He preferred it to meeting students' eyes. His ties were designed to deflect the melting glances of girl students and to enable him to watch all students without their watching him. But the dwarf went on staring and frowning until Corkoran was almost uncomfortable. In the manner of dwarfs, he had his reddish hair and beard in numbers of skinny pigtails, each one with clacking bones and tufts of red cloth plaited into it. The braids of his beard were noticeably thin and short, and the face that frowned from under the steel war helm was pink and rounded and young.

"Ruskin," the dwarf said at last in his peculiar blaring voice. The voice must be caused by resonance in the dwarf's huge, square chest, Corkoran decided. "Dwarf, artisan tribe, from Central Peaks fastness, come by the virtual manumission of apostolic strength to train on behalf of the lower orders."

"How do you mean?" Corkoran asked.

The dwarf's bushy red eyebrows went up. "How do I mean? Obvious, isn't it?"

"Not to me," Corkoran said frankly. "I understood *dwarf* and *Central Peaks*, and that was all. Start again, and say it in words that people who are not dwarfs can understand."

The dwarf sighed, boomingly. "I thought wizards were supposed to divine things," he grumbled. "All right. I'm from one of the lowest tribes in our fastness, see. Artisans. Got that? Third lowest. Drudges and whetters are lower. Six tribes above us, miners, artists, designers, jewelers, and so on. Forgemasters at the top. All ordering us about and lording it over us and making out we can't acquire the skills that give us the privileges they have. And around this time last year we got proof that this was nonsense. That was when Storn and Becula, both artisans and one a *girl*, forged a magic ring better than anything the forgemasters ever did. But the ring was turned down for treasure because they were only artisans. See? So we got angry, us artisans, and brought in drudges and whetters, and it turned out they'd made good things, too, but hadn't even submitted them as treasure because they knew they'd be turned down. Oppression, that's what it was, black oppression—"

"All right. Don't get carried away," Corkoran said. "Just explain how you come into it."

"Chosen, wasn't I?" Ruskin said. A slight,

proud smile flitted above his plaited beard. "It had to be someone young enough not to be noticed missing and good enough to benefit here. They picked me. Then each one of them, young and old, man and woman, from all three tribes, put down a piece of gold for the fees and a piece of their magic into me. That's the apostolic part. Then I came away secretly. That's what we call virtual manumission. And I'm to learn to be a proper wizard, so that when I am, I go back and *smash* those forgemasters and all the rest of them. Overthrow the injustice of the old corrupt order, see?"

And now a dwarf revolutionary! Corkoran thought. Bother! He saw that if Myrna sent out her letter to Central Peaks fastness, it would almost certainly bring an enraged party of forgemasters (and so forth) here to remove Ruskin and his fees with him. He made another note by Ruskin's name, while he asked, "Is that why you're in full armor?"

"No," Ruskin answered. "I have to come before my tutor properly dressed, don't I?" He eyed Corkoran's tie and T-shirt again and frowned.

"I advise you to leave it off in future," Corkoran told him. "Iron interferes with magic, and you won't know enough to counteract it until your second year. You're going to have trouble, anyway, if you're working with bits and pieces of other people's magic."

"Don't think so," Ruskin blared. "We dwarfs are used to that. Do it all the time. And we work with iron."

Corkoran gave him up and turned, finally, to the griffin. "You."

All this while the griffin had sat brightly swiveling an eye on each student who spoke and quivering with eagerness for her turn. Now she fairly burst forth, both wings rising and tufted tail lashing so that Felim and Olga had to move out of their way. "I'm Elda," she said happily. "Wizard Derk's daughter. I used to be his youngest child, but now I've got two younger than me: Angelo and Florence. Flo's wings are pink. She's the baby. She's *beautiful*. Angelo's wings are brown, a bit like Callette's without the stripes, and he's a magic user already. Mum says—"

"Hang on," said Corkoran. "Wizard Derk is *human*. You're a griffin. How come—"

"Everyone asks about that," Elda said sunnily. "Dad made us, you know. He put some of himself and Mum and eagle and lion—and cat for me—into an egg, and we hatched. At least, we had an egg each. There's me and Lydda and Don and Callette and Kit, who are all griffins. Shona and Blade are my human brother and sister, like Angelo and Flo, except that Shona and Blade don't have wings. Shona's married. She's gone to run that new Bardic College out on the east coast. She's got three girls and two boys, and I'm an aunt. And all the others except Mum and Dad and the babies have gone over to the West Continent in two ships, because there's a war there—only Lydda's flying, because she's a long-distance flier and she can do a hundred and fifty miles without coming down to rest, but Dad made her promise to keep in sight of the ships just in case, because Kit and Blade are the ones who can do magic. Callette—"

"But what about yourself?" Corkoran asked, managing to break in on this spate of family history.

"*What* about me?" Elda said, tipping her bright bird head to look at him out of one large orange eye. "You mean, why did Mum send me here to keep me out of mischief?"

"More or less," Corkoran said, wincing at that piercing eye. "I take it you have magic."

"Oh, yes," Elda agreed blithely. "I'm ever so magical. It keeps coming on in spurts. First of all I could only undo stasis spells, but after we saw the gods, I could do more and more. Mum and Dad have been teaching me, but they were so busy looking after the babies and the world that Mum says I got rather out of hand. When the others all went off on the ships, I got so cross and jealous that I went into the Waste and pushed a mountain out of shape. Then Mum said, 'That's enough, Elda. You're going to the University whatever your father says.' Dad still doesn't know I'm here. Mum's going to break it to him today. I expect there'll be rather a row. Dad doesn't approve of the University, you know." Elda turned her head to fix her other eye on Corkoran, firmly, as if he might try to send her home.

The thought of doing anything to a griffin who could push a mountain out of shape turned Corkoran cold and clammy. This bird—lion—female—*thing* made him feel weak. He pulled his tie straight and coughed. "Thank you, Elda," he said when his voice had come back. "I'm sure we can turn you into an excellent wizard." And bother again! He made yet another note on his list for Myrna. If Derk was angry about Elda's being here, he had certainly better not receive a demand for money. Derk had the gods behind him. Oh, dear. That made five out of six. "Right," he said. "Now we have to sort out your timetable of classes and lectures and give you all a title for the essay you're going to write for me this coming week."

He managed to do this. Then he fled, thankfully, back to his moonlab.

"He didn't say anything about the moon," Ruskin grumbled as the six new students came out into the courtyard, into golden early-autumn sunlight, which gave the old, turreted buildings a most pleasing mellow look.

"But he surely will," said Felim, and added thoughtfully, "I do not think assassins could reach me on the moon."

"Don't be too sure of that," said Lukin, who

knew what kings and emirs could do when they set their minds on a thing. "Why is the Emir—?"

Olga, who knew what it felt like to have secrets, interrupted majestically. "What have we got next? Wasn't there a lecture or something?"

"I'll see," said Elda. She hooked a talon into the bag around her neck and whisked out a timetable, then reared on her hindquarters to consult it. It already had claw holes in all four corners. "A class," she said. "Foundation Spell-casting with Wizard Wermacht in the North Lab."

"Where's that?" Claudia inquired shyly.

"And have we time for coffee first?" Olga asked.

"No, it's now," said Elda. "Over there, on the other side of this courtyard." She stowed the timetable carefully back in her bag. It was a bag she had made herself and covered with golden feathers from her last molt. You could hardly see she was wearing it. The five others gave it admiring looks as they trooped across the courtyard, past the statue of Wizard Policant, founder of the University, and most of them decided they must get a bag like that, too. Olga had been using the pockets of her fur cloak to keep papers in— everyone handed out papers to new students all the time—and Ruskin had stuffed everything down the front of his chain mail. Claudia and Felim had left all the papers behind in their rooms, not realizing they might need any of them, and Lukin had simply lost all his.

"I can see I'll have to be a bit better organized," he said ruefully. "I got used to servants."

They trooped into the stony and resounding vault of the North Lab to find most of the other first-year students already there, sparsely scattered about the rows of desks, with notebooks busily spread in front of them.

"Oh, dear," said Lukin. "Do we need notebooks as well?"

"Of course," said Olga. "What made you think we wouldn't?"

"My teacher made me learn everything by heart," Lukin explained.

"No wonder you have accidents then," Ruskin boomed. "What a way to learn!"

"It's the *old* way," Elda said. "When my brothers Kit and Blade were learning magic, Deucalion wouldn't let them write anything down. They had to recite what they'd been told in the last lesson absolutely right before he'd teach them anything new. Mind you, they used to come back seething, especially Kit."

"It is *not* so the old way!" Ruskin blared. "Dwarfs make notes and plans, and careful drawings, before they work any magic at all."

While he was speaking, the lab resounded to heavy, regular footsteps, as if a giant were walking through it, and Wizard Wermacht came striding in with his impeccably ironed robes swirling around him. Wermacht was a tall wizard, though not a giant, who kept his hair and the little pointed beard at the end of his long, fresh face beautifully trimmed. He walked heavily because that was impressive. He halted impressively behind the lectern, brought out an hourglass, and impressively turned it sand side upward. Then he waited impressively for silence.

Unfortunately Ruskin was used to heavy, rhythmic noises. He had lived among people beating anvils all his life. He failed to notice Wermacht and went on talking. "The dwarfs' way *is* the old way. It goes back to before the dawn of history."

"Shut up, you," ordered Wermacht.

Ruskin's round blue eyes flicked to Wermacht. He was used to overbearing people, too. "We'd been writing notes for centuries before we wrote down any history," he told Elda.

"I said *shut up*!" Wermacht snapped. He hit the lectern with a crack that made everyone jump and followed that up with a sizzle of magefire. "Didn't you hear me, you horrible little creature?"

Ruskin flinched along with everyone else at the noise and the flash, but at the words *horrible little creature* his face went a brighter pink and his large chest swelled. He bowed with sarcastic politeness. "Yes, but I hadn't quite finished what I was saying," he growled. His voice was now so deep that the windows buzzed.

"We're not here to listen to *you*," Wermacht

retorted. "You're only a student—you and the creature that's encouraging you—unless, of course, both of you strayed in here by mistake. I don't normally teach animals or runts in armor. Why are you dressed for battle?"

Elda's beak opened and clapped shut again. Ruskin growled, "This is what dwarfs wear."

"Not in *my* classes you don't," Wermacht snapped, and took an uneasy glance at the vibrating windows. "And can't you control your voice?"

Ruskin's face flushed beyond pink, into beetroot. "No. I can't. I'm thirty-five years old, and my voice is breaking."

"Dwarfs," said Elda, "are different."

"Although only in some things," Felim put in, leaning forward as smooth and sharp as a knife-edge. "Wizard Wermacht, no one should be singled out for personal remarks at this stage. We are all new here. We will all be making mistakes."

Felim seemed to have said the right thing. Wermacht contented himself with putting his eyebrows up and staring at Felim. And Felim stared back until, as Claudia remarked to Olga afterward, one could almost hear knives clashing. Finally Wermacht shrugged and turned to the rest of the class. "We are going to start this course by establishing the first ten laws of magic. Will you all get out your notebooks and write? Your first big heading is 'The Laws of Magic.'"

There was a scramble for paper and pens. Olga dived for her cloak pockets, Elda for her feathered bag, and Ruskin for the front of his armor. Felim looked bemused for a moment, then fumbled inside his wide sash until he found what seemed to be a letter. Ruskin passed him a stick of charcoal and was rewarded with a flashing smile of gratitude. It made Ruskin stare. Felim's narrow, rather stern face seemed to light up. Meanwhile Elda saw Claudia sitting looking lost and hastily tore her a page out of her own notebook. Claudia smiled almost as shiningly as Felim, a smile that first put two long creases in her thin cheeks and then turned the left-hand crease into a dimple, but she waved away the pen Elda tried to lend her. The words *Laws of Magic* had already appeared at the top of the torn page. Elda blinked a little.

Lukin just sat there.

"Smaller headings under that, numbered," proclaimed Wermacht. "Law One, the Law of Contagion or Part for Whole. Law Two—you back there, is your memory particularly good or something? Yes, you with the secondhand jacket."

"Me?" said Lukin. "I'm sorry. I didn't realize I'd need a notebook."

Wermacht frowned at him, dreadfully. "That was extremely stupid of you. This is basic stuff. If you don't have this written down, you're going to be lost for the rest of the time you're here. How did you expect to manage?"

"I, er, I wasn't sure. I mean—" Lukin seemed completely lost. His good-looking but sulky face grew even redder than Ruskin's had been.

"Precisely." Wermacht stroked his little pointed beard smugly. "So?"

"I was trying to conjure a notebook while you were talking," Lukin explained. "From my room."

"Oh, you think you can work advanced magic, do you?" Wermacht asked. "Then by all means go ahead and conjure." He looked meaningfully at his hourglass. "We shall wait."

At Wermacht's sarcastic tone Lukin's red face went white—white as a candle, Elda thought, sliding an eye around at him. Her brother Blade went white when he was angry, too. She scrabbled hastily to tear another page out of her notebook for him. Before she had her talons properly into the paper, however, Lukin stood up and made a jerky gesture with both hands.

Half of Wermacht's lectern vanished away downward into a deep pit that opened just in front of it. Wermacht snatched his hourglass off the splintered remains and watched grimly as most of his papers slid away downward too. Deep, distant echoings came up from the pit, along with cold, earthy air.

"Is this your idea of conjuring?" he demanded.

"I was trying," Lukin answered. Evidently he had his teeth clenched. "I was trying for a paper off your desk. To write on. Those were nearest."

"Then try again," Wermacht commanded him. "Fetch them back at once."

Lukin took a deep breath and shut his eyes. Sweat shone at the sides of his white face. Beside him Olga began scrabbling in her cloak pockets, watching Lukin anxiously sideways while she did so. Nothing happened. Wermacht sighed, angrily and theatrically. Olga's hawklike face took on a fierce, determined look. She whispered something.

A little winged monkey appeared in the air, bobbing and chittering over the remains of the lectern, almost in Wermacht's face. Wermacht recoiled, looking disgusted. All the students cried out, once with astonishment and then again when the wind fanned by the monkey's wings reached them. It smelled like a piggery. The monkey meanwhile tumbled over itself in the air and dived down into the pit.

"Is this your idea of a joke?" Wermacht snapped at Lukin. "You with the secondhand jacket! Open your eyes!"

Lukin's eyes popped open. "What do—"

He stopped as the monkey reappeared from the pit, wings beating furiously, hauling the missing part of the lectern in one hand and the papers in the other. The smell was awful.

"That's nothing to do with me," Lukin protested. "I only make holes."

The monkey tossed the piece of lectern against

the rest of it. This instantly became whole again, and it tossed the papers in a heap on top. With a long, circular movement of its tail, a rumbling and a crash and a deep growling *thunk*, like a dungeon door shutting, it closed the hole, leaving the stone floor just as it had been before Lukin tried to conjure. Then the monkey winked out of existence, gone like a soap bubble. The smell, if possible, was worse.

Olga, who had gone as white as Lukin, silently passed him a small shining notebook. Lukin stared at it as it lay across his large hand. "I can't take this! It looks really valuable!" The book seemed to have a cover of beaten gold inlaid with jewels.

"Yes, you can," Olga murmured. "You need it. It's a present."

"Thanks," Lukin said, and his face flooded red again.

Wermacht hit the newly restored lectern sharply. "Well?" he said. "Is anyone going to admit to the monkey?"

Evidently nobody was. There was a long, smelly silence.

"Tchah!" said Wermacht. He gestured, and all the windows sprang open. He piled his papers neatly in front of him on the lectern. "Let's start again, shall we? Everybody write 'The Second Law of Magic.' Come along, you in the second-hand jacket. This means you, too."

Lukin slowly sat down and gingerly pulled out

the little gold pen slotted into the back of the jeweled notebook. He opened the book, and its hinges sang a sweet golden note that made Wermacht frown. Carefully Lukin began to write neat black letters on the first small, crisp page.

The class went on and finished without further incident, except that everyone was shivering in the blasts of cold air from the open windows. When it was done, Wermacht picked up his hourglass and his papers and stalked out. Everyone relaxed.

"Who did that monkey?" was what everyone wanted to know as they streamed out into the courtyard.

"Coffee," Olga said plaintively from the midst of the milling students. "Surely we've got time for coffee now?"

"Yes," Elda said, checking. "I need a straw to drink mine."

They had coffee sitting on the steps of the refectory out of the wind, all six together. Somehow they had become a group after that morning.

"Do you know," Felim said reflectively, "I do not find Wizard Wermacht at all likable. I most earnestly hope we see him no more than once a week."

"No such luck," said Olga, who had her crumpled timetable out on her knee. "We've got him again straight after lunch. He does Herbal Studies, too."

"And Elementary Ritual tomorrow," Elda discovered, pinning down her timetable with her right talons while she managed her straw and her coffee with her left. "That's three times a week."

Ruskin hauled his timetable out from under his mail and examined it glumly. "More than that. He does Demonology and Dragonlore, too. Man's all over the place. *Two* sessions a week on Basic Magic."

"He's not likely to forget us, is he?" Lukin remarked, running his fingers over the smooth humps of the jewels in the golden notebook.

"Maybe he's not vindictive," Claudia suggested. "Just no sense of humor."

"Want to bet?" grunted Ruskin. "Lukin, may I see that notebook a moment?"

"Sure," said Lukin, handing it over. "I suppose, from his point of view, I was quite a trial to him, although he did seem to pick on people. Funny, though. When I first saw Wizard Corkoran, I thought *he* was the one I was going to hate. Stupid lightweight in silly clothes."

"Oh, I do agree!" said Olga. "Such a poser!"

"But he fades to nothing beside Wizard Wermacht." Felim agreed. "Necktie and all."

"Oh, how *can* you talk like that about Wizard Corkoran!" Elda cried out. Her tail lashed the steps. "He's *sweet*! I love him!"

They all stared at her. So did everyone else nearby. Elda's voice was strong. Claudia said cautiously, "Are you *sure*, Elda?"

"Of *course* I'm sure! I'm in love!" Elda said vehemently. "I want to pick him up and carry him about!"

They looked at her. They thought about Wizard Corkoran grasped in Elda's brawny, feathered arms, with his legs kicking and his tie trailing. Olga bit her lip. Lukin choked on his coffee, and Felim looked hard at the sky. Claudia, whose upbringing had forced her to think cautiously, remembered that Corkoran was a wizard and said, "Please *don't* pick him up, Elda."

"I wouldn't dare," Elda said regretfully. "It's just he does so remind me of my old teddy bear that Flo plays with now. But I'll be good. I'll sigh about him and look at him. I just don't want any of you criticizing him."

"Fair enough." Ruskin agreed. "You languish if you want. Thought is free. Here." He passed the little notebook back to Lukin. "Take care of this. It's dwarf work. Old, too. Some kind of virtue in it that I don't know about. Treasure standard."

"Then I'd better give it back," Lukin said guiltily to Olga.

She looked extremely haughty. "Not at all. It was a gift."

TWO

A WEEK PASSED, WHICH seemed like a
month to Corkoran's new students. They
learned and did so much. They went to
lectures delivered by Myrna, Finn, and other
wizards. They wandered bewildered in the
library, looking for the books Corkoran had told
them to read, and even found some of them.
They rushed from place to place, taking volumes
of notes during the day, and in the evenings tried
to write essays. The days seem to stretch enormously, so that they even had spare time, in
which they discovered various activities. Ruskin
took up table tennis, quite fiendishly. Olga joined
the Rowing Club, and got up at dawn every day
to jog to the lake, from which she returned
at breakfast time, ravenously hungry, looking
more than ever like a hawk-faced queen, and so

violently healthy that Claudia shuddered. Claudia was not good in the mornings. Her idea of a proper leisure activity was to join the University Choir, which met in the afternoons. Felim joined the fencing team. Lukin and Elda, who both looked athletic but were not, became members of the Chess Club and sat poring over little tables, facing one another for hours, when they should have been learning herbiaries or lists of dragons. Both were very good at chess, and each was determined to beat the other.

In that week it became increasingly evident that Lukin and Olga were a pair. They wandered about together hand in hand and sat murmuring together in corners. Except when she went rowing, Olga gave up wrapping her hair back in a scarf. Her friends at first thought that she had simply discovered she liked running her hands through its fine fair length, or tossing it about, until they noticed that Lukin at odd moments would put out a hand and lovingly stroke it. And when Lukin was not looking, Olga would stare admiringly at Lukin's somber profile and broad shoulders. Possibly she lent him money, too. At any rate, Lukin soon appeared in a nearly new jacket and unpatched trousers, though this did not stop Wermacht calling him "you in the second-hand jacket."

Wermacht, they discovered, made a point of never remembering students' names. Ruskin was always either "you with the voice" or more often "you in the armor," despite the fact that after the first day Ruskin had given up wearing armor. He now wore a tunic that, in Elda's opinion, would have been too big even for Lukin but that stretched tight around his huge dwarfish chest, and trousers that seemed too small for Elda's little brother Angelo. To make up for not wearing armor, Ruskin plaited twice the number of bones into his hair. As Claudia said, you knew he was near by the clacking.

None of the others exactly paired up at the time, though Ruskin was known to be sneaking off to the nearby Healers Hall to drink tea with a great, tall novice healer girl whom he had met in Herbal Studies—taught by Wizard Wermacht— for which the first-year healers came over from their hall. Ruskin admired this young lady greatly, although he hardly came up to her waist. And for two days Felim took up with an amazingly beautiful first-year student called Melissa, whom he had met in Basic Magic—taught by Wermacht again—until the outcry from the others became extreme.

"I mean to say, Felim, she is just totally *dumb*!" Olga exclaimed.

Lukin agreed. "Wizard Policant's statue has more sense."

"She just stands and smiles," Elda said vigorously. "She must have *some* brain, I suppose, or she wouldn't be here, but I've yet to see it. What do you say, Claudia?"

33

"I'd say she smiled at whoever admitted her," Claudia answered, thinking about it. "Wizard Finn probably. He's a pushover for that kind of thing."

"Truly?" Felim asked Claudia. "You think she is stupid?"

"Horribly," said Claudia. "Hopelessly."

Everyone tended to follow Claudia's advice. Felim nodded sadly and saw less of Melissa.

Everyone learned the gossip around the University, too. Very soon it was no secret to them that Wizard Corkoran was obsessed with getting to the moon. Elda took to stationing herself where she could see Corkoran rushing to his moonlab with the latest lurid tie flapping over his shoulder. "Oh, I wish I could help him!" she said repeatedly, standing upright to wring her golden front talons together. "I want to help him get to the moon! He's so *sweet*!"

"You need a griffin your own age," Olga told her.

"There aren't any," said Elda. "Besides, I couldn't pick a griffin up."

For a while they all called Corkoran "Elda's teddy bear."

As for Corkoran himself, that week went past at the usual pace, or maybe faster than usual. There were so many crucial experimental spells going forward in his lab, and the construction of his moonship was going so slowly, that he grudged every minute of the four hours he spent teaching. Just getting to the moon was problem enough. He had still not worked out what you did for air there either. But certain experiments had started suggesting that in airless space, soft things like human bodies were liable to come apart. Peaches certainly did. Corkoran that week imploded more peaches than he cared to think about. And peaches were beginning to be expensive now that autumn was coming on. The new load he ordered cost more than twice as much. Suppose, he wondered as he rushed along the corridors to teach his first-year group, suppose I were to give up using spells and just put an iron jacket around them? That would mean an iron jacket for me, too. I'd land on the moon looking like that dwarf Ruskin.

Here he ran full tilt into Wizard Myrna rushing the other way. Only a deft buffer spell from Myrna prevented either of them from getting hurt. Corkoran reeled against the wall, dropping books and papers. "So sorry!" he gasped. "My head was away beyond the clouds." He bent to pick up his papers. One of them was a list of his students that he had scribbled on for some reason. Oh, yes. He remembered now. And luckily Myrna was there, though looking a little shaken. "Oh, Myrna," he said, "about those letters I asked you to send to the parents of new students . . ."

Myrna closed her eyes against Corkoran's tie. It had shining green palm trees on it, somehow interlaced with scarlet bathing beauties. She had been suffering from morning sickness all that week, and she did not feel up to that tie. "Asking for money for the University," she said. "Not to worry. I sent them all off the day after our meeting."

"What? Every single one?" Corkoran said.

"Yes," said Myrna. "We'd just had a big delivery of Wizard Derk's brainy carrier pigeons, so there was no problem." She opened her eyes. "Why are you looking so worried? Those birds always get where you tell them to go."

"I know they do," Corkoran said morbidly. "No, no. I'm not worried. It's nothing. Really. Just a bit shaken. Are you all right? Good." He went on his way feeling quite anxious. But there was so obviously nothing he could do to recall those letters that the feeling did not last. Before he had reached the end of that corridor, Corkoran was telling himself that blood was thicker than water and that more than half those families were going to be so grateful to the University for telling them where their missing children were that they would probably send money, anyway. By the time he reached the tutorial room, he was back with the problem of the imploding peaches.

He could have given that tutorial standing on his head, he had done it so often. He collected the usual six essays on "What is wizards' magic?" and went on to talk about the underlying theory of magic, almost without thinking. He did notice, however, that his students seemed to have come on quite a bit, even after a mere week. They all joined in the discussion almost intelligently, except the griffin, who simply stared at him. Never mind. There was always one quiet one, though he would have expected that one to be the skinny girl, Claudia, and not the griffin. The piercing orange stare was unnerving. Nor did he understand when he happened to mention a teddy bear as an example of inert protective magic why all the students, even the griffin, fell about laughing. Still, it showed they were melding into a proper group. They accepted it, without difficulty, when he gave them the same essay to write all over again. He always did this. It saved having to think of another title, and it made them all think again. He was quite pleased as he hastened back to his lab to put peaches inside cannonballs.

His students meanwhile streamed off with the rest of the first year to the North Lab, where they were shortly listening to Wizard Wermacht's important footsteps and watching Wizard Wermacht stroke the little beard at the end of his long pink face while he gazed contemptuously around them all, ending with Lukin and Ruskin.

"No more deep holes, roaring, or monkeys today, I hope," Wermacht said. He had said this at each class, sometimes twice a day, for the last week. Felim glowered, Olga made a small, impatient sound, Ruskin and Lukin ground their teeth, and Elda's beak gave out a loud, grating *crack*. Claudia merely sighed. The rest of the students, as usual, shifted and muttered. It seemed to everyone as if Wermacht had been saying this for several years. "Notebooks out," said Wermacht. "You'll need rulers for diagrams under your first big heading."

Nobody had a ruler. They used pencils and the edges of desks rather than have another scene. So far they had got by without one by keeping as quiet as they could. But Lukin's face was blanched with rage. Ruskin's was deep pink, and he was muttering, "Oppression!" even before the top of the hourglass emptied and Wermacht's heavy feet went striding away.

"Plain damn rudeness, I call it!" Lukin snarled as they pushed their way out into the courtyard. "I'm so busy keeping my temper that I haven't time to learn anything!" Olga took his arm and patted it while she led the way across the courtyard for coffee. Olga drank coffee by the quart. She said she needed it to run in her veins. "*And* we've got the beastly man again this afternoon!" Lukin complained. He was soothed by Olga's patting, but not by much.

"And in between comes lunch," said Claudia, "which may even be worse than Wermacht."

The rest groaned. Of all of them, Claudia probably suffered most from the truly horrible food provided by the refectory. She was used to the food that the Emperor ate and the exquisite, spicy waterweeds of the Marshes. But dwarfs ate delicately, too, Ruskin said, even the lower tribes; and, Felim added, so did the Emirates. Elda craved fresh fruit; Olga yearned for fresh fish. Lukin did not mind much. The poverty of Luteria made the food there very little better than the stuff from the refectory.

"But," Lukin said, as they forced a way up the crowded refectory steps, "I would give my father's kingdom for a properly baked oatcake."

"Oatcake!" Claudia cried out, quite disgusted.

"Why not?" Olga asked. "There's little to beat it if it's made right." Her northern accent came out very strongly as she said this. It always did on the few occasions when she spoke of anything to do with her home. "Find me a fire and a griddle, Claudia, and I'll make you one."

"Yes, please!" said Lukin.

It was one of those muggily warm autumn days. Every student in the place seemed to be outside sitting on the refectory steps. Olga put their six cups of coffee on a tray and carried it over to the statue of Wizard Policant instead, where they all sat on his plinth except Elda, who spread herself out at their feet, alternately bending down to sip at her straw and raising her big golden beak to sniff the mushroom and wheat straw scent of autumn, carried in from beyond the town by the faint, muggy wind. Something in those scents excited her, she was not sure what, but it made her tail lash a little.

"A fire and a griddle," Claudia said. "If I could do it unjinxed, I'd fetch you both, Olga. Why, with all this magical ability there is in this University, doesn't anybody make the food at least *taste better*?"

"That's an idea," Ruskin grunted, banging his dangling heels against the plinth. "I'll do it as soon as I learn how. Promise. Charcoal roast and mussels with garlic. How about that?"

"Newly caught trout with parsley butter," Olga added yearningly.

"I've never had mussels," said Elda. "Would I like them?"

"You're bound to. Your beak looks made for opening shellfish," said Felim.

"And chicken pie to follow," said Claudia. "What pudding, do you think?"

"Claudia," said Lukin, "stop encouraging everyone to think of food and tell me how to deal with Wermacht. If he calls me 'you with the secondhand jacket' once more, I may find I've opened a mile-deep hole underneath him. I won't be able to help myself."

"And I might savage him"—Elda agreed— "next time he calls me an animal."

"Let's think." Claudia leaned forward, with both bony hands clasped around one of her sharp knees. Her eyes took on a green glow of thought. In some queer Marshperson way, her hair seemed to develop a life of its own, each dark lock coiling and uncoiling on her shoulders. Everyone turned to her respectfully. They had learned that when Claudia looked like this, she was going to say something valuable. "I've heard," she said, "that Wizard Wermacht is the youngest tutor on the faculty, and I suspect he's very proud of that. I think he's rather sad."

"*Sad!*" exclaimed Ruskin. His voice rose to such a hoot that students on the refectory steps jumped around to look. "I may cry!"

"Pitiful, I mean," Claudia explained. "He swanks about with those heavy feet, thinking he's so smart and clever, and he's never even noticed that those other wizards make him teach all the classes. Why do you think we're so sick of being taught by Wermacht? Because all the older ones know it's hard, boring work hammering basics into first years and they let Wizard Wermacht do it because he's too stupid to see it isn't an honor. That's what I mean by sad."

"Hmm," said Lukin. "You've got a point. But I don't think it'll hold me off forever." A grin lit his heavy face, and he flung an arm around Olga. "If I get angry enough, I may tell him he's being exploited."

Olga leaned her face against Lukin's shoulder. "Good idea."

The rest watched with friendly interest, as they had done all week. Olga was extremely beautiful. Lukin was almost handsome. Both of them were from the north. It fitted. On the other hand, Lukin was a crown prince. All of them, even Ruskin, who was still having trouble grasping human customs, felt anxious for Olga from time to time. Elda had her beak open to ask, as tactfully as possible, what King Luther would think about Olga when they heard, quite mystifyingly, the sound of a horse's hooves clopping echoingly through the courtyard. There was a great, admiring "O-o-oh!" from the refectory steps.

"Riding in here is illegal, isn't it?" asked Felim.

Well-known smells filled Elda's open beak. She clapped her beak shut and plunged around the statue, screaming. In the empty part of the courtyard beyond, a superb chestnut colt was just trotting to a halt and folding his great shining carroty wings as he did so. His rider waited for the huge pinions to be laid in order, before slinging both legs across one wing and sliding to the ground. He was a tall man with a wide, shambling sort of look. *"Dad!"* screamed Elda, and flung herself upon him. Derk steadied himself with several often-used bracing spells and only reeled back slightly as he was engulfed in long golden feathers, with Elda's talons gripping his shoulders and Elda's smooth, cool beak rubbing his face.

"Lords!" said the horse. "Suppose I was to do that!"

"None of your cheek, Filbert," Elda said over Derk's shoulder. "I haven't seen Dad for a week now. You've seen him every day. Dad, what are you *doing* here?"

"Coming to see how you were, of course," Derk replied. "I thought I'd give you a week to settle down first. How *are* things?"

"Wonderful!" Elda said rapturously. "I'm learning so many things! I mean, the food's awful, and one of the main teachers is vile, but they gave me a whole concert hall to sleep in because the other rooms are too small, and I've got *friends*, Dad! Come and meet my friends."

She disentangled herself from Derk and dragged him by one arm across to the statue of Wizard Policant. Derk smiled and let himself be dragged. Filbert, who was a colt of boundless curiosity, clopped across after them and peered around the plinth as Elda introduced the others.

Derk shook hands with Olga and then with Lukin, whom he knew well. "Hallo, Your Highness. Does this mean your father's allowed you to leave home after all?"

"No, not really," Lukin admitted, rather flushed. "I'm financing myself, though. How are your flying pigs these days, sir?"

"Making a great nuisance of themselves," said Derk, "as always." He shook hands with Felim. "How do you do? Haven't I met you before somewhere?"

"No, sir," Felim said with great firmness.

"Then you must look like someone else I've met." Derk apologized. He turned to Claudia.

"Claudia? Good gods! You were a little shrimp of a girl when I saw you last! Living in the Marshes with your mother. Do you remember me at all?"

Claudia's face lit with her happiest and most deeply dimpled smile. "I do indeed. You landed outside our dwelling on a beautiful black horse with wings."

"Beauty. My grandmother," Filbert put in, with his chin on Wizard Policant's pointed shoes.

"I hope she's still alive," said Claudia.

"Fine, for a twelve-year-old," Filbert told her. "She doesn't speak as well as me. Mara mostly rides her these days."

"No, I remember I could hardly understand her," said Claudia. "She looked tired. So did you," she said to Derk. "Tired and worried."

"Well, I was trying to be Dark Lord in those days," Derk said, "and your mother's people weren't being very helpful." He turned to Ruskin. "A dwarf, eh? Training to be a wizard. That has to be a first. I don't think there's been a dwarf wizard *ever*."

Ruskin gave a little bow from where he sat. "That is correct. I intend to be the first one. Nothing less than a wizard's powers will break the stranglehold the forgemasters have on Central Peaks society."

Derk looked thoughtful. "I've been trying to do something about that. The way things are run there now is a shocking waste of dwarf talents. But those forgemasters of yours are some of the most stiff-necked, flinty-hearted, obstinate fellows I know. I tell you what—you come to me when you're qualified and we'll try to work something out."

"Really?" Ruskin's round face beamed. "You mean that?"

"Of course, or I wouldn't have said it," said Derk. "One thing Querida taught me is that revolutions need a bit of planning. And that reminds me—"

Elda had been towering behind her father, delighted to see him getting on so well with her friends. Now she flung both feathered forelegs around his shoulders, causing him to sag a bit. "You really don't mind me being here? You're going to let me stay?"

"Well." Derk disengaged himself and sat on the plinth beside Filbert's interested nose. "Well, I can't deny that Mara and I had a bit of a set-to over it, Elda. It went on some days, in fact. Your mother pointed out that you had the talent and were at an age when everyone needs a life of her own. She also said you were big enough to toss me over a barn if you wanted."

"Oh, I wouldn't do that!" Elda cried out. She thought about it. "Or not if you let me stay here. You *will*, won't you?"

"That's mostly why I'm here," said Derk. "If you're happy and if you're sure you're learning something of value, then of course you have to stay. But I want to talk to you seriously about what you'll be learning. You should all listen to this, too," he said to the other five. "It's important." They nodded and watched Derk attentively as he went on. "For many, many years," he said, "forty years, in fact, this University was run almost entirely to turn out Wizard Guides for Mr. Chesney's tour parties. The men among the teachers were very pressed for time, too, because they had to go and be Guides themselves every autumn when the tours began. So they pared down what they taught. After a few years they were teaching almost nothing but what was needed to get a party of nonmagic users around dangerous bits of country, and these were all the fast, simple things that worked. They left out half the theory and some of the laws, and they left out all the slower, more thorough, more permanent, or more artistic ways of doing things. Above all, they discouraged students from having new ideas. You can see their point in that. It doesn't do for a Wizard Guide with twenty people to keep safe in the Waste when a monster's charging at them to stand rooted to the spot because he's thought of a new way to make diamonds. They'd all be dead quite quickly. Mr. Chesney didn't allow that kind of thing. You can see the old wizards' point. But the fact remains that for forty years they were not teaching properly."

"I believe those old wizards have retired now, sir," Felim said.

"Oh, they have." Derk agreed. "They were

worn out. But you haven't grasped my point. Six smart students like you ought to see it at once."

"I have," Filbert said, chomping his bit in a pleased way. "The ones teaching now were taught by the old ones."

"Exactly," said Derk, while the others cried out, "Oh, I *see*!" and "That's *it*!" and Olga said, "Then that's what's wrong with Wermacht."

"All that about 'your next big heading.' So schooly," said Claudia. "Because that's all he knows. Like I said, pitiful."

"Running in blinkers," Filbert suggested brightly.

"Then it's all no *use*!" Elda said tragically. "I might just as well come home."

From the look of them, the others were thinking the same. "Here now. There's no need to be so extreme," Derk said. "Who's your tutor?"

"Corkoran," said Elda. The others noticed, with considerable interest, that she did not go on and tell Derk that Corkoran reminded her of a teddy bear.

"He's the fellow who's trying to get to the moon, isn't he?" Derk asked. "That could well force him to widen his ideas a little, though he may not tell them to you, of course. You should all remember that for every one way of doing things that he tells you, there are usually ten more that he doesn't, because half of them are ways he's never heard of. The same goes for laws and theory. Remember there are more kinds of magic than there are birds in the air, and that each branch of it leads off in a hundred directions. Examine everything you're taught. Turn it upside down and sideways; then try to follow up new ways of doing it. The really old books in the library should help you, if you can find them—Policant's *Philosophy of Magic* is a good start—and then ask questions. Make your teachers think, too. It'll do them good."

"Wow!" murmured Olga.

Elda said, "I wish you'd come and said this before I'd given in my essay. I'd have done it quite differently."

"I also," said Felim.

Lukin and Ruskin were writing down "Policant, *Phil. of Mag.*" in their notebooks. Ruskin looked up under his tufty red brows. "What other old books?"

Derk told them a few. All the others fetched out paper and scribbled, looking up expectantly after each title for more. Derk concealed a smile as he met Ruskin's fierce blue glare and then Felim's glowing black one and then found Claudia's green eyes raised to his, like deep, living lamps. You could see she was half Marshfolk, he thought, looking on into Olga's long, keen gray eyes, and then Lukin's, rather similar, and both pairs gleaming with excitement. He seemed, he thought quite unrepentantly, to have started something. Then he looked upward at Elda, feeling slightly ashamed that she trusted him so devotedly.

But he met one of those grown-up orange twinkles that Elda had been surprising him with lately. "Aren't you being rather naughty?" Elda asked.

"Subversive is the word, Elda," Derk said. "Oh, yes. Your mother reminded me how beastly the food used to be here. We didn't think it could have changed. Filbert!"

Filbert obediently moved his hind legs around in a half circle until he was facing the statue and sideways on to Derk. There was a large hamper standing on his saddle. Derk heaved it down and opened it in a gush of piercing, fruity scent.

"Oranges!" squawked Elda as the lid came creaking back. "My favorite fruit!"

Everyone else but Claudia was asking, "What are they?"

"Offworld fruit," Derk said, heaving down a second hamper. "Don't give them away too freely, Elda. I've only got one grove so far. This one's lunch. Mara seems to have put in everything Lydda cooked and left in stasis for this last year. She reckoned the food might even be worse now the University's so short of money. Help yourselves."

The smells from the second hamper were so delicious that five hands and a taloned paw plunged in immediately. Murmurs of joy arose. Filbert fidgeted and made plaintive noises until Derk thoughtfully turned over buns, pies, pasties, flans and found Filbert some carrot cake, then a pork pie for himself. For a while everyone ate peacefully.

"*Is* the University short of money?" Olga asked as they munched.

"Badly so, to judge by the plaintive but stately begging letter they've just sent me," Derk said. "They tell me they're forced to ask for donations from the parents of all students."

He was a little perplexed at the consternation this produced. Claudia choked on an éclair. Lukin went deep red, Olga white. Ruskin glared around the courtyard as if he expected to be attacked, while Felim, looking ready to faint, asked, "*All* students?"

"I believe so," Derk said. But before he could ask what was worrying them all so, the courtyard echoed to heavy, striding feet. A peremptory voice called out, "You there! You with the horse!"

"Wermacht," said Olga. "This was all we needed!"

They turned around from the hamper. The refectory steps were now empty since it was lunchtime. Wermacht was standing alone, with all the folds of his robe ruler straight, halfway between the steps and the statue, outrage all over him. "It is illegal to bring a horse inside this University courtyard," he said. "Take it to the stables at once!"

Derk stood up. "If you insist."

"I *do* insist!" Wermacht said. "As a member of the Governing Body of this University, I demand

50

you get that filthy brute out of here!"

"I am *not* a filthy brute!" Filbert wheeled around and trotted toward Wermacht, quite as outraged as the wizard was. "I'm not even exactly a horse. Look." He spread his great auburn wings with a clap.

To everyone's surprise, Wermacht cringed away backward with one arm over his head. "Get it *out* of here!"

"Oh, gods! He's scared of horses!" Elda said, jigging about. "He's probably scared of me, too. Somebody else *do* something before he puts a spell on Filbert!"

Lukin had his legs braced ready to charge over there. Ruskin was already down from the plinth and running. Derk forestalled both of them by swiftly translocating himself to Filbert's flank and taking hold of the bridle. "I'm extremely sorry," he said to Wermacht. "I wasn't aware that horses were illegal here. It wasn't a rule in my day."

"Ignorance is no excuse!" Wermacht raged. He was mauve with fear and anger. "You should have *thought* of the disruption it would cause, bringing a monster like this into a place of study!"

"He's still calling me names!" Filbert objected.

Derk pulled downward hard on Filbert's bit. "Shut up. I can only repeat that I'm sorry, wizard. And I don't think there's been any disruption—"

"What do you know about it?" Wermacht

interrupted. "I don't know who you are, but I can see from the look of you that you haven't a clue about the dignity of education. Just go. Take your monster and go, before I start using magic." He shot an unloving look at Elda. "We've one monster too many here already!"

At this Derk's shoulders humped and his head bowed in a way Elda knew meant trouble.

But here Corkoran came flying across the courtyard from the Spellman Building with his palm tree tie streaming over his left shoulder. One of his senior students had seen trouble brewing from the refectory windows and sent him a warn-spell. "Oh, Wizard Derk," Corkoran panted cordially. "I am so very pleased to meet you again. You may not remember me. Corkoran. We met during the last tour." He held out a hand that quivered with his hurry.

Wermacht's reaction would have been comic if, as Olga said, it had not been so disgusting. He bowed and more or less wrung his hands with servile welcome. "Wizard *Derk*!" he said. "The famous Wizard Derk, doing us the honor to come here! Corkoran, we were just discussing, Wizard Derk and I—"

Derk shook hands with Corkoran. "Thank you for intervening," he said. "I remember you had the tour after Finn's. I was just leaving, I'm afraid. I had been thinking of discussing a donation with you—though my funds are always rather tied up in pigs and oranges and things—

but as things turn out, I don't feel like it today. Perhaps later. Unless, of course," he added, putting his foot into Filbert's stirrup, ready to mount, "my daughter has any further reason to complain of being treated as a monster. In that case I shall remove her at once."

He swung himself into the saddle. Filbert's great wings spread and clapped. Wermacht ducked as horse and rider plunged up into the air, leaving Corkoran staring upward in consternation.

"Wermacht," Corkoran said with his teeth clenched, and too quietly, he hoped, for the students around the statue to hear. "Wermacht, you have just lost us at least a thousand gold pieces. I don't know how you did it, but if you do anything like that again, you lose your job. Is that clear?"

THREE

GRIFFINS' EARS ARE exceptionally keen. Elda's had picked up what Corkoran said to Wermacht. Ruskin had heard, too. His large, hair-filled ears had evolved to guide dwarfs underground in pitch dark by picking up the movement of air in differently shaped spaces, and they were as keen as Elda's. He and Elda told the others.

"How marvelous!" Olga stretched like a great blond cat. "Then we can get Wermacht sacked anytime we need to."

"But *is* that marvelous?" Elda asked, worried. "I think I ought to stand on my own four feet—I think we *all* ought to—and deal with Wermacht ourselves."

This struck the others as being far too scrupulous. They attempted to talk Elda out of it. But by the time they had carried the hamper of oranges and the half-empty hamper of lunch to Elda's concert hall, their attention was on Felim instead. Something was wrong with him. He quivered all over. His face was gray, with a shine of sweat on it, and he had stopped speaking to anyone.

Elda picked him up and dumped him on the concert platform, which now served as her bed. "What's the matter? Are you ill?"

"Something in the hamper disagreed with him," Ruskin suggested. "Those prawn slices. They're still making me burp."

Felim shook his wan face. "No. Nothing like that." His teeth started to chatter, and he bit them closed again.

"Then tell us," coaxed Claudia. "Maybe we can help."

"It does quite often help to tell someone," Lukin said. "When I've had a really bad row with my father, I nearly always tell my sister Isodel, and you can't believe how much better that makes me feel."

Felim shook his head again. He unfastened his mouth just long enough to say, "A man should keep his trouble locked in his breast," and clamped it closed again.

"Oh, don't be so stupid!" Olga cried out. "People are always saying that kind of thing where I come from, too, and it never did anyone a bit of good. One man I knew had a fiend after him, and he never even told the magic user in

55

our—in our—anyhow, the magic user could have helped him."

"Besides, you aren't only a man, you're our friend," said Elda. "*Is* it a fiend?"

"No," gasped Felim. "Assassins. If the University has sent a demand for money to all families, then the Emir will learn that I am here and assassins will come."

"But didn't you tell Corkoran that the wards of the University would protect you?" Ruskin demanded.

"So I may have. But how do I know? I have not enough wizardry yet to know if the wards are strong enough," Felim said desperately. "Assassins are magic users. They are also deadly with weapons. I have practiced all week with the rapier, but I know this is not enough. They may break the wards and enter here. I am promised horrible magical tortures so that I die by inches. What do I *do*?"

Ruskin's face was by this time almost as gray as Felim's. "Forgemasters are magic users, too," he growled. "How strong *are* these wards?"

Everyone looked at Claudia. She came and put her hands calmingly on Felim's shaking shoulders. "Steady. Does anyone know any divination spells?"

There was a long silence, and then Lukin said, "I think we do those next term."

"A bit late. Right," said Claudia. "So we can't find out if the wards here will protect him—"

"And tell no one else, tell no one else!" Felim

almost screamed. "This is a shame I can hardly bear!"

"All right," said Claudia. "But we can quite easily put protection spells on you ourselves, you know. It's just a matter of finding out how to. There must be books in the library about it. Let's go and look."

"Er, I hate to say this," Lukin said, "but we have to go and take notes about herbs from Wermacht. Five minutes ago actually."

"Library straight after that then," said Elda. "Stick in our midst, Felim, and if any assassins turn up, we'll defend you. I can be quite dangerous if I try."

"I—I am sure you can." Felim agreed with a quivering sort of smile.

When they tiptoed hurriedly into the North Lab, Wermacht was already dictating notes to students and healers about the virtues of black hellebore, but his manner was decidedly subdued. Seeing the six belated students, he did nothing but pull his beard and mutter something that might have been "Better late than never!" Even when Elda knocked over a desk, trying to be unobtrusive, all he did was raise a sarcastic eyebrow. He did not seem to notice that Felim just sat there, unable to concentrate on black hellebore, or on fetid hellebore either.

"*That* was a relief!" said Claudia as they shot outside afterward, dragging Felim with them. "Now. Library."

They hastened across the courtyard to the grand and lofty Spellman Building. The Spellman Building, so one of the innumerable pieces of paper they had been given when they first arrived informed them, was the oldest part of the University, designed by that Wizard Policant whose statue stood in the courtyard. Once it had contained the entire University. Now its lower floor contained the Council Chamber, the main lecture hall, and the University office, all ancient stone rooms where generations of student wizards had once sat learning spells. The upper floor now held bachelor quarters for the wizards who lived in the University, and the library. Elda led the rush up the great stone stairway, hardly sparing a thought for the fact that her claws were scraping stone steps that had been climbed by a thousand famous wizards. Up to now this had awed her considerably, but she was in too much of a hurry just then.

The librarian on duty winced a bit as Elda shoved through the swing doors, followed by a gaggle of humans and a dwarf, and hurriedly strengthened the stabilizing spells. The library was spacious enough for humans, with its high ribbed ceiling and shapely clerestory windows, but the gaps between the mighty oak bookcases had only been made wide enough for two wizards in robes to pass comfortably. Elda filled the gaps, and her wingtips tended to brush the marble busts of former wizards on the ends of each bookcase. The librarian watched nervously as the group made for the Inventory.

The Inventory was a magical marvel. It looked like a desk with a set of little drawers above it. You picked the special quill pen out of the inkwell on the desk, which activated the magic, and then wrote on the parchment slotted into the sloping surface. You could write the author of a book, or its title, or just the general subject you wanted, and when you had, the Inventory hummed a tune to itself and, after a second or so, slid open one or more of its little drawers. Each drawer was labeled on the outside with the name of one of the wizards whose marble busts stood on the ends of the shelves. Inside, you would find a card with the name of the book or books you needed on it, its author, and its shelf number. The snag was that the busts of the wizards were not labeled. You had to know which statue was Eudorus, or Kline, or Slapfort, and so forth, before you could begin to find the book.

The librarian watched more and more uneasily as heads bent over the desk and drawers slid in and out. Unfortunately it was the griffin who knew the names of the busts. She seized card after card, hooked it to a talon, and set off on three legs to plunge between bookcases and back out again carrying a book. Sometimes she got the wrong side of a bookcase and backed out without a book, to plunge into the next gap along, but in either case the bust on top lurched and wobbled.

Meanwhile the whispers around the Inventory grew more agitated. Several of the students glanced toward the librarian. Eventually the dwarf announced, in a loud, buzzing whisper, "Well, I'm going to *ask* about it," and came marching up to the librarian's desk. He put his chin on top of it and asked, quite politely, "Don't you have Policant's *Philosophy of Magic*? I can't seem to find it in the Inventory."

"Well, no, you wouldn't," the librarian explained. "That's an old book. We don't keep those on the shelves."

"And"—the dwarf propped a large hand on the desk to consult a crumpled list—"I can't find *The Red Book of Costamaret*, *Cyclina on Tropism*, or *Tangential Magic* either. Are those not on the shelves, too?"

"That's right," agreed the librarian. "We don't bother with any of those these days because none of the tutors recommends them to students. The courses nowadays don't go in for theory so much."

"But that's *ridiculous*!" Ruskin boomed.

"Hush," said the librarian. "People are trying to work here."

Most of the students sitting at the tables down the center of the library were looking up indignantly. Ruskin glanced at them and scowled. But he was here to distract the librarian, not to cause a disturbance, so he continued in a hoarse, growling whisper. "*Why* don't the courses go in for theory? Does that mean you won't let me have these books then?"

"You've no need for them," the librarian said patiently. "You're a first-year student. You'll have enough to do simply learning the practical things."

"That is not true." Ruskin began beating the hand with the list in it on the desk. The librarian watched the desk tremble, apprehensively. "I am a dwarf. Dwarfs *know* the practical stuff. And I have an inquiring mind. I want to know the *other* part, the thusness of how, the color and shape of the ethos, the smell of the beyond. Without knowing this, I am setting up my anvil on sliding shale. By denying me these books, you are asking me to found my forge on a quaking bog!"

"I am not denying you those books," the librarian said hastily. "I'm simply explaining why they're not on the open shelves. Just tell me which one you want and I'll call it up for you. Policant's *Philosophy*, you said?"

Ruskin nodded, the bones in his beard plaits rattling on the desk. "And *The Red Book of Costamaret*," he added, thinking he might as well make this distraction worthwhile.

"Very well." Disapprovingly the librarian activated an obscure spell.

Ruskin, watching keenly, saw that the spell was something very advanced, that he would never be able to operate himself. There were codes and signatures in it, and arcane unbindings. Regretfully he gave up the idea of sneaking in here at night and having a good rummage through the secrets of the University. He watched the air quiver between the librarian's hands, and the quiver become a pulsing. Eventually two large leather books slid out of nowhere onto the wooden surface in front of his face. They smelled divine to Ruskin, of dust and old gloves. "Thank you," he rumbled. He sneaked a look toward the Inventory. The others had by no means finished there. Elda was just dashing off with three more cards skewered to her right front talons. He raised his list. "And *Cyclina on Tropism*, *Tangential Magic*, *Paraphysics Applied*, *Thought Theorem*, *Dysfunctions of Reality*, *Universa Qualitava*, and, er, *The Manifold of Changes*," he read in a long, throaty grumble.

"*All* of them?" the librarian exclaimed.

"Every single one, please," Ruskin husked. "And if you have any others on the same lines—"

"Your student limit is nine books," the librarian snapped, and began making gestures again.

By the time the steep pile of books arrived— *Tangential Magic* was enormous, and some of the rest almost as mighty—the others were making their way to the librarian's desk, each with a pile of slimmer volumes, to have them checked out. The librarian eyed the advancing forty-five books and said, "I shall have to report this to your tutor."

They tried not to exchange uneasy looks. Eyes

front, Claudia asked, "Why is that?"

"Because it's not normal," said the librarian.

"Oh, no, of course it isn't," Olga said resourcefully. "Corkoran wondered if you'd worry, but he wants us to get into the habit of consulting more than just one book at once."

She did not need to nudge Elda for Elda to chime in with "He's such a lovely tutor. Even his ideas are interesting."

Elda was so obviously sincere that the librarian shrugged, grumbled, "Oh, very well," and stamped all fifty-four books, with some sighing but no more threats.

They hurried with their volumes to Elda's concert hall, Ruskin almost invisible under his. Once there they spread the books out on the floor and got to work examining them for usefulness. Lukin was particularly good at this. He could pick up a book, flip through it, and know at once what was in it. Felim did nothing much but sit quivering in a ring of books, as if the books themselves gave him protection. Ruskin was even less useful. He settled himself cross-legged on Elda's bed with *The Red Book of Costamaret* open across his knees and turned its pages greedily. He would keep interrupting everyone by reading out things like "To become a wizard, it is needful to think deeper than other men on all things, possible and impossible."

"Very true. Now shut up," said Olga. "This one looks very helpful. It's got lots of diagrams."

"Put it on this pile then," said Lukin.

Eventually they had three piles of books. One, a small pile of three, turned out to be almost entirely about raising demons, which they all agreed was not helpful. "My dad raised one once when he was a student," Elda told them, "and he couldn't get it to leave. It could be a worse menace than an assassin."

The other two piles were what Lukin called the offensive and the defensive parts of the campaign, six books on spells of personal protection and thirty-six on magical alarms, traps, deadfalls, and trip spells. Claudia knelt between the two piles with her wet-looking curls disordered and her face smudged with dust. "We've got roughly three hours until supper," she said. "I reckon we should get all the protections around him first and then do as many traps as we've got time for. How do we start, Lukin?"

"Behold," boomed Ruskin as Lukin took up the top book from the small pile. "Behold the paths to the realms beyond. They are all around you and myriad."

By this time everyone was ignoring Ruskin. "Nearly all of them start with the subject inside a pentagram," Lukin said, doing his rapid page flipping. "Some of them have pentagrams chalked on the subject's forehead, feet, and hands, too."

"We'll do them all," said Claudia. "Take your shoes off, Felim."

"What color pentagrams?" Elda asked, swooping on Felim with a box of chalks.

Lukin turned pages furiously, with Olga leaning over his shoulder. "It varies," Lukin said. "Green, blue, black, red. Here's one says purple."

"Do one of each color, Elda," Claudia instructed.

"Candles," said Lukin. "That's constant, too." While Olga got up and raced off to the nearest lab for a supply of candles and Elda busily chalked a purple five-sided star on Felim's forehead, Lukin leafed through all three books again and added, "None of them says what color the pentagram around the subject should be—just that it must be drawn on the floor."

"The floor's all covered with carpet," Elda objected, drawing a green star on the sole of Felim's right foot. "Keep still, Felim."

"You're tickling!" Felim said.

"Use the top of his foot instead," Claudia suggested. "Can't one draw on a carpet with chalk?"

"Yes, but I like my carpet," said Elda.

"The method of a spell," Ruskin intoned from the platform, "is not fixed as a law is of nature but varies as a spirit varies. Consider and think, O mage, and do not do a thing only for the reason it was always done before."

"Some useful advice for a change," Elda remarked. She finished drawing on Felim, put the chalks away, and arranged the thirty-six books from Lukin's "offensive" pile into a pentagram around Felim, working with such strong concentration that her narrow golden tongue stuck out from the end of her beak. "There. That saves my nice carpet."

"The matter of nature," Ruskin proclaimed, "treated with respect, responds most readily to spells of the body."

"Oh, gods! Is he still at it?" Olga said, returning with a sack of candles from Wermacht's store cupboard. "Do shut up, Ruskin."

"Yes, come on down here, Ruskin," Lukin said, climbing to his feet. "Time to get to work. There are five points to this pattern and five of us apart from Felim, so it stands to reason we're going to need you."

Ruskin sighed and pushed *The Red Book of Costamaret* carefully off his knees. "It's blissful," he said. "It's what I always imagined a book of magic was—until I came here and found Wermacht, I mean. What do we do?"

"Everything out of these three books, I think," Lukin said. "It ought to be pretty well unbreakable if we do it all, eh, Felim?"

"One would hope." Felim agreed wanly.

They started with a ring of ninety-nine candles around the pentagram of books, this being all the candles in the sack. Because no one knew how to conjure fire to light them yet, Ruskin lit them all with his flint lighter. Then they stood one at each point of the pentagram, passing books from hand to hand to talon, reciting rhymes, shouting words of power, and attempting to make the gestures in the illustrations. One spell required Elda to hunt out her hand mirror and pass that around, too, carefully facing the glass outward to reflect enemy attacks away from Felim. In between spellings, they all looked anxiously at Felim, but he sat there stoically upright and did not seem to be coming to any harm.

"You will yell if it hurts or anything, won't you?" each of them said more than once.

"It does not, although I feel rather warm at times," Felim replied.

So they went doggedly on through all three books. It took slightly less than an hour because a number of the spells were in more than one book and some, like the mirror spell, were in all three. Nevertheless, by the end they all suddenly found they were exhausted. Elda said the last incantation and sank down on her haunches. The rest simply folded where they stood and sat panting on the carpet.

Here a truly odd thing occurred. All ninety-nine candles burned down at once, sank into puddles of wax on the carpet, and flickered out. While Elda was looking sadly at the mess, she saw, out of the end of her left eye, that Felim seemed to be shining. When she whipped her head around to look at him properly, Felim looked quite normal, but when she turned the corner of her other eye toward him, he was shining again, like a young man-shaped lantern, glowing from within. His red sash looked particularly remarkable, and so did his eyes.

Around the pentagram the others were discovering the same thing. Everyone thought they might be imagining it, and no one liked to mention it until Olga said cautiously, "Does anyone see what I see?"

"Yes," said Claudia. "My guess is that we've discovered witch sight. Felim, can you see yourself glowing?"

"I have always had witch sight," Felim said, "but I hope this effect does not last. I feel like a beacon. May I wash the chalk off now?" But the colored pentagrams had gone. Felim held out both hands to show everyone.

"It's worked!" Lukin slapped his own leg in delight. "We did it. We make a good team."

They were so pleased that much of their tiredness left them. Felim climbed rather stiffly from among the books, and they celebrated by eating oranges and the last of the food in the other hamper. Then, still munching, they took up books from the pentagram to find out ways to trap the assassins before they got near Felim.

"My brother Kit would call this overkill," Elda remarked.

"Overkill is what we're going for," said Lukin as he rapidly opened a whole row of books. "Doubled and redoubled safety. Oh-oh. Difficulty. About half of these need to be set to particular times. We have to time them for when the assassins actually get here."

"That's all right," Claudia said, peeling her sixth orange. "Oh, Elda, I do love oranges. Even Titus never has this many. We can work out when they'll get here. Felim, how long did you take on the way?"

Felim smiled. The glow was fading from him, but his confidence seemed to grow as it faded. "Nearly three weeks. But I took a poor horse and devious ways to escape detection. The assassins will travel fast by main roads. Say a week?"

"A week from whenever the letter from the University arrived," said Claudia. "Elda, when did your father get his?"

"He didn't say. But," said Elda, "if it went by one of his clever pigeons, it would take a day to Derkholm and three days to the Emirates."

"Say the letter was sent the first day of the term," Olga calculated. "Ten days then, three for the pigeon, and seven for the assassins. The day after tomorrow is the most likely. But we've enough spells here to set them for several nights, starting tomorrow and going on for the next three nights. Agreed?"

"Most for the day after tomorrow, I think," said Claudia. "Yes."

Ruskin sprang up. "Let's get to work then."

This was something Felim could do, too. They took six books apiece and worked through them, each in his or her own way. Felim worked slowly, pausing to give a wide and possibly murderous grin from time to time, and the spells he set up made a lot of use of the knife and fork from Elda's food hamper. Ruskin went methodically, with strips of orange peel and a good deal of muttering. Once or twice he dragged *The Red Book of Costamaret* over and appeared to make use of something it said. Elda and Olga both spent time before they started, choosing the right spells, murmuring things like "No, I hate slime!" and "Now that's *clever*!" and worked very quickly once they had decided what to do—very different things, to judge from Olga's heaps of crumbled yellow chalk and Elda's brisk patterns of orange peel. Lukin worked quickest of all, flipping through book after book, building patterns of crumbs or orange pips, or knotting frayed cloth from Elda's curtains, or simply whispering words. Claudia was slowest. She seemed to choose what to do by shutting her eyes and then opening a book, after which she would think long and fiercely over the pages, and it would be many minutes before she slowly plucked out one of her own hairs or carefully scraped fluff off the carpet. Once she went outside for a blade of grass, which she burned with Ruskin's lighter before going to the door again and blowing the ash away.

All of them met spells that they could tell were not working. There would be a sort of dragging heaviness, as if the whole universe were resisting what they were trying to do. They didn't let that bother them. If they did enough spells, they were sure some would work. They just went on to a new one. Among them, they set up at least sixty spells. When the refectory bell rang for supper, Elda's concert hall was littered with peculiar patterns, mingled with books, and all six of them were exhausted.

"You're going to have to walk carefully in here," Lukin said to Elda.

"It's only for a few days. I'll put a note for the cleaners," Elda said blithely. "If Felim's safe, it's *worth* it."

"Thank you," said Felim. "I am most truly grateful."

FOUR

Ruskin spent most of the night reading *The Red Book of Costamaret*, first in the buttery bar with a mug of beer, then, when they turned him out, in his own room. He fell asleep after he had finished it, but he was up at dawn, pounding on the door of Elda's concert hall for the rest of the books.

"Oh, good *gods*!" squawked Elda when the pounding was reinforced by Ruskin's voice at its loudest. "All right. I'm coming!" She flopped off her bed platform, remembered just in time that the floor was covered with spells, and spread her wings, thinking it was lucky she was a griffin. She flew to the door, too sleepy to notice that the wind from her wings was fanning some of the spells out of shape. Meanwhile the door was leaping about. "Ruskin," said Elda, wrenching it open, "please remember I can tear you apart if I want to—and I almost want to."

"I want *Cyclina on Tropism*," Ruskin said. "I need it. It's like a craving. And I'll take the rest of my books, too, while I'm here."

"Feel free," Elda said irritably, moving away from the doorway.

Ruskin rushed inside, skipped dextrously between spells, and pounced on *Cyclina*. "Do you want to read *The Red Book of Costamaret*?" he asked as he collected the rest. "It's full of the most valuable magical hints. You can have it now if you like, but I want to read it again before I have to take it back to the library."

Elda had not formed any great opinion of *The Red Book*—although it had indeed given her a hint, she realized—but she was too sleepy to refuse. "All right. Give it to me in Wermacht's class this morning. Now go away and let me go back to sleep."

Ruskin grinned and departed, looking like a rattling stack of folios balanced on two small bent legs. Elda shut her door and flew back to her bed. But she found he had woken her just enough to stop her getting back to sleep again. She lay couched on her stomach, thinking crossly about the mess her room was in. Soon she was thinking what a long time it was until breakfast and then how lucky it was that she still had some oranges. After that there was nothing for it but to get up and tread carefully about, eating an orange. After

73

that she thought she would try to get at least some of the ninety-nine pools of wax out of the carpet. That, even with efficient griffin talons, took more than half an hour of scraping and scratching, but there was still a long time until breakfast. Elda began hopping between spells, collecting the other forty-odd books from the library into piles. This was how she discovered Policant's *Philosophy of Magic*. Ruskin had missed it because it looked very much like the other, more ordinary books.

"Oh, well," said Elda. "Dad did say to read it."

She flew back to her bed with it and started to read.

It was not at all what she had expected, although she saw at once why it would appeal to her father. Policant had a way of putting together two ideas that ought not to have had anything to do with one another, and then giving them a slight twist so that they did after all go together— rather as Derk himself had done to eagle and lion to make griffin, Elda thought. To her mind, the way Policant did it was a bit forced. But Policant kept asking questions. They were all questions that made Elda say to herself, "I wouldn't ask *this* like *that*!" or, "That's not the right question; he should be asking *this*!" Before long she was wondering if Policant might not be asking the wrong questions on purpose, to make you notice the right ones. After that she was hooked. It dawned on her that she had chosen the most exciting subject in the world to study, and she read and read and read. In the end she was almost late for breakfast because she just had to finish Section Five.

She floated into the refectory, feeling utterly absentminded, but terribly alert somewhere, as if her brain had been opened up like an umbrella— or rather, a whole stack of umbrellas, some of them inside out.

"What is the matter?" Felim asked, seeing the way Elda's wings and crest kept spreading and her tail tossing.

"Nothing," said Elda. "I've just been reading Policant."

"Good, is he?" asked Lukin.

"Yes, but in a very queer way. I couldn't stop reading," Elda said.

Her friends eyed Elda's arching neck and shining eyes with some awe. "May I read him after you?" Felim inquired politely.

"You all *must*!" Elda declared. "Even you," she said to Ruskin, who looked up from *Cyclina* with his eyes unfocused and grunted.

Elda was so anxious to get back to Policant before Wermacht's class that she only spared a minute to watch Corkoran racing to his moonlab with his tie of peacock feathers floating out behind him. She stared briefly at his rushing figure and then galloped back to her concert hall.

Corkoran did not notice her at all. He had problems. Surrounding a peach with a cannonball

75

turned out to make it far too heavy. He knew he would hardly be able to walk in that much iron, even if, as his experiments suggested, he was going to feel lighter on the moon. He was thinking of magical ways to reduce the weight of iron, or maybe pare down a cannonball, and he was simply irritated when he found the neat little stickit-spell the librarian had left on his desk. So his first-year students had taken out fifty-four books? Why not? He had chosen them to teach because they might turn out to be exceptional. He forgot the matter and spent the next two days carefully dunking balls of iron into different magical solutions.

In those two days Policant went the rounds of all of Elda's friends, followed by *The Red Book of Costamaret*, followed by *Cyclina* and the rest. None of them found *The Red Book* quite as marvelous as Ruskin had, but Policant grabbed them all, and Felim became so absorbed in the wonders of *Tangential Magic*, vast as it was, that he forgot about assassins and almost forgot to go to Wermacht's classes. Olga only got him there by marching up to Felim's room and snapping her fingers between Felim's eyes and the book, almost as if she were breaking a spell. Once there in the class, Felim gazed broodingly at Wermacht and shook his head from time to time.

But Wermacht struck them all that way now they had read those books. As Olga put it, when they gathered around the statue of Wizard

Policant after classes, listening to Wermacht now was like trying to hear one raindrop in a thunderstorm. There was just so much *more* of magic. "But please don't keep shaking your head at Wermacht like that, Felim," she added. "The beastly man's coming right back into form."

This was true. For half a day after Corkoran's threat Wermacht had been almost subdued. He plugged away dictating his big headings and drawing his diagrams and hardly looked at the students at all. Then he started stroking his beard again. The following morning he called Ruskin "you with the voice"—luckily Ruskin was thinking of a really difficult idea in *Thought Theorem* and hardly noticed—and began to address Lukin as "you with the——" before he stopped and said "golden notebook." By that afternoon it seemed to have occurred to him that if he pretended Elda was not there, towering and golden at the back of the North Lab, Corkoran would have no grounds for firing him. He stalked up to the front of the class in quite his usual manner, planted his hourglass, and swung around, stroking his beard.

"This afternoon," he announced, "we were supposed to be doing conjuring flame. But someone seems to have taken all the candles. Anyone have a confession to make?" His eyes traveled over the class so accusingly that half the students cowered and appeared to be searching their souls. Olga's lovely face remained frigidly innocent.

"Right," said Wermacht, after nearly five

minutes' worth of sand had poured into the lower bulb of the hourglass. "It seems we have a hardened criminal in our midst. So we are going to do something far more difficult. All of you write down 'Raising Magefire.' Underline it. Keep your notebooks open, and all of you stand up." Seats scraped on stone as everyone rose to his or her feet. "Now hold out both hands cupped in front of you." When Elda hastily rose to her haunches, sending her desk scraping, too, in order to do this, Wermacht stroked his beard and ignored her. "Now sit down again, and write a description of the precise position you were in." Seats scraped again. Everyone scribbled. "That's it. Now stand up and adopt the position again." Wermacht stuck his thumbs into the armholes of his robe and stalked back and forth as everyone once more stood up. "Good. Higher, you with the secondhand jacket. Nearer your chin. Better. Now concentrate and find your center. You'll find that under the tenth big heading in your notes from last week. Sit down and turn back to the place. You'll find you have written—even you with the voice, look at your notes—that your center—you with the secondhand jacket, I said consult your notes—your center is a small multi-dimensional sunlike body, situated just below the breastbone in men and around the navel in women. Now stand up and locate it in yourself."

Everyone rather wearily stood up again, cupping hands and talons. But this was only the third time. Wermacht, smugly marching back and forth, had them up and down like yo-yos, until even Elda had lost count.

Finally, he said, "That's better. Now, keeping the position and concentrating on your center, smoothly transfer some of the energy from your center to between your hands."

There was a long, straining silence, while everyone tried to do this.

"Think," Wermacht said, with contemptuous patience. "Think of flame between your hands."

"Then why didn't you *say* so?" Ruskin rumbled.

"Did you say something, you with the voice?" Wermacht asked nastily.

Ruskin said nothing. He simply stood there with his face lit from beneath by the pile of purple flame cupped in his large hands. Wermacht scowled.

At that moment several students near the front gave cries of pleasure and held out little blue blobs of flame.

"*Very* good," Wermacht said patronizingly.

After that, as if it were catching, blue flames burst out all over the North Lab.

"Like wildfire," Olga said, grinding her teeth, and summoned suddenly a tall, green, twirling fire that forked at the top. The forks twisted together almost to the ceiling.

"Oh, dear!" said Lukin. He had managed to do it, too, but his blue fire was, for some reason, dancing in a little pit in the middle of his desk.

Wermacht exclaimed angrily and came striding up the lab. "Trust you lot to make a mess of it! You with the secondhand jacket, pick that flame up. Cherish it. Go on, it won't burn you. And you, girl with the long nose, pull your flame in. Think of it as smaller at once, before you make a mess of the ceiling."

Olga shot a furious look at Wermacht and managed to reduce her forked green flame to about a foot high. Lukin leaned forward and gingerly coaxed his blue flame to climb into his hands. Wermacht made an angry spread-fingered gesture over the desk, whereupon the small pit vanished.

"What is it with you?" he said to Lukin. "Do you have an affinity for deep pits, or something?" Before Lukin could reply, Wermacht turned to where Felim was nonchalantly balancing a bright sky blue spire of light on one palm. "*Both* hands, I said!"

"Is there a reason for using two hands?" Felim asked politely.

"Yes. We do moving the fire about *next* week," Wermacht told him.

Elda, all this while, had her eyes shut, hunting inside herself for her center. She had never yet been able to discover it. It made her anxious and unhappy. Nobody else seemed to have any difficulty finding the place. But now, after reading Policant, she began to ask herself, Why? And the answer was easy. Griffins were a different shape from human people. *Her* center was going to be in another place. She gave up hunting for it up and down her stomach and looked into herself all over. And there it was. A lovely, bright, spinning essence-of-Elda was whirling inside her big griffin ribs, in her chest, where she had always unconsciously known it was.

There was a tingling around her front talons.

Elda opened her eyes and gazed admiringly at the large, transparent pear shape of golden-white fire trembling between her claws. "Oh!" she said. "How beautiful!"

This left only Claudia without magefire in the entire class. Wermacht turned from Felim to find Claudia with her eyes shut and her cheeks wrinkled with effort. "No, no!" he said. "Eyes open and see the flame in your mind."

Claudia's eyes popped open and slid sideways toward Wermacht. "I shut my eyes because you were distracting me," she said. "I have a jinx, you know, and I'm finding this very difficult."

"There is no such thing as a jinx," Wermacht pronounced. "You're just misdirecting your power. Look at your cupped hands and concentrate."

"I *am*," said Claudia. "Please move away."

But Wermacht stood looming over Claudia, while everyone else stared at her until Elda expected her to scream. And just at the point when Elda herself would have screamed, Claudia said, "Oh—blah!" and took her aching hands down.

Almost everyone in the lab cried, *"There!"*

"What do you all mean, 'there'?" Claudia asked irritably.

Wermacht took hold of Claudia's skinny right arm and bent it up toward her face. "I can't think what you did," he said, "but it's there. Look."

Claudia craned around herself and stared, dumbfounded and gloomy, at the little turquoise flame hanging downward from the back of her wrist. "I told you I had a jinx," she said.

"Nonsense," said Wermacht, and strode away to the front of the class. "Withdraw the flame back to your center now," he said. This was surprisingly easy to do, even for Elda, whose heart ached at having to get rid of her lovely transparent teardrop. "Sit down," said Wermacht. Seats obediently scraped. "Write in your own words— you, too, you with the jinx. You can stop admiring your excrescence; dismiss it and sit down now."

"But I *can't*," Claudia protested. "I don't know what I did to get it."

"Then you can stand there until you do, and write your notes up afterward," Wermacht told her. "The rest of you describe the process as exactly as you can."

Everyone wrote, while Claudia stood there miserably dangling her flame, until Elda remembered her own experience and hissed across at Claudia, "Ask yourself questions, like Policant."

Claudia stared at Elda for a moment and then said, "Oh!" The flame vanished. Claudia sat down and scribbled angrily.

"I can see I'm going to be 'you with the jinx' from now on," she said to the others as they crowded out into the courtyard.

"Join the club," said Lukin. "Why doesn't somebody assassinate that man?"

Felim flinched and went gray.

"It's all right, Felim," Elda said. "You've got protections like nobody ever before."

Elda proved to be right.

Around midnight that night Corkoran locked his lab and thought about going to bed. His rooms were in the Spellman Building on the same floor as the library, along with Finn's and Dench the Bursar's, who were the only other wizards who actually lived in the University. All the rest of the staff lived in the town. Corkoran strolled across the courtyard in a chilly, fine mist that raised goose bumps below the sleeves of his T-shirt, and found the University looking its most romantic. It was utterly quiet—which, considering the usual habits of students, was quite surprising—with just a few golden lights showing in the turreted black buildings around him. These stood like cutouts against a dark blue sky, only faintly picked out in places by misty lamps from the town beyond the walls. Better still, the moon was riding above the mist, just beside the tower of the Observatory. She was only about half there, a sort of peachy slice above a faint bluish puff of cloud, and Corkoran was ravished by the sight. He stood leaning against the statue of Wizard Policant, gazing up at the place where he so longed to be. So very far away, so very difficult to get to. But his moonship was about half built now. It would only take another few years.

"I'm going to do it," he said to the statue of Wizard Policant, and slapped it on its stone legs.

As if that were a signal, a monstrous noise broke out. If you were to beat forty gongs and a hundred tin tea trays with spades and axes, while ringing ten templefuls of bells and throwing a thousand cartloads of bricks and a similar number of saucepans down from the Observatory tower, you might have some notion of the noise. Mixed in among this sound, and almost drowned by the din, a great voice seemed to be shouting. DANGER, it bellowed. INVASION.

Corkoran clutched the statue in shock for a second. The noise seemed to turn his head inside out. He was aware of distant howlings from the main gate, where the janitor, who was a were-wolf, had reacted to the shock by shifting shape, and he realized that the man was not likely to be any help. But Corkoran was after all a wizard. He knew he must do something. Although the bonging and clattering and crashing seemed to be coming from all directions, the huge, muffled voice definitely came from the Spellman Building. Corkoran clapped a noise reduction spell over his ears and sprinted for the building's main door.

FIVE

THIS HAS TO be a student joke," Corkoran muttered. He threw wide the doors of the Spellman Building and turned on all the lights without bothering with the switches. He was so astonished at what he saw that he let the doors crash shut behind him and seal themselves by magic while he stood and stared.

The grand stairway was buried under a mountain of sand. And went on being buried. Whitish yellow sand poured and pattered and cascaded and increased in volume, doubled in volume while Corkoran stared, as if it were being tipped from a giant invisible hopper. Odder still, someone seemed to be trying to climb the stairs in spite of the sand. Corkoran could see a half-buried figure floundering and struggling about a third of the way up. As far as he could tell, it was a man in tight-fitting black clothes. Corkoran saw a black-hooded head emerge from the mighty dune, then a flailing arm with a black glove on its hand, before both were covered by the inexorably pouring sand. A moment later black-clad legs appeared, frantically kicking. Those were swallowed up almost instantly. A turmoil in the sand showed Corkoran where to look next, and he saw a tight black torso briefly, rather lower down. By this time the sand was piled halfway across the stone floor of the foyer.

Corkoran wondered what to do. The older wizards had warned him before they retired that he should expect all sorts of magical pranks from the students, but so far nothing of this nature had occurred. Most students had seemed uninventive or docile, or both. Corkoran had had absolutely no experience of this kind of thing. He watched the seething sand pile ever higher and the struggling black-clad fellow appear, lower down each time, and dithered.

While he dithered, the onrushing sand swept the black-clad man down to floor level, where he staggered to his feet, tall, thin, and somehow unexpectedly menacing. Corkoran had just a glimpse of a grim, expressionless face and a black mustache before a large pit opened under the fellow's staggering black boots and the man vanished down into it with a yelp.

That, thought Corkoran, was surely not one of our students. He went to the edge of the pit and peered down. It was fairly deep, breathing out a curious fruity darkness. He could just see the pale oval of the man's face at the bottom and the dark bar of the fellow's mustache. "You're not a student here, are you?" he called down, just to be sure.

"No," said the man. "Help. Get me out."

Sand was already pattering into the pit. At this rate it would fill up enough in five minutes for the man to climb out. Corkoran could not help thinking that this was a bad idea. "Sorry," he said. "You're trespassing on University property." He stepped back and covered the pit with the Inescapable Net he used to stop air leaking from his moonship.

Then he turned his attention to the sand.

This proved to be far more of a problem. It took Corkoran three tries just to stop more of it arriving. The spell was decidedly peculiar, some kind of adaptation of a little-known deadfall spell, with a timer to it that had to be removed before the main spell could be canceled. But eventually the sand stopped coming, and Corkoran was merely faced with the small mountain of it that was there already. He raised his arms and tried to dismiss it back to the desert it had presumably come from.

It would not budge.

Feeling rather irritated by now, Corkoran performed divinatory magic. All this told him was that the sand had to be returned to the place it had come from, which he knew already. He was forced to go and pick up a handful of the gray, dusty granules, in order to perform a more difficult hands-on spell of inquiry.

"Help me!" commanded a voice from near his feet.

Corkoran whirled around and saw black-gloved fingers clinging to the underside of the Inescapable Net. The fellow had magic, and he was probably unbelievably strong, too, to have climbed right to the top of the pit. This was bad news. "No," he said. "You stay there."

"But this pit is filling with poisoned water!" the intruder panted.

Corkoran leaned over and saw the man crouched at the head of the pit, with his black boots against the rough side of it and his hands clutching the net. Below him, quite near and obviously rising, was dark, glinting liquid. The smell of it puzzled Corkoran. Some kind of fruit, he thought. The smell brought back memories of the Holy City when he was there as a Wizard Guide during the tours, and a priest of Anscher passing him a bright, round, pimply fruit. Then he had it. "It's only orange juice," he said. "Tell me who you are and what you think you're doing here, and I'll let you out."

"No," said the intruder. "My lips are sealed by oath. But you can't let me drown in orange juice. It is not a manly death."

Corkoran considered this. The man did have a

point. He sighed and cast away his handful of sand. "Bother you. You are an infernal nuisance." He levitated the Inescapable Net from the top of the pit, bringing the man upward with it. The man promptly let go of the net with one hand and grabbed Corkoran by his flowing peacock-feather tie. And twisted it. This was not simple panic. Corkoran saw a knife glitter in the man's other hand, the one still clinging to the net.

Corkoran panicked. He was suddenly in a fierce struggle, brute strength against magic, killer training against panic. Being throttled with your own tie, Corkoran found himself thinking in the midst of his terror, was quite as disgraceful as being drowned in orange juice. At that stage he was trying to throw this murderer back into the pit. But the fellow was far too strong. He hauled on the tie until Corkoran could hardly breathe, and the glittering knife crept up toward Corkoran's right eye. The only thing that saved Corkoran was the net, which was still in the way between them. Corkoran pushed back at the fellow and at the knife with every spell he could think of, and for some reason it was only the strange spells he could think of. And the struggle ended, with the murderer two inches long and imprisoned in the Inescapable Net, which had turned itself into a bag around him.

Corkoran held the bag up and looked at it, as surprised as his attacker must have been. He loosened his tie. Relief. He was shaking. "Let that be a lesson to you," he told the bag hoarsely. Then, because he could not think what else to do with it, he levitated the bag to hang on the massive light fitment that dangled from the vaulted stone ceiling, where it was at least out of the way, and turned back to the mountain of sand.

He took up a handful, murmured the spell, and then let it patter to the floor as he asked it, "What are you? Where are you from?"

A soft, spattering answer came. "We are dust from the moon."

"*Moon* dust?" Corkoran turned to the stairway and looked at the enormous pile of fine gray-white sand with astonished admiration. Moon dust. This had to be an omen. He had half a mind to let it stay there to encourage him in his work. But he realized that it would be very inconvenient. And he was the person best qualified to send it back to the moon. Yes, definitely an omen. From being shaken and sore-throated and angry, he found he had become lighthearted and almost benevolent toward whichever student had done this. It was a silly prank, but it had given him an omen.

He told the sand to go back to the moon. It vanished at once, every grain of it. Corkoran had a vision of the spell working—which was not something that often happened with him—and the sand sailing up past the Observatory tower, through the clouds, and siphoning onward in a spiral to that half-moon up there. Smiling, he turned to the pit and told that to go, too. It closed up, sploshily, with a clap and a sharp smell of oranges.

Here he became aware that the monstrous din out in the courtyard had gone away as well. Thank the gods! This must mean that the prank spell had finished now. Corkoran took the noise abatement spell off his ears and thankfully climbed the stairs, which had a clean sand-blasted look to them, on his way to bed.

At the top he encountered Wizard Dench, the Bursar. Dench came shuffling across the landing, wearing old slippers and a moth-eaten gray dressing gown. "Oh, there you are, Corkoran," he said. "I've been to your rooms to look for you." For some reason Dench was carrying a black cockerel upside down by its legs.

Corkoran stared at it, wondering if Dench was taking up black magic and if he ought to sack him on the spot. "Dench," he said, "why are you carrying a black chicken by its legs?"

"On the farm when I was a boy," Dench replied, "we always carried them this way. It's the best way to capture them. That's why I was coming to look for you. I don't know if I was dreaming or not—I was certainly asleep—but while it was climbing through my window, I got the idea it was a man. But when I woke up and looked, it was a cockerel. Running everywhere, making a dreadful noise. What do you think I should do with it?"

"Wring its neck, I should think," said

Corkoran. "It's only another student joke. The kitchen might be glad of it."

"Er, well, in that case," said Dench. "That's why I came away from the farm. I can't bear to wring necks. Could you, er—"

He held the hapless cock out to Corkoran. As Corkoran sighed and reached out to take it, the bird began twisting about, flapping its wings and screaming. Almost as if it understood, Corkoran thought.

"Hang on," he said. He seized a flailing wing and murmured the spell of inquiry again. "What are you?" he asked.

"An assassin of Ampersand," the bird replied. "And my curse on you for causing me to break my oath! A thousand, thousand curses—"

"Shut up," said Corkoran. "It's another one of them, Dench. I caught one just now on the stairs. They must be partners. I think someone knew they were coming and set up traps for them. Not to worry. I know how to deal with them now." He rapidly shrank the cockerel to the size of a bumblebee, caught it as it whirred free from Dench's fingers, and stuffed it into a bag made of Inescapable Net, which he sent to join the other one hanging from the light fitment. "There. Now we can both go to bed."

"But, Corkoran!" Dench exclaimed. "We could be dead in our beds!"

As Dench spoke, there was a thunderous banging on the main doors below. Dench

93

clutched at Corkoran's arm, and Corkoran said, "Oh, what *now*?"

"Corkoran! Dench!" It was Finn's voice, amplified by magic. *"Are you all right in there?"*

Corkoran remembered that the doors had locked behind him. He went galloping down the stairs, with Dench in his slippers flip-flopping after. When he reached the place where the pit had been, there was such a stench of oranges that Corkoran automatically detoured in case the pit opened again. It had seemed to close, but he was taking no chances. Dench, however, flip-flopped safely straight through the spot and clasped Corkoran's arm again.

"Corkoran, what is Finn doing outside at this time of night?" he demanded as Corkoran wrenched the doors open. *"And* in pajamas?" he added.

"Best not to ask," Corkoran murmured.

Finn's pajamas were a wizardly purple flecked with little stars. He was shivering in the misty night air and obviously agitated. Behind him the courtyard was filled with almost every student in the place, wearing cloaks, gowns, coats, wraps, and sweaters over their nightclothes. They raised a cheer when they saw Corkoran and Dench unharmed in the doorway.

"Thank the gods!" said Finn. "There was such a noise and such a strong sense of magic in here that we thought there must have been some sort of accident."

"There was a bit of trouble," Corkoran admitted. He gestured Finn aside and addressed the students. "It's all right, everyone. You can go back to bed now. Something tripped the alarms, that's all. But Wizard Dench and I have made sure everything is quite safe now. Return to your rooms, please, before someone catches cold. There's absolutely nothing to worry about." He started to close the doors. "Are you coming in or staying out?" he asked Finn.

"Er—" Finn's eyes flicked to an extremely beautiful student girl standing shivering in a white silk gown. Melissa, Corkoran thought. No brain. "Oh, coming in, of course," Finn said, with his teeth chattering. "I only went outside to see what was making all that noise. What *was* the trouble really?" he asked as he stepped inside.

"Nothing much," Corkoran answered airily. "Student prank. It's all over now."

He went upstairs to bed with a strong, satisfied feeling of having been rather brave and behaved rather well. It was clear to him that he had all the intrepid qualities necessary for getting to the moon and dealing with what he found when he got there. And he had had an omen. The night had not been wasted. He fell asleep designing, as his custom was, a new flamboyant picture to put on his tie tomorrow.

And it seemed to him that he jumped awake the next second.

It was gray dawn: A warn-spell was dancing

up and down his body on top of his blankets. "*Urgent from Wizard Finn*," chanted the spell. "*Urgent from Wizard Finn. Accident to one of your students. Staircase five, room three. Come quickly.*"

"Gods and little fishes!" groaned Corkoran. "Whatever next?" He surged up, swatted the spell, and climbed into jeans and a sweater. The morning was truly chilly. There was frost on Wizard Policant as Corkoran pelted crosswise through the courtyard. Staircase five was in the far corner near the main gate. The first thing Corkoran saw there was Elda. She was up on the roof, with all four sets of talons clamped on the gutter and her wings spread for balance, so that she could crane down with her head upside down through the window. Corkoran hated heights. It made him dizzy just to look at her. And he could see the gutter bending as he raced over there.

"It was *your* fault as well," she was saying into the window. "You would keep reading things out of *The Red Book*."

"It was not my fault *so*!" Ruskin's voice rasped from inside.

"Elda, get down!" Corkoran panted. "You're breaking the gutter!"

Elda's head shot right way up in shock, and she lost her balance. Corkoran gasped. But Elda simply swirled a wing and flipped her tail and landed on her feet like a cat outside the entry to the staircase. She sat up and looked soulfully at Corkoran. "I'm too big to get inside the room, you see."

"Tough." Corkoran shot past under her beak and pounded up the worn wooden stairs indoors. Room three was on the upper floor, with a second window that gave a pleasant view over the town. It was fairly bare, but full of people. Finn was there, and Olga, both of them in the blue tights and white jerkins of the Rowing Club. How *does* Finn find the energy? Corkoran wondered. Ruskin was there, standing on tiptoe to peer out the inner window at Elda. It was obvious, Corkoran thought, that Ruskin slept with all those bones in his pigtails. He could not have had time to plait them all in before he arrived here. Lukin and Claudia were there, too, red-eyed and sleepy, Lukin wrapped in Olga's fur cloak and Claudia in one of those Empire garments that always reminded Corkoran of a very large bath towel. All of them except Ruskin were staring at the thing in the middle of the room.

The thing—whatever it was—was a little taller than Lukin and quite smooth and rounded and domed. At first Corkoran thought it was made of strangely smooth tree bark, but as he went closer, he saw that the seeming bark was leather, leather in long, narrow strips with gold lettering on each strip. It reminded Corkoran of nothing so much as a beehive, but a beehive that seemed to be made of books. When he put out a finger with a magnifying spell on it to the nearest gold lettering, he found it read *Advanced Protective Magic*. Yes, definitely books. But quite the most alarming feature was the long, spear-shaped knife sticking out of one side of it.

Corkoran's touch seemed to disturb the bee-hive. It waddled uncertainly in Ruskin's direction. Dim cries and scrabbling came from deep inside it.

"He's not happy," Ruskin stated.

"Well, would you be?" Claudia asked. "He must have been in there for at least six hours."

"Who is it?" Corkoran demanded.

"Felim," said Lukin. "Assassins were after him, you see, and we tried to give the poor fellow some protections." He gave an enormous yawn that reminded Corkoran irresistibly of last night's pit.

The yawn made Corkoran realize he was as sleepy as Lukin, but he began to understand the happenings of last night. "Why did you use library books?"

"Those aren't really library books," Claudia explained. "Elda says the real books are still on the floor in her room."

"It just came out like this because stupid Elda built the pentagram out of books," Ruskin growled. "And I don't care what she says. It was *not* my fault!"

"The important question is," said Finn, "can you get it off him? I can't. *They* can't. They're not even sure how they did it."

Corkoran rubbed his bristly chin. What a way to appear before students! And here was Finn all trim and clean-shaven, just as if he had never been outside half last night in purple pajamas. "Well, it's going to take some divination then. Is the knife part of it? Whose is it?"

"The knife's nothing to do with it," Olga said. "It belongs to the man hanging by one leg outside the window."

"What?" Finn looked at Corkoran, and Corkoran stared at Olga. She seemed utterly calm.

Both wizards hurried to the window that looked out over the town.

The man dangling outside was dressed in black like Corkoran's attacker. The first part of him they saw was the sole of a black boot, which was gripped very tightly around the ankle by a thick orange rope that appeared to be welded to the windowsill. Finn put out a finger and very cautiously touched the rope. A familiar gust of oranges came to Corkoran's nostrils. "This is like a steel hawser!" Finn said wonderingly.

Hearing him speak, the dangling man raised his face, which was bright red and encased in a black hood, from the region of the lower windows. "Let me up, for pity's sake! I'm going to die like this!"

"Poor fellow!" said Finn.

"No, he isn't. I heard that sort of talk last night," said Corkoran. "But we'd better haul him up, anyway. I want an explanation. But go very carefully."

Neither of them could budge the orange rope. It defied both spells of levitation and spells of release, and after that it defied plain pulling. It was not until Ruskin came over to wrap his large hands around the rope and heave with his powerful shoulders that the hanging man began to inch up the outside wall.

"Thought so," Ruskin grunted rather proudly. "This trap's one of mine."

Corkoran got his shrinking spell ready. As soon as the black boot came up level with the windowsill, he grasped the toe of it and clapped the spell on. Then he whipped forth a bag of Inescapable Net and crammed the tiny, struggling man inside it. Even so, the assassin contrived to stab Corkoran in the thumb with his tiny dagger. "Ouch!" cried Corkoran.

A clatter from the middle of the room made them all whirl around.

The beehive had vanished. Felim was standing there, sweating and rather white, with the knife on the floor at his feet. He was waving his arms, warning them all to keep clear of it.

"Are you all right?" everyone cried out.

"More or less. It was a little hot and stuffy but very safe," Felim said. "But no one must come near this knife. Assassins always poison their weapons."

"What?" Corkoran looked at the little red blob on his thumb. He put it to his mouth to suck the blood off and then rather quickly took it away.

"I fear," Felim said apologetically, "that the knife should be destroyed and the whole floor cleansed. The poison they use is lethal."

Corkoran felt ready to faint.

"In that case," said Finn, "you get over to Healers Hall at once, Corkoran, and I'll see to the cleansing. You students all go outside. Quickly."

Corkoran vanished in a clap of inrushing air. The five students clattered down the stairs and into the courtyard, where Elda bounded up to them. "Oh, Felim, I'm so *glad*! Are you safe now? Did we get them all?"

"I am not sure," Felim said cautiously. "Assassins always work in bands of seven."

His friends looked at one another anxiously. "Corkoran must have caught at least one more of them last night," Lukin pointed out. "How many of the spells were sprung, Elda?"

"Dozens," said Elda. "My carpet looks as if someone emptied a bag of rubbish over it."

"So we *might* have caught them all?" Lukin said.

"In that case," Ruskin growled, "where are they?"

This caused more anxious looks, which deepened to real worry when Claudia said, "The big question is, If we *haven't* caught them all, does the protection go back on Felim when the next one has a go at him, or is that spell used up?"

"I think," said Olga, "we maybe ought to ask Corkoran."

"Dare we?" asked Elda. "He looked awfully annoyed. And he wasn't wearing his tie."

Ruskin, who was still annoyed with Elda, demanded, "What's his tie got to do with anything? He's still a wizard, even without a tie."

"That wasn't what I *meant*!" squawked Elda. "You—"

"Please," said Claudia. "I've got to go and get dressed. I'm freezing. The rest of you try to catch Corkoran on his way back from the healers." She went. Lukin, yawning and shivering, wrapped himself into Olga's fur cloak and went to get dressed, too. The remaining four hung about near the statue of Wizard Policant until Finn came and found them there.

Finn was angry by then. He had been deprived of Melissa and half a night's sleep, and now he had missed Rowing Club, too. He always felt out of sorts, anyway, if he missed his morning workout on the lake. Instead, he had been landed with the tricky and dangerous magic of getting rid of the assassin's knife and then cleansing Felim's floor. The fumes that came off the black, spear-shaped mark on the floorboards had made him cough and feel more than ever out of sorts. When the poison was finally banished and he clumped down the stairs to see Elda looming in the middle of the courtyard above Ruskin, Olga, and Felim, all of them in clouds of their own steamy breaths, Finn was suddenly furious. It was all their fault. He strode toward them.

"Haven't you people done enough now?" he demanded in a hoarse shout.

Corkoran meanwhile was returning from Healers Hall, feeling rather queasy from the thick green liquid the duty healer had made him drink. The duty healer had assured him that he was in no danger whatsoever. The tiny dagger had not had enough poison on its point to poison a gnat, and most of that had come out with the blood. The healer wiped away the blood and burned the cloth she used. Then she made him drink the green liquid as a precaution. But Corkoran was not convinced. Like most people who are hardly ever ill, he was quite unable to tell which were dangerous symptoms and which were not. Did his head ache, he wondered as he walked, *merely* because he was short of sleep? Or was it the deep working of venom? Why was his heart racing so? He refused to believe it was just with terror. And what caused his knees to tremble slightly as he walked? It was certainly not with relief. And *was* the sick, heavy feeling in his stomach *only* caused by the horrible green drink? Or was he about to die and waste all his moon research? He swung the little bag with the assassin in it and thought vengeful thoughts at it.

He came around the corner of the North Lab to find Finn with his legs astride and his arms folded, standing near the statue of Policant, bawling at Elda and her friends. It was so exactly what Corkoran wanted to do himself that he approached, feeling deeply appreciative.

"No, it wasn't, it was plain idiocy!" Finn was yelling. "You should have come to one of us, and we could have put *proper* protections around him. We know the correct spells. You don't. But oh, no! You had to go and be clever! And what happens? Everyone in this University loses a night's sleep, Corkoran gets poisoned, and I nearly choke. And Felim could have suffocated, of course."

"I beg your pardon," Felim objected quietly as Corkoran drew closer. "I must contradict you there, Wizard Finn. The protections put around me by my friends were far more effective than the wards of the University, and I could breathe with perfect ease."

"What do you know about the wards?" yelled Finn. "You never gave the damned things a chance! You rushed in and fooled about with books and orange peel instead. It was the merest luck the stupid things kept you safe. You *must* learn that magic is dangerous stuff! You have to go *cautiously*, step by little step, and follow the *rules*, or you could end up *dead*, or turned into a *fish*! I always tell my students they should never, *ever* do anything they haven't been taught to do!"

"Hear, hear!" said Corkoran.

Elda, who had her beak open to suggest that *someone* must have done something he hadn't been taught, or there would never have been any magic to start with, shut her beak and gazed at

Corkoran sorrowfully. Ruskin's eyebrows bunched, but the way he looked out at Corkoran from under his scowl seemed almost pitying. Olga and Felim stared straight and unconvinced. Corkoran wondered what had got into them all, but he went on firmly, "I agree with every word that Wizard Finn has said."

"I beg your—" Felim began in his usual polite way. But he stopped because the paving stones of the courtyard began to bulge upward in front of Corkoran.

Corkoran leaped backward from the bulge. "Oh, what now?" he said. As he spoke, the hillock of stonework split apart, grinding a little, to make a slimy-seeming hole. Out of it came the familiar and piercing smell of oranges, mixed with what was certainly the smell of sewers. A creature about the size of a lion squeezed out of the reeking space. It was a creature like no one there had seen before. Its skin was orange, shiny, and pimply, its head was too big for its body, and it shone with slime. In the enormous jaws of its great head it held a long, heavy bundle. This bundle it proceeded to lay lovingly at Corkoran's feet, wagging its skinny orange tail as it did so. Then it paused to gaze expectantly up into Corkoran's face. When Corkoran did nothing but look disgusted, the creature faded into nothingness, a little sadly. The stones of the courtyard closed with a thump, although the smell remained, sharp in the frosty air.

"Ugh!" said Finn. "I suppose that's another of them who tried to get in through the sewers."

Elda was jigging up and down. "That's one of mine!" she told Felim delightedly.

Corkoran looked unlovingly from Elda to the assassin lying by his toes. The man was dripping with slime and orange juice and half stunned, but he was already struggling to reach the dagger in his boot. Corkoran hastily put his foot on the man's reaching fingers and shrank him before he could do any more. As he summoned another bag of Inescapable Net, he said, "If you people have any more spells set up, go and dismantle them. Now." He scooped the assassin into the bag and strode away toward the Spellman Building.

Finn, who wanted to change out of his Rowing Club clothes, glowered at the students and followed Corkoran. By the time Finn reached the foyer of the Spellman Building, Corkoran was summoning the first two bags down from the light fitment. "You've got four of them!" Finn exclaimed. "What are you going to do with them?"

Corkoran still felt ill. He held the four little bags up at eye level so that they could both see the three tiny men and the one extremely small cockerel struggling about inside. "I think I might send them to the moon," he said vengefully. "I need to know for certain that there isn't any air up there."

"You can't do that!" Finn said, horrified. "That's a dreadful death!"

Corkoran was taken aback and rather hurt at this reaction of Finn's. He would have thought that after the bad time these people had given them all, Finn would be entirely in favor of the idea. "Why not? They're assassins. Two of them nearly killed me."

"Yes, but they're human beings, not experimental animals," Finn protested.

"That's why it's such a good idea," Corkoran explained. "I'll put them in several different designs of metal suits, so that if they don't suffocate or explode, I'll know which one's safe for me to wear."

Finn felt sick. The assassins might be professional murderers, but he was sure they did not deserve this. He knew assassins were dedicated men, who trained for years and had the same kinds of professional standards that wizards did. In their way they were honorable people. And they had surely only been doing their job in coming here. The trouble was, he thought, Corkoran was far too obsessed with the idea of getting to the moon. He wondered, not for the first time, if Corkoran might not be a little unbalanced in his mind. If he was, Finn could perfectly understand it. Working as a Wizard Guide to Mr. Chesney's tour parties tended to make you unbalanced. It had been hard, feverish work, in which none of the events had been real, except that the dangers were very real and sometimes utterly terrifying. Finn remembered the way he had felt when the tours had been stopped: almost bewildered and still expecting that he was going to have to kill someone. He had been so used to people being killed then that he had worried at the way he seemed to have become flinty-hearted about death. It looked as if Corkoran was still feeling like this. In which case, what could one say to stop him sending these unfortunate men to the moon? The trouble was, Corkoran did not think of experiments as murder. They were just stepping-stones on his way to be the first man on the moon.

Finn discovered that he knew the perfect thing to say. "Corkoran, these are *men*. If you send them to the moon, you won't be the first man to walk there."

Corkoran thought about this irritably. He realized Finn was right. "I could send the cockerel," he suggested.

"But that's really a man, too," Finn argued. "People like Querida or Derk would say you were cheating."

Corkoran sighed. Derk he thought he could deal with, but Querida was another matter. She was still the most powerful wizard in the world and still officially High Chancellor of the University. You did not do anything Querida might disapprove of. "All right," he said. "I'll think of something else." Blast Finn. These creatures had given him a bad fright and probably poisoned him. He wanted them to suffer.

He carried the four little bags to his moonlab, feeling peevish. There he hunted out the old cage where he had kept the rats that he had sent to the moon and shook the assassins into it out of the bags, carefully turning each one rat size as he did it, so that they could not squeeze between the bars. He sealed the cage with Inescapable Net and left a note on it for his assistant, telling her to feed and water the creatures once a day while he considered what to do with them. Then he forgot about them. He went away to shave and find his tie. Cherry pink irises on it today, he decided.

SIX

IN PLACES LIKE the University word gets
around. Though nobody precisely told anybody, by the end of breakfast everybody
knew that Felim was being hunted by seven
assassins—some versions said seventy—and that
Corkoran had so far caught only four of them.
Felim was surrounded by people offering sympathy and lucky amulets. He was also approached
by a lofty third-year student who offered to sell
Felim a set of eight essays, guaranteed to get top
marks, for a mere eight gold pieces. For, as the
lofty student pointed out, Felim was surely going
to be far too busy dodging assassins to do any
more work this term.

Felim, who by this time was very white, with
large dark circles under his eyes, objected politely
that he did not yet know what subjects Corkoran

was going to ask him to write essays on.

"No problem," said the lofty one. "Corkoran always sets the same essays. I bought the set from a girl who said Wermacht bought them, too, in his first year, and we all know what that did for Wermacht."

At this Felim drew himself up very tall and straight. "No, thank you. I discover that it is my duty to force Corkoran to read something different."

"It's your funeral," said the lofty one, and went away.

About the same time, the kitchen staff heard about the assassins. They all threatened to go home unless a wizard was provided at once to put protection spells on the kitchen and the refectory. "We could," claimed the cook, "be brained with our own frying pans while we work."

"Let him leave," growled Ruskin, "and the rest with him. All any of them do is to float food in grease."

Though most students shared Ruskin's opinion, none of the wizards did. Corkoran sent Wermacht to put the spells on. Wermacht stamped importantly into the kitchens and spent a refreshing half hour striding about there, intimidating the staff and ordering the cook on no account to touch either the walls or the windows once the spells were set. He then strode off, only slightly late, to teach his first-year class on Elementary Astrology.

The first-year students meanwhile waited in the North Lab with their notebooks, rulers, star charts, and compasses. Everyone but Elda was shivering. It was still a bitterly frosty, cold day, but Wizard Dench, the Bursar, had decreed that the University could not afford fires, or any other form of heating, for another month. Students were huddled in coats and cloaks, and some even wore gloves. Many wistful glances were cast at the large empty fireplace in the north wall.

"Do you suppose," someone suggested, "that we could collect rubbish and burn it there?"

"Everyone's bound to have wastepaper in their rooms," said someone else. "Anyone good at conjuring?"

Nobody was, particularly. But Ruskin discovered a wastebasket in one corner of the lab and tipped the pile of torn-up notes it contained into the grate. He got them alight, and all the students gathered around for what little warmth there was. Someone had just said that simply looking at the flames made you *feel* warmer when the chimney above the flaming pile of paper began disgorging a landslide of soot. Soot poured down into the grate, where it put out the flames but left the paper smoldering. Smoke now came billowing forth. Everyone backed away, coughing.

"Typical of this place!" exclaimed the student who had suggested the fire. "There must be a birds' ne—"

"Hush!" said everyone else.

Some of the coughing was coming from inside the chimney.

Everyone backed away in a rush, as two long black-clad legs appeared in the fireplace, groping for the ground. Melissa screamed.

And Wermacht strode into the lab just as a wildly coughing assassin ducked out from under the mantelpiece and advanced on the students with his dagger raised. There were screams from others besides Melissa. Elda, Olga, Claudia, Ruskin, and Lukin plunged amid the panic to the place where they had last seen Felim and relaxed in relief when they found him safely encased in the beehive of books again. Elda, unable to stop, charged on into the beehive and sent it reeling and blundering among the desks. A lot of desks were knocked over, some of them by Elda.

Behind Elda, the assassin reached out to take the nearest student hostage. With a certain inevitability, it was Melissa he grabbed at, and Melissa went into hysterics of terror. *"Save me! Save me!"* she screamed, and went on screaming it even though the assassin's black-gloved hand never reached her. Instead, the hand, followed by the arm, followed swiftly by the rest of the man, dissolved into little flakes of sooty ash. The flakes swirled about but hung together in a vague man shape that dithered against the mantelpiece, as if the assassin were wondering what in the world had happened to him.

The greenish blush swept across Claudia's face

as she recognized her burned-grass spell. Melissa turned, still screaming, to see what everyone was staring at and saw what seemed to be a black ashy ghost reaching for her. Screaming even harder, she rushed for the door. Since Wermacht was standing just in front of the door, stock-still and staring, Melissa rushed into Wermacht and flung her arms around him. "*Save* me!" she shrieked.

As every male person in the University afterward agreed, and this included the cook, the janitor, the porter, and half the office staff, anyone else who was lucky enough to have Melissa fling her arms around him would have made the most of it. Not Wermacht. He unwrapped Melissa and shoved her aside. He said, "This is a ridiculous fuss over nothing. You with the secondhand jacket and you with the armor, pick up those desks. And you come out from inside those books, whoever you are."

"He can't," Olga explained. "They only go away when the danger's over."

Wermacht stroked his beard smugly. "There is no danger," he said.

At this everyone gasped and tried to explain that the ghostly figure made up of whirling ashes was a trained assassin and that the fact that Felim was still inside the beehive *showed* there was danger.

"There is no danger," Wermacht repeated, against the chorus of agitated voices. "Go and sit at your desks, all of you. Corkoran will be here shortly. I have sent him a warn-spell. Wait quietly until he gets here. Let's have no more silly screaming and rushing about."

"The man's mad!" Ruskin said as everyone moved nervously to sit down.

When Corkoran swept into the North Lab with his pink iris tie streaming over one shoulder, he was slightly surprised to find all the students sitting uneasily at a somewhat uneven row of desks—uneven because a large space had to be left for the beehive standing in the middle of the lab—while Wermacht stood with his arms proudly folded beside the peculiar whirling figure on the hearth.

"Ah, Corkoran," Wermacht said in his smarmiest manner, "I've neutralized the assassin for you, as you see, but I didn't like to ash him completely without word from you, so I've kept him under my spell until you got here."

There was a gasp of pure indignation from Claudia. Her face was almost olive-colored as she whispered to Olga, "It was *my* spell! It's almost the only one I've done that *worked*!"

Corkoran was saying at the same moment, "Thanks, Wermacht. Very good of you." He had a bag of Inescapable Net ready for this one. He reached out and rather tentatively tweaked at the nearest twirling flake of ash in the creature's arm. To his relief, the assassin promptly became a two-inch-high pile of whirling dust. Corkoran blew it into his bag with a minor draft spell and no trouble at all. He stood up, smiled soothingly around at the students, and walked away.

A slight thumping made him turn in the doorway. Felim was now standing where the beehive had been. Felim's face was red, and his usually smooth black hair was sticking out in all directions, but he was grinning at Elda.

"Five down," Corkoran heard someone say as he hurried away. "Two to go." He hoped whoever said that was wrong. He had had enough alarms. And the rat cage was quite crowded when he tipped the little dust storm into it. He turned it back into a rat-size man to prevent it trying to squeeze through the bars or the net, and the cage seemed more crowded than ever. Yes, he thought, as he went back to the careful magics of the moonship, five assassins is quite enough.

An hour later the students boiled out of the North Lab into the courtyard, full of indignation. Every one of them was sufficiently attuned to magic to know that Wermacht had not cast a spell of any kind on the assassin. "Taking the credit just to suck up to Corkoran!" most of them were saying. "What a *creep*!" Even Melissa was saying it, and she was more indignant than anyone. "Did you see the way he treated me?" she kept asking. "I might have been a dog with mange!"

"I must say I am highly interested that everyone else has arrived at the same opinion of Wermacht as we have," Felim remarked. "It suggests that our judgment was sound."

"I'm just downright relieved that the protections came back around you," said Olga. "My heart stood still when I saw those legs coming down the chimney. What's the matter, Claudia?"

"Nothing—or at least I have the most dreadful mixed feelings," Claudia said. "You don't know how good it feels to do a spell that works for once! But then I think of the way it turned a person into ash and I feel dreadful! And I keep hoping Corkoran isn't going to do anything terrible to him."

"Of course he isn't," said Ruskin.

"He's probably simply going to release him into the wild or something," Lukin said soothingly. "That's the obvious thing to do. And let's hope those protections go *on* working because there are still two more assassins somewhere."

Everyone knew there were two more. The entire student population, not to speak of the kitchen staff and the janitor, spent the rest of the day jumping at sudden noises and looking nervously over their shoulders. Felim's friends arranged that he should never be alone. "But I am quite all right! The protection is better than armor," Felim protested when Ruskin insisted on coming with him every time he went to the toilet.

"Yes, but do you know how long the spell will last?" Ruskin retorted.

The rest of Felim's friends insisted that he spend the day in Elda's room, where there was space for everyone.

"I don't pretend to be a fighter," Lukin said, "but I can open a pit anytime, and Olga can fetch monsters. And if all else fails, Ruskin and Elda can take the assassins apart."

"I notice you don't mention me," Claudia said wryly, and Elda, who was couched on the floor amid the shriveling remains of the spells, carefully penning an extremely argumentative essay, looked up to say, "I don't *like* the idea of taking people apart. I never have. But I'll try."

Felim shrugged. He had wanted to be alone in his room to write his essay because, in spite of a night spent standing bolt upright in a hard shell smelling of book, he was determined to prove that he had no need to buy essays from the lofty student. His honor required it. But since there was obviously no use in arguing, he borrowed a wad of Elda's fine handmade paper and set to work. The others set to work, too. Shortly they were all scribbling busily in various parts of the concert hall, Olga at the table with Felim, Claudia in a corner because her essay required scissors and a ruler, Ruskin kneeling in front of a chair, and Lukin sprawled out on Elda's huge bed. The concert hall became more littered than ever, what with cups of coffee fetched by Olga, the mugs of beer Ruskin brought in after lunch, and the crossed-out pages that Lukin kept throwing away.

Lukin always had more trouble writing things

than the others did. It seemed to take him six crossed-out tries before he could get into his stride. But by the middle of the afternoon he, too, was going nicely. He was getting quite eloquent when he discovered, slightly to his surprise, that the one thing he needed to support his argument was something Wermacht had dictated to them back in the first week. He got out the jeweled notebook to check the exact words. And he was so surprised by what he found that he let out a sharp yelp.

Everyone jumped, thinking Lukin had met the sixth assassin. Finding Lukin simply staring at his notebook, they all relaxed and went back to writing.

Lukin went on staring. Part of what Wermacht had said was there—"Magic without definite aim is dangerous"—but it was alone in a blank page. The pages in front of it and after it were empty. When Lukin came out of his surprise enough to leaf onward he found that quite a lot of herblore and dragonlore notes were still there, but with mysterious crisp white blanks in them. His astrology notes had vanished entirely, leaving pages that looked as if they had never been written on. Almost the only thing that was complete was the page where he had tried to describe exactly how wonderful it felt to raise magefire.

Olga noticed his frantic rifflings and rustlings. "What's up?" she asked, flinging back her hair to look around at him.

"My notebook, the one you gave me," Lukin said. "More than half the pages are crisp and clean again; most of Wermacht's next big headings have gone. Is it some kind of trick book?"

Ruskin leaped up and trotted over. "Let's see." He took the little book between both large hands and leafed gently through it, grunting each time he came to a blank. "Hmm. Ah. Hmm. Dwarf magic's been at work on all the pages you wrote on, definitely. But that's all I can tell you. I don't know what the magic's meant to do, but it looks as if you'd better get yourself another notebook."

"You can borrow my notes. They're in my bag. Over there," Elda said, pointing with one wing, without for a moment stopping writing.

Lukin discovered he could remember quite well what Wermacht had said, anyway. "It's all right. Wermacht says everything so often and so loudly that it's hard to forget it. I'll buy a new notebook tomorrow. I've just about got the money."

"I didn't mean to give you a trick notebook," Olga said, distressed about it.

"You weren't to know," Claudia said. Then, realizing that Lukin had so little money that he would probably have to go without something in order to buy a new notebook, she added, "I've a spare notebook here with me. Please have that." And before Lukin could get too proud to accept, she went on quickly. "Biscuits, anyone?

Doughnuts? It's my turn to go out and buy us something."

They settled down again with doughnuts, and the day drew on almost peacefully toward evening. Felim was on his twenty-third page, Elda on her fourteenth, and even Lukin was on page six when all of a sudden there came a giant cry of "HELP! HELP!" It was carried on a general warn-spell very hastily and badly applied by someone who was evidently terribly frightened, and it jolted them all where they sat, knelt, or lay.

"Another assassin!" Ruskin boomed. "I'll stay here with him. The rest of you go and see."

They threw down their pens and raced for the courtyard, with Elda galloping ahead. There they found almost everyone else in the University dashing outside, too, even the librarian and Wizard Umberto, who were very seldom seen out of doors. Breaths rolled out of many panting mouths in the sharp air. Voices babbled, and fingers pointed into the strong blue evening sky.

"The Observatory tower," people were saying. "Two of them. Just look at that!"

Elda reared herself above the babbling crowd and stared up at the tower above the Spellman Building. Those last two assassins must have been working as a pair, perhaps hiding in the tower until nightfall. She could see them clearly against the clear sky. One was clinging to the very tip of the dome, which was spinning like a whirligig under him. The other was hooked by the seat of his tight black trousers to some kind of spike sticking out from under the dome. He was hanging face downward over nothing and struggling a little. The one on the dome was just clinging. The windows of the spinning dome were crowded with blurred, desperate student faces. Faint cries of "Help!" came down from them.

"That one on the spike is my spell," Felim said, rather proudly, from beside Elda's right wing. He had disobeyed them and rushed outside, too, with Ruskin hanging on to the end of his sash. "They must have attacked someone, or they would not have set it off. Whose is the spinning dome?"

"No idea," said Elda, but she had a swift, uneasy memory of herself flying across the room to let Ruskin in, and her wings stirring spells about. She forgot it almost at once. Corkoran was on the other side of her with Umberto, squashed up against her left wing.

"So who are those up there with them?" Corkoran was asking.

"My second-year astrology group," Umberto answered. "I'm afraid they're up there without supervision. I, er, shirked the stairs rather. Can you stop the dome's spinning from here? I can't."

"No," said Corkoran. "I tried. Someone's got to get up there to deal with it, I suppose. How's your levitation, Umberto?"

"Rotten," confessed the chubby Umberto.

Corkoran sighed and looked around for Finn. "So's mine."

Elda realized that this was her chance to be of real service to Corkoran. Her heart thumped so with excitement that for a moment she felt almost as giddy as that assassin must be—not to speak of the students. She had to open her beak wide and gulp in frosty air before she said shyly, "Excuse me, Corkoran. I could fly up there holding you if you like."

It came out rather louder than Elda intended. Faces turned to her approvingly, and someone in the background gave a small cheer. Corkoran was forced to turn and look at Elda. "So you could," he said, with quite remarkable lack of enthusiasm. He looked at Umberto and then down at himself, comparing weights. There was no doubt who was the slenderer. Corkoran sighed again. "Very well, but please don't dig your talons in. And don't drop me, or you'll have my dying curse on you before I hit the ground."

This forced Elda to say, "Of course I won't drop you. I'm terribly safe." She had never actually carried a person through the air in her life. Derk would never allow it. But it was a bit late to explain that now. Everyone in the courtyard was making enthusiastic noises; Umberto loudest of all.

Corkoran reluctantly moved over in front of Elda, and she put her talons very carefully around his chest, under his armpits. Wizard Umberto did his bit by running round in a circle, pushing people back, and crying out, "Make a space there, make a space there! The griffin needs room to take off!" People moved quickly, in an awed and worried way, until a fairly wide area was empty around Corkoran and Elda. When Elda judged it was large enough for her to spread both wings in, she flexed her wings and tensed her legs and took off. *Unghgh*. The first wing stroke was all right. The second was *leaden*. Corkoran was *heavy*. As her feet and his left the ground, Elda all but dropped straight back down. She flapped furiously. I *will* do it! she told herself. I'm huge and I'm strong and I will! All around her people were shielding faces from the wind she was making and she was still barely off the ground. Stop panicking, she told herself.

All of a sudden she was back to being five years old, when she first started to fly. She could almost hear her mother's voice. "Elda, for the gods' sakes, go steady! You always rush at things so!"

Thank you, Mum, Elda thought. She reduced her desperate fanning and tried instead for the slowest, strongest wingbeat she could manage. Almost at once she was rising above all the staring faces, and rising again, with Corkoran clutched to her chest, just as if he were really the teddy bear she used to fly around with when she was five. It was the situation she had been daydreaming about ever since that first tutorial.

Except that it was not. Corkoran did not feel in the least like a teddy. He felt wide and stiffish, with a layer of meaty plumpness around the stiffness, which, try as she might, Elda feared she was digging her talons painfully into. And coming in gusts from under her talons was a most unpleasant smell of sweat. Corkoran was sweating with distress, probably because she was hurting him with her talons. Or maybe he was scared of heights. Elda had heard some humans were. Or perhaps he was scared of the assassins. Or perhaps—Elda did not want to think this, but she suspected it was the true reason—Corkoran was scared of *her*. She told herself that, anyway, to do this when he was so frightened meant that Corkoran was being very brave, but she did wish it didn't make him *smell* so bad. And he was so heavy. Far too heavy to carry straight up to the tower in one swoop. Elda had to bank to find an updraft and circle for altitude.

"You're going the wrong way!" Corkoran said. His voice had gone rather shrill.

"Circle . . . for . . . height," Elda panted.

"Oh, I understand," said Corkoran.

Elda hoped he did understand, because she had to keep on circling until their upward path became a spiral, while the courtyard full of upturned faces, the walls and turreted roofs, the other courtyards, and the town beyond wheeled this way and that underneath them. By the time they were on a level with the madly spinning dome, Elda's forelegs ached from carrying Corkoran, and every muscle in her wings was a

different fiery pain. The trouble was, she realized, she had spent nearly three weeks almost
without flying a stroke. Kit was always telling
her you had to fly at least every other day to keep
in condition. And I will, I will! I promise! Elda
thought as she crept toward the tower with long,
laboring strokes. And it was not over yet.

"Go around to the left," Corkoran said to her.
"We'll pick off the one on the spike first. He's
helpless."

He said it with an airiness that Elda knew was
totally false. Gusts more sweat came off him.
Elda made herself think how brave he was, but
she knew, underneath, that Corkoran sweated
because he felt as helpless as the assassin, dangling in the grip of a monster half bird, half lion.
And she almost groaned aloud at what he said. In
order to get at that assassin, she was going to have
to hover, and she was bad at hovering even when
her wings didn't ache like this. Don, who was the
family expert at hovering, always laughed when
Elda tried it. Worse still, the assassin on the spike
had seen her heading for him, and he had his poisoned dagger out. He was not that helpless.

Grimly Elda backed her wings and started the
fast back-and-over hovering movement, leaving
herself enough momentum to inch slowly closer
to the man. He held his dagger forward, and his
lips were spread in a grin, because her head was
stiffly out with the effort, and he was going to get
her in the eye, she knew he was, and so did he.

And she hurt. It was horrible. Her brother Blade always said that when things were horrible, you thought of something else to keep yourself from noticing, but Elda couldn't. The dagger stabbed at her. She wove her face aside and stabbed back with her beak. Then they were fencing, dagger and beak, stab and weave, high in the air, while Elda tried to hover and tried not to drop Corkoran and tried not to get poisoned and tried not to scream. . . .

Corkoran wriggled in her grip, and she nearly yelled at him to keep still. But the assassin was quite suddenly the size of a bumblebee and dropping down into the little bag Corkoran was holding out under her neck. Of course he had to touch the person for the spell to work, Elda realized.

"That's one," Corkoran said. He sounded as strained as Elda felt. "Rise up to get above the dome now."

No, I can't! Elda thought. You don't know what you're asking! But she reminded herself that she had after all offered to do this, and somehow she got her wings out of the hover and was somehow going forward again, circling the giddy dome, up and around and up, to where the dizzily twirling final assassin sat clutching the hatch that covered the great telescope inside. He had a knife out, too. As each rotation brought him to face them, he made a threatening stab toward them with it. It was one of the big, spear-shaped knives, and it had quite a reach. As Elda winged in closer, the man even managed to stand up. Not bad for someone who ought to be too dizzy even to sit straight, Elda thought. But I've had enough of this! One thing griffins were extremely good at was the calculation of speed and angles. Elda sideslipped until the man's back was briefly toward her and then pecked him hard in the rear.

He overbalanced with a scream. Corkoran cried out, "Whoops!" and just barely managed to snatch hold of the assassin's nose as he toppled past. "There," he said. "All over." A calming sort of gesture in the opposite direction brought the dome to a grinding stop. Elda could hear cheering coming from inside the dome and distantly from the courtyard, too. "Now put me in through one of the windows," Corkoran said. "Quickly. I can't stand any more."

Elda had no breath left to speak. She simply sideslipped again until she was level with a window and did more of the beastly hovering while some of the students inside wrestled it open. She watched Corkoran topple inside over the sill, helped by numerous arms, and then toppled herself, in a half glide, down onto the roof of the Spellman Building, to lie there in an aching heap.

He might have said thank you! she kept thinking, heavy with cramps and with memories of that nasty smell of sweat. She did not feel in the least triumphant. It was more like being racked with bouts of shame. She felt a complete, useless fool. Once or twice, though, she found she was wondering how Corkoran would manage going to the moon if he was that scared of heights. She decided to stay on the roof. Anything else was too much.

Half an hour later a trapdoor beside one of the chimneys opened, and Ruskin climbed out. Elda did not look, but she could tell it was Ruskin by the clacking of his hairbones. "So there you are," he growled. "Are you in one piece?"

"I ache," Elda admitted. "All over." In my soul, too, she thought.

"And I bet he didn't say thank you, did he?" Ruskin said.

"No," said Elda.

She wanted to go on and explain that it was just that Corkoran was afraid of heights, but before she could muster the energy, Ruskin said, "There you are then. I'm beginning to think there's not much to choose between wizards and the forgemasters back home. Selfish, overbearing lot, all of them. Think the world's made just for them. There he is down in the buttery bar, being bought beer and playing the modest hero, and hasn't even mentioned you! You want to come down now? Claudia's over in Healers Hall arranging for a herbal steamroom for you. She says that's what you'll need."

"Oh, yes!" Now, it was mentioned, Elda knew this was the one thing she wanted. Hot steam.

Nice smells. Aches easing away. How clever of Claudia. She began to feel better just at the idea.

"Lukin's with Olga and Felim down in the yard, ready to help you over there when you're down," Ruskin told her. "The question is, can you glide, or shall I let you down on a rope?"

Elda found she felt a great deal better already. She slewed her head up and around until she could see Ruskin's wide, short shape above her against the sunset. There was the outline of a coil of rope over one of his massive shoulders. He really had come prepared to take her half ton or so of weight, even though he weighed barely a tenth of that himself.

"Easy enough with a rope. Dwarfs do this all the time," Ruskin explained. "Take a turn around a chimney with the rope and pay it out slowly. The others will catch you.'

A little squawk of a chuckle escaped Elda's beak. How kind. She really did have friends. But *I bet there's usually a whole team of dwarfs for something of my weight.* "It's all right, Ruskin. I can glide down. Thank you." She surged to her feet and managed to crawl across to the parapet. When she put her head over and saw the distant faces of three of her friends turned anxiously up to her in the dusk, they seemed so far down and the courtyard looked so small and dark that there was a moment when she almost understood how humans could be afraid of heights. Then she climbed on the parapet and spread her wings, and it was all right. She came down in a smooth, sloping glide, to land just beyond Olga, Lukin, and Felim, almost without stumbling.

They rushed up to her. "Elda, you were wonderful! Are you all right? Can you walk?"

"I'll be fine once I've had a steam bath," Elda assured them. She knew, somewhere behind the ache in her wings and in her forelegs, that what she was really suffering from was disillusionment, but that was something she was not ready to think of yet.

SEVEN

THE DAY AFTER Corkoran crammed the last two assassins into a cage designed for two rats and then forgot about them was an almost uneventful one. Everyone went about normal University business in quiet relief. Practically the only event of note was that Melissa met the lofty student after breakfast and purchased eight essays off him for twenty gold pieces. The lofty student got very drunk that evening, but that was hardly unusual. Ruskin grumbled about the food all day, but that was hardly unusual either. Possibly more noteworthy was the way Ruskin collected the forty-odd library books lying on Elda's floor and explained kindly to Elda (who was lying on her bed, aching rather but fiercely finishing her essay) that he would see to them for her. Then he took them back to the library.

"These have not been taken out in your name," the librarian pointed out.

"My friends asked me to bring them back for them," Ruskin rumbled. He had discovered by now that if he reduced his voice to a low, grinding rumble, people assumed he was trying to whisper and usually begged him not to. The sound made the library windows buzz and produced irritable looks from the students working at the tables. "Just give me the library slips, and I'll get out the other books they need," he grated.

"Hush. Very well. Hush," the librarian agreed, anxious only to get rid of him.

Ruskin left the library with thirty-eight new books. Every single one of them was from the Gastronomic Magic section. This puzzled the librarian a little. Only a couple of Wizard Umberto's students were doing the food magic option this term, and Corkoran never bothered with it. But there seemed no point in telling Corkoran. He had ignored the librarian's last note utterly. The librarian shrugged and went back to casting Inventory-spells.

Ruskin retreated to his own room and got down to some serious reading. Sweet peace reigned.

The following day the frosty weather gave place to rain. Elda, who had really, truly, and honestly intended to go out flying before breakfast, got up to find rainwater spouting from every gargoyle on the Spellman Building and dripping from the end of Wizard Policant's pointed nose. There was even a small waterfall sliding down one of the walls of her concert hall. She gave up and went back to bed, marveling at the way Olga still went out rowing in spite of the rain. Olga came back drenched and blue-white, but very cheerful and ravenous for breakfast.

The refectory smelled, very strongly, of fried onions. "Ooh!" said Olga. "My favorite!"

Most other people found the smell the exact opposite of what they needed first thing in the morning and contented themselves with toast, even though most oddly there were no onions being served at all. There were, however, some remarkably fine sausages and golden mounds of perfectly scrambled eggs. Olga and Elda, who needed to eat twice as much as a human, anyway, both heaped their plates high and sat down near Ruskin to enjoy eating for once.

Lukin was one of those who could only manage toast. "Great gods!" he said from the other side of Olga. "What's wrong with this toast? It's nice! Usually it's too floppy to hold and too tough to bite. I've always wondered how they got it like that. But this is just right."

Olga nudged Elda's wing and jerked her head toward Ruskin. Ruskin's plate was mounded even higher than theirs. He had six pieces of toast and a stack of pancakes dripping with syrup and butter lined up for later. He was eating with serious rapture. But his round pink face was just a little too innocent. "Shall I say anything?" Olga murmured.

Claudia had no doubts. "Ruskin," she said, "most of it's lovely. But what makes it all smell of fried onions?"

Ruskin's pink forehead wrinkled. "I don't know," he confessed. "I'm working on it. I think I'll have it sorted by lunchtime."

"Please solve it soon," Felim requested. "The smell gives me a headache. I was up far too early finishing my essay."

Essays were traditionally to be handed in after breakfast on that day. There were shelves in the Spellman Building for that purpose, each marked with a tutor's name. Tradition handed from student to student described the serious penalties for not getting an essay there in time. For the first offense you could be deprived of your voice for a week, and your hearing as well next time, and, it was claimed, repeated offenders had their magic powers removed. No one knew anyone to whom these things had actually happened largely because no one dared be late with an essay. Nobody wanted to lose the power of speech, let alone anything else. Even the most dissolute of students hurried to turn up with at least one scribbled sheet on time.

In consequence, there was quite a procession of students trotting through the rain toward the Spellman Building after breakfast, shielding wads of paper under umbrellas, cloaks, waterproof jackets, or damp shawls. Everyone who arrived in the North Lab for Wermacht's class on Basic Alchemy immediately afterward was chilled and dripping and out of breath.

"Outer garments on the cloakrack," ordered Wermacht. He was as spruce as ever, having been protected by some kind of rain-warding spell, and he tramped impatiently to and fro behind his lectern with the hourglass on it, while everyone obediently hung sopping garments on the tall, three-legged stand beside the door or hooked umbrellas to the lead-lined trough by the wall.

"Today," proclaimed Wermacht as soon as this was more or less done, "we are going to examine the mystery of the Alchemical Marriage. Write that down. Your small heading under that is 'The White with the Red.'"

People scrambled to chairs and snatched out notebooks, and then they were off, writing down the mystery as fast as they could with wet, chilly fingers, until the sand in the hourglass had trickled to the bottom, every grain of it. Lukin, in his hurry, tried to use the golden notebook, but everything he wrote apart from the big heading simply disappeared as fast as he wrote it. He gave up and got out the jaunty little calfbound notebook Claudia had given him instead. After that he was steadily behind with Wermacht's dictation and still trying to finish when the others surged to their feet and collected their still-dripping garments from the cloakrack.

Amid the bustle he heard Wermacht say peremptorily, "You with the jinx, come here."

Uh-oh, Lukin thought, and kept his ears open and his head down as he scribbled, in case Claudia was in trouble.

Claudia's wrap was at the bottom of a heap of others on the same wooden hook, and she had to wait for other students to unhook their cloaks and jackets from on top of it. If it had only been on top, she thought, she would have snatched it and run and pretended not to hear Wermacht. She wondered whether just to run anyhow, but one odd result of her mixed parentage was that she hated rain. Claudia's mother could never understand it. Marshpeople were supposed to revel in wetness. But the part that had come uppermost in Claudia here was the Empire half, and the Empire was hot and dry. Being wet made Claudia ache. Her wrap was specially charmed to keep her dry and had cost her brother, Titus, most of the taxes from a town. So she was forced to stand there waiting for it while Wermacht came striding up and seized her arm.

"Please," Claudia said, pulling away.

"I've been thinking," Wermacht said, holding on just as if she had not spoken or moved, "about this jinx of yours, and I can see now what's causing it. I can lift it very easily. Would you like me to do that?"

"No, thank you," Claudia said coldly and promptly.

Wermacht stared at her as if he could not believe his ears. "Do you mind telling me why?"

Claudia, having been brought up with the very good manners everyone had in the Empire, did not answer, "Because you told Corkoran my spell was yours, you creep!" although she was tempted to. The trouble was that *not* saying this threw her into confusion. This is often the case when someone is being too polite. Claudia did most desperately want to be rid of her jinx. It caused continual trouble when she went to the Marshes and worse trouble in the Empire. It had made the Senate declare her an Unwanted Person there, in spite of the Emperor's coming to the Senate in person to intervene. But strongly though she yearned to be rid of it, Claudia knew that this meant someone—probably a wizard—tinkering with her magical powers. And of all the wizards who might tinker, she most passionately could not bear it to be Wermacht. She had almost no idea how to say this politely.

"Because," she managed to say at length, "because, er, it's only due to misdirected power, you know."

Wermacht's outraged glare did not abate. He did not let go of her arm. "Precisely," he said. "It's simply a matter of straightening the paths of power and reaming them out a bit. I can do that in seconds."

"No," said Claudia. "Thank you, Wizard Wermacht, of course. But my—my Empire code

of morals means I have to do the straightening out for myself." And in spite of Wermacht's still hanging on to her arm, she reached haughtily for her wrap with the other hand. "*Good* morning, Wizard Wermacht."

"You are being a silly little thing!" Wermacht said. He shook her arm.

Lukin snapped his notebook shut and got up to rescue Claudia. This had gone far enough.

At the precise moment he stood up, a brilliant blue flash exploded from Wermacht's hand and into Claudia's arm. For an instant it lit up Claudia herself, her wrap stranded between her other hand and the cloakrack, and even the cloakrack itself, which seemed just for that instant to be made of blue fire. It sizzled blue on the stone ceiling and flashed in the wet footprints leading to the door. But the light had gone before Lukin could get anywhere near.

"There," Wermacht said smugly. "That didn't hurt a bit, did it?"

Lukin came up and detached Claudia's arm from Wermacht's fingers. He turned to Wermacht in his most princely manner. It was not a manner he liked to use much, but he was good at it when he did, far better than Claudia was. "Wizard Wermacht," he said regally, "that is enough. Claudia has already told you twice that she does not wish anyone to tamper with her magic. Why don't you take her word for it and leave her alone?"

Wermacht gave Lukin a puzzled frown. "What's the matter with you? I was simply lifting the jinx from her. She'll be much more comfortable now."

Lukin stared steadily back. "But she asked you not to."

"Female vapors," said Wermacht. "Female vapors." And he stalked heavily away through the doorway.

"Are you all right?" Lukin asked Claudia anxiously.

She shivered a bit as she dragged her wrap down and slowly draped it around her. "Well, I didn't feel anything particularly, if that's what you mean. I don't *feel* any different, I think—just a bit shaken."

"I'm not surprised. Wermacht's an overbearing *donkey*!" Lukin said vehemently. "Come on. You need looking after. Let me buy you a drink."

A wisp of a giggle came from Claudia. "Thank you. But what *with*?"

"Oh—" A flush surged across Lukin's face. "You'd better pay, and I'll pay you back. I might be getting some money soon."

"Not to worry," said Claudia. "Myrna's lecturing now, and I want to go. Myrna doesn't make you feel brain-dead the way Wermacht does."

"I'll come with you then," Lukin said gallantly. He was not much of a one for lectures that you didn't have to go to, but it was clear to him that Claudia needed company.

They left the North Lab together, with Claudia saying as they went, "But I'm not going to *faint* or anything silly like that!" When they were most of the way across the courtyard toward the Spellman Building, the cloakrack swayed on its three legs and began to trundle after them. It staggered over the doorsill and trundled on, lurching, some way across the courtyard. About halfway between the Lab and Wizard Policant, it stopped and stood, looking forlorn and perhaps a trifle bewildered, with raindrops hanging in rows from its curly hooks. The janitor discovered it there just before lunch and put it back inside the lab, muttering, "Darn students! Another of their jokes."

Lunch was—well—peculiar. In the refectory the smell of onions had gone, but it had been replaced by a potent scent of strawberries, which did not go well with the smell of the usual refectory stew. The stew itself, bubbling in the usual row of cauldrons, looked quite normal but, when ladled out onto plates, proved to be a strident bright green. It had strands in it, too, of darker green, along with khaki lumps and viridian morsels and a general, subtle air of sliminess. "Pond weed!" somebody shouted. "Look out for tadpoles!"

Most people declined to eat it and lunched instead off strawberry mousse and bread. Ruskin's friends, knowing a little more than most, each took a plateful. Elda and Felim both had to give up and resort to strawberry mousse and bread, too. As Felim said, it was hard to taste anything but slime through the scent of strawberry, and Ruskin had done a good job on the mousse. Lukin ate most of his, because his mind was still on Claudia. And Claudia, recognizing the dish for Marsh chowder, told Ruskin it was delicious and went back for more. While she was away at the cauldrons, Lukin told the rest of them about Wermacht and the troubling blue flash.

"Do you think he did it?" Ruskin asked. "Took away her jinx, I mean. And let me tell you, this is the best Marsh chowder *I* ever ate. You don't eat it that way, Olga. You sort of suck it in. Brings out the taste."

"He could have taken it off," Lukin said, while Olga seemed to be shuddering faintly. "But *Cyclina* and *The Red Book* both say a jinx is usually bound up with a magic user's actual power, and what I'm afraid of is that he took away her magic power, too."

"But then she'd have to leave, wouldn't she?" Elda asked, appalled. Lukin nodded.

"That is a real worry." Olga agreed, pushing her plate away. "What have we done to deserve Wermacht? Don't answer that question—particularly you, Ruskin. Nice try with the stew, shame about the smell and the color. Is it *meant* to be this slimy? Don't you think you'd better read up a bit more, or practice somewhere else, or something?"

Ruskin sighed. "I've been thinking that, too. I read the books, thought it was easy, but now I think there must be more to it than that. I'll have another go when I've worked out what it is."

When everyone left the refectory, there was almost as much green stew left piled on plates or bubbling in cauldrons as there had been to start with. A deputation of students and six angry warn-spells were sent to Corkoran about it.

Corkoran told the deputation he would see about it and went to find Finn. "Look, Finn, some student's been mucking about with the food again . . ." he began.

"And I'll give you six guesses which one," said Finn. He saw well enough that Corkoran intended him to find the culprit, and he thought that for once Corkoran could do his own dirty work. "It'll be one of your first years, Corkoran. My money's on your dwarf, but I'd take a side bet on Claudia. Wermacht's been telling me she's got some kind of jinx."

"Has she?" Corkoran had forgotten that Claudia had told him this herself. He flicked at the violet monkeys on his tie. "Look, Finn—"

"All you have to do," Finn cut in, "is to eat in the refectory tonight and trace the spell. It'll be something pretty crude. It always is."

"But I haven't—" Corkoran tried again.

"So that's your course of action," Finn said firmly. "Catch the dwarf red-handed." Seeing Corkoran about to speak again, Finn changed the subject swiftly and enthusiastically. "You know that first year of mine—Melissa? The one everyone says has no brain. I've just had a really marvelous essay from her, clear, concise, to the point, well thought-out, truly brilliant! If it weren't for your policy, I'd give it an A. I think we've all been misjudging—"

"Yes, yes," Corkoran said irritably. This was some kind of sore point with him, Finn could see. Probably none of Corkoran's precious, carefully chosen first-year students was anything like as good as expected. Too busy messing with food and assassins to do any work, Finn thought. He watched Corkoran turn peevishly away. "Then if you can't help," Corkoran said over his shoulder, "I suppose I'd better follow your advice and get indigestion in the refectory." He rushed moodily away with the purple monkeys flapping, while Finn did his best not to laugh. It was seldom he got the better of Corkoran.

Back in his lab, Corkoran sat at his bench with his back to the assassin cage and his moonship bulking by the windows, crying out to be worked on, irritably surveying the monstrous pile of paper his first-year students had dumped on him. Why couldn't young people remember someone had to *read* their eloquence? He would have to set a word limit. This was awful. Corkoran usually reckoned to whip through all the week's essays in half an hour or so and then get comfortably back to his lab work. Indeed, he had already whipped through the offerings from the second and third years. Sensible, slim essays, those were, full of the usual facts, none of them trying to explain the universe or anything silly like that. And he could have sworn that those six first years had been far too busy lately to cover more than one sheet with writing. Yet here was Felim producing thirty pages, Elda twenty-nine, Claudia the same, Olga twenty-six, and Ruskin forty—count them, *forty*! Lukin was more moderate. He had only produced ten pages, but since those were written very close in tiny black writing, Corkoran feared the worst. What had got *into* them all?

For an ignoble five minutes or so Corkoran contemplated simply returning the essays unread. But that was just the kind of thing that Querida could be counted on to discover. The griffin almost certainly knew Querida quite well. And the last thing Corkoran wanted was Querida turning up at the University to ask questions. He sighed and, shudderingly, picked up Felim's monster. Compromise. Skim through. Get the gist.

This was not easy. Felim kept quoting spells, nearly all of which Corkoran had never met before. He had to keep getting up to consult the enormous *Almanac of Magics* on the lectern beside his moonship, to make sure that Felim was not just inventing the spells. And Felim never was. All the spells seemed to be real, but Corkoran stopped consulting the *Almanac* and began skimming when he realized that with each spell Felim was pointing out that there were possibilities the maker of the spell had never thought of. Different uses for them and different sorts of magic branched off from them in a hundred directions, Felim said. He ended by saying that magic could explode into a hundred new forms no one had thought of yet—except this was hardly the end. Felim spent his last three pages suggesting the forms the new magic could take, astromagic, psychomagic, metaphysical magic, biomagy, theurgy, centromagic, anthropism, numerology, ritual magic, most of which were entirely beyond Corkoran's understanding.

He shook his head sadly. This was not modern magic. Magic these days confined itself to strictly practical things, to known facts and proven procedures. Felim argued well and wrote elegantly, but it would not do. This was some relief to Corkoran. For a while, when he first started reading this monster, he had been afraid he was going to have to break with his policy and give Felim a high mark, if only for all the research into spells Felim had done. Corkoran's policy, as Finn had reminded him, was that the University existed these days to turn out competent magic users with the skills that were needed to reorganize the world after the mess Mr. Chesney had made of it. There was no place for deep research or Felim's kind of speculations. What the world needed was run-of-the-mill *practical* magic. For

...d should be rethought from the botto[m] [u]pward....

Corkoran left off reading and gave Ruskin [a] C. Then, after some thought, he made that [a] minus for bossiness. It was as if the wretche[d] dwarf was teaching *him* instead of the other wa[y] around. He wanted, even more than he had wit[h] Elda or Olga, to give the essay an F for failed, bu[t] some of Ruskin's arguments were so persuasive that Corkoran actually caught himself wonder-ing if perhaps, maybe, he should rethink his moonshot methods.

He shoved the forty pages angrily away and snatched up Claudia's offering, which he had left until last because it looked peculiar. A glance at the light showed him that he was not going to get any of his own work done now before refectory supper, so he supposed he had better give his full attention to *this* now. It seemed to be a mass of fluttering paper slips held together by adhesion spells.

It was very peculiar. Claudia evidently held the same opinion as Felim and Elda, but she had set out to prove her opinion practically, by starting with a fairly common spell and showing how it could be made to do two different things. The first page gave the spell and then was divided into two columns, showing the two new spells. These in turn led to four—no, five—more derived spells in four columns and an attached slip of paper. And so on. Ten columns led to twenty-

this reason Corkoran had decreed that only third-year students and then only those who showed supreme practical skills should ever get an A.

He scribbled a generous B minus on Felim's monster and "Answer the question" beside it, and turned to Lukin's essay next because it was the shortest. And here was Lukin talking about the different possibilities of magic, too, in a soaring, joyful way that quite shocked Corkoran. He had thought Lukin was going to be one of your stolid plodders. But not a bit of it. Lukin talked about the boundaries and limitations set on magic, and while he agreed that some were there for safety, he thought most of them unnecessary. He pointed out a few. Take these off, he said. Experiment. Have fun with magic.

Fun? Corkoran thought. What nonsense was this? Magic at University level was *work*. You were not supposed to have fun with it. Yet here was Lukin, expressing himself rather well in his tiny black writing, suggesting that magic was there to *enjoy*. Well, he *was* a prince, Corkoran thought, and had obviously been brought up to think that magic was what you relaxed with after a day's ruling. Corkoran decided to allow for that, and awarded Lukin a C, instead of the C minus he had first intended.

He gave Olga a C, too, again quite generously, he thought. She had at least tried to answer the question "What Is Wizard's Magic?" But her essay was full of *opinions*, which again would never do. Olga's notion was that magic could not be standardized, for the gods' sake! Everyone's particular magic was influenced by that person's particular character, she said, and differed from another person's magic in the same way that handwriting differed. Furthermore, she said, a person's magic could be spoiled or improved by the way they were taught or by their upbringing. She gave one or two examples. Corkoran was quite struck by her account of a teenager who was punished for playing with air elementals and gradually became unable to speak to any elementals at all.

"Can *anyone* speak to elementals?" he murmured, and wrote "accuracy?" in the margin there. On the whole, Olga's offering irritated him even more than Lukin's did. Of *course* magic was supposed to be standardized! Corkoran's job at the University was to iron out all the differences in it.

He sighed and dragged Elda's massive offering forward. Elda was on the same tracks as Felim. What *had* they all been reading? Elda, even more than Felim, was certain that there were great tracts of magic left unexplored, and she kept giving examples that were not even in the *Almanac* of magics, which she must have learned from Derk, her father. Half the time Corkoran had no idea what she was talking about. He had never heard of gene tailoring, or zygotes, or rhyzomes either. He was a discover that Elda knew this and expla   u in carefully numbered notes at the en huge essay. And before this Elda's last pag even further than Lukin had and became less a song of praise for magic, its excitemen its possibilities. That was enough. Cor scribbled a highly irritated C minus, and dered, while he dragged Ruskin's heap of p in front of him, whether he ought not, in all h esty, to give this diatribe a straight D.

He was determined to skim Ruskin's essay But it was impossible. Ruskin was a dwarf, used to working with intricate things, and his argument was like chain mail, forged link by link. He put out a suggestion. He followed that with obvious things that led from it—things you were forced to agree to—and then he went one stage further and *Wham*! you were agreeing to something that was quite unheard of. Then Ruskin took the unheard-of idea and did the same to that. *Wham*. A new mad idea. Around and around the links Corkoran went, up and through and *wham!* through the first twenty pages. By this time he found he was humbly agreeing to a complete reorganization of the University syllabus, with theory and practical being taught together, to give more space for hugely advanced theory, and the first-year course beginning where the third year's left off; and agreeing then that magic as used today was being handled entirely wrongly

five. . . . Help! thought Corkoran, leafing on to find pages with up to fifty columns, done in tinier and tinier writing and only readable because Claudia had fitted them with an expander spell that Corkoran himself had never learned to cast. And as if this was not difficult enough—though it seemed to be meant to be helpful—the last page folded out into a huge family tree of all the spells, their branches color-coded red, green, and blue, with extra notes about how to apply them all.

"And I have to check all this?" Corkoran said aloud. Yes. Obviously he did. Claudia could be fooling him by writing complete nonsense. It took him well over an hour. When he was done, he could not help feeling an irritated sort of admiration. Some of those fifty new spells were good, new, useful things, and deriving them all from just two simple ordinary spells took a perverse sort of genius. But it was all as unheard of as Ruskin's ideas. *And* it was not a proper essay. Corkoran turned the fluttering mass over and wrote "C–. Answer the question." Genius or not, Claudia had wasted her time and his, and besides, even a genius can always do better. Perhaps he would give Claudia an A if she did this again in two years' time. Or perhaps not. He did not want any of his students going out into the world thinking they could work marvels.

It was sad, really, Corkoran thought as he stacked the steep stack of papers together. Young people came to the University full of such bright hopes, feeling the whole world was open before them. And by the end of three years most of them were simply competent magic users, scraping around to find employment that made them some money. He remembered being like this himself even. Right at the start of his first year he had thought that magic offered great things—though he could not remember now what things—and by the end he had felt he was lucky to get a job on Mr. Chesney's tours. He had come on a lot in those three years, he knew. He was sorry for his six students. But they would learn, just as he had. Meanwhile it was time to drop into the refectory for supper, where he would almost certainly be able to catch one of his young geniuses in the act of messing with the food. He would, he thought, make Wermacht come with him for moral support. Yes, that was an *excellent idea*. He set off, tie flying.

Claudia was also on her way to the refectory after choir practice. As Elda was occupying the concert hall, choir was usually held in the North Lab—Claudia was beginning to think she *lived* in that lab—from which it was only a short cross-wise sprint through the rain to the refectory. Claudia ran through the freckled light from the globes of wizard light fixed to the buildings with her wrap over her head and did not look around until she was at the top of the refectory steps, where her friends were waiting. There she happened to glance across the courtyard. And there was the wretched cloakrack from the North Lab out in the rain between the refectory steps and the statue of Wizard Policant.

Lukin had seen it, too. He had watched it come out of the lab and trundle jerkily after Claudia. "Someone's having a joke with that thing," he said, in a loud, much too hearty voice. He and Olga took a friendly grip on Claudia's arms and pulled her indoors.

Corkoran was in the refectory by then, and Wermacht, looking rather moody, with him. He spotted his first-year students as they joined the line for food in the large space being kept for them by Elda. Elda's beak switched toward Corkoran in surprise and then switched away. Her feelings about him were in utter confusion. Two days ago she would have been delighted to see Corkoran here. Now her main feeling was embarrassment. He was slumming. Why?

Corkoran left Wermacht to keep them places at a table and demurely joined the end of the food queue. He was instantly surrounded by students complaining that the rain had come through into their rooms.

"Don't tell me. Tell Wizard Dench," he told them. It was always like this, he thought. The moment he showed his face in public, people tried to keep him from his work. Another student accosted him with each step he took toward the food. The roofs were evidently in a bad way this year. But there was nothing wrong with the food when he reached it—or nothing that was not quite usual, he thought, wincing at the choice between iron-hard meat pie and vegetable cakes floating in grease. None of the wizards ever ate in the refectory if they could help it. Corkoran himself always sent out to the town's one good restaurant. A man in a crisp white apron brought him the chef's special every evening to eat in his rooms. Tonight he bravely loaded two trays with one of each choice and levitated them over to the table where Wermacht was sitting.

That table was still empty apart from Wermacht. It was like a no-go area. Students took chairs away from that table and crammed them in anywhere else rather than join Wermacht. Corkoran found this quite a relief. And Wermacht did not seem to notice. But he noticed the food. He winced. "I thought I'd got away from all this," he said. "What do we do now?"

"We eat it," Corkoran replied. "The spell's probably triggered by that."

They gloomily unwrapped cutlery and began. Nothing changed. Corkoran, as he forced his teeth through the crust of the pie, kept a wary magical eye on his six students. Felim had not joined them to eat. He had been swept away to a table full of girls, all of whom seemed very interested in him. It looked as if Felim's recent troubles had made him very popular. The rest were together, however, with Elda occupying most of one side of a table and the others leaning conspiratorially toward her. Corkoran enhanced his hearing with a spell and tried to listen to what they said, although the general din of voices and the clatter of eating were enough to defeat almost any spell. All he caught was a wisp of a remark from Lukin: ". . . just as well, Ruskin."

He was beginning to realize that he was enduring this purgatory for nothing when all the noise abruptly died away. The refectory door barged open, and a cloakrack sidled in. It was just a tall three-legged wooden thing with a ring of big wooden hooks around the top, and you would not think it capable of expressing feeling, but it nevertheless gave out an air of timid apology that was almost human. Claudia blanched greenish white and could not seem to take her eyes off the thing. Wermacht jumped a little at the sight of it, too.

Neither of them seemed to notice that the cloakrack had been followed by a number of tall, purposeful, brightly dressed men and that what had really caused the sudden silence was the row of similar men marching in from the kitchens. These were taking off their white aprons as they came and spreading out to stand around all the walls. Under the aprons every one of them carried either a loaded crossbow or a large pistol.

EIGHT

T HE FOREMOST OF the men who followed
the cloakrack through the door was tall
and wide-shouldered. Although he was
not young—nearer fifty than forty—he was still
exceedingly handsome in a thin, hawk-faced way,
and he clearly knew it. His mass of still-golden
hair was flaunted by being tied back with a black
silk scarf, and his slender waist was similarly
flaunted with a wide black sash over his scarlet
coat that emphasized its slenderness. His pistol
was decorated with gold inlay, and he held it very
steady in a hand that was decorated with a fine
ring on each finger. The men who clustered
around him were not nearly so pretty, but they all
had steady pistols, too.

Corkoran's stomach did strange things. He
looked from the steady pistols by the door to the

dozen or so crossbows and pistols around the walls and felt betrayed. "I thought," he murmured to Wermacht, "you were supposed to have put protections on the kitchens at least."

"Nobody move, nobody try to cast a spell," the handsome man said loudly, "and nobody need get hurt." Wermacht, at this, made faces at Corkoran, expressing complete bewilderment that his protections had not seemed to work. Unfortunately his grimaces caught the clear blue eyes of the handsome man. "Cover those two," he said. "Those are real wizards."

Several pistols and two crossbows swung toward the table where Corkoran and Wermacht sat. Corkoran swallowed. Wermacht was in robes, of course, so it was obvious he was a wizard. Corkoran would have liked to think that it was his air of magical authority that caused the handsome man to know him for a wizard as well, but he feared that it was more likely that the man had recognized him from somewhere. Damn it, he knew he had seen the fellow before, if only he could place him! "Who are you?" he said. "What do you want?" His voice came out a little high, but he was relieved to hear that it was almost steady.

"Don't tell me you've forgotten me!" the handsome man said, with what Corkoran found to be a rather hideous mock sympathy. "The years must be getting to you, Corkoran. I've not forgotten *you*. Surely you remember. You and I had a little set-to over money during Chesney's last tour. You tossed me in the sea. Olaf Gunnarsson. Remember?"

Olaf Gunnarsson. Of course! That evening on the docks nearly nine years ago that Corkoran had done his best to forget ever since, came back to him now like yesterday: the fishy smell of the Inland Sea, the screams of the circling gulls, the salt staining the wharf, everything. Everything, including the beat-up wooden ship towering against the sunset and Olaf towering in front of the ship on the wharf, aiming that very gold-inlaid pistol at the anxious tourists clustered behind Corkoran on the dock. Olaf had not been nearly so well groomed in those days. In fact, he had looked almost as beat up and ragged as that ship of his. He had terrified Corkoran. It was not *his* fault that someone had egged Olaf on to demand twice as much money for pretending to kidnap the tourists. But Olaf had assumed Corkoran was party to the deal. He had insisted that Corkoran was trying to pocket the extra money. Corkoran could even remember the exact insults Olaf had shouted at him and the way that Olaf's crew, from the one-legged mate to the small cabin boy, stood in a row above them on the ship and shouted insults, too. Then Olaf had said he would shoot the tourists one by one until Corkoran paid up. Corkoran had been so terrified of what Mr. Chesney might do about that that he had hurled Olaf away with the very strongest spell he could muster and gasped at the tourists to run for their lives. It was not exactly Corkoran's fault that the strength of his terror had caused him to overcook the spell. Olaf had gone whirling up over his ship, to land with a mighty splash in the water beyond, followed by all his crew. Corkoran could still hear the shouts and the splashes, like yesterday. And now the man seemed to have tracked him down.

"So you're still a pirate," he said shakily.

Olaf shook his handsome head. "Not any longer. When Chesney went, there was no profit in piracy. I'm respectable now. These days I run merchants' protection around the Inland Sea."

"You mean you're a gangster now?" Corkoran said.

Wermacht stirred beside him, genuinely horrified. "Corkoran, don't *speak* to him like that! Everyone knows Gunnarsson's a very rich man."

"Shut up," said Olaf. "Both of you shut up. I'm not here to speak to either of you. I'm here to collect my two-timing witch of a daughter. Come on, Olga. Out of there."

Corkoran slumped with relief. If *that* was all! Everyone else's eyes turned to Olga, half hidden behind Elda's right wing. Olga's face had gone so white that, what with the fairness of her hair, she looked as if there were a spotlight shining on her. Corkoran remembered that cabin boy. So he had thrown Olga into the water, too, along with her father.

Olga moved her chair until she was no longer hidden by Elda. She leaned back in it and stared across at Olaf. "How did you know I was here?"

Olaf grinned, baring very white teeth. "Your precious University was kind enough to send me a request for money. Still after the money, are you, eh, Corkoran? So I brought the boys along and came to fetch you. We've been here two days now, staking the place out, so don't feel you can get away. Come quietly and no one will get hurt."

"No," said Olga. She looked and sounded quite calm, but Elda could feel her shaking. "I'm a student now. I'm studying here."

There was a simultaneous threatening move forward by all the men standing around the walls. Olaf held up a hand, glinting with rings and a gold bracelet, to stop them. "Now, now. This is an ancient and august institution, boys. Pretend to be civilized here at least. Olga, I came prepared to be reasonable, but if you push me, I'll tell them all what you did. Then they'll kick you out."

"I didn't do anything except what I told you I'd do," Olga retorted. "You wouldn't let me train as a wizard, so I arranged it for myself. As I told you I would."

Olaf shook his golden head in mock sorrow. "Ah, Olga. Sparing with the truth. As always." His manner changed. Suddenly and frighteningly his face flushed, particularly over his hawk-like nose, and he bared his big white teeth like a skeleton's. "You howling little witchy cow of a liar! I forbade you to leave! You *disobeyed* me! *Me*—Olaf! And on top of that, you go and raid my secret island and carry off my treasure! Don't deny it! You did it!"

"I don't deny it," Olga said calmly. Lukin, who had been staring at Olaf in fascinated hatred, turned and looked at her with respect. "I did tell you I would," Olga said. "I told you quite plainly that because you'd never given me one copper of my own all my life, I'd take what I was due. I've worked for you for ten years now, Dad, raising winds and raising monsters for you when you went into the protection game, for *nothing*, not even what you pay your crew!"

"And so a dutiful daughter *should* do!" Olaf yelled. "You *robbed* me—*me*, your own *father*!"

"I only took enough to pay my fees and to live on for three years," Olga said. "There's still a lot left. Haven't you been and counted it? That's not like you, Dad."

"You *robbed* me!" Olaf howled. "That money was for my old age! The treasure was your dowry, girl!"

"Then it was mine," Olga said.

"No, it was *not*!" screamed her father. "A daughter is her father's property until he buys a husband for her. *With* her dowry! And you know very well, you thieving witch, that I had a husband all lined up for you until you robbed me and ran away!"

"My timing did have something to do with that, yes," Olga agreed.

"Hark at her!" Olaf looked around the staring students as if he knew they were bound to agree with him. "Have you *ever* heard such ungrateful disobedience? Daughters have to do what their fathers tell them."

"Only if the other side of the bargain is kept," Lukin remarked.

Olaf's glaring blue eyes, and the muzzle of his pistol, turned Lukin's way. "What was that? Speak up, whoever you are."

"I *said*"—Lukin began. He was shaking as badly as Olga—"obedience depends on—"

"He's the Crown Prince of Luteria, Dad," Olga cut in quickly.

"Oh. Then I shan't shoot him through the head," Olaf said. "Through the knee, probably, when we leave. But before that I want my money." He pointed at Corkoran. "You. Disgorge. Give me what this ungrateful hag paid you for teaching her."

Humor him, Corkoran thought. Get him to leave. "Yes, of course," he said readily. "We'll have to ask the Bursar to bring the money here, though." He had already sent several warn-spells to Wizard Dench, and to Finn, to Myrna, to Umberto, to anyone else who might be in the University. Why doesn't one of them *do* something? he thought.

To Elda, Corkoran's ready agreement was the

final item to her disillusionment with him. She could see he was soggy with fear. So was everyone there. She felt the same herself, hating Olaf, hating the men standing there, calmly aiming weapons. Elda could feel, almost as if it had already happened to her, what it was like to have a crossbow bolt in the chest. A blunt *whump*. A sharp pain. Astonishment at the thought one was going to be dead in a second. The mere idea was enough to keep Elda, and everyone else there, as still as if they were all under a stasis spell. And she could see that Olaf was what Derk would call a psychopath, who *enjoyed* shooting people. But this did not quite excuse Corkoran, who was after all a fully qualified wizard and might have tried to do *something*.

"Goo-od!" said Olaf. A long, satisfied smile made creases in his hollow cheeks. "Sensible Corkoran. Get your Bursar here then. Stand up, Olga, there's a good girl. Your husband's here, waiting for you." He put his left arm around the bulky man next to him and pulled him forward. A look of despair crossed Olga's face at the sight of him. He had a round face, missing several teeth, and a scraggy beard fringing it. His head was shaved bald, possibly to display the fact that he had earrings entirely around each ear, in golden ranks. The way he looked at Olga, the wide-legged way he walked, and the way his hands hung told everyone in the refectory that this was a man who liked beating people up and that Olga was not going to get away from him again. "Torkel," said Olaf. "My chief enforcer. You've hurt his feelings, Olga."

"I meant to," Olga said, and did not move.

At this Olaf breathed in, terribly, ready to yell again, but before he could, Melissa sprang to her feet at the table next to Olga's. "Stop it!" she cried out. "It's quite wrong! People seem to think that just because a person's female and pretty, they're not supposed to do magic and they're supposed to stay at home and have babies and be obedient and be married to a—*that* man! Why is that? Why? How would *you* like it, Mr. Olaf, if I shut you up in a house for the rest of your life and made you marry an *ogress*?"

Everyone so hated Olaf by this time that Melissa would have received a rousing cheer had anyone dared to move. Everyone's eyes shot to her, as she stood with her hands clasped to her chest and her eyes wide with feeling, looking more beautiful even than usual. Everyone thought, Well, fancy *Melissa* having the nerve! And everyone smiled at her, including Olaf, but Olaf's smile was the smile of a hungry cat with a mouse under its paw.

"A brave little beauty!" he said. "I think I'll take you with us when we leave."

"You *dare*!" Melissa cried out. Her face flushed, and she looked lovelier than ever. "I can put terrible spells on you. I know quite a few!"

Olaf smiled at her admiringly. "I'll risk that,"

he said, and turned to Torkel. "Where's that blessed priest? What are you waiting for? Do you want this wedding now, or don't you?"

Torkel nodded vigorously and beckoned someone behind them. There was a short scuffling. The current high priest of Anscher was dragged up beside Olaf with somebody's pistol held to his head.

"Stand up, Olga," Olaf said. "Come on over here this instant and be married."

Olga's face drained of color entirely as she realized just how far her father was prepared to go. She stood up, quite slowly, and looked around at all the silent, staring faces. "I thought he'd give in when he found out I meant it," she explained. "Sorry about this."

Somebody *do* something! Elda thought. She swiveled an eye at Claudia, who usually had ideas, but Claudia was still green-white and staring at that cloakrack standing on the other side of Olaf. Claudia was actually willing the cloakrack to fall sideways and knock Olaf out, but nothing happened, and Elda thought Claudia was simply paralyzed with fear. She wanted to scream.

She toyed with the idea of giving a really piercing griffin screech. But that would cause guns to go off and crossbows to twang. It was truly awful being this helpless when everyone sitting so still in the refectory was full of magic, full of skills to use that magic, full of anger, full of hatred for Olaf. As Olga walked slowly toward her father, Elda could feel the anger like an electric charge on her skin. It made her fur bristle and her feathers stand up. She could even feel the helpless anger from the people dithering outside the door on the steps. Wizards Umberto and Dench were out there, by the feel of them. They had fetched the porter and the janitor, too, but none of them had the least idea what to do.

Hey! Elda thought, when Olga was within three steps of the hulking Torkel and the piteous, gasping high priest of Anscher. Hey, I could *use* all this anger! She began gathering it in, and the magic of all the people it belonged to, pulling it in, gusts of it, blasts of it, blazing clouds of it, the indignation of Melissa, the cold fury of Felim, Ruskin's rage, the sense of outrage from the girls around Felim, Corkoran's fear and hatred, Wermacht's disgust that this could happen to *him*, the people in the Rowing Club's desire to batter Olaf's head with an oar each, and Lukin's truly formidable deep anger. It all filled Elda in instants, so that she felt like a taut, feathery balloon with it. And when she had as much of it as she could hold, she let it out at Olaf and his followers.

She could not avoid making a small pouncing movement as she sent the anger forth. Crossbows and guns snapped toward her. She made a big target after all. But the anger got there first, and it was too late. As their fingers tried to pull triggers, every pirate there was already dwindling, rushing down the walls and changing as they shrank, to become little grayish mice running away along the wainscot. The same thing happened to Olaf and his friends by the door. They did not realize they were mice straightaway. They stood in a little gray group around the skirts of the high priest's robe, staring this way and that in proud astonishment at the way the room had suddenly gone huge.

Lukin made *his* move only an instant after Elda's. There was one thing he could always rely on being able to do, and he did it. He opened a truly deep pit just inside the door. The cluster of men there had barely become mice, barely stared haughtily around, when they vanished away downward—along with the high priest, unfortunately. Olga braced both feet, leaned backward, and managed to step away from the lip of the chasm just as the cloakrack toppled into it, too.

"Hurray!" screamed Elda. "Chase the rest of them down the pit! Come on, everyone!" She went bounding after the mice running and squeaking along the walls, jumping over chairs and hurdling tables, pouncing, hunting and uttering great griffin shrieks of joy. Melissa predictably began screaming, too, and climbed on a chair with her skirt wrapped around her knees. But everyone was sympathetic after the way she had stood up to Olaf. A dozen hands reached out to steady the chair with Melissa balanced on it as Elda crashed past it both ways, chivying mice to the edge of the pit and then sending them flying over into it with swats of her great golden forefoot.

"I love mice," she said happily to Lukin, who was standing by the pit with his arms around Olga. "I used to chase them a lot when I was little."

Ruskin helped Elda chase mice. A lot of them, even so, escaped into handy crannies in the wall, but when all the visible ones had been rousted out and tumbled into the pit, Ruskin bellowed, "Somebody close this hole! *I* don't know how to! Can't somebody here close this hole and get that poor priest out of it?"

Several students came forward, but they all gave way respectfully when Corkoran pulled himself together and levitated the unfortunate priest out. Then he took pleasure in closing the pit with a vengeful *smack*. There. Let that be the last of Olaf.

The priest had hurt his leg. A party of students got in one another's way to carry him off to Healers Hall, while as soon as they opened the refectory door, Dench, Umberto, and Finn rushed inside in a gaggle, demanding to know what was going on. They joined the other party of students who went to investigate the kitchens. They found most of the kitchen staff there on the floor, tied up and gagged with dishcloths, except for the cook, who had taken a bribe from Olaf and run, it seemed. Nearly all the rest were shaken and bruised. They were led off to the healers, too.

Through all this activity Olga stood like a statue in the curve of Lukin's arms. Wizards ran to and fro, belatedly putting strong wards around the rooms, and students hurried and exclaimed, but Olga did not seem to see or hear them. She did not move until Felim came up with the very largest mug of coffee he could find and wrapped her fingers around it. Olga put the mug to her mouth and sipped. Encouraged by this sign of life, Lukin and Felim led her over to sit with Claudia. Claudia put both arms around Olga, while Elda pressed up close on her other side and Ruskin squatted in front of her. Olga came to life enough to drink most of the coffee. Then she said, "I am so sorry. I've caused everyone to have such a terrifying experience."

"But so did I," Felim pointed out. "It's not your fault, or mine."

"I don't know what you must think of me," Olga said. It was as if she had not heard Felim.

"The same as usual," said Elda.

"Except we now know why you joined the Rowing Club," Claudia said with a slight chuckle. "You spent most of your life at sea, didn't you?"

Olga slowly nodded. They watched her anxiously. This was the first time she had moved like a human being and not a zombie. "But I don't know what everyone must think of me," she repeated.

"One can't choose one's parents," Ruskin

growled, and Claudia, Lukin, and Felim added, almost together, "Unfortunately."

"But I did steal his treasure," Olga insisted. "I was the only one who knew where it was. I rowed out there at night and dug it up."

"You told me that," said Lukin, "when you lent me the money for these clothes. Remember? It must have taken real nerve. And it must have taken even more nerve to hang on to the treasure and only sell a little bit in each town you went through. Me, I'd have got rid of it all at once, even if it would have made it easier for him to trace me."

"But now *everyone* knows I'm a thief!" Olga said.

"No one I've spoken to blames you," Ruskin said. "They all say they wouldn't have dared. And it was all stolen goods, anyway, wasn't it?"

"Besides," added Claudia, "everyone knows you only took what you thought you were due."

"We-ell," said Olga, "I took a bit extra for being beaten." A tear trickled down one of her angular cheeks. She went on in a slow, faraway voice, "He didn't treat me too badly when I was his cabin boy. He only hit me then when he was drunk. He thought of me as a boy, I think. He'd always wanted a son. But it got much worse when he discovered I could raise winds. You know how when you're new to a thing, you don't always get it right, or sometimes it doesn't work at all? When that happened, he was always furious and gave me a beating. And then one day he found me playing about on land, talking to air elementals and making a lot of small whirlwinds. I told him I was practicing, but I wasn't really. Air people are—were—such fun to talk to, and I was really enjoying myself for once. And he was furious. He said it wasn't *useful*, and girls shouldn't do things that weren't any use to their menfolk. And he called me a witch and beat me half to death. It made me so ill he had to leave me behind on the next voyage, and when I got better at last, I found the air elementals couldn't hear me when I talked to them. I could only raise monsters after that. And he beat me again for not raising winds."

Out of the long silence that followed this, Elda said, "You should have taken *all* his treasure."

Olga made a gulping sound. Two more tears chased down her cheeks. "I wish," she said, "I *wish* I didn't look like him."

There was no doubt that Olga inherited her hawk looks from Olaf. Her friends exchanged glances, which somehow ended with all of them looking at Claudia. She said slowly, thinking about it, "You know, Olga, where I come from, in the Empire, all the people who do the governing and have the most money come from a very few families. This means you get a lot of people who look very much alike. My brother, Titus, has a second cousin, son of a senator, who could almost be his twin, except that no one could ever mix them up, because Porphyrio looks like the evil little twit he is, and Titus looks plain nice. And there's a dreadful tarty woman who's always causing scandals, who looks very like *me*. And I often look at these people and feel really astonished that the same features can look so different on different people. Do you see what I mean?"

Olga almost smiled. "Yes, I do. Thank you, Claudia."

Lukin was so grateful to Claudia that he wanted to reward her in some way. All he could think of was to say, "That cloakrack, it's down inside the pit. I think it's gone for good."

"I hope so," said Claudia. "I just hope my magic's not down there with it."

NINE

T HE RAIN CLEARED up in the night. In the
morning, and for the next few mornings,
since the weather turned mild and sweet
and stayed that way, Elda kept her promise to
herself and went out flying before breakfast.

She was surprised at how much she enjoyed it.
All alone with the whistling of her own wings,
she swept out across the countryside, enjoying the
sight of plowed fields, green meadows, and gray-
ing tracts of stubble wheeling below. The sun
caught sideways upon woodlands that were tint-
ing after the frost, bronze and red and almost
purple. Scents came up to her from farms, and
trickles of smoke itched her nostrils. When she
wheeled to fly back, there was the city and its
towers, golden pink in the morning sun, with the
mountains beyond flushed misty yellow with

deep blue creases in them.

The second morning her wings felt stronger, and she went further, right over to the moorlands beyond the civilized country. She was winging back from there, watching cows being driven out to pasture far below in the first farms she came to, when something glinted in the sky, over to her left, in the north. She turned her head and saw it was a dragon. It was a young one, with a lot of gold and white in it, the way the young ones had, and it seemed to be coming on a slanting course toward the University.

Elda was surprised because dragons were rare this far south. She increased her speed, hoping to be near it when it reached the city, and flew on, admiring the sight of it against the clear blue sky. So graceful, she thought. Dragons had no need to flap wings all the time the way griffins did. This one balanced its great webby wings this way and that and sailed forward on the air currents. Or did it actually *talk* to the air as Olga said she could once? Poor Olga. She was still white and quiet, and her face was all haughty with misery.

Elda's course and the young dragon's brought them closer together every minute. Elda was confident that they would meet somewhere over the University, which was in full sight now, ahead and below. Then, to her disappointment, the dragon tilted a wing, swept down and around in a half circle, and planed elegantly to earth beside a bronzed woodland some miles away. Elda watched a crowd of panic-stricken rooks and pigeons rise out of the trees as the dragon crawled into the wood and out of sight.

For a moment Elda wondered whether to fly over there and ask what it was doing. But you did not mess with dragons, particularly not the hot-tempered young ones. This one had definitely gone into hiding. So Elda flew on, rejoicing at having seen such a beautiful, unexpected thing. She came in low across the city, across the twiddly turrets and elaborate arches of Bardic College on its outskirts, and around in a great sweep over the lake. There, as she had hoped, were several long, thin boats crawling across the surface of the water like water beetles, and Wizard Finn running along the bank bellowing at them through a loud-hailer. Elda spotted the boat with Olga in it and dived down to skim just above the heads of the laboring oarswomen.

"I saw a dragon!" she shrieked.

Olga, rowing stroke, looked up and actually laughed, while behind her oars pointed every which way, crossed, clashed, and missed the water.

"Get out of it, Elda!" Wizard Finn roared from the bank.

Elda swooped up and away, chuckling, to glide in over the roofs of the city and land in the courtyard beside Wizard Policant's statue.

Olga was still laughing when she came in to breakfast, and the wild-rose pink color was back in her cheeks, as if Elda's exploit had restored her to herself. "Don't *ever* do that again!" she said to Elda. "Two of them fell in. Finn was furious. What dragon?"

Elda was about to describe it when she noticed that Claudia was simply sitting, staring, in much the same way that Olga had been doing up to now. "What's the matter, Claudia?"

Claudia just pointed at the cloakrack standing in the corner of the refectory.

"You sure it's the same one?" Ruskin asked, swiveling his stumpy body to look.

"Yes," said Claudia. "It was waiting for me at the bottom of my staircase."

"Let us experiment," said Felim.

After breakfast, which was no worse and no better for the absence of the cook, they led Claudia this way and that through the buildings, upstairs and downstairs, and found that the cloakrack faithfully followed wherever it could. In the courtyard and the corridors it trundled easily along on its three legs, always about ten feet behind Claudia. Going upstairs to the library, it fell sideways with a clatter and bumped slowly upward so long as Claudia kept moving. When she stopped, it stopped. When they shut a door on it, it waited patiently outside until somebody happened to open the door. Then it resumed its patient pursuit.

"Hmm," said Ruskin. "Why are doors an obstacle when it was able to get out of the pit?"

"That took it two days," Olga pointed out.

"But surely fairly strong magic," said Felim. "Let us test it for magic."

It was a fairly easy matter to coax the cloakrack into Elda's concert hall. There they tried all the divination spells for magic on it that they knew. Every single one was negative. Ruskin said that he was quite good at sensing magic, anyway, and put his great dwarf hands on it. After a moment he shook his head. "Not a thing," he said. Elda, after her experience in the refectory the other night, was fairly sure that she would be able to sense if there was any magic in the cloakrack, too, but she, like Ruskin, could feel nothing. It seemed simply to be neutral wood.

"At least Wermacht didn't put any of your magic in it," Olga said as they went over to the tutorial room with the cloakrack bumping along behind. "You can be thankful for that, anyway."

"Look at it this way," Lukin said when they reached the tall stone room. He slammed the door to keep the cloakrack out. "It's not doing you any harm. It's not magic itself. It's just fol- lowing you around because stupid Wermacht linked it to you rather powerfully somehow."

"Or my jinx did," Claudia said with rueful creases in her cheeks. "I'm not scared of it exactly. It's—it's just embarrassing. I won't dare go to choir practice."

"We must get Wermacht to undo what he did," said Felim.

Inevitably, when Corkoran opened the door of the tutorial room and hurried inside, the cloakrack sidled in after him. Corkoran frowned at it absently. But he was late anyhow, because so many people had stopped him on his way here to complain of mice. It seemed as if the former pirates had tunneled their way out of the pit. Corkoran wondered what everyone thought he could do about it. He was far too busy, anyway, trying to construct his moonsuit, and he did not want any more calls on his time. So he ignored the cloakrack and got straight down to handing back essays and explaining to his students that what they had been saying in them had nothing to do with the real world.

His pupils stared sadly at the marks he had given them and then equally sadly at his tie, which today had a pattern of stars and comets on it. Corkoran thought they seemed unwarrantably depressed. "What I'm trying to tell you," he said encouragingly, "is that everything has to have limitations. It's no good expecting magic to perform wonders if those wonders are against the laws of nature."

"But a lot of magic *is* against the laws of nature," Elda protested. "I couldn't fly without magic. Neither could dragons."

Lukin, the dedicated chess player, said, "You mean you have to have rules or the game won't work? But magic isn't a game. And anyway, rules can be changed."

"You're not seeing my point," Corkoran told him. "You have to use magic like a tool, for a certain set of things, and you have to operate within certain safe limits, even then, or you're in trouble. Take magic to do with time, which you'll be doing in your second year. It is known that if you speed time up or slow it down too often in the same place, you weaken the walls between universes and let all sorts of undesirable things through. It's thought that this is how Mr. Chesney got here."

They looked glum. They were too young, Corkoran thought, to understand the troubles Mr. Chesney had caused. "Or take my own work," he said. "I'm up against a law of nature at the moment, which magic has no power to change. There is no air to breathe on the moon. If I got in my moonship and went there as I am, I would suffocate, or worse, because where there is no air, my experiments have proved that the human body implodes, collapses in upon itself. I am having to design a special suit to keep myself in one piece."

"What kind of suit?" Ruskin asked.

And suddenly, to Corkoran's slight bewilderment, everyone was agog with interest. Questions were fired at him, and suggestions after those. Ruskin and Lukin discussed articulated joints for the moonsuit, which Corkoran had not realized he would need, while Olga recommended several air-spells Corkoran did not know, saying she had always kept several kinds ready in case her father's ship sank. Claudia, after some scribbling and calculating, came up with a formula for exactly how thick the metal of a moonsuit would have to be, and while Ruskin snatched her paper, checked it, and pronounced it could be thinner than that, Felim produced a scheme for surrounding the whole moon in an envelope of air. "Using your Impenetrable Net to hold it there," he explained.

"But," said Elda, "why not make the moonsuit out of Impenetrable Net, anyway? With one of Olga's air-spells on each shoulder. That's what I'd do."

While Corkoran was staring at her, wondering why this had never occurred to him, Felim observed, "You might have to stiffen the net to prevent implosion." And Claudia began calculating again just how stiff it should be.

After this Ruskin asked about the construction of the moonship in such detail and so knowledgeably that the idea began to grow in Corkoran that he might get Ruskin to finish the moonship for him. Dwarf craftsmanship was just what was needed, delicate and strong. Perhaps offer Ruskin a scholarship . . . Offer Claudia another, so that she could do his calculations . . . But before these ideas had quite ripened to a decision, Corkoran found Ruskin's eye on him, round and blue and innocent. "Pity dwarf work costs such a lot," Ruskin mused. "Such a very great deal that even the Emperor can't afford it most of the time."

Ah, well, Corkoran thought. He had enough new ideas to go on, anyway. He rushed away back to his lab, half an hour early, almost dizzy with all the possibilities his students had suggested.

There was a small square of paper lying in the middle of his lab floor. Corkoran picked it up, idly reading it as he threw it away and turned to his workbench. "MAKE US THE RIGHT SIZE," it said, in rather small letters, "AND WE GO. DO NOT, THEN BEWARE." Corkoran let it fall into his wastebin without bothering to think about it. He did not even glance toward the rat cage, where the Impenetrable Net hung off the front and the bars were forced outward. He had forgotten the assassins days ago. He got down to puzzling out articulated joints for his moonsuit.

Meanwhile a young woman was walking through the city. Every so often she stopped someone and politely inquired the way to the University. Each person she asked directed her with willing eagerness and smiled as she walked on the way he or she had pointed. She was that kind of young lady. She walked very upright in a plain cloak that swirled sedately aside to show a worn blue woolen dress, and her hair, which was on the dark side of brown, curled a little around a face that was longish and not quite pretty, but it was so full of humor and confidence and kindness that most people reacted to her as if she were a raving beauty. The porter at the University gates was no exception. He bowed to her.

"That way, my lady. Taking coffee by the statue in the main courtyard at this hour usually." And after the young lady had given him a smile that half stunned him, he said to the janitor, "Quite the most lovely lady I ever set eyes on, and I seen a few. Puts Wizard Myrna and that Melissa quite in the shade, I say."

The young lady walked on into the courtyard, where Elda and her friends were gathered around Wizard Policant and Olga had just fetched coffee.

"Forget Corkoran. He can't see beyond his tie," Lukin said to Ruskin. "How are the food-spells coming on?"

Ruskin grumped. His room was now a mess of little bowls and dishes, and tiny cooking fires in clay pots, where the smells of bread or fried fish regularly woke him during the night. "I can't seem to balance the smell with the taste yet," he confessed. "If I do get a good steak pie, it smells of lavender, or I got a lovely chowder, but it—"

Lukin gave a great shout and raced away across the courtyard. "*Isodel!*" he yelled, and flung both arms around the young lady. She hugged him back heartily.

Olga had gone white again. Elda cocked an eye at her. "His sister," she said. "My brother Blade thinks she's wonderful."

"Oh," Olga said rather faintly, and her face flooded red.

"Here," Isodel said to Lukin, handing him a worn old wallet that chinked a little. "It's not as much as we'd hoped, I'm afraid. Father suddenly decided to check up on everyone's allowance—Mother's particularly—and tell us we all spent too much. We had to account for every copper. Mother invented a charity, and I pretended there was a dress bill I'd forgotten. But we think he's getting suspicious, Lukin. He keeps asking about you. Mother and I keep saying we've seen you just this minute, and the younger ones are being magnificent, inventing things you said to them that morning, but there are so many courtiers not in the secret—like Lord Crevet, going around saying he's not seen you for weeks now—that it's getting very difficult."

Lukin experienced a deep sinking feeling somewhere just under his stomach. "The University sent out a request for donations. Did he—"

"No, that was all right," said Isodel, "though it was a narrow squeak. I'd told the loftkeeper that any pigeons that arrived from the University were to be brought to *me*, but Father was actually *in* the loft, inspecting it, when it came. Luckily Lyrian was with Father, and he realized and managed to whisper to the pigeon to fly off and look for me, so Father never saw it after all. But, Lukin, it would make things a lot easier if you could manage to nip home on a spell for a day or so and show Father you're there."

"Oh, gods!" said Lukin. "They keep us so busy here. And we haven't done translocation yet. The way I am now, I'm quite likely to arrive in the palace at the bottom of a deep pit. Or," he said, thinking about it, "at the end of a line of deep pits, between here and Luteria."

"You could borrow Endymion," Isodel suggested. "If I asked him very nicely—"

"Endymion regards himself as your own personal dragon," Lukin said. "If he wouldn't bring me here, why should he take me back? Where is he, by the way?"

"Hiding in a wood. He got shy," Isodel explained. "He hates being gawked at."

"Then you must have walked miles!" Lukin exclaimed. "Come over to the statue and sit down and meet my friends." He put an arm around her shoulders and led her to the statue, where his friends were all rather feverishly pretending not to be interested. "You've met Elda, of course. This is Ruskin, Claudia, Felim, and"—he took a deep breath—"this is Olga."

There was a weighty pause then. Isodel looked at Olga, and Olga looked at Isodel. Then both of them smiled in the same anxious-to-please way. It was clear that they liked one another but were both a little daunted by the situation. As soon as he saw this, Felim, on whom Isodel's smile worked in the usual profound way, went dashing off to fetch Isodel some coffee.

"And some food!" Lukin shouted after Felim. "Because I'll bet you had no breakfast," he said to Isodel, who confessed that this was so.

"I can't stay here more than half an hour," she added. "It's about five miles to the wood, and Endymion has to get me back for lunchtime or Father's going to ask where I am, too."

"We've got a class, anyway," Lukin said. "And I've got to talk to Wermacht about—" He looked around for the cloakrack. Claudia, Ruskin, and Olga pointed. It was standing on the other side of the statue. "And I *know* we left it inside the tutorial room," said Lukin. "But if it got out of a sealed pit, what's a mere door? It just takes a little longer. Isodel, if you think *we've* got problems, you should hear about Claudia's. And Felim's." And he told her, although he said not a word about Olga's troubles, for which everyone silently congratulated him.

Claudia had been looking from brother to sister. They were very alike, although Lukin's face was heavier and his hair darker. When they were both smiling and talking, they were more alike than ever. Claudia was puzzled, because they looked about the same age. "Are you two twins?" she asked.

They laughed. "People always ask that," said Isodel. "No, but I'm only ten months older than he is."

"She's the eldest, and she'd make a much

better monarch than me," Lukin said. "Though nothing seems to convince my father of this." Here Felim came dashing back from the refectory with a tray laden with coffee and a quantity of buns. He handed the tray to Isodel, who thanked him with a smile. "Don't you agree she'd make a good queen?" Lukin asked Felim.

"I certainly do!" Felim said devoutly. That smile had made him Isodel's for life.

"Problem," Lukin said. "Mine this time. The king, my father, has no idea that I am here learning to be a wizard. If he knew, he would not only hit the palace roof but probably also go on up through it. He thinks wizardry and kingship are two incompatible things. The rest of my family, bless them, are trying to prevent my father finding out where I am, but he is getting suspicious because he doesn't ever actually *see* me. Can any of you think of a way I can be in two places at once? Isodel's finding things really difficult."

"An illusion," Felim said promptly. "He will see you at the end of a long corridor or running ahead downstairs too fast to catch."

"No," said Ruskin. "A golem. I came across a very pretty little golem-spell the other day. You need a likeness of Lukin that this king can get close to."

Everyone looked dubious about this, knowing the success rate of Ruskin's spells lately. Isodel said diffidently, "I've seen golems. They don't behave like a real person."

"How about—" Elda and Olga began at once. Elda shut her beak, and Olga continued, "A sort of mixture of the two ideas?" and Elda exclaimed, "*I* was going to say that!"

"Yes," agreed Claudia. "That might do it. I believe such things work best on something that belongs to the person you're trying to copy. Lukin, give us a handkerchief or a button or something, and if we can get it to look like you with a simple trigger word—if somebody says your name maybe—then we can give it to Isodel—"

"And I can take it home and pass it around the family so that Father sees him in all sorts of places! Perfect!" Isodel exclaimed.

While Lukin searched himself, muttering that somehow he didn't seem to have a handkerchief, Felim said politely to Isodel, "Are you a wizard also, my lady?"

Isodel laughed. "Good lords, no!"

"She just has personal magnetism," Lukin said, giving up the handkerchief hunt and handing Claudia the torn-out inside of a pocket instead. "The kind of magnetism that has fledgling dragons swearing lifelong fidelity and courtiers falling at her feet proposing marriage twice a day."

Isodel turned decidedly pink. "It's not— I really don't encourage anyone."

"I wish I had half of it, that's all," said Lukin.

Felim's dark eyes studied Isodel, then Lukin. "Forgive me," he said in his polite way, "but I think you simply seldom choose to exercise yours."

It was Lukin's turn to blush. "Let's get on with this spell," he said.

They gathered around the torn-out pocket with their heads together, while Isodel sat on the plinth of the statue, leaning against Wizard Policant's legs, eating buns and watching. She shook her head from time to time, quite unable to see what they were doing. She was taken completely by surprise when after a minute or so Claudia said, "I think that should do it. Let's test it. Hold it out to one side of him, Olga, while Isodel says his name. Say it, Isodel."

Isodel looked at the perfectly ordinary scrap of cloth fluttering between Olga's fingers and obediently said, "Lukin?"

Immediately there were two Lukins, one standing beside the other. Isodel had no idea which one was the real one, until the one on the right scowled and said, "I don't look anything *like* that!" at which everyone laughed heartily and said, "Yes, you do!"

"Do I really look that sulky all the time?" the real Lukin asked.

Unfortunately they had by this time more than used up the extra half hour Corkoran had given them in his eagerness to get back to his lab and were ten minutes late for Wermacht's class.

Wermacht might not have noticed if Elda had not been missing. Though he had been pretending for over a week now that Elda did not exist, a blank space where a large golden griffin should be is hard to ignore. And once he had noticed that, Wermacht also noticed the five other empty spaces. As Lukin spoke, he came striding out into the courtyard to investigate.

"What do you think you're doing out here?" he demanded, and blinked a little. For a moment he seemed to be seeing two Crown Princes of Luteria. But that was before Olga gave one of them a little shake and tossed a fluttering rag to Isodel. "You are of course welcome to miss all my classes," Wermacht continued in his most sarcastic manner. "But I warn you that without my notes you'll find yourselves quite unable to answer the questions in the end-of-term exams."

"Oh, dear," sighed Claudia. "More trouble. We have to go, Isodel."

Isodel stuffed the rag into her pocket and jumped to the ground. "I'm so sorry, Wizard," she said. "It was my fault. I paid my brother an unexpected visit and made everyone forget the time. Please forgive them."

She did not smile. She simply looked earnestly into Wermacht's face. A besotted smile came over that face as she looked. Wermacht pulled his beard and straightened his shoulders. He bowed. "Oh, *that's* all right, my lady. *Anyone* would forget the time in the circumstances."

"That's very good of you," Isodel said. This time she did smile, and Wermacht almost reeled. "Thank you, Wizard," Isodel said, really meaning it.

"Not at . . . not at all, not at all, anytime," Wermacht replied devotedly.

Lukin watched with appreciation. This was how it always was with Isodel. She did not intend to make people besotted with her. It happened because she always unfailingly meant what she said. And it even worked on Wermacht, this magnetism of hers. Fine, Lukin thought. He might be able to make use of this. He kissed his sister good-bye and looked back as he followed his friends to the North Lab, partly to watch the upright figure of his favorite sister walking toward the main gate but also to check on the equally upright shape of the cloakrack. Sure enough, it gave a little jerk as Claudia moved and came trundling after her. Lukin held the door of the North Lab open so that it could trundle inside, and he sat down in time to hear Elda whisper to Ruskin, "I didn't know Wermacht was human before this!"

Ruskin replied with a sigh. "This proves I'm not. I liked her, but I prefer big fat healers."

"Er-hem!" went Wermacht, back to his ordinary behavior. "If you're quite finished talking, you with the voice, perhaps we could get on?"

Lukin grinned and set to work scribbling notes. An hour later, flexing his right hand to get the cramp out of it, he stood in Wermacht's way as Wermacht strode to the door. "Excuse me, Wizard Wermacht, can I have a word with you?"

Wermacht gave Lukin a haughty stare. "What is it?"

"My sister," said Lukin, and then, for the sake of telling the truth, pretended to lose his thread. "Isodel," he added.

Wermacht was attending instantly, bending toward Lukin and asking eagerly, "Is *that* her name?"

Lukin nodded. "Very distressed about this business with the cloakrack," he said.

"*What* business with the cloakrack?" Wermacht demanded.

Lukin pointed. Claudia, between Olga and Ruskin, was by now about ten feet out into the courtyard, jostling among the crowd of other students. As Lukin pointed, the cloakrack juddered on its three feet and began to slide after her. "She doesn't like to think it was you who did that," he said somewhat dishonestly.

Wermacht glanced irately at the cloakrack. "Who told her such nonsense?" he said. He stretched out a long arm, caught the cloakrack by its wooden upright as it slid past, and pulled hard.

Out in the courtyard Claudia screamed. Olga and Ruskin whirled around to look at Wermacht.

"That ought not to have hurt her," Wermacht said irritably.

"But it did, didn't it?" Lukin pointed out. "She's thoroughly tied to it somehow. Isodel—"

"All right, all right!" Wermacht put out both hands and felt the cloakrack all over, from its three legs, up its central pole, around the big double hooks at the top, and finally the loop at its apex. He seemed to have no more success than Ruskin and Elda had had. "*I* can't feel anything!" he snapped. "It must be her imagination." He took hold and gave the cloakrack a vicious jerk.

Claudia screamed again, in evident anguish. This time Felim came running back among the students to see what was the matter. Beyond Felim, Elda opened her wings and came coasting across everyone's heads to investigate, too.

Elda looks twice the size when she's flying! Lukin thought admiringly.

Wermacht gave Elda a thoroughly nervous look. "I shall have to think about this," he told Lukin. "Tell your sister I shall put my whole mind to the problem."

Lukin watched Wermacht stride hastily away. "Sorry," he said to Claudia. "I'd no idea it would hurt you. I was trying to get Wermacht to take whatever he did off you, but I don't think the fool *knows* what he did."

"Perhaps," suggested Olga, "we should have a go at it ourselves."

"Not just now," Claudia said. When Wermacht had pulled at the cloakrack, it had felt as if every nerve in her body was trying to come loose. She was still feeling faint and looking greenish.

"Lunch," said Ruskin.

As he spoke, the students up ahead of them began milling about and giving interested murmurs. Someone was trying to push through them toward the Spellman Building. Claudia caught one glimpse of the shining helmet on the head of this person—or rather, the purple-and-red crest of horsehair on the top of his helmet—and hid behind Elda, looking greener than ever.

She gasped. "Don't let him see me!"

Elda spread both wings a little to hide Claudia and stared above everyone's head at the advancing person. In addition to the flashing gold-colored helmet, he wore a breastplate of the same shiny metal above a neat little skirt of white kidskin with metal plates dangling on it and sandals with metal shin guards below that. His wide sword made his short scarlet cloak stick out jauntily. Elda stared down at him with interest. She had never seen anyone dressed like this in the flesh, though her sister Callette had. Callette had been to the Empire and done paintings of legionaries. Elda had seen those. But she was quite astonished when this legionary strode right up to her and, bowing his helmeted head, dropped briefly on one knee in front of her. Elda could feel Claudia quivering behind her. She had no idea what to do. She was quite relieved when the man sprang smartly to his feet and, obviously not realizing Elda could speak, asked Felim, who was nearest, "Your pardon, young sir, where do I find the headmaster of this school?"

"I fancy you must mean Wizard Corkoran," Felim told him. "Go over there, to the Spellman Building. Someone in the office there will tell you how to find him."

The man thanked him and strode away. Elda's head turned to watch him go. "Why*ever* did he kneel down like that?" she said.

Claudia gave a weak little giggle behind her. "Didn't you know? The golden griffin is the crest of the Emperor of the South. He was paying his respects to my brother, Titus."

TEN

CLAUDIA'S FRIENDS WERE slightly puzzled when Claudia said she would do without lunch and meet them in Elda's room afterward. "Do you not want to meet your brother then?" Felim asked.

"It's not my brother," was all Claudia would say, and she left at a run with the faithful cloakrack clattering after.

The others went into the refectory. Here they found that the new cook had produced a choice between the usual stew and sandwiches. "Using up leftover bread," Ruskin said, gloomily prodding packets with a large finger. "Soft as a slug in the middle and hard as nails at the edges. Wait till I get my food-spells right."

"We might take Claudia some, though," Olga suggested.

They each stuffed a packet of the sandwiches into Elda's bag and chose stew. Feeling more honest if they did without pudding—it was called fool and looked like brown custard, and no one wanted it, anyway—they left early. And stood staring in amazement at the bottom of the refectory steps as a trumpet rang out and a procession crossed the courtyard toward the Spellman Building.

First came a squad of men dressed like the legionary who had knelt to Elda, all in step, skirts swinging demurely, helmet plumes bobbing in rhythm. These were followed by a second squad. In the space between the two squads, very stately and carefully not walking in step with the soldiers, came two elderly men draped in dark purple versions of Claudia's wrap. You could tell they were important, Elda thought, because each of them had a band made of green leaves stuck end to end, like a crown, around his head. If that didn't tell you, it was obvious from the important looks on their wrinkled faces.

One of the wrinkled faces turned Elda's way. Someone barked a command. Both squads wheeled through ninety degrees, and the procession advanced on Elda, spread out in a line now, with the wrinkled men in the middle.

Lukin, muttering that his father had been at war with the Empire for the last eight years, backed out of sight behind Elda. Elda herself was so alarmed to find all these people pacing toward her that her front legs retreated toward her hind legs of their own accord, arcing her back and causing her wings to spring out on either side of her. Quite without meaning to, she bent her neck to the attack position and raised her crest. The measured steps of the advancing Empire people faltered, just slightly, at the sight.

Ruskin uttered a buzzing moan of distress and dived under Elda's outspread left wing. "*Hide* me!" he said desperately.

The change in the direction of the procession had revealed the party of dwarfs that had been following it. They were even more resplendently caparisoned than the Empire party and were standing, annoyed and deserted, scowling toward Elda.

"They've come to get me!" Ruskin's voice buzzed, muffled and feathery.

Elda made haste to bring her wings to her sides and to sit down. Her tail had been nervously lashing at Lukin's shins, and she quickly brought it around to coil in front of her feet and hide Ruskin's legs. But her crest stayed up. She was quite surprised by the surge of motherly protectiveness that swept through her. It was the feel of Ruskin huddled against her side and the sound of his voice vibrating in her wing. Mother griffins, she realized of a sudden, were meant to protect their young ones this way.

She watched alertly while the Empire party all went down on one knee before her, the wrinkled ones rather slowly and creakingly. Beyond them the dwarfs shrugged and continued on their way toward the Spellman Building. Elda was so relieved to see the dwarfs go that she said kindly to the Empire people, "Do get up, and I hope all the right things happen in the Empire."

They all jumped at hearing her speak, and even the soldiers floundered a bit getting to their feet. Once upright, they realized that the dwarf party was now ahead of them. Someone barked, "Quick, march!" and they all set off toward the Spellman Building at a walk that was nearly a sprint.

Felim gently picked up the edge of Elda's wing and peered in at the cowering Ruskin. "Why are you so very frightened?"

"Get me to Elda's room," Ruskin buzzed back, "and I'll explain."

Corkoran meanwhile was extremely irritated. Everyone seemed to be conspiring to stop him getting to work on the ideas his students had given him. First it was the high priest. Almost as soon as he was back in his lab, a healer appeared to say that the high priest's broken leg was more comfortable today and that he wished to be returned to the Holy City. Now.

You did not argue with high priests. Their gods could make things extremely uncomfortable for you if you did. So that meant that Corkoran had to find Finn and then Dench and take them over to Healers Hall, along with the ingredients of a transport spell. Holy City was a long way north, and it took three wizards to supply strength for the translocation. And it took the rest of the morning.

Corkoran rushed back to his lab, only to find the porter waiting for him with the news that a party of important dwarfs wanted to see him at once.

Corkoran sighed. "I'll see them after lunch in the Council Chamber," he said, and sent out for lunch at once, before anything else could happen. But he and his lunch had barely arrived in his rooms before he found one of the secretaries showing an Empire centurion through his door. This man saluted him, Empire fashion, with a violently outflung arm that made Corkoran start backward, and announced that the two noble senators of the Empire, Antoninus and Empedocles, were presently in the city and craved instant audience with him. Corkoran irritably decided to see them at the same time as he saw the dwarfs. Get both lots over with at once. "After lunch," he said. "In the Council Chamber." This way he might save at least a quarter of the day to get to work in.

The centurion flung an arm out again and departed. Corkoran ate his lunch slowly, making notes about his moonship as he ate and wishing he had stayed longer with his students. Ruskin had not said nearly enough. He would have to arrange some kind of special tutorial and get

Ruskin to talk about the moonship some more. Eventually, sighing at this waste of his time, Corkoran set off down the stone stairway to go to the Council Chamber.

He was halfway down the stairs when the legionaries, followed by the senators, followed by more legionaries, began streaming extremely quickly across the hallway to the Council Chamber. These were followed by a slow and stately group of dwarfs. Corkoran stopped where he was, struck by how magnificent they all were. He had intended to interview them all in his usual T-shirt and his comet-decorated tie, to show them how busy he was. But now he had serious second thoughts.

These people are rich, he thought. I sent both lots a request for money, and this is probably why they're here. I have to meet them looking as stately as they do, to show them what a fine and august place they'll be giving their support to. He sighed again as he conjured his official robes to him and climbed into them on the stairs. Ever since the tours, when Mr. Chesney had insisted that wizards all wear robes all the time, Corkoran had hated the wretched garments. Nevertheless, he went grandly down the rest of the stairs, wearing the red of a Third Level Wizard, with the hanging hood of ermine that showed he was a high official of the University, and feeling hot and disgruntled.

In the Council Chamber they all bowed to

him, and he was glad he had bothered with the robes. The two senators were in the full pomp of their Imperial senatorial purple, red borders, laurel wreaths and all, and the spacious chamber seemed crammed with all their legionaries. The dwarfs took Corkoran's breath away, with their gilded, jeweled armor, ceremonial weapons, and the precious stones swinging in the braids of their hair and beards. Two of them, whose hair was white, wore exquisite platinum coronets on their snowy heads.

Corkoran was awed by all this wealth, though he tried not to show it. He went briskly to the other side of the Council table and sat down facing them all. At this the two senators creakingly lowered themselves into seats, while the legionaries stood in massed ranks behind them. The two white-haired dwarfs also climbed into chairs, jingling faintly, and the other dwarfs crowded behind them on foot. So these standing ones were there to make the sitting dwarfs look important, just like the legionaries, Corkoran thought.

"Good afternoon, gentlemen," he said pleasantly, but in a brisk, I'm-really-very-busy tone. "What can I do for you?"

"Who are you?" demanded one of the dwarfs who were standing up.

Corkoran blinked a bit. "I'm Corkoran, Wizard Chairman of the Governing Board of the University. And you are?"

"I am Antoninus," said the left-hand senator, deftly cutting in, "Senator of the Empire. Beside me sits my colleague Senator Empedocles, and we have urgent business—"

Corkoran nodded pleasantly and turned to the dwarfs. "And you gentlemen?"

"We," said the right-hand dwarf with the coronet, "are all forgemasters from Central Peaks fastness, and we are our own soldiers." His green eyes swept sneeringly over the rigid legionaries. "We have no need to bring protection with us. I am Dobrey, son of Davelly, son of Dorkan, son of Dwain, who was founder of the tribe of forge-masters. Beside me sits Genno, son of Gart, son of Graid, son of Dwain, and behind me to my right stands Hordo, son of Harnid, son of Hennel, son of Haman, son of Dwain. And to his left stands Clodo . . ."

Corkoran listened unbelievingly as every one of the ten dwarfs was introduced by name and by descent. Senator Empedocles leaned toward Senator Antoninus to whisper, "This need to recite one's pedigree puts one in mind of a horse fair."

"What can one expect of nonhumans?" Senator Antoninus whispered back, shrugging.

Corkoran began to see he might have made a mistake to put these two groups together.

". . . And we have come here—" continued Dobrey.

"No doubt on a very great errand," Senator

Empedocles slid in deftly. Corkoran could see he was a senior veteran of committees. "But ours is pressing, Wizard. As you must know, our great Empire is the cradle and nurse of democracy, throughout all its classes and many distinctions. The Senate, to which I have the honor to belong, is but the highest of our democratic institutions, being selected by the votes of all the people on a five-yearly basis and thus being the supreme voice of the will of the people. The Emperor himself, not being so elected, on many occasions discovers the aforesaid will of the people through the votes of the Senate and is of course swayed by it. Thus I may say—though with all due diffidence, Wizard—that I and my senatorial colleague beside me represent the revealed will of the Emperor. If you follow me."

Corkoran did not follow Empedocles. He had no idea what the fellow was on about. Dobrey, sitting with his massive braceleted arms folded over his breastplate, said contemptuously, "He means his Emperor hasn't told him to come and probably doesn't know he's here. Right, Senator?"

Empedocles's wrinkled mouth pinched furiously at the corners, but he inclined his head politely to the dwarf. "This being so"—Antoninus smoothly took over—"it follows that it is imperative that you, Wizard, understand our position, or stance, if I may put it that way. Our nobly democratic institutions can only keep their integrity, integrity that is our most precious asset, if they preserve the integrity of the entire people, of our whole Imperial family, by ensuring, for their smooth operation and the maintaining of our high standards, that we take such measures toward cleanliness, unity, and normalcy as we can. Any tinge—I will not go so far as to call it a taint—of what might loosely be called anti-Imperial is to us a thing to be deplored and expunged at all costs."

Antoninus was worse than Empedocles. Corkoran looked involuntarily toward Dobrey. Dobrey's eyebrows were up, wrinkling his bulging forehead all the way up to his coronet. "Lovely," he said. "Intricate. Wizard, I think this one's on about not wanting to mix their breed. But he's said it so tangled up that he could turn around and tell you he was saying just the opposite if he needed to."

Antoninus gave Dobrey a steady snakelike stare. "My good dwarf, do you wish to make my statement for me?"

Dobrey waved a massive hand. "No, no. Carry on. This is amusing."

"We don't like half-breeds either," Genno remarked from beside him.

Corkoran suddenly discovered what they were talking about. "You mean, you've come here about Claudia," he said.

Two laureled heads gravely bowed at him. "An understanding having been reached,"

Empedocles said, "we can now proceed to outline our position more precisely. Our Imperial ruler, gracious Emperor Titus, is still quite young and has so far regrettably failed to provide for the advancement of the griffin through another glorious generation—"

"Emperor won't get married," Dobrey translated.

"And as matters stand"—Empedocles continued, ignoring this—"the chief person to profit from the reversion of the Imperial title and honors is this most unfortunate half sister. You see our problem, Wizard. Without in the least wishing to go against the august preferences of the Emperor, we would want rather to preempt them by annihilating any threat of mixed blood at the heart of the Imperium."

"With this in view," Antoninus put in, "we in the Senate were exceedingly interested in the discovery that this University is currently, and we hope temporarily, suffering a slight shortfall in its funding. The Emperor would, I am sure, in the right circumstances, be happy to put it to the vote in the Senate that the Empire relieve, to some extent, the embarrassments of a worthy institution, so that matters can be adjusted to the satisfaction of all parties."

Dobrey chuckled. "And now he's offering you a bribe."

"To hand her over so that they can snuff her," Genno explained.

Two laureled brows turned and lowered at the dwarf party.

"Or you can snuff her yourself if you'd rather," Genno added.

"This is infinitely crude," said Antoninus.

"But moderately accurate," said Empedocles.

But I think I'm going to need Claudia for my moonshot! Corkoran thought. I've never seen anyone calculate as fast as she does. This morning he had felt nearer to getting to the moon than he had ever felt before. On the other hand, there was no denying that the University needed money badly. The two different needs pulled Corkoran this way and that like the rope in a tug-of-war. He could tell Claudia to work for him or he'd let the senators have her. But there was no guarantee that Claudia was as good as she seemed. He could take the senators' money and use some of it to hire someone else who could calculate equally swiftly. But there was no guarantee that he could find anyone who could. No—hang on! There might be a way to keep Claudia *and* get the money. The senators, thanks to the dwarfs, had let him know that the Emperor had no idea they were here.

Corkoran raised his head with a regretful, sad smile. "Alas, gentlemen. You should have come and talked to me a week ago, before my fellow tutors discovered that the young lady in question, though a half-breed, is their most promising student for years. The University has already decided to award her a scholarship. Talent counts over blood here, you know. We have to retain the young lady on our books."

The senators turned and looked at one another. Antoninus raised an eyebrow. Empedocles nodded. Both old men got up. "Then we won't waste any more of your valuable time, Wizard," Empedocles said, "but merely remind you, in view of your resolve to retain the young person in question, that the Empire never sleeps, never rests."

Bother! Corkoran thought, watching the legionaries form up smartly in squads and smartly march out of the chamber with the senators pacing in their midst. That was a warning. It almost certainly meant more assassins. Still, they had dealt with one lot of assassins, so they could probably handle another—except that this time Corkoran was determined that the Emperor was going to help them do it. Just get rid of the dwarfs first. He waited until the doors had boomed shut behind the last legionary and turned to the dwarfs.

Dobrey grinned at him. "Oddly enough," he said, "we're here on a rather similar matter."

"But *we* don't beat about bushes," said Genno. "We want that Ruskin back. We'll pay in treasure or in gold bars, whichever you prefer. So how much?"

Now that the senators had left, the other eight dwarfs clearly felt no need to pretend to be an honor guard. They pulled out chairs and hopped up into them with sighs of relief. "Oh, my poor feet!" said one, Hordo, Corkoran thought, and leaned his elbows on the table. "Name your price, Wizard. You need the money. Everyone in town was telling us that your roofs leak and about how Bardic College and Healers Hall both refused you a loan last summer."

This was true, unfortunately. Corkoran was still smarting, when he thought about the matter, about how rude the bards had been. He could see no way out of this demand. And he was exasperated because he was fairly sure that he needed Ruskin to work on the moonship even more than he needed Claudia to calculate its course. He thought of losing the chance of all the exquisite dwarf handwork Ruskin could do for him and almost ground his teeth. He could *make* Ruskin do the work by threatening to sell him to these forgemasters, but only if he could see some way of inducing these dwarfs to let him keep Ruskin here. It was fairly clear that they were too blunt and shrewd to believe him for a moment if he suggested another scholarship for Ruskin. "Why?" he asked, playing for time. "What do rich, high-caste dwarfs like you want with a measly runt like Ruskin?"

"That's the nubbin of it," Dobrey said. "We're all Sons of Dwain here. Forgemasters. Artisans like Ruskin are our slaves—legally. They *belong* to us, Wizard. All the lower tribes do."

"And we can't have a slave running off like this," Genno explained. "He *has* to be taken back and publicly executed as an example to the rest, or they'll *all* think they can run off."

"Yes, I see that," Corkoran said. "But I met a lot of dwarfs while I was on the tours, forgemasters and artisans, too, and nobody ever suggested the artisans were slaves."

"Western dwarfs," Dobrey said dismissively. "Different customs. Dwain made *our* customs when he took over Central Peaks five hundred years ago. Did it legally, too, with Wizard Policant for witness. Came all the way here to this University to make sure it was lawful."

"Look in your library," said Hordo with his elbows on the table. "You'll find that agreement in your Inventory. We brought our copy with us, just to make sure. That Ruskin *belongs* to us, and you've got to give him back."

"Let's see your copy then," Corkoran said, still playing for time.

Dobrey, who was obviously the senior forgemaster, fetched a folded parchment from the front of his ornamental gold breastplate. It was brown with age and almost clattered with stiffness as Corkoran took it and spread it out. Yes, there it was, all in order, with Policant's crabbed black signature beside the University seal at the bottom and a swirl that deciphered as "Dwain" at the other corner. "Artisans, miners, drudges . . . agree to form clans, these clans to be the sole property of forgemasters . . . this agreement in exchange for certain spells of protection donated by the University in consideration of one ton of gold . . . said spells only known to forgemasters and of proven value against the demons of the deep. . . ."

So this was why the low-caste dwarfs sold themselves, Corkoran thought. Silly thing to do. But it clearly brought the University quite a profit. Wizard Policant must have been a smooth operator. "Do you still have the spells, or much trouble with demons?" he asked, wondering if he could offer to renew the spells in exchange for Ruskin.

Dobrey coughed. "Er-hem. Naturally we've still got the spells, but between you and me, Wizard, those demons were what you might call a legal figment. A lot of the dwarfs *thought* there were demons in the lower galleries, so it came to the same thing. And that doesn't alter the agreement one bit."

"Of course not," Corkoran agreed. So the only thing for it seemed to be to operate as smoothly as old Policant and ask for a ton of gold this time, too. Then give half of it back in exchange for a team of artisans to work on the moonship. Who might do the work much faster than Ruskin on his own, anyway. "Well, then . . ." Corkoran began.

The big doors of the Council Chamber swung open, and Lukin came in. Olga was with him, very stately in her fur cloak. Lukin had a stately air to him as well, even more than Olga did. Knowing how important this was, Lukin had struggled against his usual desire not to be prince or king of anywhere and had managed to pull over himself all the royal magnetism he usually left to Isodel. "Good day, forgemasters," he said, every inch a prince.

"Oh, go away!" Corkoran said irritably. "Two of my students," he explained to the interested dwarfs.

"My business," Lukin stated firmly and majestically, "is with the forgemasters." Before Corkoran could say any more, he said to the dwarfs, "I am the Crown Prince of Luteria, and I find myself in need of a servitor in this place. By an oversight, I left my man behind in Luteria. I've come to buy Ruskin from you as a replacement."

The dwarfs all put back their braided and helmeted heads and bellowed with laughter. "And what, lad, do you think you could offer us that we don't have twice as much of, anyway?" Dobrey asked, with his face all creased up in amusement. "If you're talking gold, forget it. Precious jewels, fine work, the same goes."

"I'm serious," Lukin said. "I've come to make you an offer you can't refuse."

Corkoran prudently decided to keep out of this. He could hardly lose. If Lukin won, he had Ruskin to work on the moonship and money from the Emperor Titus, anyway. If the forgemasters refused the bargain, whatever it was, there would be even more money and a team of artisans into the bargain. He sat back.

"You'd have to be offering something pretty valuable, lad," Genno observed.

"I am," Lukin said with his chin haughtily raised, and hoped mightily that this was true. It was a mad gamble that he and Olga were trying, from a plan hatched with difficulty while Ruskin was almost incoherent with terror, and Claudia just as bad and no help at all. It all depended on Elda's sudden conviction that the small golden notebook was very valuable indeed. Why else, Elda said, had it been among Olaf's hidden treasures? At which Felim had looked thoughtful and asked Olga why she had kept it instead of selling it with the rest of the treasure she had taken. Olga was not sure, except that she felt drawn to it somehow. At which Felim nodded to Elda and said it was quite probably some sort of magical virtue in the notebook that made Olga feel this way.

The plan they hurriedly hatched after that depended on the senators' leaving before the dwarfs. Because, as Felim pointed out, senators were rich people, too, and they didn't want the matter confused by a senator becoming covetous and wanting either Ruskin or the notebook for himself. So would the senators be likely to get their word in first? "Oh, they will, they will!" Claudia had cried out, with her teeth chattering.

"They always do." Felim had sped off to watch and returned with the welcome news that the senators were just leaving. Lukin and Olga had sprinted to the Council Chamber with only the sketchiest notion of what they were to say.

To Lukin's relief, the dwarfs were decidedly interested. All their round, shrewd eyes were fixed on him. "So what is it you're offering?" Genno said.

"This." Lukin took a few steps forward and, in a careless, royal way, fetched the small golden notebook out of his pocket.

There was a long, penetrating silence, while all the dwarfs' eyes narrowed to focus on the book. "It looks," Dobrey said at length with unconvincing casualness, "like dwarf work from here. Can I see it close, lad?"

"If it *is* dwarf work," Genno said, clattering his ornaments as he shrugged to show how unconcerned he was, "*if* it is, and I don't say it *is*, mind, it'll have a virtue of some kind. What does it do, lad—if it does anything, that is?"

This really might be going to work. Lukin tried to keep calm. "I don't know. It's queer. All I know is that most of the things I write in it just disappear."

A very slight tremble of excitement affected all the dwarfs. One of them actually licked his lips. Dobrey held out a large hand, blistered and discolored on its palm and lumpy along its fingers. Old and important he might be, but he evidently still worked at a forge. "Show, lad."

Lukin took hold of the notebook by one delicately molded corner and held it out so that Olga could take hold of a corner, too. Together they went along behind the row of dwarfs—like assistants at an auction, Lukin thought—holding the book open so that each dwarf could turn the small, crisp pages. Most of them seemed particularly interested in the page containing the half sentence from Wermacht's first class, but others checked the gaps in the notes about herbs, and others leafed all through. Once or twice either Olga or Lukin had to let go for someone to examine the work on the cover and grunt enigmatically. When every dwarf had seen his fill, Dobrey leaned back in his chair.

"Just how did you come by this, lad?"

It was said as though Dobrey thought Lukin had stolen the book. But Ruskin, shaking with fear so that Lukin could hardly understand him, had assured Lukin that this manner of question would be the second part of the process. If there *was* a process, which Ruskin appeared to doubt miserably. Lukin looked Dobrey haughtily in the eye and replied, "It was given me as an engagement present by my bride-to-be, Olga Olafsdaughter here. It was part of her dowry. Please tell them, Olga."

The shrewd, round eyes all turned to Olga then. Olga colored up and seemed very uncomfortable. "My father was a pirate," she said, in a flat, wooden way. "Olaf Gunnarsson. This book was part of his private treasure. He took this book and a lot of other things from a dwarf ship that I saw him rob and sink on the Inland Sea."

Genno turned and slapped Dobrey ringingly on his armored back. "It *is*! It *is*!"

The great chamber echoed with his voice and the huge delighted voices of the others. "It really *is*! It's the Book of Truth! We got it, and those fool Westerners have *lost* it!"

Dobrey looked up at Lukin. "It's the only book of its kind," he said. "They made it, these Western dwarfs, a good thousand years back, to record only the truth. That's why your notes went missing. None of them were true. It's one of the Great Treasures, this book. You can have Ruskin and welcome for this, lad. You can have the whole tribe of artisans with him, for all I care."

"Steady on!" said Hordo, whose elbows were still on the table. "Don't get carried away and sell off all our workers, Dobrey."

"Just Ruskin then. Hand us the book," said Dobrey, stretching out his hand again.

Corkoran realized that it would be prudent to intervene here, before he lost Ruskin *and* the money. "Er-hem!" he said. "Before you give it to him, Lukin, I think you should get the bargain down in writing and make sure they all sign it."

Lukin's eyes, turning to Corkoran for an instant, seemed to say, "Why weren't you any help before this?" Corkoran was surprised to feel his face heating up. Well, he was quite hot in these wretched robes.

"Yes, of course. Get it in writing—I was forgetting. It's the excitement," Dobrey said shamelessly. "Anyone thought to bring writing stuff? Sealing wax? What a pity. Never mind."

Corkoran wordlessly conjured a sheet of parchment, pens, ink, a lighted candle, and a lump of sealing wax to the table in front of the dwarfs. Dobrey looked at it all regretfully. "Run out of excuses, haven't I? You'd better write it, lad. We'll sign and seal."

Lukin grinned a bit. An important part of his education as a prince had been in how to draw up treaties and contracts that were properly binding. Dobrey was not going to get anything this way either. Lukin pulled the parchment over to the end of the table and wrote, quickly but very carefully, two copies and signed his name on both. He passed the parchments along to the dwarfs, who all read with narrowed eyes and signed without comment, except for Genno, who asked in a hurt way, "Now why did you go and put in all this about 'and all magic he now commands,' lad?"

"I gathered that he borrowed a lot of magic from the rest of his tribe," Lukin explained, as haughty and princelike as he could be. "He's of no use to me without that."

"Oh, don't *haggle*, Genno!" Dobrey bellowed as he stamped hot red wax with the great ring on his forefinger. "We've got the best bargain we'll ever get in a thousand years, *and* you know it! Shake." He offered his great, rough hand to Lukin again, who shook it with hearty relief. "If only you knew, lad," Dobrey said, "just what you've signed away here! What a treasure!" He clutched the notebook lovingly to his breastplate as he climbed down from his chair. Genno snatched up one copy of the agreement and stuffed it inside his armor, before climbing down, too.

The dwarfs were all leaving at last. The rest of them, even Hordo, who had been looking like a fixture, were clattering down to their feet and marching in a cheerful body to the door. Corkoran sprang up, too. "Nice work, Lukin, Olga," he said. Then he fairly pelted out by the back way to the pigeon loft. A clever pigeon could get to the Emperor long before those senators were near the Empire. On the other hand, the senators had almost certainly sent a pigeon of their own. You could hire them from several lofts in the city. Corkoran knew he had to get his version off to the Emperor as soon as possible. A lot of money hung on it.

The janitor met him at the base of the ladder, looking worried. "I was just coming to find you. Been a bit of a frackshaw up there, there has."

"Oh, what *now*?" Corkoran started up the ladder, nearly fell off it when his robes tangled around his feet, and angrily conjured the robes away, back to his rooms. He arrived in the dim wooden loft with the janitor panting at his heels.

All the small, rounded pigeon doors at the end were open, letting in a chilly draft and enough light to show gray feathers and splashes of blood everywhere. Two pigeons lay on their backs with their pink claws uppermost, dead, right by Corkoran's feet. Beyond them was the corpse of a mouse that seemed to have been pecked to death.

"I ain't been drinking," said the janitor.

"I'm sure you haven't," Corkoran said, stunned.

"You got to believe what I saw," the janitor asserted. "I heard this noise, see, as I was on my rounds, and I climbs up to investigate. And—you got to believe this—there was battle and mayhem going on, hordes of mice going for the pigeons and the pigeons flying every which way and some of them fighting back. So I jumps inside here and shouts, and the mice all run away down between the floorboards. Then—you *got* to believe this!— I see a lot of little tiny men at the end there. Climbing about opening the pigeon doors, some were, and some of them was pushing pigeons out through the doors and two of them were fixing a message to another pigeon. When they sees I see them, they push that pigeon out, too, and run for it. Wriggle down cracks in the floor, just like the mice. And I've not touched a drop of drink, I swear."

"Tell me," asked Corkoran, "were these little men dressed all over in black?"

"They were and all," said the janitor. "That's why I didn't see them first off."

"Then I believe you completely," said Corkoran. He looked glumly around the shambles in the loft. The assassins had teamed up with the ex-pirates, by the look of things, and from what the janitor had seen, the assassins had just sent a pigeon for reinforcements, while making sure there were no pigeons that the University could send for help. Corkoran shivered. For a moment he was almost tempted to send Finn or Wermacht to ask Querida to come here quickly. But no. Querida was such a tyrant. She was almost certain, if she came, to reorganize the University around him, and she would start by canceling his moonshot, Corkoran knew it. Much better to manage by himself. He had dealt with assassins and pirates once. He could do it again. "Are there any pigeons left at all?" he asked the janitor.

There was a stirring in the rafters over his head. "Croo. Some of us. Up here," a warbling voice replied.

Corkoran raised mage light in one hand and discovered five decidedly battered birds crouched along the highest beam. Some of his anxiety left him. "I'm going to put the strongest possible protections around you—particularly you," he said, pointing to the one that seemed the least battered. "I need you to take a message for me." The bird hunched a bit but obediently fluttered down to the rail beside the message desk. "You," Corkoran said to the janitor, "go and get all the mousetraps you can find and set them up all around this loft."

"Think that'll work?" the janitor asked dubiously. "These looked to be brainy mice."

"They'll work when I've put spells on them," Corkoran said grimly. "Killer-spells."

"Right." The janitor collected the three corpses for disposal and clumped away down the ladder.

Corkoran got to work putting protection around the remaining pigeons. He enhanced it upon his chosen pigeon and then, since the bird did look very battered, added a strong speed-spell as well. The ink for writing messages had been spilled in the affray, and all the little slips of paper had been torn up. The assassins had been making darned sure no one could send for help. Too bad. Corkoran conjured more ink and paper. Then he wrote a careful and accurate account of his conversation with the two senators, their hints and their offer of money, and dwelt particularly on their final threat, citing the dwarfs as witnesses to the whole interview. He addressed it to Emperor Titus. He did not ask the Emperor for money or for help from any assassins the senators planned to send. That would have been crude. He was sure he could rely on the Emperor's gratitude for both.

"Now," he said as he fixed the flimsy paper

into the tube on the bird's leg, "you are to take this to Condita in the Empire and deliver it to Emperor Titus. The Emperor in *person* and no one else. Have you got that?"

"I'll try," croodled the bird. "I've heard they bag you in butterfly nets and take you to the Senate down there."

"Avoid that," said Corkoran. "Find the Emperor." He took the pigeon's warm, light bulk in both hands and carried it to the open pigeon doors. "Don't let anyone lay hands on you until you find the Emperor." He let the bird climb to the small doorstep and watched it wing rather wearily away.

The janitor arrived back then with an armload of mousetraps. Corkoran spent quite a time setting them up with some distinctly vicious spells, while the four remaining pigeons craned down from their beam to watch. When Corkoran finally climbed away down the ladder, the birds exchanged looks, crooned at one another, and fluttered down to the doors. Corkoran had hardly reached the bottom of the ladder before the pigeons were gone, too, winging painfully away to Derkholm.

The sun was setting by the time Corkoran reached his lab. He turned on the lights with a sigh of relief. And stood with his hand on the switches, appalled. The assassins and their mouse allies had been here, too. His notes and calculations had been gnawed into confetti-sized scraps and tossed about in heaps. His experiments for the moonsuit had been broken and spilled and emptied all over the floor. But worst and most heartbreaking of all, his precious moonship, his carefully designed and cherished moonship, which had taken him three years and untold amounts of money to build—and had been two-thirds finished by now—had been hacked to bits. Shining shards of it lay in a heap by the window. Corkoran could see hundreds of very small gleaming sword cuts on each shard. Those assassins must have sat in their cage, day by day, learning exactly what things were most important to him.

Corkoran stared at it all numbly.

ELEVEN

LUKIN HELD THE door of Elda's concert hall open for Olga, then shut it and leaned against it while Olga slowly shed her cloak. He felt weak. The others, scattered around the room, watched him anxiously.

"Phew!" he said. "You hit the bull's-eye, Elda. Ruskin, you are legally my slave, and I've got a bill of sale to prove it." He flourished his signed and sealed parchment. "Regard yourself as a citizen of Luteria from now on."

"*Wey*-HAY!" Ruskin bounded to his small legs, pigtails flying, and did a clacking dance of triumph with Felim. In the course of it the cloakrack got knocked over. Claudia let it lie. Her position was nothing like so certain as Ruskin's. The fact that no legionaries had come to arrest her was small comfort. The senators could be starting extradition proceedings in the city at this moment. She huddled among the cushions on the stage, wondering what to do about it.

"You stick close to me," Elda told her, picking up the cloakrack. "Fetch your things, and sleep in here from now on. I can handle those soldiers."

Olga was not joining in the rejoicing any more than Claudia was. She was standing near the door beside the dropped furry heap of her cloak, staring into nowhere. "I think," Lukin said to her, "that I handled those dwarfs rather well."

"Do you?" Olga said.

"Yes, I *do*," Lukin said, hurt by her lack of enthusiasm. "Dwarfs are such tricksy beggars. You have to pin them down in all directions. I was afraid they were going to sheer off even before the bargaining started, when you were telling them how you got the notebook. You sounded so wooden, as if you were reciting a lesson you'd learned or something."

Olga whirled around on him in a swirl of hair. "Oh, did I? Mr. Crown Prince Lukin! And how *was* I supposed to behave when you were lording around telling lies about dowries and brides-to-be? Was I supposed to simper? Was I supposed to say, 'Oh, yes, Lukin's father's just dying to have a pirate in the family. And a *mouse*'?"

Lukin was perplexed. Olga looked so angry. He could not understand why her eyes were brimming with tears when everything had gone so well. "You know I had to say something like that to give the book a proper provenance. They wouldn't have accepted that it was mine to sell if I hadn't. You *know* I didn't mean a word of it."

"All right, don't rub it in!" Olga screamed at him.

"I'm not," Lukin said, trying to be reasonable. "I thought we were friends enough and understood one another enough that you could accept what I had to say and back me up. I'm sorry if it annoyed you, but we had to rescue Ruskin."

"I'm not *talking* about Ruskin!" Olga yelled. "You might at least have *warned* me!"

"Then I'm sure I don't know what you *are* talking about!" Lukin snapped. "You're being as bat-headed as Melissa. You must have realized, when I asked you to come with me, that I was going to have to spin a yarn of some kind."

"Oh!" Olga gasped. "That *does* it! I never want to speak to you again, ever in my life! Never!" She burst into tears. Crying so hard that she could barely see what she was doing, she fumbled the door open, flung it wide, and ran away. She was crying such volumes of tears that Lukin could see drops whirling out on either side of her flying hair, shining like rainbows for an instant, before the door swung back and slammed in his face.

"What's got into her?" he asked his friends slightly irritably.

They stared solemnly back. Claudia, realizing this was a time to forget her own troubles, climbed off the stage and went to join Elda. The cloakrack jiggled across the carpet after her. Everyone ignored it. "Don't you really know?" Claudia asked Lukin.

"No," said Lukin, and it seemed to him he was being entirely honest. "I haven't a clue."

"Then we can't tell you. Think about it," Claudia said.

Everyone waited while Lukin thought. His first thought was that his friends were being as unreasonable as Olga had been. Here he was, having behaved like a prince for once and rescued Ruskin, and instead of telling him how clever he had been, they were asking him to *think*. It made no sense. But while he thought that, his immense satisfaction at rescuing Ruskin began to melt and crack a little. Uncomfortable feelings began to wriggle out from under it. Perhaps he had ridden roughshod over Olga a little. But behaving like a prince *made* you do that. He found he needed to move about, so he went and handed Ruskin the signed and sealed parchment. "There," he said, and then, before he could stop himself, "Did she really mean that, about never speaking to me again?"

Everyone knew Olga, her pride and her straightforwardness, and they answered, "Yes!" in chorus, and continued to watch him.

"Don't all *stare* at me like that!" Lukin said irritably. He wondered whether to go away like Olga and be alone for a while. But as soon as he thought of being alone, by himself entirely, he began to see that there was a great yawning pit inside him, of *hurt* that Olga did not want him anymore. Olga had become the person he relied on. She understood him. She knew when he was making a joke and when he was being serious; that was why it was so *astounding* that she had not seemed to know he was lying to the dwarfs when she had been his staunch ally in all the other troubles. She had lent—no, *given*—him money for clothes. She had handed him a priceless notebook without hesitation in Wermacht's first class, and she had conjured up a smelly monkey to help him, though—as she had confessed to him later—she truly hated calling up monsters; it made her feel unclean. So why, why had she run off now? He had not known she could be so feckless. "Do you think perhaps I should go after her and talk to her?" he asked.

"That depends on what you want to say to her," Claudia answered.

Then I won't bother, Lukin thought. She'd just shout at me again. And for himself, he suspected that he would whine and complain to Olga that he *needed* her, which would annoy Olga and make Lukin ashamed of himself. But then, when he started to think of needing Olga, he discovered that the need was really there, much deeper and much stronger and likely to go on for much longer than he had ever believed such a need could. And he began, dimly, to see why

Olga had been so upset. She had after all been born to a very different family from Lukin's. But I don't care two hoots about her beastly father! he told himself angrily. In fact, I'd quite happily set an enormous infallible mousetrap for him personally. But he knew this was not really what this was all about. He sighed. "But I've no idea where she's gone," he said.

"Aren't you training to be a wizard then?" Ruskin asked him.

Lukin frowned at him.

"Ruskin means," said Elda, "that if you're linked to Olga in any way, then you can *know* where she's gone."

Lukin thought about this, too, while everyone again watched him expectantly. At length the heavy look cleared off Lukin's face, and he smiled. "On the roof of the Spellman Building," he said. "More or less where Elda was."

Olga was indeed on the roof. Climbing up the narrow wooden staircase to the trapdoor beside the chimney, tears whisking off her chin and soaking her hair as she went, felt just like the many, many times she had climbed to the masthead after Olaf had beaten her. Just the same, she thought. I'm alone again. As usual. She coiled up by the chimney, which gave her some small shelter from the cold breeze up there, and she cried. She cried for herself, for her father, and for Lukin—Lukin, who she had thought had such great kindness and depths and affection under

that rather sulky face of his and who obviously
had not. Or not for Olga. She had seen that, fully
and truly, while Lukin was putting on his crown
prince face for the dwarfs. Aristocratic, haughty,
and *so* polite. Considerate to people lower than he
was—and most people *were* lower, of course.
Olga was lower than most. Waterfront riffraff
she would have been, had Olaf not stolen that
ship after Olga's mother died.

And she cried. Oblivious of the cold breeze,
which kept wrapping itself around her in strands
and plastering her hair into her mouth, she cried
and cried.

Oh, what is the matter? the breeze cried back.
Speak to us! Please speak to us again!

Olga opened her wet and swollen eyes and
stared at the air elementals wrapping themselves
around her. They were long, silky, scarflike
beings, and quite transparent, with anxious bird-
like eyes. *Elda's eyes remind me of theirs,* Olga
thought. *That must be why I like her so much.*
"What's happened? I can see you!" she said. Her
voice sounded thick and awful. "I can *hear* you
again! Why haven't you talked to me all this
time?"

But we did! they cried back. Their voices were
like the delicate moan of wind in wires. *We
talked, but you never seemed to hear us. You never
cried.*

Nor had she, Olga realized. That first time
when Olaf had beaten her half to death, she had

refused to make a noise or shed a tear. Somehow it had been important not to. And after that it was as if the tears had gone underground in her and got lost in a place she could never find. "I think I got too proud to cry," she told the elementals. "I wasn't going to let him know he hurt me."

But what has hurt you now? they asked.

"Lukin," Olga gulped.

We'll go and blow him away for you, they offered.

"Oh, no," she said quickly. "I don't want him hurt. It looks as if I'll just have to leave the University."

We don't understand, they said.

Human reasons for things had always been beyond them, she thought, and actually almost chuckled at some of the misunderstandings. That huge storm which had blown their ship right across the Inland Sea to Farness because Olga had told them that Olaf had refused to let her dress as a boy any longer. They had been trying to blow Olaf overboard, they said. At least that postponed the change of clothes. You couldn't buy anything on Farness, let alone skirts.

The door by the chimney opened, and Lukin climbed out. "Oh dear," he said, seeing Olga's swollen face and tear-drenched hair. "I'm sorry." He was, as he spoke, almost sure that he could see long, transparent creatures spiraling about her. Next moment he was utterly sure. The things dived upward and streamed around his head

230

until his eyes watered and he thought his hair would blow off. "Hey!" he said. "You can talk to air elementals again! That's marvelous. Call them off."

"Why are you here?" Olga said. "Can you see them, too?"

"Of course I can," Lukin said, batting at the creatures, which made no difference at all. "They're making themselves rather obvious. Call them *off*. I came—well—because I love you."

"They don't always do what I— *What* did you say?" said Olga.

"I love you," Lukin repeated. It seemed truer than ever the second time he said it. "I don't care whether your father's one of the Emperor's elephants or chief bullfrog in the Marshes, I'd still love you. You're Olga. And I brought you your cloak. Here." He dragged the heavy fur out through the trapdoor and draped it around her. Somehow, while doing so, Lukin himself became wrapped around Olga, too. They stayed that way for quite some time, while the air elementals wreathed a joyous, windy, open pattern around the pair of them. Eventually Lukin said, with his chin on Olga's smooth fair head, "Mind you, if he ran across the roof at this moment, I'd stamp on him."

Olga shuddered. "Don't. I still, well, love him, in a twisty sort of way."

"I can understand that," Lukin said, because he had his own father in mind, too, and he did not mention his plans for a mousetrap.

News. Visitors. Excitement! the elementals began crying out, swooping between the chimney and the parapet.

"They always know when something unusual is going on," Olga said, disentangling herself. "Let's look."

"If it's more senators or another batch of dwarfs, I don't want to know," Lukin said, following her to the parapet.

Down in the courtyard the first thing they saw was Melissa, racing past the statue, pursued by a little mob of mice and screaming, "Oh, *save* me!" The response was immediate. Students, not all of them male, hurried out of doorways all around the courtyard and stamped and shouted to scare the mice off. One student threw fire at them. Another rather spoiled that by trying to douse the mice in water. Lukin watched hopefully, but all the mice got away.

"That girl is such a wimp," he said.

"No, she's not," said Olga. "Just stupid, and it's not her fault she was born that way. She knows she was, and she's trying to do something about it. I respect that. Those other girls helping her respect her for it, too."

This sounded like the Olga Lukin knew. He turned to grin at her, then ducked as an enormous shadow boomed overhead. Wing feathers clattered as great wings cupped themselves to brake and a crowd of air elementals spilled out from under, screaming with the fun of it.

"See? They did know," Olga said as she and Lukin leaned over the parapet to watch a great brown griffin come gently to the ground beside Wizard Policant's statue and fold her cream-barred wings down on her lion's back. She towered above the statue.

"That," Lukin said, awed, "must be quite the biggest griffin ever. I think her name's Callette."

Next moment there were violent griffin shrieks from the concert hall. Its door banged open, and Elda streaked across the courtyard, shrieking, "Callette! Callette, you're *back*! Are the others back, too? This is my sister Callette!" she screamed at Ruskin, who was coming after her at a bowling run on his short legs, followed by Felim at an awed trot.

The students who had come out to help Melissa stopped on their way back indoors and stared. Windows and doorways filled with more interested faces.

"I'm going down," said Olga. "I want to meet her. Coming?"

By the time they had clattered down the stairs and into the courtyard, both griffins were inside a crowd and Elda was saying happily to everyone, "She's ever so clever. She's *rich*. She makes beautiful, artistic things called gizmos, and people buy them for ever so much money, don't they, Callette? Thieves Guild bought nine last year, and before that the dragons bought twenty and—

Oh, *here* are Olga and Lukin! Well, you've met Lukin once, I know, but this is Olga, Callette."

Elda, Lukin was rather bemused to see, only looked like a small-medium size beside Callette. "You probably don't remember me," he said diffidently to Callette.

Callette's large brown nearest eye inspected him. "Yes, I do. You were small, and your knees were black. You'd fallen down a pit." The eye went on to inspect Olga, and then Callette's head turned so that both eyes could look at her. "What a very beautiful human you are. Can I paint you sometime?"

"Olga's—" Elda began.

"Shut up." Callette pushed her face and beak affectionately along Elda's feathery neck. "You do talk so. You haven't let me tell you why I came."

"To see me," Elda guessed happily.

"Well, I did miss you." Callette sounded a little surprised, saying this. "Quite a bit. But I really came to tell you that Lydda's married."

"What?" screamed Elda. "Who *to*? *When*?"

"Who's Lydda?" Ruskin rumbled.

"Her sister. One of the other griffins," Lukin whispered.

"Last week, over on the other continent," said Callette. "Kit and Don and I all went to the wedding. Blade was the only human there. There are quite a lot of griffins across the ocean, in big families. Lydda's is called Harrek Acker. Acker's a high-up fighting family, though they do have a few wizards in it, too. They gave a very good wedding out on the plains just before we started for home. Tremendous amounts of food."

Elda spread her wings and jumped up and down. "Callette, tell it *properly*! You never *do*! How did Lydda meet this Acker person? Does she *like* him at all?"

"Like him!" said Callette. "It was the soppiest thing I ever saw. We were still on the boats then, but we could see the land, and Lydda was going to fly there, so she was in the air. But there was this war on. That was why we were there, to try to stop it. And it turned out that there were griffins on both sides in this war, as well as humans, and Harrek was flying patrols for his side. He saw our boats and came over. Or down, I think. He was up near the clouds. The first thing we knew, there was this smallish whitish griffin diving in on Lydda. He has a hooked beak and bent-back wings. They say that's how a real fighter looks. And Lydda yelled and turned upside down to meet him. She says that's how you fight, and it was instinct. But instead of fighting, they sort of spread, wing tip to wing tip, and went over and over in the air." Callette shrugged, in a rattle of feathers. "We didn't know *what* was going on. Kit and I both took off to help, but before we got anywhere near, they both yelled out that this was their mating flight and to go away. Love at first sight, Lydda said."

There was a sigh of sentiment from most of the listening students. Lukin hugged Olga to his side.

"Huh!" said Callette. "Neither of them was any use at all after that. Mooning about. Twining necks. Rubbing beaks. We had to settle the war without them. Mind you, Don was almost as bad by the end. Females coming out of his ears."

"And Kit?" Elda asked with acute interest.

Callette put her beak in the air and rolled her eyes. "Kit? There aren't too many black griffins over there. They think he is *so* handsome. Girls were flopping out of the sky and fainting at his feet."

"But did he *like* any of them?" Elda asked.

Callette considered. "Not so's you'd notice," she conceded. "His head didn't get half as swelled as I'd expected. He told me he wanted to get the world straightened out before he settled down."

Elda giggled. Somebody at the back of the crowd called out, "How about you? Did you meet anyone?"

Callette's tail lashed irritably. "None of them are big enough." She turned pointedly toward Elda. "Elda, Mum's gone into a complete fuss about Lydda. That's why I said I'd come and tell you. Mum says she's *got* to go there and check that Lydda's happy. Dad said he'd go, too. They're taking Flo and Angelo and going as soon as we can find them a boat. Blade's over at the coast seeing about that now. Kit's at home trying to calm Mum down. Kit says to tell you he and Blade will try to come over to see you after that—today if they can. You're not upset like Mum, are you?"

"I don't *think* so," Elda said, though it seemed very strange to have another sister married. "Is this Harrek good enough for her?"

"You sound just like Mum," Callette said. "He's fine. Nice. Aristocratic, the way families stand over there. Not *very* stupid. It's Lydda's life. I quite like him."

But Lydda might have waited until the rest of her family could get there, Elda thought. She knew just how Mum must be feeling. Anxious, rather hurt and left out, and suspecting that Kit had organized it all, saying grandly that *he* would deal with their parents. Oh, well. As long as Lydda was happy . . .

She was smelling griffin quite strongly all the while she was thinking this. It was not Callette's sweet, familiar, feathery smell. This was unwashed griffin, dirty. Kit? But Kit kept himself as clean and well preened as Callette did. Don, however, was not always as fond of washing as he might be. "Where's Don then?" Elda asked.

"Still at sea," Callette told her. "His boat didn't have a wizard—" Her head jolted up. She had smelled dirty griffin, too. "Oh, *gods*!" she said. "I don't *believe* this! I warned that Flury— Get all these people out of here, quickly!" Callette rounded on the gathered students, wings up, beak outstretched, eyes glaring, tail slashing, looking so menacing that even Elda backed away. "All of you clear out of this courtyard. There's a griffin coming who isn't nice. Go on. Shoo!"

"Why? What's wrong with this griffin?" Claudia asked. She had ventured out to gaze at Callette, too, calculating that someone Callette's size could protect her from any number of legionaries and probably the whole Senate as well, and was standing behind Elda with the cloakrack faithfully at her side.

"Everything's wrong with him," said Callette. "I hate him. He makes me go soft and squeamish inside." The smell was stronger now. Ruskin and Olga had both caught it and were making faces. Everyone else was still standing, staring, innocent and unbelieving. Callette's head switched back and forth in exasperation. She swiveled back at Elda. "You're a wizard. Make me go invisible or something. Come on. Quickly. Maybe he'll go away if he thinks I'm not here. *Quick!*"

Callette was so agitated and so obviously in earnest that Elda turned anxiously to her friends. "How *do* I?"

"Willing her to disappear, do you think?" Olga suggested.

"If we all try willing together, maybe," Felim added.

"Let's try. *Everyone* will Callette invisible!" Elda said. She put her head down and willed, hard and urgently. Beside her Claudia, Olga, and

Lukin linked arms and willed, too. Felim hauled Melissa in on the other side of Elda and put his head down beside hers. The distant raucous scream of griffin voices came clearly on the wind. This caused most of the other students there to realize that Callette had not been making a fuss about nothing. After glancing uneasily in the direction of the screams, almost everyone put his or her head down and willed.

Callette's enormous shape was suddenly not there. She did not blur or fade. She simply winked out of sight like a burst bubble. She seemed to be gone so completely that Elda raised her beak and sniffed anxiously. Under the now almost overpowering smell of alien griffin, Callette's scent was still faintly there.

"She really is just invisible, I think," Elda said uncertainly.

"Just in time," Ruskin said, pointing.

Not one but five big winged shapes were wheeling through the air above the Spellman Building, screaming remarks to one another as they came. No one could catch the words, but it was evident from the tone that violent, derisive things were being said. The yell with which the foremost griffin folded his wings and plunged to the courtyard made hearts lurch and goose pimples rise on backs. Elda felt her hackles wrench themselves upright, from her tail to her crest. Nearly all the students stampeded for safety as the first griffin plopped to the ground, and the next plummeted screaming after, and the next after that. Each one was at least as big as Callette, and all, as Callette had said, were not nice creatures in any way.

Elda stampeded with the rest and found herself, along with Ruskin, rushing hard into something huge and soft and warm, in the region of the statue of Wizard Policant. Realizing she had run into Callette, she backed hurriedly off, only to find that she and Ruskin were almost alone in the courtyard with the alien griffins. Claudia was the only other person out there. Claudia had tripped over the wretched cloakrack, realized when she picked herself up that there was no more time to run in, and was now on one knee with both hands wrapped around the central pole of the cloakrack and the hook-laden head of it aimed aggressively at the nearest griffin, in the manner of an Empire legionary pointing a spear. Though doorways and windows were full of anxious faces, the three of them were the only ones in the open, if you did not count Callette, and Callette was clearly lying low.

The griffins had landed here and there about the courtyard, apparently randomly, but somehow in positions where they cut Elda and her friends off from every doorway. Elda did not need to turn her head to see the ragged brown-and-white male behind her, looming in front of the door of her concert hall. Being able to see behind you was an advantage that griffins had over humans, but as Elda realized now, it was no advantage at all with other griffins. They were all so large, too, at least as big as Callette, and filled the air with raffish aggressiveness. Otherwise they were an ill-matched lot. The main one, who was now strutting toward Elda, jeeringly swinging his tail, was streaky chestnut with a shaggy dark brown crest and bold yellow eyes. Another was pigeon colors, but so unkempt that the pinks and greens on his gray neck barely showed at all. One was plain dull brown, and the fifth ought to have been white, but he was so dirty he looked yellowish. At any other time Elda would have been marveling that there should turn out to be so many kinds of griffin, but here and now she was plain scared.

"Where's Callette?" the strutting griffin demanded. "I know she came this way. She doesn't escape Jessak Atreck just by crossing the ocean."

"You can see she's not here," said Elda.

The griffin's yellow eyes flicked around the courtyard. "She's hiding. There are at least four doors here big enough for her to get through."

"Want me to search the place, Jessak?" the off-white griffin asked.

Jessak looked at Elda with his scruffy head on one side and pretended to consider. "No. This little yellow cat can tell me. Can't you, runtlet?"

"No," said Elda. "Even if I could, I wouldn't."

Jessak's answer to this was to extend his neck,

so that it became improbably long and scrawny, with chestnut feathers sticking out all around it, until his beak was pointing into the middle of Elda's forehead and his yellow eyes were glaring into hers. He raised a forefoot and pretended to scratch his beak, showing talons at least twice the size of Elda's and wickedly sharp. "Yes, you will, runtlet."

Claudia tried to distract Jessak by calling out, rather shrilly, "What do you want with Callette, anyway?"

Jessak did not bother to move or answer, but the brown-and-white griffin said, "Jessak's sworn to marry Callette and teach her manners. She scratched his—"

"Shut up!" said Jessak, still glaring at Elda.

"It's a funny kind of human, anyway," grumbled the brown-and-white griffin. "Greenish. Shall I tear it up?"

"When I've got Callette," said Jessak. "You want to keep your eyes, yellow cat, you tell me where she is."

Elda simply remained as still as a statue, as still as a cat at a mousehole, and did not answer. Her scalp and the line of her backbone ached, her hackles were up so high. She understood exactly why Callette had said this griffin made her feel soft and squeamish inside. The smell of him, the way he glared, and the great eagle-lion shape of him were making strong primitive demands that Elda had never met before. He made her, like a cat or a bird, or even like a lioness, want to lie down and give in. Her insides crawled with what seemed to be lust. But griffins were a higher order of being than cats or eagles, as Elda remembered Mum's firmly telling her once when she caught Elda chasing mice, and the way Jessak was deliberately making her feel was beginning to enrage her.

Behind the brown-and-white griffin, in the doorway of the concert hall, Felim, Olga, and Lukin rather frantically tried a third spell. They had tried to open one of Lukin's pits under each griffin, and then to turn the invaders into mice, and now they tried a simple banishment spell. This one had no effect on the invaders either. "I do not understand this," Felim whispered. "They seem to have some kind of magical immunity."

Ruskin, standing beside Elda, had discovered the same thing and then remembered that dwarflore stated that griffins in the old days could not be touched by magic. "These griffins are throwbacks," he rumbled disgustedly. "*Cave* griffins! Why don't they just go away?"

Jessak's beak stabbed around at Ruskin with incredible speed. Ruskin sprang backward. Elda, beginning to be really angry, clapped her right wing over the dwarf and hauled him against her flank, glaring at Jessak while she did so. The other griffins snapped their beaks, clapped their wings, and screamed with amusement.

"Ho, ho, ho!" howled the pigeon-colored one.

"*She's* ready to be a mother, isn't she? Can I have her, Jessak?"

That did it. Elda's building rage erupted and exploded at the full pitch of her lungs. She had a very powerful voice. As Derk had often ruefully pointed out, the youngest in a family of vociferous griffins had to be the loudest in order to get heard at all. "You disgusting crew of horrible little *birds*! You barge in here, you strut about, you do your best to bully and frighten everyone, and you haven't even the decency to wash! Or even preen. You *stink*! And then you have the cheek to think that my sister would have anything to do with you! *You*, when you're so filthy and so rude and haven't *three* brain cells among the lot of you, you think you can come in here and lord it over decent people. . . ."

There was a lot more than this. Once Elda got going, she got going with a vengeance. Jessak, still with his neck stretched out, put his head on one side and pretended to admire her, which made Elda angrier than ever.

"Even your ancestral *pigeon* would be ashamed of you!" she screamed. "The half-breed vulture you have for a grandmother must be writhing in her muck heap. And your mother, who was obviously a street-walking baboon or an unusually stupid civet cat, probably died of humiliation long ago!"

There was a sound like a whip crack beside her. Air blasted Elda's wing feathers sideways.

And, to Elda's enormous relief, her human brother Blade appeared beside her. "Carry on, Elda," he said. "Keep their attention. You're doing wonderfully. We got your message. Kit'll be here in a moment."

TWELVE

ELDA FILLED HER lungs joyfully and screamed again. "Your grandfathers were all *rats*, and *they* were educated by jackals!"

But Jessak and his friends were no longer listening. They were looking at Blade and drawing together into a huddle in what looked very like dismay. "You again!" said Jessak.

Blade folded his arms and tapped with one booted foot. "Yes. Me again. I warned you when they exiled you that if you came over here, I'd make you sorry. And I will. I give you a count of ten to get out of this place. One. Two."

Elda looked fondly down at Blade as he stood and counted. Blade these days was tall and rather thin, with straight, fairish hair and a straight, fairish face that usually held the same mild, friendly look that his father, Derk's, did. You would not think to look at him that he was one of the four most powerful wizards in the world. Elda just wished she could learn to be anything like so good.

"Five. Six," said Blade. "Seven."

Elda noticed that Blade was keeping half an eye on the evening sky above the Spellman Building as he counted. She kept half an eye there, too. Blade and Kit usually worked as a pair. Sure enough, there was a dark bird-shaped speck against the sunset there, and it grew very rapidly larger and darker. Kit was flying flat out.

"Eight," said Blade. "Nine."

"You can't frighten us. We're immune to magic," the off-white griffin said unconvincingly.

Blade raised his eyebrows. "Ten," he said.

And Kit came hurtling down past the Observatory tower and over the parapet like a diving black demon, shouting thunderously. "GET AWAY FROM MY SISTER, YOU GODFORSAKEN REJECTS!" Fire blasted up from the courtyard where the invading griffins stood. Blade grinned and added his magic to Kit's. The result was that all four griffins were shot into the air as if a bomb were under them. Kit flung a further sheet of fire beneath them as they rose, causing them to scream as one griffin and flap their singeing wings desperately. Blade sped them on their way with another blast of magic. They clapped their tails between their legs and flew madly to get away.

"BLASTED RIFFRAFF!" Kit thundered over his

shoulder at them as he landed.

That was neat, Elda thought. You don't magic *them*, because it doesn't take, so you magic the air underneath them. Then she had a moment when she thought, Only *four* griffins? And *what* message? But she forgot those questions in her total delight at seeing her brothers again. She raised both wings, letting a rather overheated-looking Ruskin tumble out, and wrapped Blade in her pinions. "Love you, Blade!"

"Me, too," Blade said, butting her with his head, griffin fashion. He slapped her flank. "You had a good shout, didn't you? Those gangsters were looking almost respectful when I got here."

Elda chuckled as she galloped over to Kit. Kit was so glad to see her that he actually twined his neck with Elda's, which was a thing he very rarely did. Elda rejoiced in the well-known clean smell of his feathers and the sleek shine of his pantherlike sides. The only pale part of Kit was his great buff-colored beak. And his yellow eyes, of course, which were just now returning from angry black to ordinary gold. But she had forgotten how huge he was, bigger than Callette, bigger than Jessak by some way. He made her feel as small as Ruskin.

"Are all the griffins on the other continent as nasty as those ones?" she asked Kit, with a worried thought about Lydda.

"Lords, no!" Kit paced toward Blade, looking rather satisfied, and Elda trotted beside him, wondering why Kit did not seem to notice that there was still one foreign griffin left, the plain brown one, crouched in the opposite corner of the courtyard in the shadow of the refectory steps. "Most of the griffins there are nice people," Kit said. "Those lot were the dregs. Outlaws. But don't worry. I don't think they'll come back in a hurry."

"What did they get outlawed for?" Elda asked, flicking an anxious glance at the motionless brown griffin in the corner.

"Not just for stalking Callette, I can tell you!" Kit said as they reached Blade. "They enjoy tearing humans and griffins apart. They had themselves real fun during the war."

"And everyone over there is far too civilized to get rid of them properly," Blade told Elda. She could see he was disgusted about it. "Jessak's family got lawyers, and the lawyers argued that they were throwbacks to primitive griffins and couldn't help themselves. So they exiled them instead. We ran into them just before that, when Jessak got a thing about Callette."

"Lawyers!" snorted Kit. "Where *is* Callette, anyway? She said she—"

Kit said this at the precise moment that he walked into the invisible Callette. Callette surged and squawked. Kit reared up and back, hugely astonished.

"*What* the—"

"You *trod* on me!" Callette said out of

nowhere. "Clumsy oaf!"

Elda and Ruskin became helpless with laughter. So did Claudia. She had been getting up, clutching the cloakrack for support for her very shaky legs. Now she clung to it and giggled.

"Where *are* you?" Kit demanded of the air.

"How do *I* know? I can't see myself to tell you!" Callette retorted.

"She asked us to make her invisible because she didn't want Jessak to see her," Claudia explained, as well as she could for laughing.

"Fair enough," said Blade. He was grinning, too.

Kit was not amused. "Trust you to do something really stupid, Callette! Where *are* you, for goodness' sake?" He scythed at the air with both front sets of talons, walking cautiously forward on two legs like somebody playing blindman's buff. "How can I turn you back if I don't know where you are?"

"But I don't know— Now you trod on my *tail*!" Callette howled. There was an invisible turmoil. Kit canted sideways, carried by an unseen body almost as big as he was, and tried to save himself falling by wrapping his talons around the statue of Wizard Policant. There was a sharp *crack*. Wizard Policant swayed, broke off at the ankles, and fell, first with a padded *whump*—"OUCH!" cried Callette. "Now look what you've done, you fool!"—and then with a stony *crash*, when he rolled on the ground by Kit's feet. Kit, like a giant-size startled cat, skittered away sideways and stood in an affronted arch.

Claudia whooped and pointed.

"What's the matter?" Blade asked her anxiously.

"His." Claudia swallowed. "His." She managed to get the rest out between laughs in a hurried, chesty drone. "His feet. In pointy shoes. *Oh!*" She gave a whine of laughter and slid down the cloakrack, shaking.

Blade looked at Wizard Policant's feet standing all by themselves on the plinth and collapsed, too. The lights around the courtyard came on just then, showing the wide space full of people again. Everyone who had run away from Jessak and his friends was now outside once more, very curious to see two of the world's strongest wizards, and most of them were laughing at Wizard Policant's feet, too. After a moment even Kit saw the funny side of it.

"Hey, look!" someone called out. "You can see Callette's shadow!"

This was true. The shadow was large and ruffled and spread in several directions. Its heads swung about as Callette realized she could see it as well and then raised blurred multiple wings and waved a forefoot or so.

"She seems to be all right," said Blade. "Come on. Let's get her visible." Everyone at once backed away considerably. "Oh, no," Blade told them. "Whoever made her this way has to help, or it'll take us all night. Who did do it?"

Everyone there exchanged looks and realized that they had all done it. They all stepped forward again. Claudia hauled herself up the cloakrack and tried to stop laughing.

"Look," Blade said to her kindly, "do you really need that thing? Can I put it over by the wall for you?"

"I, er, I'm not sure it'll stretch that far," Claudia confessed.

Lukin hastened over. "It won't go more than ten yards away from her," he explained. "She's tied to it magically somehow."

Blade reached up and felt the wooden hooks around the top of the cloakrack. "So she is! Kit, come and have a look at this! I've never met anything like it."

Kit, who was attempting to arrange the students in a circle around Callette's multiple shadow, left off for the moment and came over to plant a massive taloned, handlike forefoot on the top of the cloakrack. "What *is* this? This is the most cockeyed spell I ever met! It's all back to front and sideways. Who did it?"

"Wermacht," said Lukin.

"Who?" said Blade.

"Whoever he is, he's a fool," said Kit. "This is going to take some unraveling." He and Blade began prowling around Claudia and the cloakrack, muttering technicalities, while Claudia stood there like someone holding the pole in a maypole dance, looking self-conscious.

Elda saw that they were going to be some time. She left her place in the circle and began tiptoeing away toward the dark corner by the refectory steps. "We'll need your name," she heard Kit saying behind her, and Claudia replying that she was Claudia Antonina. At which Blade exclaimed, "Then you must be Emperor Titus's sister! I *thought* I'd seen you before!"

"Only once." Claudia's voice came distantly to Elda. "When I was fourteen."

The dull brown griffin had not moved. He was sitting the way cats do, with his forelegs tucked under him and his back hunched, and his wings in a brown glittery swath above that. He seemed much smaller in this position. His face was level with Elda's, very dull and meek. His heavy-lidded eyes were half shut. Elda would have thought he was asleep, except that she could see his eyes shine as they turned to look at her. She was surprised to find that his smell was quite clean, or only as sweaty as you might expect from a griffin who had just flown here from the coast.

"Who are you?" she demanded. "Why are you still here?"

"Me?" he said, sounding rather surprised. "I'm Flury. I'm very inoffensive really. You mustn't be alarmed. I stayed because I thought it was interesting here."

"Why hasn't anyone else noticed you?" Elda said.

"I hoped nobody would," Flury answered modestly. "I'm good at lying low."

He was certainly quite a contrast with Jessak, but he was so dull and meek that Elda found him rather exasperating. "You mean you're lying low because you're an outlaw?" she asked with a bit of a snap.

"No," Flury said. "At least nobody told me I was an outlaw."

"Then why were you with Jessak?" Elda asked suspiciously.

"He's a sort of distant relative," Flury explained. "The family wanted me to look after him."

"Look *after* him!" Elda could think of nothing more unlikely.

Flury hunched himself a little tighter, apologetically. "It does seem senseless, doesn't it? What could *I* do to stop him getting into trouble? But they're a very influential family, you know. Jessak should have been executed, really, for war crimes, but they got him exiled instead and then employed me to go with him."

"Are you a fighting griffin then?" Elda asked.

"Not really," said Flury.

"A lawyer then?" said Elda.

"Not particularly," said Flury.

"But," said Elda, exasperated by now, "if you're being paid to be with them, why have you let them fly off without you?"

"I couldn't stop them, could I?" Flury pointed

out meekly. "They seemed rather set on leaving in a hurry. Do you think the people in charge here would let me be a student if I asked?"

"Probably not," said Elda. "You have to train to be a wizard in order to study here. Do you want to do that?"

"Not enormously," Flury said. "No."

"Well then," said Elda, more exasperated than ever, "you'd better fly after Jessak and his friends. They're bound to be causing trouble by now."

"Not at night," said Flury. "Besides, my contract ended when I brought them here. You'd better go back to your friends. They'll be needing you any moment."

This appeared to be true. Kit and Blade were now asking everyone where Wermacht was. They seemed to have decided they could only raise the spell on the cloakrack with Wermacht there to help. "He's not here," various people said. "He'll have gone home by now. He lives in town."

"Where does he live? I can fly there and fetch him—by the scruff of his neck if necessary," Kit said.

But nobody knew. As several students pointed out, apologetically. Wermacht was not one of those tutors you wanted much to do with outside classes. If it had been Finn, now, or Myrna.

"Bother this!" said Kit. "Blade, we really do have to get home."

"I know." Blade turned to Claudia. "Look, I'm

awfully sorry about this. Do you mind waiting a day or so until we've got my parents safely on their way? We'll come back then, during teaching hours, so that this Wermacht's bound to be here, and make sure he untangles you properly, I promise. Will you be all right until then?"

"Perfectly," Claudia said bravely. The cloakrack after all was the least of her worries. If the Senate wanted her dead before she became enough of a wizard to protect herself, then what was a cloakrack here or there? When Blade came back, she thought she might summon courage to ask him to protect her, but privately, not out in the courtyard in front of everyone like this. Meanwhile she intended to stick to Elda like a burr.

"Right." Blade smiled at her, and as Elda slid back to her place between Olga and Felim, he turned to the matter of making Callette visible again.

"And about time, too!" Callette said from somewhere near the fallen statue.

"It won't take a moment," Kit said, huge and glistening like tar beyond the ring of students. "This is simple—just strong because so many people did it. All join hands. That's right. Now concentrate on Callette as you last saw her."

Everyone did so, while Kit and Blade raced in a clockwise circle outside the ring of concentrating students. And it was almost as if they turned Callette on like a light. She reappeared, large and ruffled and cross, in a momentary blaze of evening sunlight, as everyone had last seen her, her barred wings rosily gleaming and her big brown eyes catching nonexistent orange sunset. By the time she had lifted each foot and turned her head to inspect both wings, the glow had faded to the normal dimness from the courtyard lights.

"Thanks," she said gruffly. Her tail lashed. "Blaze of glory."

"And now we really must go," Blade said. "See you soon, Elda, Claudia." He translocated away, vanishing with a whistle of inrushing air.

Kit and Callette had to travel in a less wizardly way. Both spread their great wings, braced their legs, and leaped upward in a windy tolling of wing feathers and a downdraft that tossed everyone's hair. "Bye!" Callette called downward. Everyone clustered around the ruined statue to wave good-bye. Ruskin jumped onto the empty plinth to get a last sight of the huge dark bodies wheeling around to gain height against the blue-black sky. Olga and Lukin stood on the fallen statue. Elda gazed upward and sighed. She had not realized how much she had been missing her family until they were gone again.

"You know," Ruskin boomed thoughtfully, "it must be possible to make a wing-spell."

Lukin laughed. "Get your food-spells right first."

A strong, sour voice spoke from under his feet.

"*Would* you be so good as to lift me back to my pedestal now? It feels most uncomfortable lying here without my feet."

Olga and Lukin hastily jumped off the statue. Ruskin knelt on the plinth and stared down at it. Everyone else backed away. "That *was* Wizard Policant speaking, was it?" someone asked, Melissa probably.

"Of course it was, you silly minx," said the statue.

There was no question of it this time. Everyone near saw the stone lips move. "Then we had better put him back," said Felim.

This was not easy. As Felim said later in the buttery bar, Wizard Policant probably weighed nearly a ton, and without Elda's strength and Ruskin's knowledge of how to move stone, they might never have done it. It took ten people using the cloakrack as a lever to raise Wizard Policant enough for Elda and Ruskin to grasp him near his stony middle and haul him up—while everyone else dropped the cloakrack and pushed—until he was lying across his plinth. At this stage several people tried casting weight-reducing spells, but Wizard Policant seemed as immune to magic as Jessak had been. They had to use brute strength to get him upright. Then as many of the strongest people who could crowd onto the plinth had the difficult task of guiding Wizard Policant's broken legs into the shattered ends of his ankles, while Elda hovered strenuously above, with Wizard Policant's pointed hat grasped in all four feet.

Stone rasped. People panted, Elda loudest of all. Everyone's sweat plopped down onto the plinth like rain. And Wizard Policant himself intoned, "To your right . . . A fraction backward . . . Now half an inch left . . . Forward, and right an eighth of an inch . . . Rotate me a very small amount clockwise . . . No, too far . . . The other way . . . Hold it there . . . Now *down*."

They dumped him with a crash. Elda shot upward, wondering if she would ever be able to walk again. Everyone on the plinth balanced upright, trembling. "Is that it?" Claudia asked from the ground.

"Yes," said Wizard Policant. "Thank you." Upon that he became completely a statue again. Though a number of people asked him anxiously if he was all right now, he did not reply.

As Elda sank shakily to the ground, Ruskin crouched and ran his big hands around the statue's legs where the break had been. "Seamless," he said. "Not a sign of any join."

"He must have been a very powerful wizard," Felim said soberly. "I cannot, frankly, see any of our present teachers being able to do this."

Everyone murmured agreement as they climbed off the plinth. Lukin wiped his sweating forehead with the back of his hand. "Phew!" he said. "Quite a day! I don't know about the rest of you, but I've just remembered I've got some money now, and I'm going to the buttery for a drink."

They all went. They forgot supper and ate sandwiches from the buttery, after which they spent the rest of the evening there. Elda couched against the wall where the now extremely battered cloakrack was propped, sipping beer through a straw and wondering what humans saw in it, while Claudia leaned against Elda, feeling safe at least for the moment, and Ruskin, perched on a bar stool to bring him level with everyone else, told Felim more and more loudly how it might be possible to make wings and enchant them so that a dwarf might fly. Lukin simply grinned and wrapped his arm around Olga.

Much later, when the students had dispersed with much happy shouting and quite a lot of discordant singing, Finn walked purposefully through the courtyard—disturbing as he went a crowd of mice gathered around a dropped sandwich—and down to the main gate, where he let himself out by the small postern. He would try the White Lion first, he thought, and then the Golden Eagle and the Mage. If he drew blanks there, it would have to be the Red Wizard, the Blue Boar, the Green Dwarf, and the Griffin, followed by the Dragon, the Pumphouse, and Tilley's Wines, and after that some of the lower taverns. The city had a great many inns and several big hotels, such as the Imperial Arms and the Harping Bard, where the senators and the dwarfs had probably stayed. It promised to be a long night.

But Finn was lucky. Corkoran was in the White Lion, sitting at a table filled with carefully lined-up wine bottles and a half-full one in front of him. In the rest of the room all the chairs had been put on top of the tables and the landlord was leaning on the bar, looking tired and impatient.

"Come on, Corkoran," Finn said. "Time to go home."

"Got no home," said Corkoran. "Not anymore. Turned out to starve when I was fifteen. Tours sacked the place. Walked all the way to the University."

"The University," Finn said, "*is* your home now. You're head of it. Remember?"

"Not. That's Querida," said Corkoran. "I'm only Chairman of the Board."

"That's the same thing these days," Finn pointed out. "Come along, Corkoran, we need you. We had a plague of griffins this afternoon, and there was no one in authority to deal with them. One of them knocked down the statue of Policant."

"Mice," said Corkoran. "You must be drunk, Finn. Mice is what we've got a plague of. Mice don't knock down statues. They eat moonships."

Finn sighed. "You were probably on your tenth bottle at that stage. Come along back now. You've drunk quite enough, and the landlord wants to close."

"Can't," said Corkoran. "Won't. Got no reason to do anything anymore, Finn. My moonshot's over. Finished. Everything eaten and cut to pieces."

"I know," Finn said sympathetically. "I went to your lab to look for you. It was those assassins, wasn't it?"

"You should have let me dump them on the moon!" Corkoran cried out. "It's all your fault, Finn!"

"I should have taken them off you and sent them back to Ampersand," Finn said. "I'm sorry now that I didn't. But it's no use crying over spilled milk, Corkoran—"

"I'm not crying," Corkoran explained. "I'm drowning my sorrows."

"You certainly are!" Finn agreed, looking at the rows of bottles. "For the last time, Corkoran, are you coming back with me or not? You're giving a lecture tomorrow, and *I'm* not going to give it for you."

"Myrna will," Corkoran said. "Nice obliging woman. Ask her if you don't want to do it."

"Oh!" said Finn. "*Bother* you then!" He activated the transport spell he had brought with him, with the result that Corkoran woke up in his own bed the next day, fully dressed and feeling like death and without the slightest idea how he got there.

THIRTEEN

WHILE THESE THINGS were going on in the University, pigeons from it were winging in several directions. One speeding eastward passed quite low above the string of ten dwarfs, riding ponies and celebrating as they rode. They laughed and raised their jeweled cups to it.

"That could be ours," said Dobrey.

"Nonsense," said Genno. "We sent ours before we left."

"Well, anyway," Dobrey said complacently, "the other forgemasters will have our news long before we get home. Fellow tribesmen, we are now the richest fastness in the world. People will come from all over the world and pay gold to learn the truth from this book."

"We'll drink to that!" shouted the rest.

Two pigeons meanwhile flew south. One was wounded, but still gained steadily on the pigeon sent by the senators. The largest number of pigeons, however, went west. The biggest group flew in a miserable gaggle and were followed by four others almost as miserable. Derk had told them all, before he hired them out, that if anyone hurt or mistreated them, they were to come straight home to Derkholm. So this was what they were doing. They passed underneath Callette, winging the other way, and shortly after that under five griffin strangers flying after her. A while later Kit came thundering over them. They found this dimly reassuring. Everything that flew respected Kit these days. They arrived in the Derkholm pigeon loft more or less at the same moment that Blade—having translocated in from the coast, saying he had just had a message for help from the University, which was what sent Kit thundering off there—kissed his distraught mother's cheek, told her he had to go and help Kit but that they would both be back for supper, and translocated out there himself.

The other pigeons were horrified at the condition of the fugitives. They set up such a din that Old George, who was on his way to feed them, anyway, almost ran up the ladder. He ran down again almost at once and raced off to find Derk. Derk was on the terrace with his two winged youngest children, a vast terrace that had sometime ago been covered with a protective spell that kept out the weather but did not stop anyone from walking or flying through it, so that all the griffins could join in family life there.

"Those pigeons," Old George panted. "That lot you sent to the University. About half of them's come back in a terrible state! Bleeding. Feathers missing. One's going to lose an eye if you don't do something quick!"

Derk was quite glad of the distraction. Mara had just dashed indoors crying about Lydda, and he was not sure what to do about either of them. He was upset by Lydda's sudden marriage himself, anyway. He felt quite as bad as he had on the day Shona took herself off to the East Coast with her Geoffrey. He did not feel he could help Mara at all.

"Go and kiss your mother better," he said to Angelo and Florence, and pelted for the loft.

Here at least he could do something. Derk tutted to himself sadly as he stabilized the wounded eye, patched wounds, stopped bleeding, and set feathers growing again. What an awful way to treat harmless, valuable birds! He was puzzled as well as upset by the story they told him. What were these very small men directing fighting mice? Why had they disabled the pigeons and then shoved them out through the doors? It was probably no wonder that Elda had sent to Blade for help. At least, with Kit and Blade on their way there, he needn't worry about Elda now. But something was very wrong. What were the senior wizards doing to let this sort of

265

thing happen there?

He thought about this while he regenerated the eye and caused another pigeon to regrow a severed foot. When he was finished, he went down and saddled up Filbert. Then he went into the house to find Mara. She was upstairs in the main bedroom, surrounded by open suitcases and heaps of clothing and somewhat impeded by Florence, who was fluttering about her, "helping." "Oh, good," she said as Derk entered. "Find me as many of your shirts that are clean as you can."

He could see she had taken refuge in packing. That was a relief. "Yes, when I get back," he said. "I'm just off to see Querida."

"But you don't like her. Flo, put that *down*," Mara said. "Why? Flo, if I have to tell you again, you'll be sorry. Is it the University? I heard Old George saying— Flo, I *warned you*. Can't Kit and Blade see about it? Right, Florence. That is *it*. Go and play with Angelo. Now."

Florence, who knew when a parent really meant what she said, drifted to the door. She also knew that Angelo was in a bad mood. Angelo's great hero was Blade, and he had got Blade back just that day only to have Blade disappear twice in quick succession. He did not want a mere sister. "I don't want to play with Angelo. He's making pies in the bath. He's *dirty*."

"Oh, don't go and tell me tales, or I really shall run up the wall!" Mara said. "Out!" And as

Florence reluctantly fluttered away, lower lip stuck out and trembling at the tyranny of mothers, Mara protested, "But, Derk, it's nearly nightfall! Can't you go tomorrow?"

"I thought you wanted us all to leave tomorrow," Derk said.

"I did, I did! I *do*!" Mara said. "But I'm not sure we can get packed by then. What's the matter? Is something really wrong at the University? I do wish I hadn't let Querida persuade me to send Elda off there now. Elda could have come over the ocean with us then."

"I wish you hadn't packed her off there, too," Derk said, frowning. "When a place sends half my pigeons back hacked to bits, you wonder about it, Mara, you really do. I'm going to ask Querida to take a good long look at it while we're away. I'll be back for supper, I promise."

"That makes you and Blade and Kit *and* Callette, all making the same promise," Mara said. "All right. We'll be late eating, anyway. I won't be able to start conjuring food until I've sorted out these clothes and sorted out whatever Angelo's up to, I suppose."

Derk kissed her and left before she made him sort Angelo out for her. Mara was much better at managing winged children than he was. "Make the most of this," he told Filbert as Filbert's strong chestnut wings carried him northward. "It could be your last proper flight before the voyage."

"I know," Filbert answered gloomily. "I'm not looking forward to over a week on a boat. There's seasickness. You know horses can't be sick, don't you?"

"Teach your grandmother," said Derk. "We're stowing all you horses on deck. If you get seasick, just take a short flight—unless there's a storm, of course."

"I might get swept into the sea!" Filbert protested.

"So swim," said Derk. "And wait for someone to throw you a rope. All horses can swim."

"I *could* be the exception," Filbert said nervously. "I've never tried."

While Filbert flew northward, further north still, in the kingdom of Luteria, King Luther suddenly canceled the usual arrangements for supper in the Great Hall with the court and decreed a family meal in the Small Dining Chamber instead. It was the sight of Isodel slipping late and guiltily into the Great Hall for lunch that decided him.

She's been seeing an unsuitable lover! King Luther found himself thinking. He was ashamed of this thought almost as soon as he had it. He knew very well that every man Isodel encountered instantly became her would-be lover, suitable or unsuitable, and he was fairly certain that Isodel had so far not responded to any of them. But he didn't *know* she had not. There was always going to be a time when she *did* respond, and he gloomily expected it to be to someone quite wrong. He did not know his daughter any longer, that was the problem. He did not know any of his children these days. Lukin seemed to have been avoiding him for weeks. And the other four were big with some secret that made them giggle in corners or rush breathlessly away on hidden errands when he came anywhere near them.

To some extent King Luther blamed Mr. Chesney for this. Chesney's tours had caused Luther's wife, Queen Irida, to leave him and live in hiding with her children for safety. She had come back once the tours had stopped, saying— and he believed her—that it *was* only the tours that had made her do it and that she did in fact love him. Then he was able to get to know his children all over again. But there had been that gap. This gap maybe accounted for the way he felt that all six of his children were becoming total strangers to him now.

Consequently, he waited to be sure that all his children were actually in the castle and would not have time to duck out again. When he had glimpsed even the elusive Lukin turning a distant corner beside Isodel, he gave his orders and put up with the dismay of the cooks and servers in a good cause.

Twenty minutes later everyone gathered in the Small Dining Chamber around an expanse of slightly yellowed and darned white tablecloth and slightly chipped crystal. They were all warmly dressed, since the Small Dining Chamber breathed chilly dampness from each of its stone walls, despite a newly lit fire, and they had done their best to smarten themselves up. None of their clothes were new, and the result was still slightly shabby. King Luther sighed as he looked around at them, wishing the kingdom could afford to dress its royal family more suitably. Isodel, particularly, deserved better than plain blue wool and a threadbare silk shawl. And little Emana, who showed signs of growing up to rival Isodel, could do with dresses that had not gone through two older sisters before her. As for the boys . . .

Here he met his wife's alarmed eyes and realized that they were, all of them, extremely nervous at this sudden family dinner. "It's all right," he said. "I'm not going to eat you." He murmured the customary thanks to the gods and sat down. Everyone else but Lukin pulled out chairs and sat down, too. Lukin was unaccountably still standing beside his mother. "Sit down, Lukin," his father said.

As the servers came forward with oatmeal soup—oatmeal figured a lot in the palace diet, partly from poverty, partly from tradition—Lukin sidled around the corner of the table in a rather curious way to the empty chair nearest the queen. The yellowish tablecloth billowed. Beside the empty chair Princess Erola made a sort of snatching movement and Lukin appeared to sit down. But King Luther could have sworn that just for an eyeblink, Lukin had vanished completely. A server leaning to place a bowl of soup got in the way at a crucial moment, however, and King Luther could not be sure.

That wretched boy has been doing magic again! he thought. And in spite of all I said to him! But as this was supposed to be a friendly family supper, King Luther ate his soup and asked Isodel pleasantly how she had spent her day.

Isodel looked as if she wished he had asked her anything else. "Oh, I, er, took a nice long flight on Endymion. Right over the mountains, you know."

"And this made you late for lunch?" asked her father.

Isodel colored heavily. "Yes," she admitted. "Endymion misjudged the time."

Since Isodel was obviously so uncomfortable, King Luther considerately turned to his two younger sons and asked them the same question. Lyrian replied that they had had lessons in the morning.

"But the afternoon was much more interes—" Logan said, and stopped with a yelp. It looked to King Luther as if Princess Emana had most uncharacteristically jabbed him with a fork. "I was only going to say," Prince Logan said, glowering at his sister, "that we had a good game of hide-and-seek."

"Big mouth," muttered Emana.

"I conclude you were playing somewhere you shouldn't have been," King Luther said tolerantly, and he turned to Erola. Beyond Erola, Lukin was just sitting there in front of his untouched soup. "What's the matter, Lukin? Aren't you hungry?" King Luther asked.

The glances his children exchanged with one another and with their mother seemed almost panic-stricken, until Emana said, "He just doesn't like oatmeal soup."

"He told me that, too," Lyrian said, with such a strong air of relief that King Luther was puzzled. "This morning," Lyrian added earnestly.

"While you were in your lessons?" asked the king.

Lyrian went white. "No. At breakfast. Yes. Breakfast, it must have been breakfast."

"Can't you speak for yourself, Lukin?" King Luther asked.

Again there was the barely hidden panic. Queen Irida said, "I think Lukin has overtaxed his throat somehow, my love. I'm worried about him."

"Do you mean he's made a magical hole in his *throat* now?" the king demanded.

"Oh, no, no, no, nothing like that!" Irida said faintly.

A look of cleverness came over Prince Logan's

face. "He did do some magic, though. That may be it." The cleverness died away, and panic replaced it as his father looked at him. "You know how you can drink magical potions," he said wildly. "Accidentally. It was brown, and Lukin probably thought it was coffee." As the king continued to stare at him, he added desperately, "Or gravy. Maybe it was *only* gravy. Strong gravy, of course."

"What on earth are you talking about?" said King Luther.

"He's just inventing things again," said Emana, glaring warningly at Logan.

"I am not!" Logan retorted, near to tears. "I always tell the exact truth. Lukin made me promise to last year!"

This caused his father to look at the motionless, silent Lukin again.

"You know, Mother," Erola said abruptly, "I think it would be best if I took Lukin to his room. And helped him lie down, you know. He doesn't seem well."

"Excellent idea!" Queen Irida said, with extraordinary heartiness.

"Just a moment," King Luther said as Erola was pushing back her chair. He would have been a fool indeed not to have realized by now that his family was trying to keep something from him, and he was not a fool. "Lukin, come over here and let me have a look at you before you go."

Looks of desperation were exchanged on the

other side of the table. On Lukin's side the table-cloth billowed again. Erola and Lyrian both acquired distant, concentrating looks, and Lukin first jumped from his chair and then came sideways in jerks behind Erola. When he reached Lyrian's chair, he did another of those momentary blinks out of existence but swiftly reappeared and came on strongly sideways again, accompanied by more billowing from the tablecloth, to stand at last obediently beside the king's chair.

"Hmm," said King Luther, and put out his large blue-knuckled forefinger. Not wholly to his surprise, this finger went right through Lukin. "This is a simulacrum, isn't it?" he said. "What's going on? Where is Lukin?"

Nobody answered. Lyrian sighed slightly, and the false Lukin disappeared.

"*Answer* me!" barked King Luther. "I have a right to be told where Lukin is. I'm not an ogre, you know."

"Or not more than half the time," Lyrian murmured.

King Luther pretended not to hear Lyrian, but this did not improve his temper. He raised his hurt, gloomy face to look at his wife. She was staring at him from her end of the table as if he had an arrow trained on her heart. "Irida, you seem to be leading this conspiracy. Be so good as to tell me where Lukin really is."

Irida licked her dry lips and pushed away her soup. "I—I'm sorry, my dear. He's at the

University. He—he had my mother's money, you know."

"*Is* he?" King Luther said with the sarcastic calm of extreme fury. "Is he now? Against my express orders and with the connivance of the rest of you. And I suppose you were late for lunch, Isodel, because you'd sneaked off to see him." Isodel simply nodded. "No wonder"—King Luther continued—"that I haven't set eyes on the boy for the best part of a month! Well, well. I shall just have to set out myself tomorrow and fetch him back. In chains if necessary."

"Oh, no!" gasped Irida.

"Oh, *yes*, madam," said King Luther. "You may handle the kingdom while I'm away. Though it may be that I'm a fool to trust you even with that."

"Luther!" Irida exclaimed.

The king ignored her and rang for the servers. When they hastened in, he gave orders for a squad of guards to be ready to ride with him at dawn. "And I want a watch kept on the pigeon loft," he said. "No one—*no one*—except myself is to be allowed into it." At this the glances Isodel and Lyrian had been exchanging fell glumly to the tablecloth. King Luther saw this. "And I shall need to speak to the Chancellor," he added. "None of my sons or my daughters is to receive any money while I'm away, and my queen only precisely what is needed for running the country. Now please bring on the second course."

He then savagely ate the rest of his supper, while his family picked at theirs. All of them had the sense not to pretend to be ill in order to dash to the pigeon loft, he was glad to see. He smiled grimly into his oatmeal dessert. Perhaps he did know his family after all. He knew exactly what was going to happen next. He ate cheese and then some fruit, vengefully, in order to spin out their suffering. Finally, he pushed back his chair and strode from the Dining Chamber without another word. Sure enough, behind him Isodel and Irida broke into frantic whispering.

"But, Mother, it's *worse* than that! Olga——" he heard as the door was swinging shut.

King Luther hastened then, with long strides, but not quite running, through stone corridors and down the dank spiral stairs that led to the garden court where Endymion had chosen to take up residence. The young dragon was there as he expected, coiled up by the stone seat, finishing the sheep he had had for supper. The last of the daylight shot gold and copper gleams from Endymion's baby scales as he moved aside politely so that the king could sit on the seat and get his breath back.

A mere half second later, so that King Luther barely had time to lounge back in the seat breathing normally as if he had been there for quite a while, Isodel pelted into the garden with her skirts hauled up around her knees and her shabby shawl flying. The light was so bright on the dragon that she did not notice her father at all.

"Oh, Endymion, finish your sheep quickly!" she panted. "We have to go to the University again at once!"

"Do you indeed?" asked King Luther, and Isodel jumped nearly a yard sideways. "You can come with me, on horseback, tomorrow morning, if you really want to go."

Isodel glared at him. She opened her mouth angrily, then shut it again and arranged her shawl. "No, thank you. I'd prefer to stay here and support Mother."

"Then you must certainly come with me," said her father, "or the gods know what fresh plots you'll be hatching."

"You intend," asked Isodel, "for everyone to be as miserable as you can possibly make them?"

"How well you understand me," said King Luther. "You accompany me; the rest stay here without money for exactly that reason. Isodel, you know I'm not normally a tyrant, but you've all forfeited my trust this evening, you and Lukin most of all."

Isodel stood very straight. Her hands, arranging her shawl, pulled it downward so fiercely that it jolted her head forward. "Not a tyrant!" she said. "What trust?"

Her father stared at her gloomily, wondering what had gone wrong. It was as if he and the rest of his family had somehow missed one another in the dark. Nevertheless, he did not intend to let them get away with this evening's capers. He turned to the dragon. "You'll have to leave Luteria, Endymion," he said. "Now."

Endymion, who had been studiously bolting his sheep and keeping out of this trouble, turned a large green eye toward him in surprise. "Why is that?"

"Because I, the King, command it," said King Luther. "Because I know you'll help Isodel on the sly if you're here."

"But," Endymion said smugly, "I am sworn to Isodel, not to you, sire."

"You're not old enough, as dragons go, to swear to anyone," King Luther told him. "I know dragonlore, and I know you count as a hatchling still—and a runaway hatchling at that. I'm quite well acquainted with your king, as it happens, and I'm about to send off a pigeon to him, telling him where you are."

A roll of immature smoky flame came from Endymion's mouth, causing the sheep's wool to sizzle and stink. "You wouldn't!"

"I would and I will," said King Luther. "The next place I go is the pigeon loft. If you go now, you can arrive ahead of the pigeon and pretend you came back voluntarily."

"This is not nice of you," Endymion said. "Very well." He rose limberly to his feet and settled his wings with a rattle. Very gently he nosed at Isodel's stiff face. "I shall come back later, my princess," he said. Then he raised his wings, which, like sails, caught the wind off the mountains and lifted him at once. With a mere tilting of them, he was up and circling and ghosting away as a darkness against the darkening sky.

Tears were pouring down Isodel's face. "I shall do my best to make the journey as miserable for you as it will be for me!" she promised.

King Luther nodded, seeing that she meant it. He supposed he would survive it. He was used to being rather unhappy.

The pigeon flying east reached its destination around then. Since Ampersand was a long way south of Luteria, night had already fallen over the many painted spires, domes, and spiked cupolas of the Emir's palace. The Emir himself had wandered into one of his gardens after dinner to gaze up at the waxing moon and enjoy the slight, sad fragrance of autumn. The pigeon was brought to him there, nestled bright-eyed in the hands of a servitor. Other servitors followed with lights, so that the Emir could see to read the message it carried, and his vizier personally accompanied them, to extract the tiny slip of paper from the tube on the bird's leg and hand it, bowing, to the Emir.

The Emir accepted the message, unfolded it, and peered. Lights were instantly and anxiously brought closer. "This writing is quite unacceptably small," the Emir complained.

The vizier snapped his fingers. A servitor

handed the Emir a pair of spectacles. The Emir put them on and once more raised the slip of paper. This time he seemed able to read it. Everyone relaxed.

Prematurely. The Emir's face became suffused so darkly with blood as he read that the vizier secretly signed to a servitor to run for a healer. This was regardless of the fact that the Emir always categorically refused to see a healer. For the last couple of months the Emir's heart had been giving cause for concern, and the vizier had taken the precaution of having a healer always within call, just in case. As the servitor streaked off, the Emir uttered such a shriek of rage that the man stopped as if he had been shot.

"Villainous swine!" howled the Emir. "Order me my guard, my camels, and my weapons! I must go at once to raze that infamous University to the ground!"

"In person, gracious lord?" the vizier ventured to inquire.

"In person, of *course*!" snarled the Emir. "Those wizards have stained my honor twice now. This time those sons of dubious ancestry have also dishonored seven of my best assassins. I shall not let this pass!"

"But would it not be better, gracious lord," pleaded the vizier, thinking of heart attacks, chaos, and crisis and, most of all, of twenty-two sons of the Emir, none of whom had yet been designated as heir to Ampersand and who were all increasingly annoyed about it, "would it not be more convenient to set off at dawn tomorrow? Your guard would be better prepared and your gracious self much fresher." You might even have thought better of it, he thought, but did not of course dare say.

The Emir pulled his lower lip, scowling, and considered. The vizier made sense. In a hasty departure, someone always forgot something, and he was determined that his vengeance on the University should be meticulously complete. He intended to take the University apart, stone by stone, and its wizards limb from limb. "You are right," he conceded. "We will start an hour before dawn tomorrow." But he wanted to take something apart *now*. He looked around and saw valued servitors staring at him earnestly under lights that trembled slightly. Taking them apart would be a waste. New ones would have to be trained. Then his eye fell on the pigeon. "Take that bird out of my sight and wring its neck!" he commanded before he turned on his heel and strode back indoors. The peace of the garden was ruined now.

The servitor obediently carried the pigeon away through the garden. One did not wring the necks of birds in the Emir's private quarters. The pigeon had the sense not to show that it had understood everything that had been said. It was, after all, one of Derk's clever pigeons, and most of its round body was brain. It continued to nestle trustingly in the man's hands, until they reached the stable yard, where the servitor shifted his grip, preparing to take hold of the pigeon's neck and twist it. As soon as it felt the man's hands move, the pigeon clapped its wings mightily, struggled, pecked, clawed with its feet, and finally burst upward from between the servitor's palms, to swoop—in the greatest relief—to the very top of the stable minaret. The man watched it go philosophically. Perhaps he had in mind the fact that the pigeon was the hired-out property of a very famous wizard. Perhaps he felt that the Emir had been unjust. At any rate he made no attempt to recapture the bird. It was able to roost undisturbed on the minaret all night, and when dawn was only a suggestion at the bottom of the sky and the stable yard began to bustle with men running and shouting orders, clashing weapons, protesting camels, and bundles of supplies, the pigeon took to its wings and flapped briskly westward toward Derkholm.

FOURTEEN

HIGH CHANCELLOR QUERIDA, who was very small, very wrinkled, and so old that she looked greenish, had been enjoying herself hugely until the moment she looked up and saw Derk approaching on Filbert. She had found a cottage on the edge of the Waste, all by itself among swelling hills, which was the cottage of her dreams. Alone there, except for her three large tabby cats, she spent most of her days working to reduce the Waste to proper farming country again. It was utterly satisfying. She caused pools of unspeakable slime to dry up, she anchored the roving carnivorous trees into clumps of woodland and made them change their diet, and she turned the savagely mutated beasts back to what they should have been. It amused her extremely when creatures with crocodile teeth and wings suddenly found they were really rabbits. The looks on their faces were quite comical.

These activities of course released quantities of unpleasant magic. Querida spent pleasurable weeks setting up spells in her cottage attics that caught this magic, converted it to neutrality, and sent it out into the world again. Some part of the magic she made proactively good, and each time this was sent out it changed the world, just a little, into what it might have been had not Mr. Chesney come along with his tours. It was the kind of learned but practical magic that Querida most enjoyed. And it confirmed her in her opinion that she was still the strongest wizard in the world. Kit and Blade, though probably as strong, were too young, in Querida's opinion, to influence the very earth that they lived on.

By now almost a third of the Waste had been returned to woods, meadows, and unpolluted streams. Querida was looking forward to tackling the mountains in the middle, where there were some very knotty and interesting nasty things. Some of these had been disturbed by Elda. Querida had not been pleased about that. She had taken swift steps to get Elda packed off somewhere where she could do no harm. In the meantime, before she took on the mountains, Querida allowed herself the leisure to spend her evenings gardening. She was at work planning and planting a flower bed for spring in front of her cottage, with her cats rather crossly curled up in the grass nearby, when she looked up to see Derk descending toward her in the sunset.

It ought to have been a pretty sight. Filbert's wings shone red in the red light, with fringes of golden light caught in their edges, but Querida took one look and straightened up crossly. "Here comes trouble!" she said. She did not like Derk any more than he liked her. Her cats, as one cat, stood up and mewed. "Yes, yes, I'll feed you when he's gone," Querida told them, and watched Filbert slant down to land beyond her. Deep hoofprints all over my lawn! she thought. "Well?" she said to Derk.

"I can't stay long," Derk said. This was important to both of them. Derk felt happier, saying it. Querida relaxed a little, hearing it. Derk explained about Lydda's sudden marriage and Mara's deep, worried need to take ship at once to find out if the marriage would work.

"The young are always thoughtless," Querida said. "How is my friend Callette?"

"Grumpy," said Derk. "She got stalked by some sort of well-born griffin hoodlums, and she says she's glad to be back. But I really came here about the University." He told her about the wounded pigeons and what they had said. "So I was hoping you could find time to translocate over there and see what's going on," he concluded.

Querida was exasperated. She had *known*

Derk would do something like this to her. He always did. It was this way he had of jogging her almost nonexistent conscience that made her dislike him so. "I can't possibly go until tomorrow," she snapped.

"Can't you manage just one quick trip now?" Derk pleaded.

Querida was forced to find reasons for delaying, and once she had uttered them, she found they were very good reasons, anyway. "No," she said. "This needs careful thinking about. All the years I was at the University, when you were a student there yourself, even at the height of Mr. Chesney's activities, something like this simply *could not* have happened there. The ambient magics that act as wards for the University would have prevented it. When I left these younger wizards in charge, I assumed they would maintain the wards in the usual way. But they obviously haven't. I need to think how to handle that before I go rushing over there."

"Then you'll translocate there first thing tomorrow?" Derk asked her anxiously.

"No again," Querida snapped. "I shall travel there by pony trap, as I came." Seeing Derk's expression and realizing he was probably worrying about Elda, she explained, "The obvious answer to these ferocious mice is a set of competent cats. My three cats are excellent mousers, but they hate translocating. Either they escape on the way, or they arrive so put out that they're useless for days. They have to travel with dignity or not at all."

"But you *will* go tomorrow," Derk said.

"I will go tomorrow," Querida promised. With irritated relief she watched Filbert take off again.

She spent the rest of the evening considering what to do about the University. A place like the University was essential to the world, or the whole globe would be full of untrained wizards heaving mountains about like Elda, or worse, raising demons and getting those demons to teach them further shocking things to do. And such a place, full of strong but untaught magics, needed to have strong wizards at the head of it. "I think I made a mistake when I organized that Governing Board," Querida admitted; she could admit to a mistake privately, at least. "The place really needs a powerful Chancellor." But she could think of no one suitable to be Chancellor except herself. And she had had her fill of running the University. She wanted to get on with her work in the Waste. "Perhaps I'd better bring some of those older wizards out of retirement," she mused. "They won't be happy about it, but they can do the job."

Very early next morning she prudently harnessed Hobnob, the pony, to the trap first, before the unavoidable and spirited hour necessary to get her cats into baskets. Like all cats, Querida's three were largely immune to magic. They took one look at the baskets and dived under furniture, and the only way to fetch them out was to haul them out by hand. Then they fought like fiends when they were anywhere near the baskets.

But it was done at last. Querida shook the reins and clucked to Hobnob, and the trap set off bumping down the grassy track southward, with the three cats fulminating in baskets behind Querida. At the rate the pony traveled, it would have taken nearly three weeks to get within sight of the University. Querida intended to cheat a bit, naturally. She meant to phase in a small translocation every few miles and cut the journey down by half. As long as the cats, and the pony, too, *thought* they were traveling in the normal way, she could get away with quite a bit of cheating. The question was, How much?

She began testing the air as she drove for the rumors it brought. Rumors came to her in the form of long, silky bands that wrapped themselves around her, whispering. For all her power and all her learning, Querida did not recognize them as air elementals. She simply thought of them as rumors. They whispered to her of griffins, pirates, assassins, worry, sabotage, bloodshed, more bloodshed, armed men from the north, more armed men to the east and the south, and of magic misused.

"Good gracious!" said Querida. "This sounds like the bad old days again!"

She encouraged Hobnob to trot and took them all forward several times further than she had intended—so far forward, in fact, that they were already on the edge of the peaceful farming lands. The track was almost a road here, wide and dry and rutted, running between meadows that swelled up on either side.

Almost instantly the pony tossed his head and tried to stop. The cats threw themselves around in their baskets, growling. Querida assumed that in her sudden alarm at the rumors, she had not phased in their translocation smoothly enough and pushed Hobnob onward with a sharp little spell. They swept around a curve in the track, and here the pony did stop, shivering. Another meadow swelled above them, and this one was littered with dead cows. And not just littered, Querida thought, shivering, too. Strewn with bleeding pieces of cow was a better description. Someone or something had pulled heads off cows, torn cows open and spread them about, and, in one or two places, apparently dropped cows on rocks and smashed them to pulpy meat. The smell of fresh blood filled the air, and the meadow was loud with buzzing flies, hordes of crows and ravens, and the screams of a few vulturelike scavengers that had clearly been fetched from the Waste by the scent.

"Is this a rogue dragon, I wonder?" Querida murmured. As she had no doubts about her ability to handle a dragon, or even several dragons, she began sending forth a peremptory summoning spell for the one who had done this to come and explain itself at once.

She had not completed the spell when the cow killers arrived. Shrieking to one another that here was more fun now, they soared from the opposite hillside and planed in over Querida's head, pinions whistling, to land with aggressive thumps in the road all around the pony trap. They towered over it, squawking with laughter when the pony squealed and tried to rear and the cats went mad in their baskets.

Querida quieted Hobnob and did her best to calm the cats, while she looked around at four unpleasant stranger griffins. They smelled disgusting. She hardly needed to see the blood on their beaks and the shreds of meat caught on their talons to know what had killed those cows.

"Why have you slaughtered a herd of cows?" she demanded, hissing with anger.

The largest and most raffish griffin bent his ungroomed chestnut head to look at her. "A little green human!" he said. "Funny the way humans here seem to turn green when they see us. They must do it when they're frightened or something."

No one had dared comment on Querida's skin color for half a century now. She became angrier than ever. "I asked you a *question*!" she hissed. "Who are you? Why did you slaughter these cattle? You couldn't possibly eat this number. It was just wanton killing."

"Wanton killing is what we do, little green lady," said the chestnut griffin. "We can't help ourselves. We're throwbacks. We're like primitive griffins were. Sad, isn't it?"

"Nonsense!" said Querida. "Of course you can help yourselves. Every creature with a brain can decide *not* to do something if it tries."

The chestnut griffin jerked his head up and stared down his beak at her, venomously.

"You mustn't speak to Jessak like that," said the off-white griffin, "or he'll take you apart."

"And your pony," added the dove-colored one.

Querida wrinkled her nose at both of them. Their coloring made it so obvious how dirty they were. "I spoke exactly as he deserved," she said, "though rather too politely. He's simply a spoiled bully. Where are you all from? I don't recall seeing you before."

"From? We flew here from the University," the ragged brown-and-white griffin replied. "Jessak was angry because he couldn't find Callette."

"Jessak's from a very good family across the ocean," the off-white one explained. "Callette shouldn't have thwarted him. *You* shouldn't thwart him. He gets angry when that happens."

"Which explains why he took it out on innocent cows, does it?" Querida said. "What an extremely stupid and craven thing to do!"

At this Jessak dropped to all fours and went

prowling around the pony trap, taking care that one of his ill-smelling wings slapped across Querida's face on the way. "I've had enough of this little green human," he said. "Time to start disassembling her. I think I'll begin with *this*." He plunged a large feathered forearm into the cart and seized the nearest cat basket.

If Jessak had not done that, he might have survived. Up till then Querida had simply been angry and disgusted. She had been considering transforming these four unpleasant creatures into rabbits and had only hesitated because she realized that this might not improve the local breed of rabbit. But her cats were the three things she loved most in the world. The sight of her Sabrina all blown out and growling, with her eyes glaring through the side of the basket, black and wide with terror, dangling aloft on the end of unkempt bloody talons, was too much for Querida. She saw red. She surprised herself—as much as the griffins—by yelling out four words that shook the universe.

Everything became a little dizzy and blurred for a moment. When the universe righted itself, Querida found herself, to her great relief, still sitting in the pony trap with Hobnob still between the shafts, surrounded by four enormous statues of griffins. The nearest statue still held a cat basket dangling from its talons with—again to Querida's relief—a live and furious cat in it. Rather shakily Querida climbed back along the pony trap and carefully unhooked Sabrina. Sabrina spit at her.

"I don't blame you," Querida said. "I didn't intend to let you in for anything like this." She put the basket back in the cart and turned to take up the reins again. This was where she realized that the whitish griffin statue and the grayish one were blocking the road. "Bother!" she said. "Move!" But they just stood there, with expression of surprise and puzzlement all over their stone faces.

It took Querida half an hour to discover spells that would topple them out of the way, but topple they did in the end, one in each direction, to leave just enough room in between for the cart to edge through. In the process the whitish statue broke in two and the gray statue's beak came off, but Querida did not find it in her heart to feel at all sorry. She shook the reins. The pony was sweating and moved only slowly.

"I know, Hobnob, I know!" Querida told him. "I feel just the same. But we have to find the folk who own these cows and explain what happened. If I manage that properly, they might let us rest in their farm for a while."

Around the time that Hobnob trudged off again, the two pigeons that had headed south reached Condita, capital city of the Empire. The uninjured pigeon planed demurely down to the marble pigeon walk along the front of the

Senatorial Office Building, where a hand came out of a window and grabbed it at once. The wounded bird fluttered away to a complex of marble roofs and colonnades nearby. It landed rather heavily on the hidden lead top of the largest structure, where it limped cautiously along, peering through gutter holes, until it found the inner courtyard it was looking for. Then it took off again, went into a dive, and thumped to the top of the arbor of yellowing vines, where Emperor Titus was sitting over a last cup of coffee. The table in front of him was covered with pieces of broken bread, as if the Emperor had crumbled his breakfast without much appetite. The pigeon eyed the crumbs wistfully while it compared the person below with the magical memories Corkoran had planted in its brain.

Emperor Titus, tallish, thinnish, age twenty-five, darkish hair, jagged profile, mild expression, correctly clothed in Imperial wrap of white with a purple border with a raised golden design of griffins. Yes. This was the correct recipient. The pigeon refreshed itself with an overripe grape from the arbor while it made sure the Emperor was alone.

The Emperor was alone because he was lingering over his breakfast. As soon as his coffee cup was empty, someone would know and people would descend upon him with a mass of things he was supposed to do, most of which he was fairly sure were pointless. These days the Senate did all the governing. Titus simply signed laws. He had once told Claudia that the Empire nowadays thought of the Emperor as a sort of rubber stamp on legs.

"Behave differently then!" Claudia had told him. "Show them who's Emperor."

But Titus had shaken his head and explained that he could not offend the senators, most of whom were old enough to be his father and closely related to him into the bargain. The people would be shocked if he tried.

"I don't think so," Claudia said. "I think they'd cheer you in the streets."

Titus could not believe this. The people *believed* in the Senate. He sighed over his coffee now. This was the kind of talk that got Claudia so hated by the Senate. He was glad he had managed to get her away to the University, where she would be safe, but he did miss her very badly.

The pigeon flopped out of the vine leaves and staggered among the breadcrumbs.

Titus nearly jumped out of his skin. "Gods! You gave me a shock!" he said.

"Apologize," croaked the pigeon. "Message. Your eyes only."

Titus picked it up to get to the message tube on its leg and exclaimed again. The bird was covered all over with tiny stab wounds and bleeding from a bigger cut under one wing that must have hurt like mad when it flew. Hoping it had not had to come far, he pulled Corkoran's message out and unrolled it.

Afterward, he said he felt as if the top of his head had come off. For a moment or so he was in such a fury that he all but leaped up yelling for vengeance, guards, executioners, his army, lawyers, judges, people with knobkerries, and anyone else who could do something to Antoninus and Empedocles, even if they only beat them over the head with plowshares and saucepans. But he had been brought up to control himself. So he simply sat with his hands clenched so hard on his knees that he found big bruises there later, watching the pigeon hobble about, wolfing breadcrumbs. After a minute he thoughtfully pushed his goblet of water over so that the pigeon could sip from it. Antoninus and Empedocles belonged to opposing parties in the Senate. It followed that the entire Senate was behind this visit of theirs to the University. Very well.

"How did you get those wounds?" he asked the pigeon when he could speak without screaming.

"Small men with swords. Angry mice," it replied. "Stopping us from going with messages."

"At the University?" Titus asked.

"Yes," said the pigeon, and gobbled another piece of bread.

Dwarfs attacking pigeons? Titus wondered. If things like that were going on at the University, the wizards there were not keeping Claudia safe as they should. This put the final touch to Titus's fury, which, because he had sat there containing it, was by now a smooth, calm, planning rage. He looked up to see the daily bevy of people approaching him. For a moment his eyes were so blurred with anger that he could hardly see them. He blinked firmly and focused his rage.

Most of those approaching were elderly scribes clutching armloads of scrolls. With them were the Steward of the Imperial Household and the Captain of the Emperor's Personal Guard, and behind them came the Imperial Cook, to ask the Emperor what it was his pleasure to eat today, the Master of the Imperial Stables, the Imperial Tailor, the Master of the Imperial Wardrobe, the Imperial Lawgiver, and finally the Imperial Historian, who was supposed to record the day's events. They were followed by six servants to clear away the Imperial breakfast.

Emperor Titus stood up to meet them, smiling his usual mild smile. The captain first, he thought, because the Personal Guards were all nephews and grandsons of senators. They usually had a lovely life getting drunk and idling about. Not today, though, Titus hoped. "Captain Postumus," he said, "it's just dawned on me that I haven't inspected the Guard for over a month. Perhaps you'd better have them parade in the exercise court in—shall we say?—half an hour. I may be a little late getting to you there, but I'll be along as soon as I've finished with these other gentlemen."

A hastily muted expression of dismay crossed the aristocratic face of Captain Postumus, but he dropped elegantly to one knee, murmuring, "As my Emperor pleases," and rose to leave.

"Oh, and Postumus," said Titus, after the Captain had taken two steps, "while you're on your way, could you ask General Agricola to step by here for a word with me? Tell him I've had an idea about the southern legions."

"My pleasure, Imperial Majesty." Postumus ducked a knee again and strode elegantly away.

Titus turned to the Imperial Stablemaster. "Eponus, I shall need my horse when I review the Guard, won't I? Can you have Griffin and Tiberius saddled for me? I'll choose which of them I'll ride when I come to the stables."

The Stablemaster ducked a stiff knee and left, too.

So far so good, Titus thought. Nothing had been out of the ordinary yet. The next part would be. Titus was relying on his usual mild, courteous manner to carry him through that. He beckoned the Imperial Steward aside and turned apologetically to the rest, all of whom, including half the scribes, were paid followers of the Senate. "Would you gentlemen mind waiting for me in the large office? I'll be with you as soon as I can."

Knees ducked. A chorus of "Pleasure, Imperial Majesty" was uttered, and everyone except the servants turned to leave. The servants hovered doubtfully.

"Please go on with your work," Titus told them pleasantly. He swept the pigeon up into a fold of his wrap and approached the steward, while the servants busily cleared the table, well within hearing. "Sempronius," he said to the steward, "would you mind terribly sending my healer to me?"

The steward went white with concern. "Your Imperial Majesty is unwell? I swear, Majesty, that the utmost precautions against poison are taken at all times."

"I'm sure it's nothing like that," Titus said truthfully. "I just don't feel quite the same today."

"I'll fetch the healer at once, Majesty." The steward hurried away, bustling the listening servants with him.

Titus allowed himself a small grin. Now there would be an obvious explanation when he failed to turn up at any of his appointments. He strolled out of the arbor and along the garden in the mild autumn sunlight, while he waited for the healer and General Agricola, and his anger continued to grow. Claudia was practically his only friend in the Empire, and the Senate was trying to kill her! Titus had had a miserably solemn and lonely childhood until his Imperial father had married again and Claudia had been born. Titus could hardly remember laughing at all before he was nine years old, when the small greenish baby lying in the Imperial cradle had crowed with delighted laughter when he bent over her. And from the moment she was a year old, Claudia had been his friend and ally, the person he told things to, the person he could laugh with. For this he had forgiven her the fact that she came with a strange, discontented stepmother whom he still very much disliked. For this, too, he had covered up for Claudia when she was in trouble, particularly when her strange jinxed magic started to cause peculiar things to happen. Then he found that Claudia was covering up for him in return. By the time Claudia was grown up, they were firmer friends than ever. Titus had defended Claudia in the Senate when it tried to declare her a public enemy, with her jinx as its excuse, and had made sure that the Personal Guard held their tongues in front of her. The Personal Guard had total contempt for Claudia's mixed blood and made no secret of it. And for this, Titus promised himself, his Personal Guard was going to stand waiting, to attention, in full polished kit, drawn up in ranks in the exercise yard, for as long as he could contrive to leave them there. He was glad to see that the day promised to be nice and hot.

The healer approached and coughed. Titus whirled around, with the pigeon clutched to him. Planning the sort of things he was planning made even an Emperor nervous. "Your Imperial Majesty asked for me?" the healer said.

Titus, who was hardly ever ill, barely knew the man. He had no idea if he was a follower of the Senate or not, but he had an idea that healers were forbidden to take sides, and he hoped this was the case here. The man was tall, thin, and haughty, which did not promise too well. Too bad. Reminding himself that he was still the Emperor, Titus said, "Yes, I did, but not for myself. I want you to heal this pigeon, please."

The healer started backward, disdainfully. "Imperial Majesty! I heal people, not *birds*!"

"Well, it can't be that different," said Titus, "can it? And this is a valuable pigeon, one of Wizard Derk's clever ones. I don't wish the Empire to cause offense to Wizard Derk."

The healer compressed his lips irritably. "This brings the gods into it, so I dare not refuse. Let me see the creature, Majesty." Titus carefully passed the pigeon over. The healer took it in his cupped hands and bent over it. "But this bird is bleeding all over! It should never have been sent out in this condition."

"My feeling exactly," said Titus. "I shall send a strong reprimand to the Senatorial Office. Whoever sent it out is going to feel my extreme displeasure." He thought the pigeon rolled an approving pink eye at him for saying this.

The healer brought the pigeon level with his chin and concentrated for half a minute. "There," he said, clearly trying not to look surprised at how easy it had been. "No problem at all, Majesty." He passed the pigeon back, brighter-eyed and no longer bleeding.

"Thank you," the pigeon crooned.

The healer jumped. "I didn't know they talked! Will that be all, my Emperor?"

"Yes, thank you," said Titus, who could see General Agricola advancing through the garden. "And of course I won't mention that you had to stoop to bird healing. People might laugh if it got about. Please feel yourself free to say that I had a trifling sore throat."

"Thank you, *indeed*, my Emperor." The healer bowed, most gratefully, and hurried away.

That seems to be all right! Titus thought. He put the pigeon carefully into the fork of a tree, where it started to preen vigorously, and strode to meet the general of his Imperial legions.

"My Emperor!" General Agricola said, almost before they were within hearing distance of one another. "I was going to try to see you if you hadn't sent for me." Agricola was one of the very few Empire veterans left over from the days of the tours. Titus had personally promoted him from the ranks when King Luther had declared war on the Empire at the end of the last tour. Agricola was wide and thick-legged, with a scar across his big nose, and not tall, in the way ordinary soldiers tended to look, but he was a very good general. Titus hoped he was loyal to the Empire. The trouble was that "the Empire" could as easily mean the Senate as well as the Emperor. The next few seconds would show just which Agricola was loyal to. "So what did you need me for?" Agricola asked.

"A number of things," said Titus, "none of them to do with the southern legions, actually. First, the noble senators Antoninus and Empedocles are on their way back to the Empire from the University. I would like you to have trusted men patrolling the northern border to arrest them as soon as they appear."

A slight smile began to spread on Agricola's tense face. Titus saw it and began to hope. "On what charge should the noble senators be detained, my Emperor?" Agricola asked.

"High treason, of course," said Titus. "If they happen to resist arrest and happen to get killed, it won't bother me. But if the bast—er, noble lords come quietly, I want Antoninus put in the dungeons at Tivolo and Empedocles at the top of the tower in Averno, and anyone who tries to bring them messages or help them in any way to be executed out of hand. The noble lords will be there awaiting trial, you see."

Agricola's smile spread a little. Titus began to believe that the man might really be loyal to the Emperor. "How long are they to wait until they come to trial, my Emperor?"

"Let's see." Titus was surprised, in a remote way, at how vicious he was feeling. "Antoninus is seventy, and Empedocles is sixty-eight. Let's have them wait twenty years. That should do it. The second thing I want is a troop of cavalry loyal to me personally. Have I got anyone who is?"

The smile was all over Agricola's face now. It was going to be all right. "*All* the legions are loyal to you personally, my Emperor, except the senatorial legion, of course. Where and when do you want your cavalry?"

"Waiting for me in half an hour at the north gate of the city. Tell them to bring supplies for a week's fast travel," Titus said, "and a spare mount each. I'll join them with mine. And they're to tell the gate guards they haven't seen us."

Agricola's smile faded a little. "May I ask where—"

"The University," said Titus. "I've got to make sure Claudia's safe. I'll go by back roads so as not to run into the senators. The third thing is, Can you tell me what the Senate's doing at the moment?"

Agricola's smile was gone, replaced by the tense look with which he had arrived. "They're in full session as I speak. They called all the senators in, even sick old Silvanus."

"Oh, *good*!" said Titus. "I was sure they must have had a pigeon, too."

The tense and worried look Agricola gave him was also a little puzzled. "I can't say that I'd call it *good*, my Emperor, with respect. Rumor is that they're debating impeaching you. They called in the lawyers and the judges, too, to make the things legal, I hear. That's why I wanted to see you, Majesty."

So that's it! Titus thought. This wasn't just aimed at Claudia. They've been after *me* as well, all along. What a fool I've been! "Impeachment of me on the ground that I'm secretly training a wizard with the aim of becoming a tyrant?"

Agricola nodded. "Something like that. Whatever sticks, I think."

"Then come with me," said Titus. He strode out of the garden and crosswise through the Imperial Palace, taking a route through unfrequented courts and little-visited parade grounds, where he and Agricola were least likely to be seen or overheard. "The fourth thing I was going to ask you for," he said as they strode, "is that I want the Senate House surrounded while they're all in there and everyone inside it put under arrest. I want them all in solitary confinement—no calls for lawyers or family visits permitted—until I get back from the University."

Agricola was grinning again. "One slight problem there," he said, marching beside the Emperor. "Senate's been arresting hundreds of tax dodgers lately. Prison's nearly full."

"I know," said Titus. "Set them free. Put all the senators in their place. I want martial law declared until I get back, with you in command, so you have full authority to do it. We're on our way to get the proper documents for it now."

"This," said Agricola, marching like clockwork, "is beginning to be the best day of my life.

I've been praying—everyone's been praying—that you'd get around to doing this before the Senate got around to deposing you. But it would help to have some crime to charge the senators with, something to stop them from screaming *too* loudly."

"We're on our way to get that now, too," said Titus.

They crossed the final, smallest courtyard and went toward the dilapidated building in its corner. It was built of marble, like the rest of the palace, but the marble was yellow and rusty in streaks where the stone had cracked and the roof had leaked. Titus pushed open the plain wooden door and ushered Agricola into a plain wooden room where a hundred depressed-looking clerks sat at long tables, each with an abacus and a pile of papers. Titus sniffed the air. He loved the warm smell of wood and dry rot in here. He had come here most days as a boy. Claudia had learned to calculate here and made her first attempt at magic in this room, which had somehow managed to twist half the abacuses into knots.

The rattle of beads and the scratch of pens stopped as they came in. Heads turned respectfully, not to the Emperor—to Titus's amusement—but toward Agricola, the Imperial General in Chief. The head of this place, Titus's old friend Cornelius, approached doubtfully, scratching his bald patch with a quill pen, which was a well-known habit of his. "The General in Chief needs something from the office of the Imperial Auditor?" he asked Titus. "My Emperor, I should add."

"Yes, something for me," Titus told him. "I want an exact audit of the accounts of every single member of the Senate. If the accounts look clean, dig. They've all been cheating the Empire for years, and I want proof of it."

Cornelius's pen paused above his head. "What? Even your uncles?" he said.

"Particularly my uncles," said Titus. "The general here is going to send a squad of legionaries with each team of accountants. He has my orders to arrest all senators' bodyguards and any member of a senator's family who tries to interfere with the audit."

"Or I have now," Agricola murmured.

"And I want you to get to work in the next half hour," Titus finished.

Cornelius tossed his pen aside. He clasped his hands and looked up at the worm-eaten rafters for a moment. "I think," he said, "that I could cry with joy. But I'll need documents of authorization."

"You can write them out for me here," said Titus, "and I'll sign and seal them now—and at the same time, I'd like you to write out the Declaration of Martial Law. Could you do both in the short form? I'm in a hurry."

Cornelius calculated, looking along the rows

of his clerks. "We'll need—let me see— All of you do two copies of both, that's two hundred of each. Get writing, everybody. Short forms are on the end shelf. Somebody find the Great Seal and the sealing wax. Hurry!"

There was a scurrying for parchment, and for forms to copy, a slapping as parchment went down on the tables, followed by the quiet, swift scritting of pens. Titus caught the boy who fetched the Great Seal and sent him off to lock the door of the large office, where those who had come to him after breakfast were, he hoped, still waiting.

"Nice thought," commented Agricola. "But I think your cook's honest, or you wouldn't be standing here. That reminds me: your Personal Guard. Those boys are bound to make trouble when I start arresting their granddads."

Titus smiled blissfully. "They're standing in rows in the exercise yard, waiting for me to inspect them. Just detail someone to keep going to them with a message that I'm on my way. With luck you can keep them there all day."

Agricola laughed about this all the time Titus was signing the parchments and passing them to Cornelius to have the Great Seal properly affixed to each. He was still grinning as he collected the sheaf of orders for martial law in both his muscular arms, gave them a shake to make sure the red disks with griffin rampant on them all hung down one side, and put his square chin on the heap to hold it down. He looked sideways at the heap of audit orders left on the table. "Squads to accompany the auditors will be here in ten minutes," he promised Cornelius. He nodded to the rows of grinning clerks. "Good hunting," he said as he followed the Emperor outside. "Pigeons," he added to Titus while they hurried across the yard, "to the rest of the legions to get them here soonest, while the home-based legions surround the Senate. Senatorial legion to be confined to barracks now, and the Personal Guard the same as soon as they smell a rat. Criers to announce martial law. Do me a favor, my Emperor, and come back soon, because it's going to be chaos, rumors, and mayhem until you do."

"I'll try," Titus promised, and pelted for the stable yard. He took both horses, telling the surprised groom that he had still not made up his mind which to ride, and arrived at the north gate almost at the same time as his cavalry escort.

The pigeon meanwhile, having fed and preened and found itself in perfect health, took off for home. It circled the palace once to find its direction, passing over soldiers seething in all directions, except for some finely dressed ones who were standing in rows in a big space, looking rather hot and bored, and then, finding north, it turned toward Derkholm. It sheered away from the Senate building, having no wish for someone to scoop it up in a butterfly net. There were soldiers on its roof by then, and more quietly gathering in the roads all around it, but the rest of the city seemed full of ordinary, busy people in the usual way. Just outside Condita, the pigeon flew over a small troop of Imperial horsemen trotting secretly and sedately through an industrial suburb and dipped its wings in greeting. Titus waved cheerfully back. He was wondering just how long the Personal Guard would stand in the sun before someone came and told them that the Emperor was missing, believed poisoned. That was when Agricola would really have his hands full.

FIFTEEN

AT THE UNIVERSITY Corkoran sat in his ruined lab, wondering whether to end it all. Sometimes he held his throbbing head in both hands—this was on the occasions it seemed about to fall apart in segments, like one of Derk's oranges—and sometimes he simply stared miserably at the remains of his sabotaged moonship. A lot of the time he just stared at the wall. It seemed a yellow sort of color that he did not remember its usually being. He was thinking that when he had the energy, he would climb to the top of the Observatory tower and throw himself off, when someone opened the lab door.

"I told you I didn't need you," he said, assuming it was his assistant.

"You haven't told me anything yet," the intruder replied.

It was a much larger voice than Corkoran's assistant's, with windy undertones and shrill overtones that made Corkoran shudder. He turned around—too quickly; it made him yelp— and saw the front parts of a strange griffin sticking through the doorway. He remembered uneasily then that Finn had said something about a plague of griffins. But at least the creature was a soothing shade of brown. Even its unusual heavy-lidded eyes were a restful mud color, and its feathers, though crisply glossy, were no harder to look at than the crust of a loaf. "What do you want?" Corkoran said. "Who are you?"

The griffin ducked its great head apologetically. "I'm Flury. I want to join up as a student here."

"You can't," Corkoran told him. Or was it her? It was hard to tell from just the front view. "You're too late. Term has already started. You'll have to wait until next autumn now."

"But I didn't know. I'm from the other continent," Flury protested. "Can't you make an allowance for that?"

The voice grated on Corkoran. It was too big. "No," he said. "Apply next spring with proof of magical attainments, and we'll see what we can do. I suppose you do have some magical abilities?"

Flury looked shy. "Some," he admitted.

"And you'll find the fees are quite high," said Corkoran. "Have you money?"

"Quite a lot," Flury admitted bashfully.

"Good. Then come back next spring," said Corkoran. "Now go away."

There was a fraught pause. The door frame creaked. "I can't," Flury said. "I'm stuck."

"Oh, ye gods!" said Corkoran. They really shouldn't trouble him with griffins when he felt like death and had just remembered he had a lecture to give. He needed help. And consideration. At this it occurred to him that Healers Hall had headache remedies. They had soft hands and soothing voices, too. That was what he needed. Hoping that if he took no notice and went away, Flury would prove to be a monstrous hallucination, Corkoran stood up and translocated to find a healer.

Seeing the room suddenly empty, Flury shrugged, causing the door frame to jiggle. "Oh, well," he said. "I tried." He put his head sideways, listening in case Corkoran was on his way back with levers or spells to get him out of the doorway. When it was apparent that Corkoran had simply forgotten him, Flury shook himself loose from the door frame and advanced into the lab. He was now about the size of a small lion. This put his beak at an entirely convenient height for sniffing along benches at the ruins of the moonsuit experiments. These puzzled him extremely. So did the torn-up calculations on the floor. He picked quite a few up, held them together where they seemed to fit, and examined them. He shook his head, baffled. Then he found the rat cage, with the Inescapable Net still hanging off it and its bars bent. He put his beak right inside it and closed his eyes to analyze the smells he found there.

"Ah," he said. "That's what I've been smelling. They were here for some time before they got out and started lurking. Can't say that I blame them really."

He then padded across to the remains of the moonship and spent some time carefully inspecting what was left of it. He nodded sadly. "Waste of effort," he said. "It would never have flown anywhere, anyway."

Then he padded away and carefully shut the door behind him.

Elda was surprised to see Flury at Corkoran's lecture, bulking huge and beach-leaf brown near the back. It was surprising also that no one else seemed to notice him and even more surprising that he fitted in. The lecture hall was crammed. By breakfast time every student in the University knew that Corkoran's moonship was in ruins and Corkoran himself devastated.

Breakfast had been a disaster because the mice had got into the kitchens. Aided by vigorous miniature assassins, they had got into all the cupboards and even into the cold store, where they sucked eggs, chewed bacon, squeezed fruit, poured out milk, and split open bags of cereal. Almost the only thing left to eat was bread—

which had luckily been set to rise in a heavy iron oven—and there was only black coffee to drink.

"Thank goodness for coffee!" said Olga. "My father never did like it."

Felim and Ruskin at once set about designing a foolproof mousetrap—nor were they the only ones; even Melissa was inventing one—and the rest were rather inclined to blame Elda for making the mice in the first place, which made Elda very uncomfortable and guilty. "Mice were just what came into my head!" she explained. "Someone had to do *something*!"

"Leave her alone," said Claudia, who had spent the night on the floor of Elda's concert hall and felt she owed Elda protection in return. "Nobody else did anything."

"Lukin did," said Olga.

"But he makes deep holes all the time, anyway, so that hardly counts," said Claudia.

The news about the moonship was almost a welcome distraction. It caused a wave of sympathy for Corkoran. Even those who felt, like Lukin, that Corkoran was poor stuff (with an unfortunate taste in ties) were determined to show that they were sorry about the sabotage. Every student who could get there, and a few novice healers, crowded into the main lecture hall to show Corkoran moral support.

Corkoran felt quite touched. He was usually lucky to get an audience of five, all female and all gazing adoringly. To find everyone cared this much cheered him considerably. Nevertheless, as he set about delivering the lecture he always delivered at this stage in the term, he knew he was doing it with much less than his usual verve.

He *does* look devastated, Elda thought. Corkoran's face was yellow-pale, and she could see his hands shaking. Even his tie was pallid, full of washed-out–looking white and yellow daisies. In a guilty, illogical way, Elda felt that this might be her fault for not finding Corkoran charming anymore. And though she knew this was probably nonsense, she found herself thinking urgently of some way to make it up to him. She heard very little of the lecture because as soon as she began thinking, she had her inspiration.

It took her until after lunch (another disaster) to find courage to mention her idea to her friends. But as they were gathered around Wizard Policant, waiting to go into Wermacht's class, she blurted it out. "Couldn't we get him to the moon somehow?"

They looked at her understandingly. They had all known that Elda would be more upset about Corkoran than anyone else. They had been worrying about her.

"I don't like to see him looking so miserable," Elda explained.

"I know what you mean," Felim said kindly. "I wonder." He fell into deep thought.

Olga, for her part, tried to put the realities of life before Elda. "I know what you mean, too," she said, "but I've seen my father with enough hangovers to know why he looked so bad."

"We can't let him take to drink!" Elda pleaded.

Lukin laughed. "You must be the most soft-hearted griffin in the world! Teddy bears and moons! Come on, Elda. Everyone else is going into the North Lab." He politely helped Claudia reel in her cloakrack. Claudia had discovered that it was easier if she kept the cloakrack close to her. Since it was going to follow her, anyway, she reasoned that keeping one hand on it as she walked was pleasanter than getting jolted every time the cloakrack stuck on a doorstep.

She parked it beside her desk in the North Lab. Elda sat protectively beside Claudia. Then she turned her head and saw Flury again. He was sitting behind a desk without a chair, just as Elda was herself, with his feathery forearms on the desktop and his talons clasped, staring around with keen interest. He looked very bright and keen and glossy and nothing like as big as he had looked in Corkoran's lecture. Elda began to wonder why he was different every time she saw him. Then she wondered why it was that no one seemed to see him but herself. She was in such a guilty, perturbed mood that it began to seem to her that Flury might be some kind of hallucination that followed her around like Claudia's cloakrack to punish her for not loving Corkoran anymore, or perhaps for turning the pirates into mice, or perhaps for both.

Here Wermacht strode in and put a stop to thinking. "Write down your next big heading," he commanded. "Moving Magefire About." Elda saw Flury looking around anxiously at everyone else's busy notebook. "Now," said Wermacht. "All of you stand up and call up magefire as you learned to do last week."

Elda had been looking forward to holding her lovely teardrop of light again. She jumped up eagerly and cannoned into Claudia in her hurry. Claudia, who was not looking forward to this at all, was getting up rather slowly. She was off-balance when Elda bumped her and staggered sideways into the cloakrack, which fell with a clatter into the aisle beside the desks.

Wermacht exclaimed with annoyance. He came striding up the aisle and picked the cloakrack up before Claudia could reach it. He banged it upright. "Are you *still* going around with this thing, you with a jinx?"

"Yes, of course I am," Claudia retorted. "You connected me to it. You should know."

"Nonsense," said Wermacht. "It's entirely your own doing. You attempted a spell beyond your powers, and you bungled it." He leaned in a lordly attitude with one hand on the cloakrack and the other stroking his beard, smiling contemptuously down on Claudia. While Claudia was gasping at the injustice, he said, "It's all in your mind, you know. Really deep down you *want* to be tied to this cloakrack."

"I do *not!*" Claudia asserted.

"Oh, but you do." Wermacht was smiling pityingly now. "Make an effort, girl. Free yourself from the shackles of your own timidity. You only want this object around for a sense of security."

Claudia gaped at him. "I—I—I—"

Flury came quietly up behind Wermacht and tapped him on one shoulder. No one had seen Flury move. No one, not even Elda, knew how he got where he was, but there he was, towering over Wermacht and wearing his usual apologetic look. There was quite a gasp from everyone, because this was the first time anyone but Elda had seen Flury at all. Wermacht whirled around, found himself staring into Flury's chest feathers, and seemed wholly irate that he had to stare upward to see Flury's face, somewhere near the ceiling. "Excuse me," Flury said, "but what you just said can't be right. As soon as you touched that hatrack, I could tell that it was your spell that did it."

"*My* spell!" Wermacht exclaimed.

Flury nodded. "I'm afraid so. I'm sorry. Nobody likes to be caught out in a mistake, do they?"

Wermacht drew himself up, looking surprisingly small under Flury's beak. "I have made no mistake. I'll show you. I'll attempt to take this silly girl's spell off and *show* you it's not mine!"

"Yes," Flury said mildly. "Do that."

Wermacht glared at him and turned to put both hands on two of the cloakrack's battered wooden hooks. He grasped them firmly, closed his eyes, and concentrated. The next instant, both Wermacht and the cloakrack were surrounded in a bluish lightning flash. There was a strong smell of ozone. The instant after that, Wermacht and the cloakrack appeared to melt into one another, folding downward as they melted. By the time everyone had blinked and exclaimed, the only thing left of Wermacht or the cloakrack was a large, leather-topped bar stool standing in the aisle on four chunky wooden legs.

"Oh, dear," Flury said, blinking with the rest of them. "I'd no idea that was going to happen." Elda, all the same, had the feeling that he was not nearly as surprised as he claimed to be.

Claudia's immediate action was to retreat experimentally to the other side of the lab. To her enormous relief, the bar stool made no move to follow her. It just stood there, looking woebegone. The reaction of everyone else was almost as swift and entirely practical. Everyone except Elda put notebooks back into bags and pens into pockets, and while Elda was staring at Flury and realizing that he was no sort of hallucination at all, everyone else was cheerfully making for the door. They were almost there when Flury said, "Why are you all going? Don't you *want* to learn magic?"

"Yes, of course we do," someone told him joyfully, "but no one can learn magic from a bar stool."

"*I* can teach you, though," Flury said, looking hurt and injured.

The students looked at one another. Somehow they all found that they did not like to hurt Flury's feelings. They shrugged, turned around, and sat at the desks again, where they resignedly got out notebooks. Flury prowled to the front and sat on his haunches by the lectern, still big, but not quite as big as he had been when he towered over Wermacht. He looked at the students. They stared dubiously back.

"What have you done so far?" Flury asked them. "Setting wards? Pattern magic? Power sharing? Conjuring? Numerology? Theurgy? Scrying? Raising lone power?" Heads were shaken at each question. "Conjuring fire then?" Flury asked as if this were a last resort. "Levitation then? Translocation? Crystallography? Bespelling objects?" Heads were shaken again. No one knew what half these things were. "May I look at one of your notebooks to see what you *have* done then?" Flury asked rather hopelessly.

Melissa, who was as obliging as she was beautiful, handed him hers. Flury flicked over pages covered with Melissa's round writing with little hearts for dots over the *i*s and frowned. A frown on even a mild-faced griffin like Flury was a menacing thing. Everyone sat very still, except for Elda, who was used to Kit. Mara often said that when Kit frowned, the universe cracked. Elda simply twiddled her talons and wondered how, and why, Flury was never the same size for more than five minutes. He was about her own size, or a little larger, as he flicked pages and frowned. "Wermacht seems to take a lot of classes," he murmured. "You should have got through more than this." Eventually he handed the notebook back. "Well," he said, "I'd better invent some way of making up for lost time. If you don't mind pushing these desks back and standing in a ring holding hands, we'll set wards by sharing power and kill two humans with one stone."

Notebooks were put away again, and everyone rather cautiously did as Flury suggested. The caution was reasonable, Elda thought. Flury was obviously a wizard as well as a griffin. But after that she and everyone else were so absorbed and busy that no one had time to feel nervous, and the rest of the hour passed before they were aware. They used their joined power to raise wards around the North Lab in six ways that Flury said were elementary and they should have known already. Then they used their joined power to scry. All of them saw, clear as clear, as if they were inside the various rooms, Corkoran sitting in his lab, the librarian resetting Inventory-spells, and the buttery bar with a few idle students in there drinking beer. Flury said the results would be better when they learned to use crystals. Then he had them conjure into the North Lab all the bar stools that no one was actually sitting on. After that the hour was suddenly over. The top of Wermacht's hourglass was empty of every grain and the bottom full of sand.

"Do you know, I actually *learned* something!" Melissa was heard proclaiming in surprised tones while everyone was leaving.

Someone returned all the stools to the buttery bar, including Wermacht, although nobody liked to sit on Wermacht until the bar became crowded later that evening. He was easily distinguishable by being taller and gloomier than any of the other stools. Elda, who was couched comfortably against the wall with a straw in her beak and Claudia leaning on her beaming because she was free of that cloakrack at last, looked at that stool and wondered if Flury had intended this to happen to Wermacht. Flury was a total mystery, she thought. Around her everyone else talked of mousetraps or the moon. Ruskin had designed what he felt was the perfect mousetrap, until Olga pointed out, with what seemed to be family feeling, that these mice had human brains.

"Hmm," Ruskin grunted. "You have a point there. I'll think again." And he joined Felim in considering how to send Corkoran to the moon.

Felim seemed to be becoming obsessed with the moonshot. Elda was embarrassed. "You don't need to worry about it," she protested.

"But it is a superb intellectual problem," Felim said. "The things we learned this afternoon, particularly the notion of several people combining powers, is, I think, the key to the problem."

"You mean, several people combining to do something like translocation?" Lukin asked.

"It beats me why Corkoran didn't plan to translocate there, anyway," Ruskin growled. "It's the obvious way."

"Do you think that maybe he can't?" Claudia suggested. "Oh, no, we saw him translocate, didn't we, Olga, the day Felim was inside the books?"

"Yes, but he probably can't go very far," Elda said. "My dad can't. He can only go five miles at his best. The moon's further than that, isn't it?"

Felim laughed. "Many thousands of miles further. This is why a boost from several people is certainly necessary."

"But remember there's no air there," Olga put in. "You'd need to translocate him in an enclosed bubble of air and you'd have to be sure there was *enough* air for him. How would you do that?"

"By compressing it?" Lukin suggested. "If you had the outside of your bubble made of squashed-up air that could be gradually released, that would hold the bubble firm, too, wouldn't it?"

"Darned good idea!" Ruskin said. He and Claudia began calculations to find out how much air Corkoran would need, while Lukin worked out spells that might compress it, and Felim tried

to calculate how many people it would take combining their powers to send the lot as far as the
moon.

They're *all* doing it! Elda thought. And
they're only doing it because they think I'm still
in love with Corkoran. She would have squirmed
if Claudia had not been leaning on her. It seemed
too late to explain that she was simply *sorry* for
Corkoran. She spent the whole of the next day in
a state of mingled guilt and embarrassment,
while calculations and discussions went on obses-
sively around her, until she simply had to explain
to someone.

"You don't need to send Corkoran to the moon
just because I said so," she said to Lukin as they
sat facing one another across a chessboard at
Chess Club that evening.

Lukin moved a knight and took it back again
quickly as he saw Elda would have his queen if
he moved it. "It's not on your *orders*, if that's what
you think. You just produced the right idea. It's
to *show* Corkoran that our adaptation of spells
really does work. Felim simply couldn't believe it
when Corkoran gave him such a low mark for his
essay, he said he filled it with the best stuff he
knew and Corkoran simply spat in his face. He
says it's his honor at stake. And Ruskin was
stunned. Did you see his face when he looked at
his mark? Or Claudia's? Claudia went grass
green, and her eyes seemed to swallow up the rest
of her face."

"What about you and Olga, though?" Elda slyly moved her queen one square.

"Seen that!" said Lukin, moving up a high priest. "Olga was furious. Corkoran had the cheek to say there probably wasn't such a thing as air elementals. It really upset her. And I've always thought Corkoran needs *showing* that he's running in blinkers."

"Filbert hates blinkers," Elda agreed. "I was a bit sad about my essay, too, but that wasn't why I thought of sending Corkoran to the moon."

"I know," Lukin said kindly. "You're far too nice, Elda. And then Flury comes along and shows us how to combine power and that was that. Check."

"Mate," replied Elda, moving her queen back to where it had been. While Lukin was cursing at having missed what she was doing, she wondered if Flury had intended to put this idea into their heads and just what Flury was up to.

She kept encountering Flury all over the University after that. He was in the library when she went to take back most of Ruskin's food-spell books in order to fetch Felim a stack of volumes on astronomy. When she backed out of the astronomy section, she saw Flury, looking very small and drab, humbly approaching the librarian's desk. He was asking anxiously for a copy of Wermacht's teaching timetable then, but when she came up to the desk herself with Felim's books, he was saying, "Then I'll ask in the office.

Thank you. Can you give me any books on the founding of the University, or a biography of Wizard Policant at all?" The librarian seemed to accept that Flury was another griffin student and gave him two books without question. Elda had no idea what Flury wanted them for.

The next time she met him, Flury seemed to be searching along the edges of the courtyard, as if he had lost something. "What are you looking for?" Elda asked him.

"I thought I might catch some mice," he told her.

Elda was not sure by now that anything Flury said about himself was true, but she said, "They won't go near you. Griffins have too much cat in them."

"I daresay you're right," Flury said dejectedly.

Elda hated people to agree with her in this dismal way. She explained rather tartly, "The mice get in all the students' rooms, but they never get into mine. I smell of danger to them."

This was true. Claudia vouched for it to Ruskin, and the next day Ruskin implored Elda to sleep in his room. His food-spells had all been eaten. Felim looked up from his calculations and said, "It would be much more use if Elda were to sleep in the kitchens." Wizard Dench, horrified at the waste of food, had been and put guard-spells on all the cupboards and the cold store, but the mice still got in.

"Don't be silly," said Elda. "You know I can't

get up Ruskin's stairs *or* squeeze through the kitchen door."

Felim once again looked up from his scribbling. Elda assumed he was doing his usual equations, full of $x = yz$ or things that looked like big tick marks, until he said, "Does *daffodil* rhyme with *Isodel*, do you think?"

"No!" said everyone, and Olga added to Lukin, "If ever I saw a heart-whole woman, it's your sister, Lukin."

"Yes, Felim, honestly," Lukin said. "Everyone who sees Isodel falls madly in love with her, but she hardly even notices."

"That is beside the point," Felim answered loftily. "To write poems to a cruel love is the height of artistry." Then, while Lukin was muttering that this was what they *all* said, Felim added, "About the mice. The assassins are certainly in partnership with the mice and assassins are usually magic users, if only in a small way. So they can certainly circumvent the Bursar's spells."

"Then *I'll* go and cast some spells on the kitchen!" Ruskin said, exasperated.

"You couldn't do worse than Wizard Dench," Claudia agreed in her driest way. "Come on, everyone. We've got a class. I'm interested to see if it's Flury or a bar stool taking it."

It was Flury. Flury seemed to be taking all Wermacht's classes, always with the same apologetic air, which seemed to suggest he was only humbly filling in until someone turned Wermacht back again, but always teaching things that Wermacht had never even mentioned. He was taking the second- and third-year classes, too. Elda discovered he was when second- and third-year students began to turn up among the first-year classes, saying Flury had told them to come and catch up on the basics.

"Has Corkoran asked you to take Wermacht's place then?" Elda asked Flury.

"I did speak to Corkoran, yes," Flury said. "This University is not in a very thriving way, you know. Are your brothers likely to visit again soon?"

"Blade and Kit?' said Elda, instantly distracted from Flury's activities. "They *said* so. I don't know what's keeping them."

It had taken Kit, Blade, and Callette, too, more time and effort than they believed possible to get their parents, and Florence and Angelo, and all the horses, and the winged runt piglet that Derk was rearing by hand, plus all the luggage Mara thought necessary, safely to the coast and then onto a ship. It was some days after Elda spoke to Flury before they were through and could return to Derkholm at last. There Callette said she was exhausted. "It's keeping my temper for a whole week," she said, and she went away to sleep in the spiky gothic den she had built for herself beside the Derkholm stables.

Kit and Blade, who did not find their parents quite as annoying as Callette did, looked at one another. Kit said, "We said we'd see Elda."

"And I promised to do something about that girl with the cloakrack," Blade said. "That's been worrying me."

"Let's go now then," said Kit, and took off for the University in a thunder of wings. Blade waited on the terrace, with his feet up on a chair, drinking a quiet mug of tea, until experience told him that Kit would have the University in sight. Then he sighed, stood up and stretched, and translocated there, too.

That day Flury had given Wermacht's class on Basic Ritual and was now moseying around the backyards of the University in his usual way. One way or another he had explored nearly all of them. This particular yard backed onto the empty stables Flury had found to sleep in, but to get there, Flury had had to fly in over the stable roof. There seemed to be no door or gate to the yard at all. But once he was there, he discovered that it also backed onto the kitchens. "Ah," Flury said.

Lion-size and sleepy-looking, Flury wandered about the weedy flagstones, scratching idly at little piles of rubbish, turning over old horseshoes and pieces of crockery, always getting closer to the larger pile of rubbish in one corner. When he was close enough to it, he pounced. Mice ran out of it in all directions, squealing. Flury took no notice of them and dug with both sets of talons. There followed a few seconds of violent activity, and then Flury stood back on his haunches, becoming the larger size that was probably natural to him, holding a bundle of small, black-clad human figures. Ignoring the way they shouted shrilly and writhed and struggled, he calmly sorted through them.

"Six," he said. "Assassins always go in sevens, I heard. Where's the other one?"

Six small black arms pointed. Flury turned his head down to look at the tiny black cockerel almost between his hind legs. "I see," he said. "That doesn't seem quite fair." Spreading his wings for balance, he picked the cockerel up with his left back talons. He brought that leg up to his front ones and transferred the chicken to the bundle of assassins he already held. As soon as it reached its companions, it became a small man dressed in black, too, who seemed to be struggling not to cry. "That's better," Flury said as he uncurled himself. "And I suppose you'll all be wanting to be your proper size now."

The small men became very eloquent about this. Their arms waved, and their voices shrilled.

"Yes, all right," Flury said. "But I'm afraid there's a catch. You'll be the right size ten miles from here. If you come any closer, you'll be small again."

The small men, at this, became even more eloquent.

Flury shook his head. The tiny voices were making his ears buzz. "I don't care if you haven't fulfilled your mission. You seem to me to have done enough. The wretched fellow is wandering about looking as if a house has fallen on him." Ignoring the assassins' further attempts to scream that *Corkoran was not the target!,* he spread his wings and flew out into the countryside with them. There were several farms about ten miles off where Flury had been cadging food, and he wanted his lunch.

He had described Corkoran exactly. Around the time Flury was finishing an excellent lunch, Corkoran was shambling around the edge of the main courtyard on his way to the White Lion, oblivious of students streaming out of Myrna's lecture. Corkoran had forgotten all about teaching this last week. Most of his students had realized and considerately not turned up. Corkoran was not interested in that or in anything much any longer. He barely looked up when a great black griffin coasted down to land beside Wizard Policant. Nor did he look around when Kit's arrival was followed by the whipcrack of Blade appearing. Elda's happy shrieks of greeting only made him wince.

"Oh. You've got rid of the cloakrack," Blade said to Claudia. He felt rather cheated.

Claudia saw how he felt. "It was another accident," she said. "The wizard who did it is now a bar stool." She chuckled about it. Her eyes glowed, and a delighted greenish dimple appeared in one cheek.

Blade gazed at her laughing face and discovered that he did not mind too much about the cloakrack. He said, "Oh, no! Really?" and laughed, too.

But here Felim and Ruskin advanced on Blade and Kit with sheets of paper. "We think it may be possible to translocate a man to the moon," Felim said, "by a combined boost of shared power. Would either of you agree?"

"In a bubble of air," Ruskin said, holding up a page of drawings. "Like so."

As Blade took the papers with considerable interest and Kit leaned over his shoulder to look at them, too, Olga explained, "Elda was terribly upset when Corkoran's moonship was destroyed. She got us thinking of other ways to get him there."

Griffins do not blush. Elda wriggled and felt ashamed. "He looked so devastated," she said, wishing she had never, ever told anyone that Corkoran reminded her of a teddy bear. "But you don't have to bother," she added earnestly.

"Well, I can't see why anyone would *want* to go to the moon myself," Blade said, "But this looks as if it could work. Kit's got the strongest boost of anyone I know. What do you think, Kit?"

"Let's take another look at that air bubble," Kit said. "We wouldn't want to kill him." He skewered Ruskin's page of drawings on a talon and studied it closely. "I'd double this," he said at length. "You always need a safety margin, and it would make the outside harder if you packed more compressed air in. What say, Blade? No time like the present. Isn't that Corkoran over by the main gate? Shall I fetch him here?"

Claudia said swiftly, "He might find that a bit overwhelming."

"We'll go," said Olga.

Corkoran was on his way through the gate when running feet approached him. He looked around with slow surprise at Olga on one side of him and Lukin, very breathless, on the other.

"You do still want to go to the moon, don't you?" Lukin panted.

Now they were having a joke with him, Corkoran thought.

"If you do," Olga said, tossing a sheet of her hair off her face, "Kit and Blade can send you there now."

Kit and Blade, Corkoran thought. Two of the most powerful wizards there were. He looked back over his shoulder, and there indeed *was* Kit, with Blade looking child-size against him, conferring with Ruskin, who looked child-size against Blade, all of them passing pieces of paper about. Felim stood beside Elda, evidently explaining, with strong, spell-like gestures of his brown hands, and Claudia was beside Felim, nodding. Perhaps Olga meant what she said. Perhaps this thing was possible after all.

Corkoran straightened his plain white tie.

"Let's give it a try, anyway," he said.

They led him back to the statue, where Kit explained quite briefly what they meant to do and then braced himself low on the ground with his legs spread for balance. Blade swiftly organized the rest of them into a ring around Corkoran, so that Elda was clasping Kit's right foreleg and Ruskin his left one, and Blade himself took the final place facing Kit, between Claudia and Felim, while Lukin and Olga stretched their arms wide on the sides to make the ring as even as possible. "Go," Blade said.

The air bubble began to form around Corkoran. He looked at it, marveling. It was expanding and hardening to a beautiful misty blueness when Flury came flying gently back across the Spellman Building. As soon as he saw what was going on by the statue, he gave a shriek of horror and went into a dive.

"*No!*" he screamed. "Not with whatshername in there!" He hit the courtyard in what was probably the worst landing a grown griffin had ever made and, stumbling, legs sliding in four directions, wings beating for balance, tried to hurry toward the statue. "*Stop!*" he shrieked.

As he shrieked, the misty blue bubble expanded to enclose everyone around Corkoran. Flury could see all their heads turn to look at it and the mystified expressions on their faces for an instant. Then the bubble vanished, blasting Flury backward with the force of its going.

He picked himself up miserably and hobbled toward the statue. "That'll teach me to teach people things, won't it?" he said, and looked uselessly up into the cloudy sky. "I suppose they've *all* gone to the moon now."

"No," said the statue of Wizard Policant. "They missed the moon."

Flury limped another step and stared into the statue's stone face. "Er, did you speak?"

"Yes. I said that they missed the moon," the statue replied. "Two of them had jinxes. It's been irritating me profoundly that no one's done anything about them."

"Did they take enough air?" Flury demanded.

"Enough air for what?" asked the statue. "I've no idea where they've gone."

SIXTEEN

QUERIDA ARRIVED AT lunchtime. As the house she owned in the city was let out to a friend, she went straight to Healers Hall, where she arranged stabling for Hobnob and lodging for herself, and then made sure that she was invited to lunch there. She entered the University an hour later at the head of a procession of three young healers, each of whom carefully carried a cat basket.

Flury peered down at her from the roof of the Spellman Building. He could see at once who and what she was. But Querida's expression was that of a snake looking for something to sink its fangs into. He decided to give her a while to get settled.

Querida made straight for the Council Chamber. When Flury crawled in there, at his very smallest and meekest and least noticeable,

337

there were already three dead mice laid in a row under the table by Querida's tiny feet. Querida had piles of paper and ledgers in front of her on the table, together with a saucer of milk— Sabrina having refused utterly to eat on the floor after the trials of the journey—and she had Wizard Dench and Wizard Finn standing on either side of her. Both wizards looked thoroughly miserable.

"I can just about forgive the upper floor of this building being turned into luxury flats for wizards," Querida was saying, "but the two other things I will *never* forgive. Dench, be kind enough to explain how you came to let Corkoran squander all this money."

Wizard Dench squirmed. "The moonshot, you know. It's a very prestigious project."

"Prestigious!" hissed Querida. "*Prestigious!* Corkoran is no more able to get to the moon than *you* are. *And* you know it!"

Flury went smaller yet and tiptoed away to a corner. He could tell he had not given Querida nearly enough time to get settled.

"As for you, Finn," Querida continued, "had you *no* idea that the wards here— Who are *you*?" she snapped at Flury. "You there! Stop crawling about like that!"

Flury stopped and turned to her respectfully. This was a wizard to be reckoned with. Very few people could see him unless he wanted them to. "I'm Flury, ma'am."

Querida frowned. "Flury?"

"Flurian Atreck," Flury admitted. "And I'm afraid I've got some more upsetting news—"

Querida's brows went up. "The wizard? I've heard of you, though I had no idea you were a griffin. And I'm sorry. If you were hoping for some kind of high-powered conference with wizards of this continent, you'll have to wait. We have a crisis here. The University wards are all but down."

"I know, ma'am," said Flury. "That's why I stayed here. I was in charge of four exiled griffins, you see, with a contract from my government to get them painlessly neutralized—"

Sharp as a striking snake, Querida demanded, "Was one of them called Jessak?" Flury nodded. "Then I do not love you, Flurian," she said. "You sent them to me, didn't you?"

"Not exactly," Flury protested. "I laid it on them to go where they would be neutralized. It was a tricky matter, ma'am, because they were largely immune to magic, and I couldn't neutralize them myself because they were distant cousins. I brought them here first, thinking the University would be full of people who could do it, and I had rather a shock when I found that the place was pretty nearly powerless. I had to call for help, or young Elda would have been hurt. Then when they'd gone, I stayed to see if I could restore the power here. But I can't. I think it's because Corkoran refused to enroll me as a member."

Querida looked at the ribbed stone ceiling. "Typical. I get angrier with Corkoran with every minute that passes. Finn, you were about to say where you think Corkoran is, I think."

"No, I wasn't," Finn said. "He's, er, he's unavailable."

"Nonsense!" hissed Querida. "Unless he's really gone to the moon, that is."

"That's just the trouble," Flury said unhappily. "He has. Only I think they missed."

They knew they had missed when they saw the moon whip past in the distance. Corkoran moaned at the sight. His teeth chattered in his gray face, and he clutched his arms around himself, trying not to look at the deep stars in the black sky outside the bubble or at the tiny, shrinking blue ball of the earth. "I was always afraid of heights!" he said, not for the first time.

"Do shut up!" Elda snapped at him. She was slightly ashamed of snapping, but she was having a harder time than Corkoran, being so much bigger. She had never expected not to be able to stand with her feet or push with her wings. Kit was trying to wedge her in, but he had nothing to brace on either. They were slowly wheeling over and over inside the sphere, along with everyone else wheeling in different ways, and it was making Elda feel sick. She had not expected the extreme cold either. It was eating through fur and feathers, into her wings particularly, until she felt she was turning into a block of ice. Ruskin was resourcefully muttering heat spells, and Blade was backing him up, but the sphere seemed to shed the heat as fast as they made it. And there was no way to thicken the outside because, as they quickly discovered, there was nothing out here to thicken it with.

"We forgot heat and neglected to provide gravity," Felim said, shivering ruefully. "Is there perhaps some means of reversing ourselves?"

"I'd need something to kick off from before I could turn us," Kit said.

Corkoran moaned again. "We won't find anything now before the air runs out."

They all looked anxiously at what they could see of the compressed air at the rim of the sphere. It was almost impossible to tell how thick it was. The blue haze looked different from every angle. Elda supposed it was a comfort to know there was still some there. "Do, please, try not to be so depressing," Olga said to Corkoran. "Think how lucky it is that we all came, too. You'd hate to be all alone."

"But you're using the air *up*!" said Corkoran. "All of you. The griffins most of all. You're *killing* me!"

Nobody tried to point out to Corkoran that he had been wanting to travel like this for years, or that they had been trying to please him— or, anyway, show him it could be done. They were all too anxious. Ruskin did mutter, from the midst of his heat spells, something about ungrateful bunny rabbits, and Blade, still sending Ruskin power, said, "You know, I just don't understand. This is really only a simple translocation. Normally when you translocate, you get there almost at once."

"We must be going rather a long way then," Lukin said.

He had hardly spoken when they were there, wherever it was. With merest soft grinding, the sphere stopped. It was up to its middle into red stony earth, and the sun was blinding across them from a sky that was a curious color, between pink and blue. Despite the sunlight, it was still severely cold. They all scrambled to their feet and stared anxiously over bare desert into a distance that struck them as being rather too near. Their long, peculiar shadows stretched halfway to the horizon. As they stared, the sunlight grew stronger and the sky pinker, and they all somehow began to grasp that it was dawn here. Just as the sun grew strong enough to hide the veiled stars behind the pinkness, two rather small moons hurtled across the sky.

This seemed to be the last straw for Corkoran. He put his hands to his face and screamed.

"A screaming wizard is *all* we need!" Kit said, and he slapped a stasis spell on Corkoran. Corkoran's eyes bulged with horror, but at least his screaming stopped.

"Ah, that's not kind," said Claudia.

"You're right," Kit admitted. "It's not his fault he's useless." He took the stasis off and made Corkoran unconscious instead. Nobody protested.

"Apologies," Blade said as Corkoran flopped to the rounded floor. He did not fall nearly as heavily as they might have expected. Blade frowned about this as he said to Claudia, "Kit and I have just come from a war, and I'm afraid we both got used to being ruthless. Why were you the only person who wasn't scared stiff on the way here?"

Claudia flushed a dark olive and looked down so that her hair coiled in and hid her face. "It's my jinx," she said. "It's mostly a travel jinx. I always have trouble traveling, but I always get where I was going in the end. So I knew we'd arrive *somewhere*, you see."

"You might," said Kit, "have warned us you had a jinx. Was that what made that spell on the cloakrack so tangled?"

"I think so," Claudia admitted, with her head still down.

"*And* collected us all together and dumped us in this hole?" Kit persisted.

"Er," said Lukin, "some of that was probably mine. I always make a pit of some kind when I do any magic."

"Don't criticize this hole," Ruskin said, huskily even for him. "I reckon we freeze or burn here without it. Wherever here is," he added. "We ought all to keep well down inside it."

As everyone hurriedly sat or crouched down, Felim said, "This is a lesson to me not to rely on my honor to rule my actions. I am well served. I thought I was right and Corkoran was wrong, and look where we are now!"

Kit, who knew how it felt to have your pride crushed, said, "You *were* right. We got here. It just needed a bit more thinking through. Nobody reckoned on two jinxes either. If we had, we'd be on the moon at this moment. Where do you think we *are*?"

Felim seemed slightly comforted. "All the same," he said, "I shall be more cautious in the future if we ever get away. As to where this is, I have a feeling that Corkoran was screaming because he knew. Should we rouse him and ask him?"

Blade looked at Corkoran curled up among their legs. "We may have to," he said, "if we can't work it out for ourselves. The problem is that I have to know where I am in order to go somewhere else. Kit can push me, but I take us. Kit, when we do go, reckon for everything being lighter here, won't you?"

Ruskin slapped his knee so hard that his hand bounced. "Now that is the attitude I like! Not *if*, but *when* we go. That's positive wizarding, that is!"

"We were taught that way," said Blade. "But I don't want to sit and watch the world go past the way the moon did. Before we do anything else, we're going to unravel these jinxes."

"Air?" asked Kit. "Doesn't that come first? Is there any air here at all?"

Olga edged forward. "Maybe I can ask," she said. When everyone turned to her in confusion, she pushed her hair back and said, "Well, you see, there are some very queer sorts of elementals looking in at us from the sides of this pit. They're awfully interested, and they might help."

Naturally everyone craned to look at the sides of the pit. Not all of them could see the beings Olga meant. Of those who could see them, Ruskin and Lukin had the least trouble. Kit and Elda kept turning their heads this way and that because, from the very tails of their eyes, they *thought* they could see faces there, like clods of earth with round pebblelike eyes, but when either of them turned to look full on, there was just reddish earth. Claudia thought she glimpsed one face, but that was all. Blade and Felim saw nothing but dry, stony earth, anyway.

Olga shut her eyes and tried to listen to the dry, stony voices. It was like hearing a foreign language that was mostly clicks and faint pattering, a language Olga felt she had once learned and then forgotten. As she listened, the words seemed to come back to her slowly. "They want to know," she said after a while, "if we really are from the blue world. The air elementals in the bubble with us say we are, and they can't believe it. I've told them we are. And they say this is the red world."

Everyone started speaking at once. "Ye gods! We're on the Red Planet!" Blade exclaimed. "The dragons call it Mars," said Kit. "Oh, *damn* my jinx!" wailed Claudia. "We came a *long* way out of our way then!" Felim remarked. "How do we get *back*?" demanded Elda. "How much air do our air elementals say we've got?" Ruskin asked urgently, and Lukin said, "Can't you use our elementals to translate for you?"

"I don't want to hurt their feelings," Olga answered Lukin. "I'm getting what they say more clearly now. Now they're saying that we seem awfully big and soft. They're wondering about the way the light from the sun is going right through us."

They all noticed at once that it was getting very hot in the bubble now that the sun was climbing. Kit said, "Oh, lawks!" and a thing like a huge umbrella shot out of the bubble top and hovered over it. Unfortunately it took some of their precious air with it as it opened. They all heard the *whoosh* and exchanged anxious looks in the sudden shadow. The pit now felt icy. Warm drops of water formed under the umbrella and went running down the bubble inside and out. This made the rim of compressed air much easier to see. It was much less than half as thick as it had been.

"All huddle together," said Blade. "I daren't do another warmth-working. I think magic may use more air than anything else does."

They all moved closer together, except Olga, who remained leaning against the wet side of the bubble. She said dreamily, "Now they're saying they haven't seen melted water for thousands of years. They're fascinated. I asked about air here. They say the air elementals are all frozen, too."

It was getting fairly stuffy in the damp shade. "Ask them to send us some air," Ruskin said, "before we smother. I've been in mines with more air than this!"

Olga listened again. "There's an argument about that," she said, to everyone's dismay. "The air ones want to come. They want to see our world. But the earth ones say it's not fair. They want to see the blue world, too."

"Tell one of them to get in here with us," Blade suggested tensely. "I can make a link between it and the rest of them, so that they see what it sees."

There was a long, long pause. Then Olga pushed her hair back and held out both hands. What looked like a simple clod of the reddish earth detached itself from the surface of the pit and hopped like a toad, straight through the surface of the bubble and into Olga's hands. She held it up to her face, smiling, as if she were holding a kitten. "I can make the link," she told Blade. "No need to worry. The air ones are coming now."

There was a pattering and a pinging from all over the outside of the bubble and a frothy rushing-feeling from underneath where they all sat. Little bright bits like snowflakes came swirling in under the umbrella, and from the sides and bottom of the pit, and attached themselves to the outer surface of the sphere like iron filings clinging to a magnet. In seconds there was a thick layer of them all around, whitish and shining. They all felt they were inside a snowdrift. The light was dim and pinkish blue. But it was noticeably easier to breathe.

"Thank you," Ruskin said devoutly. "Tell them thank you, Olga." His face suddenly streamed with sweat, and sweat dripped in the plaits of his beard. They all looked at him and looked away quickly, realizing that being without air was a dwarf's most hideous nightmare. Ruskin had been living in that nightmare until this moment.

As frozen air elementals continued to patter onto the outside of the sphere, and the earth clod sat between Olga's hands exuding smug excitement, Blade turned to Claudia. "What exactly does your jinx do?"

Claudia spread her thin olive palms out expressively. "This! It messes everything up. Twists it. Everything, particularly magic. It's at its very worst when I travel, but it's terribly ingenious, too, so that I can't guard against it. Something different happens every time. I've had snowstorms in summer and landslides and flash floods and things struck by lightning. People go to the wrong place to meet me, or we miss the supply cart, or the road subsides and we have to go around it. Or the horses go lame or trees fall across the track or, or . . . I'll tell you, coming to the University, I lost our map—I think *ants* ate it!—and we went miles out of our way to the east, until the road just ended in a cliff. So we turned back. The legionaries said they'd try to get me back to Condita—they'd gone all grim and sarcastic, the way people do after a taste of my jinx—but instead we blundered into a wet forest full of alligators and went north avoiding that. And then it rained and rained, and when the rain stopped, we saw the University city on the horizon. So we went there. Luckily Titus had made us set off in plenty of time. He always does these days. And I did get there in the end, because that's the way it works."

"Let's get this straight," said Blade. "You weren't using magic to travel with, were you?"

"Of course not," said Claudia. "The legionaries would have hated it."

"Perhaps she should have been," Kit suggested. "It sounds like a powerful translocation talent that's got bent out of shape somehow."

"It *does*," Blade agreed thoughtfully. "And when she does put magic consciously with traveling, it brings us to another planet. It's strong all right."

"But other magic things go wrong, too," Claudia pointed out.

"Well, they would," Blade explained. "Everyone has one or maybe two major abilities. Olga's is talking to things I can't even see, for instance. And if the major talent gets deformed somehow, all the rest goes wrong, too."

Olga, with her face pink in the strange shadowy light, looked at Lukin and murmured, "That explains my monsters."

Blade sat with his knees up, chin in hands, elbows on bony knees, staring thoughtfully at Claudia. She looked miserably away from him. "Sorry," Blade said. "You've realized, have you? It's your feelings that are deforming your magic."

"I refuse," Claudia said, with her head bent. "I *refuse* utterly to believe that Wermacht was right!"

"I don't know what Wermacht said," said Blade. "But it's an awful pity. You feel to me as if you ought to be as strong as Querida really. Let me think—I've been to Condita lots of times, but I only ever met you there once. You must have been away a lot."

Claudia nodded. "I expect I was away in the Marshes with my mother. She insisted I spent half my time with her."

"And which did you like best, the Empire or the Marshes?" Blade asked her.

Claudia began to speak. "I—" she said, and then put both hands to her face and stopped. "I always tried to kid myself," she began again, "that I liked both of them equally. But now that it seems important to admit it, I know I *hated* both of them equally. I mean, I'm fond of Mother, or I would be if she ever stopped grumbling, and I adore Titus, but when I'm in the Marshes, everyone and everything make it plain to me that I'm Empire born and don't fit, and when I'm in the Empire, it's worse, because they think of me as dirty Marshwoman—scum, marsh slime, all that. Are you trying to make me admit that my jinx is because I'm a half-breed?' There were tears in her eyes, big and shiny and greenish in the peculiar snowdrift light.

Blade shook his head emphatically. "No, no, no. Mixes usually make stronger magic. Look at Kit and Elda: They're lion, eagle, human, and cat. No, what I'm getting at is that you've spent most of your life shuttling between two places you hated, and you probably have a fiercely strong translocation talent, anyway, so of *course* it went wrong. It was your way of kicking and screaming as they dragged you back and forth."

The tears in Claudia's eyes spilled out and rolled down her narrow cheeks. "Of *course* that's what it is! I should have seen. But—what do I do about it?"

"Forget your childhood. It's over," said Blade. "You can be a wizard now and go anywhere and do anything you want."

Claudia stared at him, still with her hands to her tear-marked cheeks. A slow smile of relief began to spread on what could be seen of her face. "Oh!" she said, and took a deep breath of the chilly, heady new air. As she did so, Blade gave

Kit a slight nod. Kit's mighty talons reached out and tweaked.

"Got it," he said, whisking something invisible away through the snowy side of the sphere. "One jinx gone. One to go."

"I know all about mine," Lukin said defensively. "Mine happens because I don't want to be a king. When I think about ruling, I just want to dig myself a deep pit and stay in it. So it's quite obvious and natural that whenever I do magic, I make a hole in something. There's nothing anyone can do about that."

Felim had listened appreciatively as Blade coaxed Claudia's jinx out of her. Now he leaned forward and joined in. "Why do you not want to be a king?" he asked. "This continues to puzzle me, for I know that in my case I would far rather be a wizard, but I know that *you* have another kind of mind that spreads wider than a wish to sit and study spells."

Lukin blinked a bit. He thought. "You have to be so strict if you're a king," he said at last, rather fretfully. "Everything has to be just so, because you have to set an example, and there's no money—and by the time I'd get to be king, there'll be even *less* money—and we can't ever seem to heat the castle, and nothing ever really goes *right* because the tours laid the kingdom to waste, and—"

"Hang on," said Blade. "You're talking about the way things *are*, in Luteria, and the way your father behaves, not about being a king. Just because your father's the gloomiest man I know, it doesn't follow that *you* have to be."

"Or mismanage money the way he does," added Kit.

Ruskin who, as a dwarf and a future citizen of Luteria, had been attending to this keenly, looked deeply shocked. "Mismanages money?"

Lukin said angrily, "He *doesn't* mismanage money! There just isn't any!"

"Our dad's always saying he does," Elda chipped in. "Derk says King Luther seems to think it's beneath him even to *think* about making money."

Lukin became angrier still. "My father can't breed winged horses or make a mint of money out of clever pigeons, the way yours can!"

"Yes," said Kit. "But *you* could."

Lukin glared at him. His teeth were so tightly clenched that the muscles bulging in his cheeks, in the strange light, made his face look like a wide, sinister skull. Kit glared calmly back. "I wish you weren't bigger than me!" Lukin said without taking his teeth apart.

"Hold your hammer," said Ruskin. "I'm with Felim here. I don't understand. You met the forgemasters. They love their power. They'd kill to keep it. Why don't you?"

Lukin shrugged and unclenched his teeth a little. "It doesn't bother me. I don't have any power."

"So you went to train as a wizard in order to get some," Blade said. "Fair enough. Then what *don't* you like? The responsibility? I'd have thought you'd quite like being the one in charge."

"I would," Lukin admitted. "Only I'm not, am I? To listen to my father, you'd think I was still ten years old. It's not his fault. He missed a whole hunk of our lives when Mother took us away into the country because of the tours, and he still hasn't caught up. There's a gap—" He stopped suddenly.

Olga looked up from the happy clod cradled in her fingers and surveyed Lukin through the hanging sheet of her hair. "I *knew* you'd see it in the end," she said. "Remember magic doesn't *think* in a reasonable way, the way people do. Yours just peppers everything you do with that gap your father doesn't notice, trying to *show* him you're grown-up now. Doesn't it? Didn't you tell me you first started making pits when the tours stopped and you came home?"

Something seemed to drain out of Lukin. He slumped. "When I was ten," he said. "I'd been looking after everyone before that: Mother, the younger ones, even Isodel a lot of the time. Isodel and I did the cooking and cleaned the cottage because Mother didn't know how to. Then we went home, and I got treated as if I were five years old!"

Blade caught the whatever it was that drained out of Lukin and posted it quickly through the ice-covered wall, in among the peering pebble-eyed faces. "There," he said. "Thanks. Don't get too upset, Lukin. I don't know why it always has to *hurt* to get things straight, but it always does." He gave a look of apology to Claudia, who sat with her head pensively hanging, on the other side of Lukin.

She saw the look through her coiling hair. She giggled. "You sound just like Flury!"

"I always want to wring Flury's neck when he looks like that," Elda agreed. "It really irritates me!"

"Especially when you know that not one cringe of it is real," Claudia said. "You did what you had to do, Blade. Don't crawl to us about it."

"How come you know Flury?" Kit asked in considerable astonishment.

"Later," said Blade. "I want to try and get us back now. All of you concentrate hard on home, please. If we miss again, we'll probably be dead."

The ringing of the bell on the pigeon loft made Callette growl sleepily and crawl out of her majestic shed. She had promised Derk that she would see to any messages that came while he was away, even though she had *known* they would come the moment she fell asleep. She prowled around the stable buildings to the loft ladder, muttering grumpily. She was far too big to get up the ladder, had been for years. She solved this the way she always did, by standing on

355

her hind legs with her front talons clutching the top rung of the ladder, while she pushed her head inside the loft.

"Which of you just came in?" she said to the dimness in there.

Two pigeons promptly presented themselves. Both looked exceedingly cheerful at being home. Both had beakfuls of grain. They swallowed hastily as Callette glowered at them.

"The Emperor of the South has arrested his Senate and gone to the University with his horse soldiers," crooned the pigeon on the left.

"The Emir of Ampersand has gone to the University with his army," croodled the pigeon to Callette's right. "He says he will take it all apart."

"Hmm," said Callette. "Thanks. I suppose I'd better fly over there and warn them. You two go back to your lunch." She got herself down to the ground by climbing her front talons down the ladder, puzzling about this news. She found it hard to believe. There was no reason that she knew for anyone to make war on the University. Even during the tours no one had attacked the place. But the pigeons always told the truth, though they did sometimes get hold of the wrong end of the stick. "Fly over there and check," she told herself as she reached the ground. "Bother!"

"Oh, *there* you are!" Don's voice rang out behind her. "Where's everybody else?"

Callette whirled around. The stable yard was packed with griffins, with Don in front of them, huge and glad and golden. Callette gaped. Derk always said that Callette's mind worked like nobody else's. She supposed that was true, for she discovered that her way of being quite intensely delighted to see her brother again was to decide to make a big golden model of him. Now. At once. A model of the perfect griffin, enormous and shapely and bright, like a huge male version of Elda, except that Don was so—so *uncomplicated* somehow. Callette's talons twitched to get modeling. Don completely outshone the gaggle of smaller griffins behind him. Most of those were girls, anyway.

"Huh!" said Callette. "Did you bring your whole fan club with you? Or are some of them Kit's?"

Don laughed. "They all wanted to see what it's like over here."

Callette slowly took in the sheer number of griffins packed in behind Don. Or wanted to found a colony, she thought. "How did you get on the boat?"

"Took turns flying and resting on the deck, of course," Don told her happily. "One of the fan club's yours."

"What!" Callette watched a griffin who was only three-quarters of Don's size come sliding out from behind Don. He was gray and white and brown, with barred wings like her own, and a very sleek, self-possessed person whose large black eyes seemed brighter and more perceptive

357

than those of the other griffins. "Oh, no," said
Callette. "Not Cazak again. Don, that's not fair!"
And like an offended cat, she turned her back on
the whole crowd and sat staring at the ladder
with her tail angrily beating.

Cazak was perhaps not quite as confident as
he looked. He hesitated. "Go on," Don said to
him. "I *know* she's just being stupid about you.
She'd fly away if she really meant it."

Cazak advanced. Callette heard his talons
clicking on the ground and said, "Go away.
You're too *small*."

Cazak, with some caution, poked his head
over Callette's winged shoulder so that he could
look her in one eye. She turned her head away.
"Come on, Callette," Cazak said. "You know
most males are my size. *We* never let that bother
us. Why should *you*?"

"Because!" snapped Callette.

The griffins crowded behind Don exchanged
looks, knowing perfectly well that Callette could
have put out one of Cazak's eyes if she had
wanted to, but none of them dared speak.
Griffins were used to being far more public about
these things than humans were.

"Promise at least to let me paint that picture of
you," Cazak said.

Callette bent and nibbled absently at one of the
rungs of the ladder. She had, she knew, felt
acutely out of sorts ever since she came home,
downright crotchety, in fact. Now she suddenly

felt fine—peaceful inside, happy really. Cazak must be why. How *stupid*! The wooden rung snapped. "Bother!" she said. "Now you made me break the ladder. All right, *paint* your picture. Then we'll see. I may hate you."

Cazak laughed. "No, you won't. Callette, I love you even more when you're being grumpy!"

"You can't start painting yet," said Callette. "I really and truly have to go to the University and warn them. There may be an emergency there. That's where Blade and Kit are," she told Don over her shoulder, "visiting Elda."

"Then we'll go with you," Don said. "There are enough of us here to deal with most emergencies."

SEVENTEEN

A T THE UNIVERSITY there were now fourteen dead mice laid out under the council table and most of the teaching staff were gathered around Querida. There was as yet no sign of any new emergency. Querida, taking the very reasonable line that no one could do anything about the missed moonshot, was dealing with other matters instead. The wards were proving very hard to restore. They seemed to resist anything that Querida did. Consequently, she was in a very sharp temper as she leafed through piles of essays and exam papers.

"Why is it that nobody ever gives any mark higher than a B?" she demanded. "Why are they nearly *all* given a B, for that matter? Half of these deserve to fail, to my mind. Finn?"

Finn, who was having a miserable afternoon,

replied as he had replied many times before, "Corkoran had this policy, you see, that we should turn out as many working wizards as——"

He broke off in some relief as Sabrina came trotting in with the fifteenth mouse. "Good cat!" said Querida. "By 'working wizards,' Corkoran meant half-trained magic users, I gather. He means to clutter the world with incompetent warlocks who can't tell a spell from a shopping list, does he? I think it's getting a little stuffy and mouseish in here. All of you come outside for a breath of fresh air."

Flury followed the procession as it trooped out into the courtyard. Because he was by now feeling sorry for Finn, and for Myrna and Umberto, though not so much for Dench and some of the others, he said, "While we're out here, ma'am, perhaps you'd like to take a look at Wizard Wermacht?"

"Oh, yes," said Querida. "Thank you for the reminder, Flury. Myrna, run and fetch Wermacht—no, you're pregnant, aren't you? What a silly state to be in. Then Finn must——"

Flury galloped off before Finn was forced to take any more orders and returned on three legs, lugging the bar stool. He set it down in front of Querida with a clatter. She looked at it. Everyone else looked at it. It stood there.

"Wermacht!" Querida called sharply. "Come on out!" Nothing happened. Querida began to mutter and work on it. Finally she went so far as to lay her little, withered hands on the leather seat, saying as she did so, "Umberto, what are you staring at? Everyone, help me! This wizard was clearly an utter bungler, and I can't do this alone."

"Er—" said Umberto.

"Who *is* this Wermacht, anyway?" Querida demanded. "*I* never met him."

"He graduated two years ago with top marks," Finn explained. "Never fell below a B, and—"

"Don't tell me!" Querida snapped. "Corkoran had this policy!"

"Er—" Umberto began again.

"Flury!" Querida said, exasperated. Bar stool or man, this Wermacht was going to have to be fired, along with Dench and six others almost equally incompetent. And Corkoran, before any of the others. It was a real nuisance having to find lecturers to take their places. Even if she called the old wizards out of retirement, she would still have to do some of the teaching herself, which was *maddening* when she wanted to be working on the Waste. "Flury, can you do anything about this Wermacht person?"

"I'm afraid not, ma'am," Flury said glumly. "I've tried. I thought I ought to try because I encouraged him to get like this in the first place."

"Will you *stop* apologizing!" Querida hissed.

"Er—Querida," Umberto managed to say, while Querida was taking a breath before she told Flury just what she thought of griffins who made wizards turn themselves into bar stools and then *crawled* about it. Like Elda, she found Flury's humility highly irritating. "Querida, I think we're about to have an international crisis. King Luther and Emperor Titus—"

Querida spared an unbelieving look across the courtyard. There, sure enough, to the left stood Emperor Titus beside his unfurled banner of the golden griffin on the purple ground, surrounded by neat ranks of glistening soldiery. Titus had his arms folded and his legs astride in a thoroughly warlike posture. He was staring across at the rigid figure of King Luther on the right. King Luther only had six soldiers and Isodel to support him, but he had his arms folded, too, and the glare he was giving Titus more than made up for his lack of an army. It looked as though the only thing that was stopping an immediate small war was the crowd of interested students flocking into the courtyard to see what was going on.

"Why didn't you *tell* me?" Querida snarled at Umberto. Even she knew that this was unfair. But she always hated being taken by surprise. She picked up the bar stool and passed it to Dench. "Take him back to the buttery. If the man isn't wizard enough to get himself out of it, he'll just have to stay that way." Then, well aware that King Luther and Emperor Titus had detested one another ever since the last battle of the last tour, she set off at a hasty but dignified walk to keep the two apart.

As she went, the man that each of the two

angry rulers had sent to question the students came back and whispered to his monarch. Titus and Luther both spared an incredulous glance at the sky before they went back to glaring at one another. Evidently they had just been told that Claudia and Lukin had gone to the moon, and neither believed a word of it.

Querida looked at the sky, too, rather hopelessly. It was overcast, covered with matte gray clouds, and likely to rain before long. Querida sighed. The roofs would leak again, and she would be forced to invite the Emperor and the King into the Council Chamber, where they would encounter a row of dead mice— Oh, no, it just wouldn't do! "Can you hold the rain off?" she asked Flury, who was the only one daring enough to cross the court beside her.

"I'll try," Flury said in the humble way that so annoyed her. His head cocked sideways. His manner changed. His head, his bright brown crest, and his wings came up. His tail lashed, and his feet braced. Somehow he seemed twice the size. "Don't move!" he said. "Don't take another step!"

He was so commanding that Querida actually obeyed. She stood still, and because Flury was staring at the sky, she looked up again, too. Her ears caught the sound that Flury had heard a few seconds ago. It was a distant, whining roar, rapidly growing louder. As Querida searched for the source of it, the clouds above the gate tower boiled into whiteness and parted to let a great flaming object through. The roar rose to screaming thunder as the burning sphere hurtled apparently straight toward Querida, lighting the tower, the courtyard, and everyone standing in it a lurid yellow-white like a small sun. Querida had scarcely time to think, It's going to hit me! before it was there, down on the courtyard in front of the statue of Wizard Policant, deafeningly but light as a feather. The blast of its coming made everyone stagger. Wizard Policant rocked on his pedestal, and Querida would have been thrown over backward if Flury had not hastily backed around behind her. Smoke belched up from the stones of the courtyard, covered the sphere so that it looked like the sun in a storm cloud, and then burned away, leaving a smell of hot lava.

In utter, deafening silence after that, Querida leaned into Flury's warm, stiff feathers and watched the outer part of the sphere turn from fiery orange to yellow and then to an almost frozen white. The whiteness steamed and twined away from it in spirals as all the air elementals from the Red Planet who had not been boiled away above the clouds set off eagerly to explore the blue world. The misty blue inner lining of the sphere fell away outward like orange peel then, to reveal two dank and gasping griffins, one sweating dwarf, and six humans, one of these clutching a clod of earth and all of them except Corkoran white and strained from the frantic magic-working they had had to do in order to survive reentry.

Kit was quivering all over, but he spared a flicker of strength to revive Corkoran before he sank down beside Elda on the nice, cool stone, which had melted to a marble smoothness and then been frozen solid again by the departure of the air elementals.

Corkoran staggered upright, looking anguished. His face was yellow and baggy with horror, and his eyes rolled. His usually spruce yellow hair was in tangles. His tie was gray. Seeing Querida gathering herself together and marching toward him, he moaned. He had hoped that he had just been having a bad dream and had now woken up. Now he knew he was still in it, and it was a nightmare.

Flury advanced, too. "Are you all right?"

Kit was so tired that his voice came out as a small squawk. "I'll live."

Elda realized that Flury was really speaking to her. "Fine, now that I know we're not all dead," she replied. Flury, she saw, was not looking humble at all. She wondered why. She thought it suited him much better to be about Kit's size, with his crest up and his eyes keenly open. This was much more how she had all along supposed—without knowing she supposed it—that Flury should really look. She so much approved of him this way that she added happily, "I'm so glad to be back! I love the whole world!"

"Isn't the world a little much to take on all at

once?" Flury said rather wistfully.

Behind them Querida seized on the best chance she would ever have to get rid of Corkoran privately and quickly, without having to take the blame for him. As she had appointed Corkoran Chairman herself, she knew very well that quite a lot of people were likely to say this showed she was getting too old to be High Chancellor. So she had to get in first, before they did. "Corkoran, you don't look well," she announced.

Corkoran was not surprised. He felt dreadful.

"I think you've been overworking," Querida continued, much to his surprise. "Would you please me and translocate to Chell City for a long holiday? Tell Wizard Bettony that you're replacing her there for the moment and ask her to come here and talk to me." Bettony had taught at the University for years, during the tours. She was not the ideal replacement for Corkoran, and she would hate having to leave Chell, but she was the best person Querida could think of. Seeing Corkoran staring at her, she added, "You'll like Chell. They make wine there. And the Duchess of Chell is very rich. If you talk to her nicely, she might set you up with a new moonlab there."

Corkoran shuddered. Going to the moon meant floating in a nightmare of vertigo inside a tiny freezing bubble, with nothing but black emptiness outside pockmarked with huge, unmoving stars. He had gone off the moon. It had looked so small as they had hurtled past. You would have to stand with your feet close together, balanced on the very top of it, he knew now, or you would stick out sideways into emptiness. The idea made him want to scream again. On the other hand, he knew all about the wine they made in Chell. "You're right," he said. "I do need a rest." He could only translocate two miles at the most, which meant he would arrive in Chell in the middle of the night, so he thought he had better go now, before Querida changed her mind and made him deal with all these soldiers. "I'll give Bettony your message," he said, and translocated in a mild draft of air. The sigh of relief that Querida gave then made more of a wind than Corkoran's going.

Titus had left his soldiers and was hurrying toward Claudia. Claudia was leaning on Wizard Policant's pedestal, thankful to have survived and even more thankful for the light, free feeling of being without her jinx. She saw Titus when he was halfway to her, exclaimed, and ran toward him. Brother and sister met with a clash of Titus's armor and hurled their arms around one another.

Lukin meanwhile took Olga's arm and nodded toward King Luther. Olga, seeing Isodel there, staring toward the other side of the courtyard, realized who this tall, gloomy man must be and squared her shoulders. She lodged the clod of earth carefully between Wizard Policant's pointed shoes and went over to King Luther with

Lukin, trying to feel brave. Ruskin followed them. Behind them, quite unnoticed by anyone, Wizard Policant bent down and picked the clod up. He stood up, holding it in both hands, in silent, wondering conversation with it.

"Father," said Lukin, "I would like you to meet Olga Olafsdaughter. We're going to be married when we've both qualified as wizards." Olga looked at him with admiration. She had not thought Lukin would dare say this much.

King Luther gazed somewhere above Lukin's head. "Someone on the roof," he said. "Student stupidity, I suppose. No, Lukin. Out of the question. I'm here to fetch you home."

"Your Majesty," boomed Ruskin, "Olga Olafsdaughter is a very rich woman. She owns an island with a pirate's hoard in it."

"I suppose I do," Olga said faintly.

King Luther bent his gloomy head to discover Ruskin's face somewhere about level with Lukin's waist. "Who," he said, "are you?"

"Ruskin, Your Majesty, lately of Central Peaks fastness, now one of Your Majesty's subjects." Ruskin bowed. His sweat-soaked braids rattled. "Lukin owns me. I'm his slave. He bought me from the forgemasters a couple of weeks ago."

King Luther did look properly at Lukin then. He discovered his son to be damp-haired and tired, but looking back at him in a very straight and serious way. He also noticed that Olga was an extremely beautiful girl. His first notion of denouncing Olga as on the catch for a prince dissolved almost instantly as he saw the way her dreadfully muddy hand twined in Lukin's and the way she and Lukin looked at one another. So he simply ignored all that. "We don't have slaves in Luteria," he said.

"I was going to ask you about that," Lukin said. "I believe it takes a Pronuncial from the Throne to free a slave, doesn't it?"

"Yes, probably," King Luther said coldly. "I brought a spare horse for you, Lukin—"

"I hope"—Ruskin interrupted in his most blaring voice—"that Your Majesty intends to keep me as a subject of Luteria. I must be one of the few people who knows where the gold deposits are there."

"*What* gold deposits?" King Luther asked, distracted.

"Enormous ones," Ruskin boomed airily, and then dropped his voice to the jarring whisper he had perfected for the library. "Majesty, when I was bringing the tribute from our fastness during the last tour, I met a dwarf at Derkholm called Dworkin, who was from that fastness just on the border of Luteria. Your Majesty may know him." King Luther shook his head, resisting the need to block his ears as well. "Well, they aren't truly Your Majesty's subjects," Ruskin conceded, still in the dreadful whisper. "Anyway, this Dworkin, who was a subchief and knew what he was talking about, said that Luteria was sitting on some of the biggest gold deposits in the world. It quite broke Dworkin's heart," he added, seeing King Luther's six soldiers looking at him avidly, "because these deposits run *very deep* and very thick, and he couldn't get in to mine them without Your Majesty's getting to know—and he knew, of course, that these deposits really *belong to the crown*—and he couldn't see himself keeping it secret, not in the hundred years of mining it'd take to get all the gold out. But if Your Majesty gives me, as one of your loyal subjects, permission, I can find that gold. As a dwarf *and* a wizard I'd have no problem. And Lukin— when's he's a wizard, too—can make the mine shafts."

Lukin pinched his mouth together in order not to laugh.

"He's certainly good at making holes in things," King Luther agreed dourly.

"Ah, but they've cured him of that here already, Your Majesty," Ruskin said, in what passed for his normal voice now, much to the King's relief. "Next he has to learn to sink pits to *order*. That'll take him the next three years, but after that he and I are both at your service, Your Majesty."

"On condition that I marry Olga first," Lukin put in.

King Luther looked up at Lukin and down at Ruskin, grimly. "What if I refuse?"

"Then I inherit a needlessly poor kingdom,

obviously," Lukin said. "I'd hate that. But I'd hate even more not being friends with you."

There was a pause while King Luther looked from his son to his soldiers, who were all staring before them so correctly that they looked like fish, and realized that Luteria was going to be riddled with amateur mine shafts unless he took some action. The only person who seemed genuinely uninterested was Isodel. She seemed to be in some kind of dream, with a strange, happy smile on her face.

It was during this pause that Kit put his head up to take in more air. He still felt as if he could never get enough of it. And his beak tasted singed. "Funny," he croaked to Elda. "There's a row of men in spiked helmets up on that roof."

Everyone within hearing whirled to look up at the Spellman Building. Sure enough, the parapet there bristled with helmets and the ends of weapons. Querida felt depressed. Kit was obviously too tired to be much help, and she was not sure she could manage an army on her own. Blade seemed to have slithered out of sight, the way he often did.

Felim sprang up from beside Elda and spun around to look at the other roofs. They also bristled with spiked helmets and weapons. Felim dodged around the statue of Wizard Policant, so that he could see the main gates. They were just being thrown wide, and the Emir was storming through them, walking with that forward lunging stride that always means trouble, with more soldiers at his back.

"This is idiocy!" Felim exclaimed. He set off for the gates at a sprint.

"Oh, dear!" Elda groaned. She dragged herself up and crawled off to help.

Blade, meanwhile, was edging over to the Emperor and his sister. Titus and Claudia still had their arms clasped around one another, but more loosely now. Claudia's laugh was ringing out delightedly. "Honestly, Titus? The *lot* of them?" she was saying. "It'll do them such good to sit in prison. They sent so many people there themselves. But I still don't know how you *dared*!"

As Blade edged up closer, Titus answered, a trifle guiltily, "Because I'd never been so angry in my life, I suppose."

This is going to be impossible, Blade thought. He felt very tired, wholly apprehensive, and thoroughly determined. He remembered once, eight years ago, thinking that something must happen to soften people's brains between the ages of fourteen and twenty, but he had never once, even when he met Isodel, discovered exactly what that something was. Now he had, eight years later, and it was awful.

Here Elda dragged herself past, with Felim sprinting ahead of her, and things became slightly less awful. Claudia said, "Stay here, Titus. I must go and look after Elda for a minute. I don't think spaceflight agrees with griffins." And she hurried after Elda.

Blade walked sideways up to the Emperor. He had always liked Titus, and he knew him quite well these days. But it was still hard to know what to say. Blade settled for the most official way he could manage, because Titus was, after all, an emperor, and blurted it out. "Er, Titus, er, Imperial Majesty, would you give me leave to pay my addresses to your sister, Claudia. Er, court her, you know?"

"Eh?" said Titus.

Gods! thought Blade. He's gone all haughty, and who's to blame him! This is hopeless! But when he looked at the Emperor, he saw that Titus had probably not been listening. The Emperor was staring across the courtyard. Blade looked where Titus was looking and saw Isodel. Evidently whatever Isodel did to men had infected Titus, too, except that for some extraordinary reason Isodel was staring back at Titus. The yearning, painful, happy unhappiness on both their faces made Blade's chest twist. It was so exactly what he was feeling himself. "Did you hear what I said?" he asked Titus.

Titus jumped a little. "Perfectly," he lied. Then, because he had been trained all his life to listen even when his attention was somewhere else, he somehow recalled exactly what Blade had said. He frowned. Blade watched the Emperor's straight eyebrows meeting over his Imperial nose and felt his own heart sink. "Claudia? Really? My sister?" Titus said. This sounded very forbidding. But Titus went on, talking in jerks. Blade saw that the Emperor was thinking very slowly, with his mind almost entirely on Isodel and the fact that he and Isodel's father had been at war for eight years, and waited, hardly daring to breathe. "She's far above you in birth, Blade," Titus began. Then he added, "But you were appointed by the gods, weren't you? And you're a wizard. You could keep Claudia safe. I have to let some of the senators out of prison sometime. But Claudia's her own person. I don't even know if she likes you."

"Neither do I," Blade said sadly.

"You're a wizard," Titus repeated. He grabbed Blade's arm crushingly. "She's his daughter, isn't she? King Luther. Get him to agree that I can marry her, and I'll back you with Claudia in every way I can."

"Done," Blade said promptly. Now I'm going to have to perform a miracle! he thought as Titus started to drag him across the courtyard.

"I don't even know her name!" Titus said, faltering a little.

"Isodel," said Blade.

"How lovely!" Titus dragged Blade onward. "What a perfect name!"

As Blade and Titus went toward King Luther, Flury was scudding after Elda and Claudia. He arrived beside Felim and the Emir almost as they did, but no one but Elda noticed him. Elda spared him a glance while she and Claudia waited anxiously for Felim to become encased in the beehive of books again. Both were extremely dismayed when nothing of the kind occurred. Felim dashed up to the Emir and stopped. The Emir halted his troops with a gesture and stopped, too. And the two of them stood face to face yelling at one another.

"Perhaps the spell's worn off," Claudia suggested.

"And *you* had the nerve to send assassins!" Felim was screaming.

"Do you think we should try to put it on again?" Elda asked as the Emir screamed back.

"What do you *take* me for?" the Emir howled. "If I make a threat, my honor demands I *keep* it! *You* had the nerve to disobey me! I *told* you I had no objection to your sitting in your study all day. I told you you could learn to be a hundred wizards! But I told you to stay at *home*!"

"And I told you never to try to bully me!" Felim yelled. "Son of a she-camel!"

"I told you I wish you to be Emir after me!" bawled the Emir. "Son of a mangy nanny goat!"

"This shall never be!" Felim screamed. "The she-camel had mange, too!"

The two of them then embarked on a shouted description of the nature of one another's grandmothers, all of whom seemed to have been several different animals, each with a number of startling diseases. Claudia and Elda stared. They had not realized that the polite and clever Felim could be like this. Claudia watched the two dark-browed faces, roaring insults at one another, and realized that they were surprisingly alike. The noses were the same, as well as the brows, although Felim's nose was smooth and young.

"Is he perhaps the Emir's son?" she said to Elda. The Emir, red-blotched and haggard, certainly looked old enough to be Felim's father.

A slight, tired smile came to the ends of Elda's beak. She knew this kind of scene rather well. Scenes like it happened at Derkholm whenever Kit and Shona happened to be at home together. "No," she said. "Brothers."

Here Felim returned to the thread of the discourse, just as Shona always did, and yelled, rather hoarsely, "Besides, you have twenty-two sons to become Emir after you! Choose among *them*!"

"Not I!" bawled the Emir. "I dislike every one of them! I have told you this a hundred times!"

At this Felim calmed down suddenly and stated, "It is not a question of *liking* but of suitability. I have told you this many hundred times."

This seemed to end the argument. The Emir, equally suddenly, became calm, too. He reached out and gripped Felim by his upper arms. "Oh, my brother, I have missed you so badly," he said. "No one shouts at me as you do. No one dares. Will you not come home?"

"No," said Felim with utter finality.

The Emir accepted this. He nodded, and sighed, just as Kit always did when Shona had the last word. "In that case," he said, "please step into the shelter of this gateway while my army slaughters everyone here. I do not wish you to be hurt."

Flury leaned down and tapped the Emir on his shoulder. "Excuse me," he said. "I can't let you do that."

Everyone except Elda jumped violently. Flury, at that moment, towered twelve feet above the Emir, who was a tall man, and no one but Elda had seen him before this. The Emir started backward, and his face became a strange leaden gray color. Felim said quickly, "Please abate your height and step back, Flury. My brother's heart has been giving us concern for three years now."

"But I can't let him *kill* everyone!" Flury protested.

Simultaneously the Emir protested, "There is nothing *wrong* with my heart!"

"Nevertheless"—Felim smiled lovingly and took the Emir by one arm—"you will not give the signal to attack, my brother, until you have been with me to Healers Hall. It is only a step away. Come with me."

"Why should I?" demanded the Emir.

"Because," said Felim, beginning to lead him gently away, "I need you to live for another three years, until I am a qualified wizard. I do not wish to be snatched home because you have named me your heir. At the end of those three years I promise I will come to you with a spell of potent divination and choose which of my nephews is most suitable to be emir. Meanwhile there are here the best healers in the world. Come."

Flury dropped to all fours and stared.

"Of twenty-two sons," the Emir said sadly as he walked, "none is satisfactory."

"Hassan," Felim replied, "has qualities, and it is a pity that Assif and Abdul are twins, for one cannot choose between them. Sayeed is firm."

"But cruel," said the Emir. "And Imram is indolent."

"Not where his racing camels are concerned," said Felim. "And Hamid or Noureddin would proceed with justice. All my nephews have something to recommend them."

This had the air of an absorbing discussion that the brothers had often had—so much so, that when cracking and creaking, followed by crashing and loud cries, proclaimed that the roof had given way under the Emir's soldiery, just above Felim's room, neither brother even glanced that way. The Emir said, "True, but they are always balanced by an undesirable trait." And they walked on, discussing other names.

"Well, I'll be . . . .!" said Flury. He looked suspiciously at Elda and Claudia, who were leaning together, both in fits of laughter.

Claudia took her head out of Elda's wing and

looked around for Titus, to tell him about all this, and found him, much to her surprise, on the other side of the courtyard beside King Luther. Hoping that this did not mean more trouble, she hurried over to him.

As Claudia arrived, Lukin was saying, "I am *not* trying to make conditions, Father. I just want to learn enough wizardry to help—"

He broke off, and Claudia shut her mouth on what she had been going to say to Titus. Both of them felt the pressure of some kind of magic as Blade slid himself into the group beside Lukin. Blade spared a glance toward the Emir's soldiers, floundering among the broken rafters of the roof opposite, and decided that what he had to say to King Luther was more important. Nobody up there seemed to be hurt. "Your Majesty," he said, "do forgive the interruption. The emperor Titus begs to wonder if the princess Isodel would consent to be introduced to him."

Before King Luther could speak, Isodel said, "Oh, *yes!*" and went toward Titus with both hands out. Then, realizing that she did not really know him, she took her hands down and said wonderingly, "Are you the Emperor of the South then?"

Titus seized her hands, anyway. "Yes," he said. They stood face to face, staring at one another and marveling. "I hope you're good at governing," Titus said then. "I've just imprisoned most of the people who usually do it."

"Quite good," Isodel said, "and very economical. You sound as if you have an emergency. Do you want us to set out now or wait till tomorrow?"

"Tomorrow will do," Titus said. "We'd have time to get married before we leave then."

"Father can marry us," Isodel told him. "The throne of Luteria has priestly functions. Lukin can give me away. Does your palace have room for a medium-small dragon?"

King Luther watched and listened with his teeth clenched to prevent his jaw from dropping. "I don't," he said to Ruskin, "I simply don't know my children."

"Ah, Your Majesty," Ruskin rumbled, "you might want to consider stopping calling them your children and referring to them instead as your sons and daughters."

King Luther stared down at Ruskin. The grim anger on his face froze and slowly melted to thoughtfulness and finally to understanding. "I should like," he said stiffly to Ruskin, "to appoint you advisor to the throne when your education here is finished. At any rate my queen and I would be happy to welcome you at the castle during the holidays, along with Lukin and Olga."

Lukin and Olga were just turning delightedly to one another when the griffins arrived. The empty gray sky was suddenly filled with winged shapes, the whistle of pinions, and the excited babble of many griffin voices. Something like the very largest rookery you could ever imagine, Claudia thought, staring upward in amazement, along with nearly everyone else. The noise quickly gave way to the muffled boom and blast of cupped wings as first Don, then Callette, then Cazak, then griffin after griffin came down to land in the courtyard, shouting greetings to Kit as they came. Elda screamed with excitement. In spite of what Callette had told her, she had never imagined there could be so many of her own kind in the world. Kit leaped up to meet them all, shouting like a trumpet. Everyone else hurriedly cleared off to the sides of the courtyard, except for Querida. Querida found herself stranded beside Wizard Policant's statue and stuck there as the place filled with more and more griffins, each one folding wings with a clapping rustle and then galloping aside to let other griffins land: white griffins, yellow griffins, speckled and brown-barred ones, gray griffins, chestnut ones, and several who were almost blue. The courtyard was very shortly a mass of gleefully snapping beaks, great round eyes, switching tails, and tossing wing feathers.

Those of the Emir's unfortunate soldiers who were not halfway through a roof hastily threw themselves flat. When, after a minute or so, they saw that the griffins were not attacking them, most of them climbed down the outside walls and streamed off indecisively to guard Healers Hall instead. This was a great relief to Titus's small squad of unmounted cavalry. They had thought they were going to have to fight to protect their Emperor, knowing they would lose.

"This," said Wizard Policant to Querida, "is where I step in, I think. Roofs are easy to mend, but it is very much harder to stop a battle. I am so glad we were not called upon to do that."

Querida, rather hoping she was dreaming, looked up and found that the stone of the statue was splitting into irregular shapes, like dry mud cracking. The same thing seemed to be happening to the plinth she was clutching, revealing a yellow, buttery shine under her fingers. Upon the statue, like dry mud, each piece of stone shrank, curled up at the corners and fell away. Inside it there seemed to be a live person in wizard's robes, as elderly as she was but very much a living one.

Wizard Policant shook himself, and the last dry piece fell off him into powder. "The enchantment was tied to the wards of the University," he explained. "When they go down, I return to take up my post as Head here. There was a prophecy made that this was only to happen in the Year of the Griffin. Unkind persons held that this meant never, griffins in my time being thought to be mythical creatures, but I see that the prophecy was quite correct. I do hope you yourself will not mind stepping aside to work with me as Chancellor?"

"Not at all," Querida said a trifle faintly. "It'll

be a great relief." Of all the enchantments she had seen in her long life, this one astounded her most. But she was recovering rapidly. "You do realize," she said, in quite her usual manner, "that two-thirds of the teaching staff here will have to be fired?"

"Of course," said Policant. "I *have* been here on the spot for years after all. Will you be so kind as to summon every wizard on this continent here tomorrow? Except Corkoran, of course. We shall choose new staff from among them."

"They may not want to come," Querida warned him.

"No, but they will come. That is part of the enchantment, too," Policant told her. "Now I wish to say a word to everyone present here."

There was a sharp rapping noise, rather like a stick rapping a lectern, only much louder. Everyone, human and griffin, turned to where Wizard Policant stood on his pedestal, high above them. Everyone could somehow see him, even those who happened to have a griffin in the way.

"May I have your attention, please?" Wizard Policant's amplified voice said. "I am Policant, once Head of this University, now Head of it again. We shall of course in future run this place both as a means of educating wizards of true power and as the center for magical research it was designed to be. Meanwhile the power vested in me gives me the right to perform all cere-monies, civil, magical, and religious. It is therefore my pleasure to officiate at the marriage of Isodel, Princess of Luteria, and Titus Antoninus, Emperor of the South. If these young people will step forward, I shall be happy to pronounce them man and wife."

Everyone cheered. They had all expected a long and pompous speech. During the noise Wizard Policant asked, much more quietly, "Will somebody fetch me something to step down upon, please?" He bent down and passed Querida a clod of red earth. 'Take great care of this. It is a person from another planet who wishes to see this one. I judge that she, he, or it will see more of the world with you than by staying here with me."

As a student dashed into the buttery bar and seized the nearest stool, which happened to be Wermacht, for Policant to step on, and the griffins crowded aside to let Isodel and Titus walk toward the pedestal of the statue, the barkeeper looked up to find Flury looming over him.

"Set up every barrel you've got," Flury said, "and I'll conjure you more wine. There's going to be rather a big party. Griffins drink a great deal."

"Oh?" said the barkeeper, out of long knowledge of students. "And who's going to pay?"

"The University," said Flury. "The pedestal of that statue is solid gold."

At about this time the forgemasters on their ponies were riding into the ravine that led to the Central Peaks fastness. All of them, ponies included, were relieved to see they would be there before nightfall.

"Am I glad to be home!" said Genno. "Feet up by a nice fire and an artisan girl bringing me supper!"

"And rich. Rich beyond the dreams of average!" Dobrey answered. He flourished the Book of Truth, which had never left his hand for the entire journey.

Arrows ripped down around them from the heights. One of the ponies reared.

"Stop right there!" shouted a female voice from the left-hand cliffs.

Dobrey looked around to see that they were inside a small hedge of arrows, each one sticking upright in the ground. "Nice shooting," he remarked to Genno. "Who is that up there?"

"Rooska, by the voice. That's Ruskin's cousin—or sister, I forget," Genno said. "She's got half her clan up there with her. The other half's up on the other side."

"Come down off there, Rooska!" Dobrey shouted upward. "What are you playing at?"

"Not playing at all, forgemaster." Rooska's voice rang back. "We artisans have taken over the fastness. We're all equals here now. The ones who wouldn't be equal are dead. Where's Ruskin?"

"Sold him for the biggest treasure on earth," Dobrey boomed, waving the book again. "Come on, Rooska. Stop this nonsense. We're all tired."

"Ruskin's *alive* then?" someone else shouted from the opposite cliff. "Swear?"

"Swear it!" all the forgemasters chorused.

Genno added a further shout. "Sold to the Crown Prince of Luteria, if you must know. Now come on down and open the fastness for us!"

"You don't *understand*!" Rooska bawled. "There's been a revolution. You're not in *charge* any longer. Because Ruskin's alive, we'll let you live, but you've got to *leave*. Go on. Go *away*!"

The forgemasters exchanged looks of true dismay. It began to dawn on them that the home comforts they had been looking forward to might not be available.

"We can settle this quietly!" Dobrey yelled. "You *need* us! You need the spells against the demons of the deep!"

"No one's seen a demon in six hundred years!" someone yelled back. "It's all a big fraud!"

That voice was followed by massed yells from both sides of the ravine. *"Frauds! Get out!"* and this merged into a chant, "GET OUT NOW, GET OUT NOW, GET OUT NOW!" The chanting was backed up by more arrows, all of which fell inside the first ones, uncomfortably close to the forge-masters. And Rooska screamed a descant to the chant: *"We'll kill you if you're still here tomorrow!"*

Dobrey looked drearily from the other forge-masters to the book in his hand. "They don't care. They didn't listen when I waved the greatest treasure on earth at them. If there *were* any

demons, they deserve to be infested with them."
He sighed deeply. "Come, fellow forgemasters. If
we hurry, we can get to Deeping fastness by mid-
night. They'll take us in there if we give them the
Book of Truth." He sighed even more deeply.
"The most expensive lodgings in the world."

Followed by the chant and by yells and hoots
and catcalls, the forgemasters turned their ponies
around and plodded off again.

Sometime later, when the party in the
University was in full swing, Blade fetched Flury
another glass tankard of wine with a fresh straw
in it, and sat down on the refectory steps, level
with Flury's head, to drink his own.

"Flury, if you don't mind my asking, what are
you doing here?"

Flury rested his feathered elbow on
Wermacht, who was still a bar stool, and sipped
at the wine. "I thought you knew my government
sent me with Jessak," he said. "He was the prime
minister's son, you know. I'm sorry I had to send
to you for help."

"Oh, it was *you*, was it? I thought it was Elda.
But I know that innocent tone, too," said Blade.
"I mean, why did you *stay* here, at the
University?"

"I quite like teaching—and everyone was
being so badly taught," Flury replied, and put his
head on one side to gaze across the courtyard.

Blade followed his gaze, across crowds of

laughing human heads, some in helmets and some bare, over bottles and tankards being passed among bobbing griffin beaks and swaying wings, across dancing griffins and singing humans, all under a few flecks of rain, bright in the lights of the courtyard, which even Wizard Policant seemed unable to hold back, and found that Flury's gaze ended at Wizard Policant's golden pedestal. Olga and Claudia were sitting on the pedestal, back to back, with Elda pressed against them on one side and Lukin crowded in on the other. Ruskin and Felim were sitting leaning on the pedestal at their feet. All six of them were singing, five of them very badly. Blade could hear Claudia's sweet, strong notes coming out over the din. For a moment he lost himself in thoughts of her thin, greenish face with its smile that creased into a dimple, her bright, intelligent eyes, her strangely coiling hair, and the way she laughed at things in spite of having had the sort of life that should make her severe and solemn. She was laughing now as she sang. Then a particularly discordant squawk from Elda made him wince. Elda never could hold a tune, Blade thought. And at this he understood Flury. Elda, of course.

"She's pretty young still," he told Flury.

"She can always see me," Flury said. "I tell myself that's a good sign until I realize how much she despises me."

"She doesn't like you being humble. She told me," Blade said.

"Oh." Flury was surprised. "I thought that was proper courting behavior. But she's used to Kit, I suppose. Blade, she's so beautiful that I *ache*."

"I know the feeling," Blade said.

Flury shot him a bright-eyed look. "I believe," he said slowly, "that both our ladies have some growing and adjusting to do. Yours, if that terrifying Querida is any guide, has breeding that leads to some fairly powerful magic. That takes growing into."

Blade stared fuzzily at Flury. In all the years he had known Querida and that green skin color of hers, he had never realized that Querida had Marshfolk blood. Well, well. That accounted for a lot. "And Elda's young for her age," he said. "We shall just have to keep visiting and hoping. Do you want me to find you work over here that your government will agree to, so that you can stay here and wait?"

Flury's eyes twinkled, almost luminously. "Yes, please."

They solemnly clinked glasses.